D1065170

ONE-EYED KINGS

WILLIAM S. COHEN

ONE-EYED KINGS

NAN A. TALESE
DOUBLEDAY
New York London Toronto Sydney Auckland

PUBLISHED BY DOUBLEDAY
a division of
Bantam Doubleday Dell Publishing Group, Inc.
666 Fifth Avenue, New York, New York 10103

DOUBLEDAY and the portrayal of an anchor
with a dolphin are trademarks of
Doubleday, a division of Bantam Doubleday Dell
Publishing Group, Inc.

This novel is a work of fiction. Any references to real people, events, establishments, organizations, or locales are intended only to give the fiction a sense of reality and authenticity; the depiction of events and actions involving the CIA, FBI, KGB, and Mossad is the product of the author's imagination and should not be construed as being factual, or even probable. Other names, characters, and incidents are either the product of the author's imagination or are used fictitiously, as are those fictionalized events and incidents which involve real persons and did not occur or are set in the future.

Book design by Anne Ling

Library of Congress Cataloging-in-Publication Data

Cohen, William S.
    One-eyed kings / William S. Cohen. — 1st ed.
        p.   cm.
    I. Title.
PS3553.043405   1991
813'.54—dc20   90-22786
                                                              CIP

ISBN 0-385-23962-9

Copyright © 1991 by William S. Cohen

All Rights Reserved
Printed in the United States of America
May 1991
1   3   5   7   9   10   8   6   4   2
FIRST EDITION

To the Better Angels

ACKNOWLEDGMENTS

ACKNOWLEDGMENTS

I am indebted to many people in the telling of this story.

First, my thanks to my agent and enduring friend, Bill Adler, for his support. I am especially grateful to my editor Nan Talese, her assistant Jesse Cohen, and copy editor Liz Duvall who provided me with many insightful observations and recommendations.

Special appreciation goes to my friend Tom Allen whose advice and encouragement helped me through the lonely hours whenever doubts began to gather.

I am also indebted to John Wiseman who walked with me (figuratively) through the streets of Jerusalem.

Finally, my gratitude goes to my sons, Kevin and Christopher, for their support and encouragement.

ONE-EYED KINGS

PART 1

ONE-EYED
KINGS

PART I

"Everything is plausible here, because nothing is real."

—*The Black Book,* Lawrence Durrell

1

"JEBALIYA'S NOT THE end of the earth," Zvika Posner said bitterly, "but you can see it from here."

It was hard for Avram Koshinsky to hear Posner over the roar of the army jeep as it bucked along the potholed streets of one of Gaza's most violent Palestinian refugee camps. But he picked up enough of Posner's words to acknowledge the joke.

"Yes, Zvika. You are right. This place stinks. It is a sewer."

At that moment the jeep splashed through a large puddle of brown water, which splattered on the windshield and the clothing of the four men behind it.

"Slow down, you crazy bastard!" Posner cried out. "You're covering us with PLO shit. I just had my goddamned uniform cleaned." He continued to blurt out a stream of expletives at the driver, who smiled sardonically and continued to accelerate down the narrow dirt streets.

It was a routine patrol by a small reserve unit of the Israel Defense Forces. But of course nothing was ever routine in Jebaliya. The camp's streets were littered with rubble. The smell of burning tires saturated the air. Rats bigger than cats could be seen slinking through the garbage that was strewn everywhere. The rats were arrogant and unafraid. *Like the people here,* Posner thought.

As the jeep slowed, a group of young Palestinians flashed in front of the patrol, their faces covered by the traditional headdress, the kaffiyeh. They taunted the Israelis, daring them to drop their guns and hurling rocks at them, hoping the Israelis would chase them down the dark streets. "Zionist bastards!" they yelled. "Hitler was right! He should have burned all of you!"

Another joined in the fusillade, crying, "We will finish what Hitler started!"

The others laughed lewdly. One boy, not more than six years old, threw a rock that smashed out the right headlamp of the jeep. Posner fired a burst from his machine gun into the air. The boys scattered, still laughing.

"For Christ's sake, Posner," the young lieutenant in the front seat of the jeep shouted, "hold your fire. You know the goddamned rules!"

Yes, Posner knew the rules. No live ammunition unless his life was in danger. No rubber bullets fired at children. Never mind that his life was in danger every time he entered Jebaliya. Never mind that those children could knock your eyes out with their standard-issue slingshots.

And now the goddamned politicians in the Knesset were demanding investigations into army brutality! *Why don't they investigate the Palestinian mothers who send their children out to stone us, hoping one of them will be maimed or killed? Why don't they condemn the lunatics who beat to death any Palestinian who advocates restraint or refuses to participate in the* intifada?

Posner was consumed with bitterness. He couldn't understand why Koshinsky did not seem to share his anger. The younger man had immigrated from the Soviet Union three months earlier. Maybe it was simply a cultural gap. Koshinsky was not particularly talkative or social. He carried out his assignments with little of the cursing or complaining that was so common with the other reservists. He was a contained man who shared little of himself with Posner and the others.

It was an odd thing. Politically, Koshinsky was much further to the right than Posner. He was a staunch member of the Likud Party, but was critical of what he thought was Likud's soft line in dealing with the *intifada*. Once, during a patrol, he had confided that if the choice were his, he would bulldoze every refugee camp in Gaza and the West Bank all the way to Amman.

The jeep lurched as the driver dropped into yet a lower gear. Posner was rocked to his left and nearly out of the rear of the jeep. As he started to curse the driver, he saw flashes of fire coming from an open window in a housing compound, so he began yelling at the driver to speed up. Too late. Slugs from automatic weapons slammed into the jeep's engine block, stopping it as if it had hit a stone wall. Both men in the front seat were hit and lay bleeding to death. They were exposed to the continuing stream of fire coming from the window. Their screams only seemed to stimulate the sadistic yells from the darkened compound.

Fear gripped Posner's stomach. He could hear the bullets shredding the bodies of his friends. He felt bile rise up in his throat. How many were there? Shit. Bullets tore into the jeep's tires, exploding them.

Koshinsky tapped Posner on his helmet and passed him a tear-gas gun. "Drop some gas in through the first- and second-floor windows over there. When they come puking their guts out, we'll cut them apart. No prisoners. No witnesses."

Posner nodded. Fear had passed. He loaded the gas grenade onto his rifle and fired. Then another, and another. Smoke poured out of the hovel across the street. Guns went silent. Posner was in a rage. He began to fire canisters into all the buildings around him.

But where were the people? Why didn't they come running out into the street so he and Koshinsky could massacre them? Why was there no coughing, no puking? Why was there only an eerie silence?

He turned in bewilderment toward Koshinsky, who had strapped on his gas mask. Koshinsky motioned for Posner to do the same.

Posner dropped his rifle and began to slip his mask over his face. He did not notice that Koshinsky had moved behind him.

The blow across the back of his neck was so swift, so hard, that Posner had no time even to scream into his mask. Already in a kneeling position, he simply toppled over face-first into the foul-smelling dirt.

Koshinsky, moving quickly, snapped his truncheon back onto

his belt and then reached down and removed Posner's helmet. Raising a ten-pound rock high above his head with both hands, he hurled it directly onto Posner's head, crushing his skull. Then he reached into the front of the jeep and activated a battery-powered portable radio.

Manufacturing desperation in his voice, Koshinsky yelled, *"Gold Star! Gold Star!* This is *Burning Bush.* Jebaliya. Fourth quadrant. Three hundred meters from the gas pumps. We have been ambushed. There has been a massacre. Help!"

2

THERE COULD BE NO mistake about it. President Eric Hollendale, sitting ramrod straight in his high-backed leather chair in the Cabinet Room, was fighting hard to control his anger. And barely winning.

Eric Hollendale had thick, close-cropped hair that was prematurely gray, very nearly white. His Scandinavian face, however, was ruddy and almost unlined. The combination was dramatic, conveying at once a telegenic vigor and reassuring maturity.

Forty years ago, fresh out of college, Hollendale had fought as a Marine in the Korean War. After completing his three-year commitment, he went off to engage in jungle warfare on Wall Street as a bond salesman. Eight years later he achieved a partnership in Strauss, Jenkins, & Fedder, a top brokerage firm. Abruptly—his partners thought quixotically—he moved to Chicago, where he turned his skills to the futures market. He formed his own company, buying and selling commodities whose future value was as speculative as a weather prediction. Hog bellies. Soybeans. Costa Rican cattle.

He made millions. And spent them. On houses—a thirty-acre

estate in Lake Forest, Illinois, a Palm Beach vacation home, a six-teen-room condominium in Vail. And on boats, art, jets, globe-trot-ting vacations. *Fortune* magazine listed him among the top fifty CEOs in America. *People* put him on the cover. Heralded as one of a new breed of businessmen who combined bottom-line profitability with progressive notions of social equity, he was soon mentioned as gubernatorial material, a possible future president.

The puffery had fueled Hollendale's ambitions. Bigger bank accounts and larger corporate jets no longer sated him. Mercantile power was no match for the power to move people and events. The real trading, he decided, was to be done on Pennsylvania Avenue. After two terms as governor of Illinois, he mounted a media-ori-ented, back-to-business-basics, pride-in-America campaign that car-ried him right into the White House.

None of the dark-suited men now in the room—Vice President John Manfred Lewis, Secretary of Defense Martin Price, CIA Direc-tor Jack Bickford, Secretary of State George Shanahan, National Security Adviser Butch Naylor, White House Chief of Staff Clayton Skillings, and General Allen Kastenmayer, chairman of the Joint Chiefs of Staff—dared to engage in the usual premeeting banter.

The President took a final sip from his coffee cup and dabbed his mouth with a linen napkin, then looked directly across the long, oblong, leather-inlaid table at his Secretary of State.

"What have the Israelis done to us now?" He meant "to *me.*" Hollendale assumed that everything that happened in Israel was a provocation directed personally at him.

"It's not exactly clear yet, Mr. President," Shanahan said in his deep and sonorous voice, which sounded rather like that of a professional radio announcer. "I spoke with Israel's Foreign Minis-ter, Etan Narkiss, early this morning, and he said they were still trying to sort everything out."

"Come on, George," Hollendale snapped, slamming a rolled-up copy of the morning's Washington *Post* on the table. "What in hell's there to sort out? They killed nearly fifty unarmed Palestinians last night. Gassed them to death!"

"Mr. President," Bickford interjected, attempting to defuse Hollendale's anger, "from the initial reports I've seen, it looks like a repeat of what happened in Tbilisi back in May of 1989. Soviet soldiers tried to control a group of demonstrators with chloropicrin.

We use the same stuff as a fumigant to kill rodents and insects. It's too early to tell, but it's likely that there was an overconcentration of the chemical."

"Just a case of poor quality control at the factory? That's about what I expect from those great analysts of yours, sitting on their fat asses out at Langley!" Hollendale exclaimed. "Well, you try to sell that at the United Nations today." He shook his head in disgust. "We're going to get hit with a resolution to condemn Israel in the Security Council this morning, and frankly, I don't know whether I'm going to veto it. I may just decide to vote for it."

For several seconds no one responded. Not until the silence became embarrassing. Finally Secretary of State Shanahan spoke, carefully, so as not to rebuff the President. "I share your anger, Mr. President, but I think you should take a longer view. This may be a case where inside a tragedy lies an opportunity . . ."

Hollendale tilted his head quizzically, a gesture that encouraged Shanahan to continue.

"You've got a summit meeting coming up in mid-August, just after Congress goes into its summer recess. You're going to sign a major chemical weapons agreement with the Soviet Union. Already I've been getting word that the Senate Intelligence Committee—particularly its chairman, Sean Falcone—is preparing to raise some hell over the verification aspects of the agreement."

Martin Price was tempted to shout "And well they should!" but maintained his silence. Shanahan never let the facts, or danger to American security, get in the way of a deal with the Russians. But that was a battle that Price would have to fight with Shanahan another time. He and General Kastenmayer had more bad news to bring to the President immediately after this meeting, and he didn't want to dissipate any of the good will he would have to call on in Hollendale.

Shanahan noticed how the President's mood had shifted. Color had flowed back to Hollendale's face, although he was still clearly angry. Shanahan continued his line of reasoning with increased confidence. "The Gaza massacre, as it's already been called, will do two things. First, it will give you increased leverage over Prime Minister Shimon Gerstel in forcing the Israelis to negotiate a land-for-peace settlement with the Palestinians, and second, it will help remove any obstacles to the chemical weapons agreement in the Senate. Who knows, we may even be in a position to force the other twenty nations who have chemical weapons to agree to eliminate their stockpiles. This could turn into a real bonanza for you as leader in the effort to remove this threat to the human race."

Hollendale scanned the faces of the men around the table. They suddenly looked as blank as the marble-eyed busts of George Washington and Benjamin Franklin that sat in stony silence at the end of the room. He skipped quickly past that of his Vice President, John Manfred Lewis, a former governor of New York who had been forced on him by party professionals.

Only Clayton Skillings, Hollendale's chief of staff, spoke up, reaffirming Shanahan's optimism. "I think the Secretary makes a lot of sense."

Butch Naylor nodded in agreement.

"George, are you recommending that I veto the UN resolution?" Hollendale asked.

Shanahan cleared his throat, as if to assure that his voice would achieve the precise timbre of certitude. "Yes, Mr. President, but only after I make it clear to the Israeli Foreign Minister that this is going to cost them."

Shanahan's argument appealed to the President. Maybe calamity and opportunity were the two sides of this coin. A silk purse out of a sow's ear. Old proverbs had their place in politics.

"All right, gentlemen," Hollendale said, pushing his chair away from the table, signaling that the meeting was over. "I want to give it some more thought." What the President meant was that he wanted to confer with Harry Polanski, the FBI director. Much to the resentment of those in the room, Polanski was the President's closest confidant, the one who was never reluctant to give advice, even when his grasp might exceed his knowledge.

After the meeting in the Cabinet Room ended, Martin Price walked with General Kastenmayer back to Butch Naylor's office in the northwestern corner of the West Wing of the White House. The three men sat there and drank coffee for the next half-hour, reviewing the President's reaction to events in Israel.

Then they descended a narrow set of carpeted stairs to the basement level, moved past a uniformed officer sitting behind a dark glass-topped desk, and entered the Situation Room. Moments later Eric Hollendale arrived, looking far less troubled than he had in the Cabinet Room.

The four men sat in modern soft leather chairs around a highly polished teak table. Although the room's title conjured up notions of grand proportions, the area actually was quite small, not even as large as a family-sized poolroom. Three walls were paneled and a curtain was drawn across the fourth; behind this staff members monitored telephones and computer and television screens. In one corner a black Plexiglas bubble was affixed to the ceiling, camouflaging a videocamera that could be activated to record proceedings in the room. There was, however, to be no record that this meeting ever occurred.

"Mr. President," Secretary Price said, "I know this has been a rough day already, but I'm afraid there's more bad news for us in Israel. Something that has far more important consequences than what happened last night. I've asked General Kastenmayer to brief you and Butch on this and respectfully ask that this matter be extremely closely held. No one else is to know for the time being."

Hollendale asked, "Shouldn't Jack Bickford be in on this?"

"No, Mr. President. This involves a highly compartmentalized defense program. I've asked General Kastenmayer first to bring you up to date on SUNDANCER. This program, as you know, offers us the greatest breakthrough we could hope for in satellite reconnaissance, acquisition, and targeting technology." Price turned to the President's top military adviser and signaled for him to begin.

Allen Kastenmayer was a thin, slightly built, balding man who had the mien and pallor of a clergyman. He was soft-spoken, utterly devoid of that gruff "only Air Force spoken here" bombast that afflicted so many military officers. His toughness was all on the inside.

"It's incredibly technical," he began. "I'll skip all the azimuths and pixels and put it in shirt-sleeve English.

"We have the capability now to hang an infrared bird approximately 22,300 miles in geosynchronous orbit in space." Kastenmayer's face flushed slightly as he caught himself slipping into scientific terms immediately. "That means it will stay in a fixed position relative to the earth's surface. It will cover about a quarter of the planet at all times. The satellite will scan the earth's surface, searching for unusual levels of heat.

"It will be able to separate the heat from natural and artificial ground clutter—industrial and commercial activities, even dump sites. It will be able to spot cruise missile or ICBM tests anywhere in the Soviet Union—Kola Peninsula, Tyuratam, or Plesetsk, you name it—and distinguish decoys from real missiles. And track thousands of them simultaneously.

"The upshot of all this is that if the Soviets ever try to launch a sneak attack on us, we're going to be able to knock out their missiles almost as soon as they leave their launching pads and platforms, and then put the Bear in total darkness. He wouldn't know where the next nuclear bolt, aimed right at his heart, was coming from."

"Come on, Allen. Even the Air Force must admit that the threat's down now. I like SUNDANCER for keeping an eye on them. But let's cut the old bolt-from-the-blue bullshit."

"Will do, Mr. President. But they've still got eight or nine thousand strategic warheads they can lay on us like a Joe Montana pass."

Kastenmayer, chastened by Hollendale's admonition, was careful to couch the rest of his description of the program in defensive terms. He did not have to elaborate that in this case, America's technological shield could easily be turned into a preemptively striking sword.

"And what part do our Israeli *friends* have in all of this?" Hollendale inquired, scratching on a notepad that he had every intention of destroying.

"They've got the space-based laser gun."

"Well, it sounds to me like everything is on track, General. What's the reason for the urgency of this briefing?" The President's tone took on an edge of impatience, implying that the others could have discussed this with Naylor without bothering him.

"We've got a major problem, sir. We believe this technology has been leaking right into the Soviets' hands."

"What?" Hollendale erupted.

"There is great danger that every promise offered by SUN-DANCER is being broken by someone's greed or fanaticism."

"What's the evidence, General?" Hollendale's voice had

dropped to little more than a whisper, which told Naylor that he was fighting to hold down his anger.

"A defector. Vyacheslav Kamamenov."

"Is the intelligence community united on the validity of his information?"

"No, sir. Not yet. The CIA doesn't accept his bona fides yet. And they don't understand his references to SUNDANCER."

"You think he's legitimate?"

"Yes, sir. I've spent a good many hours with the analysts over at the Defense Intelligence Agency. DIA thinks he's straight. We recruited him back in 1979, when he was a visiting scholar at MIT, up in Cambridge. After he returned to Moscow, he was admitted as a member of the Academy of Sciences. He's been one of the leading Soviet scientists assigned to work on their strategic defense programs—which, as you know, are more vigorous than our own. He knows about the tests we've been conducting with our friends. And he says the data are coming through a Soviet agent in Israel known as *Canaan.*"

"Jesus Christ." Hollendale turned to Naylor, a look of incredulity in his eyes. "Do you believe it, Butch? *Canaan?*"

Naylor nodded, his lips tight. "It's possible, Mr. President."

"There are several other possibilities, sir," Kastenmayer continued. "The leaks could be coming from the contractors. They have excellent security control, but it's always possible that one of their scientists has been compromised. The Soviets pay a lot more money than they did in the old days."

"Yeah," Naylor could not resist adding, "thanks to all the credits and guaranteed loans we've been giving them. We're financing their espionage in our own country."

"What about those divas on the Hill?" This was Hollendale's favorite way of referring to members of Congress. Not one of them could pass a refrigerator light without breaking into an instant analysis of the late-night news, he thought. God, how they liked to strut and pontificate. Oh, they had power, too, the power to delay, defer, paralyze . . . But they wanted no responsibility! No, the only way to get things done was to take action first and talk about it later. There weren't many chances to do this. But if he acted and was successful, Hollendale knew they'd fall into line and heap him with praise. If he failed, there would be a stampede to the press galleries to condemn him. Either at his throat or at his feet. So be it. He wasn't going to let a bunch of pygmies tie the presidency into knots with all their phony, soul-searching timidities . . .

"Also possible," responded Kastenmayer. "But there are only a few who know about SUNDANCER's . . . targeting capabilities. They have a conceptual understanding, but no technical information of any specificity."

"But," Naylor injected, "conceptual knowledge would be enough to alert technical people within the intelligence community to things to look for."

Kastenmayer nodded in agreement. "That's right, Butch. There could be a tandem arrangement, with neither person evoking anyone's suspicions. A congressman or a senator could furnish the technical man—or woman—with the code-word keys that unlock the computer's safe."

"But it's also possible that it's someone in our own shop. That could include as many as a hundred people."

Naylor knew that Kastenmayer's last comment had set fire to the President's smoldering emotions.

"Goddammit! General, I can't even hold a Cabinet meeting without its appearing verbatim in the Washington *Post* the next day. I swear to God that some of my own people are backstabbing me. Either that or the chandeliers are wired!" Hollendale was building up to one of his patented rages. He slammed the notepad down and pushed his chair away from the conference table. After pacing halfway around the table, cursing between clenched teeth, he returned to his seat across from Kastenmayer, possessed of a sudden unexpected calm.

"What are my options, General?"

Naylor looked at the man he called Iceman in guarded moments. He had seen this transformation before. Hollendale was a bundle of emotional contradictions, capable of erupting over the most trivial and insignificant matters but then running cold as icewater when the White House pillars seemed about to crumble.

Look at him now, Naylor thought, admiration spreading across his face. *Cool sonofabitch.* The economy was heating up. The jackals on Wall Street were demanding tax cuts; Congress was on a rampage over corporate greed. South Korea just announced that it was shutting down our army base in Seoul, and pressure was on to get out of

Okinawa. On top of all this came the news of the Gaza massacre. Now this. And Iceman didn't even break a sweat.

"There aren't many, sir," Kastenmayer said, "and none of them are good. We can scale back the funding of the program for the next fiscal-year budget and cite congressional cuts in the defense budget as the reason. This would cause serious layoffs for the contractor and succeed in producing cost escalations if we decide to ramp the program back up. Second, you could call the Israeli Prime Minister, tell him about the problem, and ask him to investigate."

"Investigate!" Hollendale exploded again. "First they gas some Palestinians and say, 'Sorry, we made a little mistake at the pharmacy.' Now they've got a damn traitor working for the Russians, and we're going to ask them to help us find him? Why don't we make it real simple—they turn over the spy or we turn off the spigot on SUNDANCER. A straight quid pro quo. What choice would Gerstel have but to deal?"

Naylor decided to intercede. "He could argue that the spy story is phony, a back-door deception designed by the Arabists at the State Department. And he has a lot of support in this country, Mr. President. Maybe fifty or a hundred political action committees. They carry a lot of weight with Congress."

"I don't think so, Butch. He's got too much at stake with our foreign assistance package this year." There was a trace of menace in Hollendale's voice. "After what happened in Gaza last night, I don't think he's in a position to influence American public opinion. And the divas won't take on public opinion on this one."

"Or," Naylor continued, adding another option, "in the worst-case scenario, the existence of SUNDANCER could be leaked to the press. If Congress were to learn of all the . . . facets of the program—well, it could be . . . difficult. Very difficult."

"Gerstel would do that to me? Some friend!"

"None better, Mr. President. He wouldn't do it. One of his political enemies would. Gerstel has carried a lot of heavy mail for us that no one else would touch. We pull out and he's gone. He's been criticized by his right wing for being soft on the Palestinians and a lapdog of the United States. They'd ridicule him by saying that's the way we treat lapdogs. The Israelis play politics like it's roller derby—with brass knuckles. We can't cut him off. Without Gerstel, there's a real possibility that we'd lose the only hope for moderation in the Likud. How would you like to do business with the Kach? They became even more militant after Rabbi Kahane's assassination. Or the Sicarri—the Daggermen? They threatened to kill Yitzhak Shamir one time for making too many concessions to the PLO. They probably wouldn't hesitate to go after Gerstel."

Kastenmayer offered one final thought. "Mr. President, it's possible that Kamamenov's defection is not genuine."

"But you said you think it is."

"I do. I'm just exploring all the possibilities. This might be an attempt by the Soviets to stop the program—about which they have speculations but no information—by introducing doubts about its security. If they turned Kamamenov, they may be using him to spread disinformation."

"In which case, General?"

"In which case my recommendation is that we continue doing business as usual for the time being."

"Now I'm really confused," Hollendale said, his shoulders sagging, exasperation—or was it despair?—creeping back into his voice.

"It gets complicated, Mr. President. But basically, if we react too quickly to Kamamenov, the Soviets will conclude that we think he's a phony."

"But what difference does that make? If they've forced us to cut back or stop the program, haven't they succeeded?"

"Not necessarily," Kastenmayer responded, almost seeming to enjoy the regimen of mental gymnastics he was putting the President through. "They'll think that any changes are mere cosmetics. The program will continue, forcing them to intensify efforts to stop it."

"All right. I think I understand what you're saying. If we take no immediate action in response to Kamamenov, then the Soviets will conclude that we're taking him seriously and that ultimately we'll have to change or cancel the program. But this will buy us some time."

"Yes, sir."

"This mind-game bullshit is terrific for all the cloak-and-dagger boys in this town, General. But what if Kamamenov is genuine and we do nothing to stop the program? Aren't we pouring billions right down a rat hole?"

Kastenmayer paused for a long time. "That's precisely the dilemma, Mr. President."

"The bottom line in this is that we have to find *Canaan*—if he exists—without telling the Israelis. Is that it, General?"

Looking directly at his commander-in-chief, Kastenmayer said, "Yes, sir. If we can find *Canaan,* we can continue to fund SUNDANCER. If we can't, we'll have to kill it. And with the congressional budget clock running, we don't have very much time."

3

A TALL, SLAT-THIN MAN whose receding hairline accentuated his large ears walked along the beach. The man wore khaki pants and a cable-knit sweater over a blue open-neck shirt. Shoeless, he carried a favorite piece of driftwood as a large walking stick, giving him, from a distance, the silhouette of a gaunt prophet from another age.

Avi Nesher, Mossad's counterintelligence chief, loved his morning walk on the beach, just after sunrise, when the day was fresh and the soft winds off the Mediterranean cleared his thoughts. The waves on the water caught the dawn and looked as if they were on fire.

He lived his life in a byzantine construction of cycles and epicycles of deception. Striding barefoot in the sand, Nesher appeared to be a man alone, just getting a bit of exercise. This, too, was a deception. At either end of the long beach, three men dressed in dark clothes scanned the full length of the shoreline with powerful binoculars. They carried Uzis and .45-caliber automatic pistols. Two others were stationed atop the Concorde and Sheraton hotels. Holding high-powered rifles, they watched the ocean for any signs of life in the water or any sudden movement along Retsif Herbert Samuel Street, which ran parallel to the beach. PLO assassins might emerge from the city, or from the sea as swimmers or frogmen.

Nesher needed to feel the salt and warmth of the Mediterranean, to witness the flock of sea birds scurrying in the sand searching for food. Always there was the sad cry of the gulls, the whisper of conscience.

It was not conscience that was troubling Nesher today, however. Just confusion. For two days his office had been pure bedlam: phones constantly ringing, men dashing about, classified cables piling up on his desk. Explanations demanded. None offered.

The Prime Minister had been in a rage. He fired Menachem Haretz, the deputy minister of defense, over the Gaza disaster. The official word to the public was that it was a tragic mistake. But Nesher knew it was no mistake. It was murder.

Someone had poured tabun, a deadly poison, into the tear-gas canisters. The Defense Minister put out a cover story that it had been a miscalculation, an overconcentration of chloropicrin. The cover story would not hold forever. Eventually the truth would get out. Then there would be another round of accusations. More denunciations. More resolutions in the United Nations, the house of murderous hypocrites!

But who could have done it? And why? Not Posner. From all that Nesher knew, Posner had been a model reservist. He had bitched a lot about duty in the Gaza, but who didn't? Besides, he had no access to Israeli chemical stockpiles. The switch had to have been made at one of the storage sites. And if that was the case, it had to have been the act of an extremist. Or—the thought that Nesher kept pushing from his mind—one of subversion, an act designed to humiliate Israel, provide comparisons to the Nazis. That would mean the perpetrator was someone who hated Israel more than Nesher hated the PLO . . .

Words floated in his mind. Evanescence. Impermanence. His thoughts were always on Israel, a small nation 210 miles long and 45 miles wide, smaller than the state of Massachusetts, surrounded by one hundred million Arabs who were coming like a floodtide. Young Israelis frolicked in their freedom, speaking of peace, while all around them their enemies were preparing for war.

For Nesher, Israel had gone soft, drifting off to the appeasement of the left. Decadence had set in. Western music had corrupted the young men and women. They thought of sex and material pleasures more than security. They wanted to "understand the legitimate grievances of the Palestinians," they said. "Give them land, so we may have peace," said the stupid university students who, under criticism from the Western world, had begun to feel guilty about the miracle the Israelis had achieved.

Nesher had cause to complain. As a line officer in Israel's three major wars, he had earned the reputation of a brilliant military tactician, and his bravery and improvisational genius on the battlefield had helped save Israel from defeat at the hands of the Egyptians in the 1973 Yom Kippur War. He had also lost an eye to a piece of shrapnel. Instead of a patch (another hero's trademark) he wore a glass eye.

General Eli Zeira had been convinced that Anwar Sadat would never go to war against Israel. He either ignored or dismissed the significance of reports that heavy armor, along with bridge-building and amphibious equipment, was being moved along the Suez. Port Fuad was bustling with activity. On the Damascus plains, the Syrians had moved antiaircraft missiles into operational status. Until October 5, 1973, the day before the Yom Kippur War began, Zeira believed that war was not imminent. His acknowledgment of error came grudgingly and very nearly too late. Nesher had compensated for Zeira's stubbornness, or stupidity—whatever it was. Golda Meir pronounced him a military hero.

At one time Nesher had been an avowed anti-Soviet. The Soviets had armed Israel's enemies—Egypt, Syria, Jordan, Iraq, Lebanon, the PLO. But the United States, with its wealth and technological superiority, gave more than enough security to assure defeat of the Arabs. Lately, however, America's resolve and support were not what they once had been. Sure, America gave Israel the Patriot missile *after* the Iraqi Scuds had hit Tel Aviv. And then even before the war with Iraq was over, the United States announced its support for an International Peace Conference!

The United States had promised to help Israel develop an antimissile system; now Israel, having spent four years in its research and development, was faced with the possibility that the United

States might cancel the project under pressure of left-wing zombies, those idiots who demanded more money for social programs and dreamed of white pigeons and olive branches as the core of America's foreign policy. Dead pigeons. That's what America had in store for the Israelis.

That was not the only change. The French and the British, along with the United States, had become major suppliers of modern weaponry to the so-called moderate Arab states. Nesher laughed bitterly. And the Chinese—once Israel had supplied them with military technology, but now the Chinese were using Western technology to modernize their economy while shipping intermediate-range missiles to every Saudi or sultan who professed the need to defend his countrymen against Iran and Iraq. That's what certain Arabs cried to the West, while laughing up their tunics to the rest of the Arab world. Zion was their target, not Tehran or a bombed-out Baghdad.

There were other important changes taking place. The Soviet Union had changed its policy toward Israel at last. As a result of Nesher's covert efforts, the Soviets had in the past three years released more than three hundred thousand Soviet Jews to Israel and would release that many this year alone. And Israel needed more Jewish settlers, those who had known hardship, those who would be unwilling to sell out their new homeland so that the Palestinians could wage war against them.

Nesher had been a member of the Israeli delegation that had traveled to Vienna in 1989 for a preliminary meeting on establishing better relations with the Soviet Union. During that conference, he had struck what he believed to be a vein of gold. It was there that he met a man named Ptor Kornienko. Kornienko indicated that the Soviets were willing to help Israel by forewarning them of certain planned operations by the Muslim radicals in south Lebanon and giving them information on new weapons acquired by the Saudis and the Gulf states.

Nesher knew the meeting with Kornienko had been no accident. The Soviets were desperate. Their empire was disintegrating. They were making a virtue of necessity in letting Soviet Jews come to Israel. But the Jews were not coming fast enough for Nesher. There was a new surge of anti-Semitism in Russia. The Russians needed to blame someone for their despair. The danger was that the

Pamyat, the anti-Semitic right-wing group, would shut the gates before all of Nesher's people could emigrate. The Pamyat's members made no effort to hide their intentions. They were planning pogroms against the *zhidy*, the Yids. Nesher was not going to permit another *Kristallnacht* by these new Nazis who preached racial purity and searched for Jewish blood back to the tenth generation. It was Nesher who overcame Arab pressure tactics designed to throttle direct flights from the Soviet Union to Tel Aviv.

There was, of course, a price he would have to pay to Kornienko. There was always a price. But to Nesher it was a small one.

Last week Kornienko had warned Nesher that, according to a high-level source he had in the U.S. State Department, the Americans had placed an agent in the Mossad. This traitor could undermine Israel's emerging relations with the Soviet Union. He had to be identified . . .

At that moment, something caused Nesher to spin to his right and glance upward. A shadow was falling toward him, something large, indistinct against the early light. He stepped back, reeling, his right arm raised to ward off an impending blow. A small cry, more of a gasp, escaped his lips as he fell backward into the wet sand. He heard a soft thud and waited intuitively for a detonation that would kill or, worse, maim him. Nothing. He looked up and started to laugh, first with relief, then with embarrassment. It was a gull, headless now thanks to a bullet from Zvi Evron's .308 rifle. The gull had been carrying an empty milk carton. On the rooftop of the Concorde Hotel, Zvi had thought it might be a rat, a piece of garbage, or a small bomb that could be remotely triggered. Zvi took no chances.

Brushing off his pants, watching the gull's blood drain into the sand, Nesher decided he could not take any chances either.

A week later Nesher traveled to Paris to meet with Yitzhak Rafiah, a former Israeli ambassador to the United States, now ambassador to France. Nesher repeated the statement that had begun his conversation with Rafiah: "Let me say it again. Perhaps you did not hear me. There is a U.S. agent in Israeli intelligence."

"And I repeat to you," Rafiah said, "I do not see this as important. I find this fact to be one of those typical tit-for-tat games you are forever playing."

"No, Yitzhak. You know it is different. For us it is a matter of survival. We have no margin for error. We have no choice. You think the Americans are merely friendly observers? They have new clients in the Middle East." What had been thoughts a week before on the beach were now words that Nesher barked at Rafiah. "They sold out and recognized the PLO—terrorists who plot our destruction. After years of helping arm Saddam Hussein, they caved in to the Saudis and gave them the M1A1 tanks and upgraded F-15 planes they wanted. And now the Egyptians are demanding more high-performance aircraft."

"Avi, I know all of this. But I assure you, they are still our friends."

When dealing with others, Rafiah sometimes played the role of the foppish diplomat, a pencil-pusher who enjoyed the trappings of ambassadorship. But with Nesher he wore no masks. Nesher had pointedly asked for a beer—*Israeli* beer—when Rafiah had offered him a drink. Rafiah sipped a vintage French wine. They sat in his office, a showcase of modern, Israeli-crafted furniture and decor. A wide window looked out on a quiet, tree-shaded street. To Nesher's critical eye, the window was not bulletproof.

Rafiah's career had included twelve years in Aman, the Israel Defense Forces intelligence branch, a rival of the Mossad. Aman officers did not endorse the Mossad's self-proclaimed omniscience.

Nesher decided to twist the information given to him earlier by Ptor Kornienko. Standing now, his right index finger stabbing the air, he said, "We must know who this man is. It is important to Israeli security. This is no game, Mr. Ambassador, I assure you. We know that this bastard is a double agent, and he is feeding highly secret technical information, provided by the United States, *to the Soviets.* We cannot afford to have this technology fall into Soviet hands. So we need to get the name. We need to establish the identity. This will be a most difficult task. But I am sure that your American friends can do it."

"I am astonished at your naïveté, Avi," Rafiah said. "That is not the sort of information they have access to."

"All we need is this one piece of vital information. Tell them it is vital that they help us."

"And you're telling me that the Prime Minister has authorized this? He wants me to do it?"

Nesher nodded gravely, not once taking his eyes from Rafiah. One more lie in this conversation did not matter.

"I will try, Avi. I can make no promises. But I will try."

4

Iᴛ ᴡᴀs ᴀ ᴄᴏᴏʟ sᴘʀɪɴɢ day. But as Joshua Stock approached the northwest entrance to the White House, the knot in his stomach felt hot.

The call had come last night. Its suddenness had startled him. Ordinarily, most senators looked forward to a meeting in the Oval Office. Being seen entering the West Wing of the White House by the national press corps camped outside elevated a senator's prestige, even if only momentarily. Such a meeting implied that the President wished to share confidential information with his guest or to extract a concession from him. It didn't matter whether the senator was to gain or give something. That he was in a position to do either signified his importance.

But Stock took no pride in meeting with Eric Hollendale, the first Democrat to win the presidency since Jimmy Carter. The two men had been friendly at one time. But friction and distrust had displaced their friendship.

During his campaign for the presidency, Hollendale, with Stock's help, had carried the state of Florida. In no small measure, his victory was ensured by his pledge of unqualified support for

Israel. But once elected he had begun to step away from his commitment. Short steps at first: a nuance here, a slight shift there. Then came the bold proclamation for a new peace plan. The need for a more balanced approach. Recognition of the legitimate rights of Palestinians. A return by Israel to defensible borders. More arms sales to moderate Arab nations.

At the gate Stock showed his identification card to a large uniformed officer who scanned his clipboard in search of Stock, Joshua. After looking at the photo on the laminated card, then glancing at Stock, he motioned the new Cadillac convertible through the gates. Stock parked his car along the long paved driveway that led to the portico of the West Wing. He locked his car door, distrustful even behind closed iron gates. There was no telling whether one of the White House reporters might be tempted to search through the papers sitting on his dashboard.

He strode from his car toward the portico. His walk, not quite athletic, was characteristically vigorous. He still exuded confidence even as it began to drain from him. At the portico he exchanged a good morning with the ramrod-stiff Marine guard, who snapped to a salute.

A large black man stepped from a small room just inside the double-doored entranceway. "Can I take your coat and briefcase, Senator?" It was not so much a question as a demand. The request was a polite way of reminding visitors about the need for security.

Stock slipped from his lined Burberry trenchcoat and handed it to the man. He was hesitant to turn over his thick leather attaché case, because he had been kept waiting on more than one occasion and could use the time to catch up on his correspondence in the open reception room. He glanced over to the captain's tables in front of the two couches and saw that they were covered with the Washington *Post*, the New York *Times*, and the *Wall Street Journal*—more than enough reading material to keep him busy. He handed over his case and moved to the side of the receptionist's desk.

Katherine White, the President's secretary, was a thin-boned woman who tied her gray-streaked hair in a bun and secured her glasses to a beaded chain draped around her delicate neck. Smiling pleasantly, she pushed her intercom and announced Stock's arrival. The President would be with him in a few moments, he was told.

Stock sat on the couch, picked up the *Times*, and read not a word. Glancing through the pages, he was having trouble controlling the tremble in his fingers. No major arms sales were pending for approval by Congress. No judicial appointments requested by Stock were up for negotiation with the administration. He tried to think of every conceivable issue that could be of concern to Hollendale.

He stood up and turned around. He studied the large painting of George Washington crossing the ice-caked Delaware in a nearly swamped rowboat. Then he walked across the room to look at a dark, red-tinted landscape by Alvan Fisher. The scene depicted two Indian scouts poised on a slight ridge, about to be swallowed by the coming night.

He returned to the sofa. His orderly mind continued to rifle through the possible reasons for presidential interest in him. There could be only one reason, he told himself.

Always it had been the same pitch: Hollendale had committed his administration to selling advanced weaponry to one of the moderate Arab states, and he needed to have visible supporters of Israel "belly up to the bar," as his chief of staff, Clayton Skillings, crudely put it, to support his authority. Any loss or diminution of the President's power would weaken the United States in negotiating with other countries. It was forever a case of global gamesmanship in which the future of the free world hung in the balance. "Would you weaken the presidency out of blind loyalty to Israel? Don't you understand that a weakened United States can only weaken Israel?"

It was always phrased rhetorically, seemingly innocent in its wide-eyed directness. But the question was hardly innocent or direct. In fact, it was not a question. It was a threat. Once, Skillings had uttered a direct threat: "Support the President on this or I'll cut Israel's annual wish list down so far, Uncle Scrooge will look like one of Santa's helpers."

The technique worked with most senators. Not with Stock. Of course he was loyal to the United States. Yes, he wanted the President to remain strong. But why arm the enemies of our friends? No, Stock always had reasoned, he was not going to be a marionette whose arms and legs went flopping whenever Hollendale pulled on his patriotic strings.

An aide appeared and led Stock through a door. As he was escorted past the Roosevelt Room—filled with paintings and statues of the great Rough Rider and his New Dealer cousin—Stock could feel beads of sweat form under his arms and run in silent rivulets down his sides. He wanted to stop, to go to the lavatory. But there was no time. He experienced the oddest sensation that the corridor was starting to shrink perceptibly, its walls and ceiling moving closer. Though the floor was covered with a thick, deep pile carpet, he imagined that he could hear his feet striking concrete. Footfalls echoing. Why? Why was his heart pounding so?

Surprisingly, the President was alone.

Hollendale greeted Stock affably, asked if he would like some coffee, and escorted him to the sitting area opposite his ornate mahogany desk. Stock politely turned down the coffee. There was the customary exchange of pleasantries, small talk that Stock knew was masking Hollendale's agenda and his own anxiety.

An awkward momentary silence presaged the disappearance of cordiality. Hollendale's voice dropped lower, took on a sudden edge. "Joshua, we've got a problem." He paused. Was he going to lecture Stock over the tragedy in Gaza and demand that Stock help him by publicly supporting his efforts to force the Israelis to negotiate with the PLO?

Then the door to the Oval Office suddenly opened. "I've asked the director to join us. I thought it would be better to discuss this . . . difficult matter frankly. Perhaps the director can give us some guidance on how we might proceed. Harry, why don't you explain the situation to Senator Stock?"

Harry Polanski, director of the FBI, could have passed for a sumo wrestler. He always shook hands as if he were testing the density of a victim's metacarpals. He took law enforcement very seriously. People took him the same way. When Stock thrust out his hand and braced for the usual test, Polanski kept his hand at his side, turned away, and sat in a stuffed chair. Stock remained standing.

Unlike Hollendale, Polanski did not begin with preliminaries. "Senator," he said, "we've been reviewing a matter with the intelligence community. Information has developed that makes it necessary for us to talk."

Stock shifted his eyes from Polanski to the green-tinted bulletproof window behind the President's desk. Hollendale, sipping coffee, let the silence hang in the air.

Finally Polanski said, "I think there is a way out of a serious problem, Senator. One that will be helpful to us and to you."

Stock turned to the President. Hollendale looked down at a file folder. "If this has anything to do with the Intelligence Committee, I would assume that the DCI would be present," Stock said. It was a typical Joshua Stock remark, designed to put down Polanski and build up the director of the Central Intelligence Agency.

Polanski hoisted his bulk out of the chair. "Mr. President," he said, "I think this is a conversation that the senator and I should hold in the Situation Room."

The President nodded, and Polanski led the way out of the Oval Office and down a narrow corridor under the watchful eyes of the Secret Service. Walking next to him, Stock felt like a prisoner.

Late that night, alone in his Senate office, Stock hunched over the keyboard of a computer next to his desk. *My understanding,* he typed, *is that not even the DCI knows about this,* and he began to recount what had happened in the Situation Room.

Joshua Stock knew that he could not tell Sean Falcone about the White House meeting that had taken place three days earlier. But he also knew that he had to see his friend, had to give him a sense of the ordeal that had become Stock's public and private life.

They met in a side room of Falcone's Senate office suite. The room was designed for the invited visitor who did not want to be logged in by a receptionist and then run the gauntlet of staff offices and cubicles to get to the senator's large, formal office. The discreet visitor slipped into the side room through an unmarked hall door which had been unlocked for the occasion.

"You look like hell, you know," Falcone said, laughing and ceremoniously pulling out a chair for Stock. Falcone sprawled on a worn leather couch that his administrative assistant had banished to the side room during a redecoration of his office.

"Thanks a lot," Stock replied. "But on my worst days I've got to look better than you."

They both spoke a crude truth. Stock, who wore a Florida tan as an advertisement for the state he represented, was tense and nervous.

They chatted for a few minutes, and Stock began to relax. To Falcone's surprise, he asked permission to smoke. He lit what Falcone recognized as his friend's old favorite, a genuine Cuban, supplied by a wealthy Miami supporter.

"You're smoking again, Josh. How long were you off? Five months?"

"Six months, seven days," Stock said. He managed a quick smile. "I haven't had the nerve to tell Cleo. I sneak out into the garage when she's asleep, grab a smoke, then spray a lot of air freshener."

"You'll never fool Cleo about anything, Josh."

"I certainly know *that* better than anyone else." Again a quick smile. Then Stock said, "There is one thing I want to tell you, Sean. And only you."

Instinctively, both men leaned forward, huddling against the microphones that so many Washingtonians imagine but never see.

"All I can say is that I am working on something. Something known only to my computer and me. I—I started working on it three days ago. I want you to know this. That's all. Just remember that date—April 15." He stood and took a step toward the door.

"Hold on, Josh," Falcone said, rising from the couch. "That's not enough for me. If it's committee business—"

"It's *not* committee business," Stock said, his hand on the doorknob. "Not your committee. And I hope to hell the day doesn't come when it might have to become your business."

5

WASHINGTON'S FAHREN-
heit readings had climbed into the nineties, melting away the last
traces of spring. Joshua Stock stared into the full-length mirror on
the inner side of his closet door. He was thin, he thought, too thin,
and beginning to look anemic.

Cleo was becoming alarmed. Stock dismissed the weight loss.
Too much caffeine and too little sleep, he told her. It was the busiest
part of the congressional season. A senator's wife ought to know that
by now. Things would ease up. A recess was due soon. A vacation on
Cape Cod or at Kennebunkport would restore every lost ounce, he
said unconvincingly.

Stock felt as if he were on the verge of a breakdown, stemming
from that April day at the White House.

At first it had seemed the right thing, the patriotic thing to do.
But doubt began to haunt his nights. The plan—he wondered
whether the President knew or wanted to know of it—was risky. Of
course, if the President authorized him to go through with it, there
was no violation. But what if the plan went up in smoke? What if
Hollendale disavowed any knowledge? Stock assumed that his con-

versations with Polanski had been either videotaped or recorded. But the tapes could be easily destroyed—or, worse, altered so that only Polanski's phony accusations remained.

Night after night he lay awake staring at the shadows rippling on the bedroom ceiling, dark ghosts mocking him, taunting him. He tried to fix in his mind the precise point when his life began to change irreversibly. He kept going back to the moment when he had met his lover at the French embassy, four months ago.

Her image flooded his thoughts. She was beautiful, bewitching. He tried to force her from his mind, for fear that he might utter her name in his sleep. But she kept slipping back, transfixing him with her piercing eyes. In the darkness, he could smell her perfume. He followed it, his mind mingling with the rising vapor, back to the embassy's cocktail reception.

He had never seen a woman so extraordinarily voluptuous. Her white Ungaro dress clung to her body, revealing high, taut breasts, firm buttocks, and long, tapered legs. Her dark hair fell about her face and shoulders in soft, full waves. Her brown eyes ignited his emotions like a flame touching dry, brittle wood. No woman had excited him like that in years.

He moved casually along the line of familiar faces that frequented those Washington parties that demand attendance. But there had been nothing random about his movements that night. He had been an animal in stalk of prey, positioning himself strategically so that if the woman turned to her right, she would have to see him, to meet his eyes.

She was talking with several men, whose wives looked understandably uncomfortable in her presence. The ambassador for the Organization of American States whispered something in her ear. She tossed the glorious head back and laughed. Stock felt an absurd stirring of jealousy. Then she turned, her wide smile revealing teeth that were white and even, and looked directly at him. Their eyes locked for only a moment, but he was sure that she had read his mind.

He introduced himself, took her hand in his, and squeezed it firmly. There could be no mistake; the message he was sending her was hardly subtle. In his frankness, though, there was an undeniable excitement that he knew was attractive. She said her name was Elise Morney. She was from Morocco. Just visiting relatives for a few days.

Stock felt suddenly lost. A few days. Hardly enough time to say hello. He told her that one could not begin to see Washington, not to mention the United States, in just a few days. Surely she could stay longer? It was a plea rather than a question. He hoped that his voice did not reveal his sense of urgency.

Cleo was occupied with talking to the French ambassador's wife, but he could not afford to appear too interested in this perfect —oh, so perfect—stranger without raising eyebrows. On more than one occasion, Stock had observed that beauty was not an asset for a woman in Washington, if she was single. She became a threat to the other women and to the established rule that title and position are all. To dally too long talking to this woman might set off speculation that he was interested in more than polite conversation.

Stock ignored intuitive, long-cultivated caution. He inquired, trying to make his question innocent, where she was staying. The Willard? Lovely hotel. Perhaps he could call her for lunch one day soon? Wonderful. And off he went to fetch his wife, wondering if her intuition would somehow detect the desire roiling within him.

Thus began his first and only love affair. He knew it was wrong, that it violated an oath of fidelity he considered sacred. But his marriage had gone flat. Perhaps it was only a midseason slump, but whether from anger or from loneliness, Cleo had either pushed or pulled herself into absurd self-indulgence. Jewelry, clothes. Shopping sprees in New York. A new Mercedes 500 SL. Becoming the patron of a local artist. She clung to her possessions as if they constituted her life-support system. His civility toward her had become almost a diplomatic initiative, sex an obligation. He worked later, traveled more. Home was no longer a refuge but more like a hospice.

Elise ignited him, accelerated his heartbeat until his heart threatened to break through his chest. It was as if the first bloom of spring had appeared and turned his barren world a new and shimmering green. Soon, with Elise, he laughed again and took joy in life's smaller pleasures: a night in New York, a drive to Annapolis, a room at a bed-and-breakfast in the mountains of West Virginia. Moments stolen from calendars filled in by staff assistants. There were more than small pleasures. There was a new excitement—a thrill intensified by the illicitness of the relationship, by the sheer brevity of their moments together.

He tried to be discreet. They did not see each other constantly. Elise would be in Washington for no more than ten days during the course of a month. Then she would disappear to God knew where. Her absence intensified Stock's obsession. He looked at his calendar, seeing each day without her as a little death.

"Elise, Elise . . ." he whispered in his sleep. The words were soft, muffled, not quite intelligible. Once, to Cleo, it sounded as if he were saying *please, please.*

6

As HE STARED UP AT the thin shafts of light filtering through the high arched windows of his office, a sense of quiet despair tugged at Anatoly Voronsky's mind. He was the President of the Union of Soviet Socialist Republics, the General Secretary of the Communist Party, the most powerful man in all of Eurasia.

Outwardly, Voronsky presented a confident, charismatic personality. At the age of fifty-four, with a full head of silver hair that was combed back from a widow's peak in soft waves, he looked as if he could play a starring movie role as the leader of the United States. The fact that he spoke flawless English endeared him to the Western press and helped give him star status. Gone was the image of table-thumping peasants with bad breath and baggy suits. Voronsky possessed a lawyer's grasp of detail and nuance and a poet's ability to express the hopes and aspirations of his people in soaring language.

Yet for all the image and the accolades, Voronsky was wracked by doubt and frustration. Like his predecessor, Mikhail Gorbachev, he knew that vast, far-reaching changes were imperative for his country. Stalin still held the Soviet people hostage in his death grip, committing murder from his crypt. Radical measures were necessary to produce more consumer goods of higher quality for domestic consumption and foreign export. But productivity was a word reserved for military programs and athletes in training. Bureaucracy barricaded the present like the stone walls surrounding the Kremlin.

The Supreme Soviet, filled though it was with new faces, had held onto old dogmas and would commit only to half-measures. Half-measures in turn had forced the Soviet people to hobble into the future, while the United States, Japan—damn, even South Korea and Taiwan—ran at full stride, their microchip computers measuring every vital step in the process. Gorbachev's much-vaunted reform measures had crumbled from insufficient support, leaving in place the decaying pillars of central planning—and rage among the disillusioned citizens.

Gorbachev had had energy, imagination, courage. But despite his enthusiasm for *perestroika,* he knew little about economics. And he had been naïve. He had never anticipated the difficulties he would encounter in invigorating his country, shaking his people from their lethargy, calling on them for more work, more sacrifice, when there was no Napoleon, no Kaiser Wilhelm II, no Hitler rushing toward them.

Gorbachev's insistence on quality control in production lines had succeeded only in disrupting production. The disruption had produced only doubt and resistance to the call for quality. Harder work was needed to produce greater quantities of consumer goods, but harder work required greater rewards. And none could be offered in the short run. *That's the rub of it,* Voronsky mused, *the distance between the short and the long run. There are a thousand graveyards in between . . .*

Under pressure from the populist president of the Republic of Russia, Boris Yeltsin, to adopt more radical economic measures, Gorbachev watched his popularity fade while his country slid inexorably toward utter chaos. Having previously proved to be a master at open-field running, zigzagging first to the political left, then back to the right, Gorbachev reversed his course again. Rejecting the advice of his Prime Minister, Nikolai I. Ryzhkov, he embraced most—but not all—of the radical "500 Days" plan pushed by Yeltsin. Ryzhkov was humiliated, while Yeltsin complained that Gorbachev was undermining the plan by retaining central authority in Moscow to tax and print currency. In giving up his plan to restructure socialism while refusing to embrace radical reform fully, Gorbachev lost the support of his followers and adversaries alike.

Initially Voronsky had shown grudging support for his mentor's policies. But as expectations grew beyond reach and production lines yielded less, Voronsky began to shift back to the philosophical center, then to the right. Gorbachev had pleaded with him not to turn away. But Voronsky could sense the change in the political winds, and he saw no future in tying his fate to Gorbachev's. Call it expediency. Voronsky called it survival.

Ryzhkov's warnings proved prophetic. Those accustomed to the old centralized planning system became frightened, confused. Inflation roared out of control. Unemployment—a notion antithetical to all Soviet ideology and experience—jumped to intolerable levels as unprofitable plants closed. Riots broke out in bread lines. Communities were torn apart. Fathers turned against their sons, the young against the old, each generation casting blame on the other. Reformers cried that the dead hand of communism was strangling them. Others retorted that before Gorbachev they had never gone without bread, meat, cigarettes, hope . . . Gorbachev was driven from power in a riptide of anger.

Boris Yeltsin struggled to turn back the forces of repression. But while delivering a passionate speech at a Moscow rally, he collapsed suddenly and died. Authorities said that Yeltsin, who had a history of heart problems, had suffered a heart attack. A reporter from a Soviet newspaper, *Top Secret*, however, charged that the KGB had murdered him by using a remotely controlled electromagnetic device to alter his heartbeat. But the reporter had no proof. And even if proof existed, he had no court or jury to present it to. The KGB and the military were in full control, and they viewed reformers as traitors to the cause of preserving the motherland. They argued that Mikhail Gorbachev's experiment with a "new openness" had been subverted by Western mischief-makers. More liberty had turned into more license, more license into anarchy. The Union of Soviet Socialist Republics was on the verge of total disintegration. A return to sterner measures was required if it was to survive.

Conservative leaders turned to Voronsky, who had endeared himself to their cause with his writings and rhetoric. They saw in

him an opportunity to present to the world a vigorous young leader
with more traditional values. Reform was to be a central part of his
agenda, but it was more evolutionary in concept, more stabilizing in
practice than Mikhail Gorbachev's. Surely the West could understand the need to restrain ethnic violence, to restore law and order.
Surely Anatoly Voronsky could persuade Western leaders of the
virtue of restraint. A velvet voice and a gentle manner would help
soften the repressive blows of necessity.

It was a lie that Voronsky had embraced. He knew that freedom, once tasted, could not be denied. That the sufferings of World
War II could no longer chain Soviet citizens into permanent servi-
tude. That in spite of the huge reductions in armed forces in Europe,
the Soviet military was still dragging the entire economy into an
abyss.

But more than truth, Voronsky wanted power. He had slipped
on a public mask, a false face—one that he wore with increasing
discomfort.

Voronsky sighed, weariness overcoming him just as his work-
day was beginning. He glanced at the obligatory portrait of Lenin
that hung in his office, evidence of the fealty he pretended to hold
for the only Soviet leader who had survived Gorbachev's depreda-
tions. Among the Soviet people, however, even Lenin was becoming
an object of ridicule and contempt. Voronsky wondered how long it
would take those who followed him to drag him, figuratively,
through the streets and the history books of the Soviet Union. And
how long before that would occur?

He slapped down the thick stack of briefing papers that was
placed on his desk by six every morning. More bad news. More crop
failures. Cases of diphtheria were up. Thousands were dying from
drinking jet fuel. AIDS was spreading. Civil disorders continued in
the Ukraine and Georgia, following shortages of milk and flour.

Pushing himself away from his large, ornate desk, its top inlaid
with rich brown leather, Voronsky moved to the bookcase that lined
the wall to the right of his desk. He plucked off a shelf at eye level a
book containing some of Yevgeny Yevtushenko's older poems. He
turned to a dog-eared page, as if there was a need to verify Yevtushenko's warning that Stalin was "just pretending to be dead."

A knock, soft, as if the bones in the hand might break, interrupted his thoughts. "My, my, Mr. President, poetry before coffee

and *Pravda* have been served is an ambiguous sign." The voice was
lightly mocking.

"Ah, Oleg, come—come in," Voronsky said, trying to wipe
away traces of his depression with a wave of his hand.

His old confidant, a key adviser on the Presidential Council,
had already entered the room and made note of the book Voronsky
had closed and put back on the shelf. Oleg Kutznetzov was a short
man whose flaccid face and pear-shaped body revealed that he had
long ago yielded to culinary extravagance. Dark horn-rimmed
glasses looped over a long beaky nose magnified sad eyes that were
nearly enveloped in puffy sacs. Voronsky thought that though
Kutznetzov disliked animals, a hound would have been a perfect
companion for him.

"I was looking for a little inspiration, Oleg. A few quotes that I
might work into a speech that I am to make in Geneva next week.
You know how Genia was always writing about the 'invisible threads
that bind humanity.' The theme always seems to make Western eyes
go wet."

Kutznetzov remained silent for several seconds, watching
Voronsky knowingly. Then he moved to the wall of books. "There
are other poets for that, Mr. President." He reached for a volume.
"Here, here is Voznesensky." Then he pointed to a book on a shelf
too high for him to reach. "Bella Akhmadulina—her words soar.
They take wing, like a white dove." Kutznetzov flipped through the
book's pages, then returned it to its place. He walked back, waddled
really, to the chair in front of the President's desk.

"Oleg," Voronsky said, indicating with an uplifted hand for
Kutznetzov to sit down. "Occasionally I get discouraged by the reports that keep coming. There seems to be no relief from the bad
news."

"Mr. President, these are difficult times, but they must be
placed in perspective. Look at the United States. Would you trade
with them right now, hmmm? For their past, perhaps. But their
future? America is the world's largest debtor. It is the most violent,
crime-infested nation in the world. It has five percent of the world's
population and consumes fifty percent of the world's cocaine. Of the
ten largest banks, not one is in America; all belong to Japan. Our
high school students study physics and algebra for five years, chem-

istry, biology, calculus. Most American students know nothing of physics and chemistry. Only a handful study calculus . . ."

Voronsky could feel a smile breaking involuntarily across his face. Though now in his eighties, Kutznetzov, who had studied at Columbia University in New York in the late 1940s, could still rattle off statistics with the confident precision of a professor.

Enough. "Oleg, you know what they say—only a bore or an economist will cite statistics before sunrise."

Shrugging his shoulders, Kutznetzov asked, "So why did you ask to see me?" He poured himself a cup of strong black tea from a porcelain decanter on Voronsky's desk.

"I need your advice, Oleg. General Viktor Borovlev is pressing me to set up a meeting with the council soon." Voronsky swiveled around in his chair, slid a door back on his credenza, and snapped on a switch. Immediately the high-ceilinged room was filled with operatic voices. It was Verdi's *Nabucco*. Voronsky moved his chair around beside Kutznetzov and bent forward, huddling with him. "It is about BURAQ."

"BURAQ? I thought that Gorbachev canceled that crazy plan."

"So did I. Apparently Borovlev didn't bury it. He just put it on the shelf. Now he's revived it and wants to move to the final phase." Voronsky's voice dropped to a mere whisper. He did not remind Kutznetzov that he had initially indicated his support for the program in order to curry favor with Borovlev.

"Why?" Kutznetzov asked, sharing his friend's anxiety.

"He says for three reasons: 'Saddam Hussein. Saddam Hussein. Saddam Hussein.' "

"Meaning?"

"Who ever knows precisely what Borovlev means? You know how he operates. He traffics in ambiguities, and thinks it makes him appear prophetic."

"What do *you* think he means, Anatoly?"

"Oh, that Saddam was a genius to gobble up Kuwait and a fool not to move right into Riyadh when he had the chance."

"Ah, I see," Kutznetzov said as he paced, then walked in small circles, with his hands clasped behind his back—a hound transformed into a penguin. "So he's convinced that BURAQ will give us what Saddam lost. Bah."

Kutznetzov turned around, then lowered himself into the chair in front of Voronsky's desk. "Anatoly, even if the plan were not sheer madness, the timing is all wrong. We are doing very well with the United States and the Western Europeans. Even the Japanese."

"Precisely. But he is adamant. And I think he has the support of Yuri Volokov and possibly Dmitri Matrosov." Like Borovlev, they were members of the President's Security Council.

"Any who disagree?"

"Only Nikolai Semenovich Truskin."

"What about Dmitri Matrosov?"

"I think his personal views are close to Borovlev's. But so far he's remained neutral because the GRU continues its tug-of-war with the KGB. Also, Oleg, there is no doubt in my mind that Borovlev's hand was involved in the massacre in Gaza in April. At first I accepted the Israeli explanation of an error. But now I've been informed that Borovlev was behind it. That he is moving ahead with BURAQ on his own."

Kutznetzov's eyes moved rapidly from side to side. "Then you must be careful. Borovlev is ambitious and dangerous. He appeals to the worst instincts of the ideologues. Truskin does not carry enough weight with the rest of the members."

"Do you think I should challenge him?"

"Not yet. It may not be necessary. First, force him to state why he would accelerate the plan now—the risks and rewards. See how that plays with the others. If there seem to be any doubters other than Truskin, you might have a good chance to defeat him."

"And if there are none?"

"Stall for time. You still are the one who must approve the final decision."

No, Voronsky thought. *The decision is not always mine, not unless things have gone wrong. Then the decision and blame are mine.*

Kutznetzov finished his struggle to get up from his chair, shook Voronsky's hand, and started to leave. He opened the door, then looked back. "And Mr. President," he said with the affection of a father for a son, "I know you like to have the Italians tailor your suits. And I know how much you dislike the Germans. But I would suggest"—he smiled, pointing to the ceiling—"that Wagner would make better listening for you and all your guests."

7

Washington, June 25

STOCK TOOK HIS SEAT
in Room 219 of the Hart Senate Office Building. Spreading out stiff-
spined black looseleaf notebooks labeled TOP SECRET in bold red
letters, he nodded to his friend Sean Falcone. "Morning, Mr. Chairman," he said, bowing in a pantomime of servant to master as
Falcone banged his gavel on a small wooden block, signaling the
beginning of the secret briefing.

Only members of the Senate Intelligence Committee were permitted to enter the dark cavern where the nation's innermost secrets
were kept. The room resembled a cubist vision of a crypt. The low
ceilings were held up by thick, angular stanchions. The walls, un-
decorated except for a map of the world and the insignia of the
Central Intelligence Agency, the FBI, and four other intelligence
services, were painted light gray, divided by a bright yellow stripe.
A small, horseshoe-shaped dais accommodating the committee's fifteen members faced a witness table. There were thirty fabric-cov-
ered aluminum chairs available for intelligence experts and others
summoned to the committee's secret sessions.

Curiosity alone would be a compelling force for a senator to attend a committee hearing. But it was rare for all members to be present during meetings, and rarer still for more than a few to remain until a hearing's conclusion. Senators had too many conflicting responsibilities; other hearings, meetings, and conferences demanded their attention and their votes. Staff members remained in the room, observing, judging, and memorizing testimony. But a great deal could be missed by staff members, who might not have access to the full spectrum of intelligence activities—or the experience of a senator. Perhaps this is why critics snidely called "intelligence oversight" an oxymoron.

Falcone believed that the secret nature of the committee's hearings inevitably produced low attendance. The public had no way of knowing who did or did not attend the sessions, whereas senators' presence at the open meetings of other committees was a matter of record. A mean-spirited practice had developed in the Senate: both Republicans and Democrats had begun to keep attendance records, which were brandished about during elections as evidence of absenteeism. As a result, senators went racing about peli-mell to their various committees. They stopped long enough to be recorded as present and to ask one or two questions, then left, hell-bent for the next meeting. Their attendance was recorded, but their attention was rarely captured. Attendance records for the Intelligence Committee could not be released, so there was no pressure to attend, no accountability to an inquiring press or angry constituency.

Actually, Falcone and his vice chairman, John Christy, preferred a light attendance. They did not hold all of the committee members in high regard, thinking them either too willing to accede to every Agency request or too enthusiastic in their opposition to anything that bore the stamp TOP SECRET. The fewer members present, the greater the leaders' power and latitude to speak on behalf of the full committee.

Falcone noted five empty chairs flanking him on the dais. Today's agenda was important. They were going to be briefed on "black programs," projects that were so highly classified that only a very limited number of people in the entire government knew of their existence. Money had to be authorized and appropriated for the projects, and under the Constitution, that required action by Congress, but the projects had to be hidden in such a fashion that most members of Congress had no idea where the money was going.

The military's black programs went to key members of the Armed Services Committee, the CIA's to the Intelligence Committee.

In the hearings, the programs were described in terms of validated requirements, technical feasibility, and cost estimates. Their complexity exceeded the technical grasp of most senators, and the request for funding was routinely approved, with the rationale that America was pushing the scientific envelope, breaking into new and exotic dimensions of technology that promised to keep us years ahead of the Soviets and Chinese.

Falcone greeted Roger Oberdorf, the deputy director of the CIA, and the other witnesses seated at the table.

Oberdorf thanked Falcone and indicated that he would provide the committee with an overview of the new black programs under development. "If there are any questions about the technical aspects of the programs, General Atkins is prepared to respond," Oberdorf said.

Dale Atkins, who sat at attention in his blue Air Force uniform with two rows of ribbons, was the National Security Agency's director of research and development. NSA was charged with intercepting and interpreting signals intelligence, which ranged from radio and electronic signals emitted during Soviet and Chinese missile tests to conversations taking place in Soviet President Anatoly Voronsky's dacha, limousine, or bathroom. Few words in the world were secure from NSA's giant ears. A laser beam directed against a distant building could peel a conversation from inside as easily as a blade could strip away wallpaper. Satellites deep in space could listen to radio conversations as if they were on an old-fashioned party line. The ability to listen to conversations and decode radio signals could provide the United States with virtually unlimited advantages in carrying out preemptive air strikes or sabotage. The NSA's worldwide array of equipment could also disrupt an opponent's command and control systems through jamming and electronic pulsing.

Oberdorf asked that the lights be flicked off. A slide projector hummed to life and an artist's schematic drawings filled the white screen that stood behind the committee's official reporter. He kept a verbatim record of the hearing by whispering testimony into a small, cone-shaped instrument that gave him the appearance of a man calmly breathing into an oxygen mask.

"One of the more promising projects in this year's budget, code-named DECIMAL DEWEY, is a computer chip that can be installed in an office copying machine. The chip will be capable of transmitting images of documents, as they are being copied, instantaneously back to Langley from anywhere in the world." Oberdorf's lips gave the faintest evidence of a smile as he said *anywhere.* Anywhere meant China and the U.S.S.R., two countries that in the past had preferred carbon paper to Xerox machines. Now the photocopying revolution had reached them. "The copying machine provides the power to the chip, so it requires no batteries and its outgoing signal is absolutely undetectable. The data are transmitted through a chain of satellites back to CIA headquarters. Big Bertha scans the data to determine the document format—"

"Excuse me, Director Oberdorf," Senator Sam Magee interrupted. "What do you mean by 'document format'?"

"Whether it is textual data or nontextual data, such as diagrams, graphs, architectural drawings, engineering sketches, that sort of thing. Or a combination of the two."

"Thank you," Magee said, apologizing for interrupting Oberdorf. "It wasn't clear to me what you meant."

A lot of things were unclear to Sam Magee, who was not regarded as one of the Senate's shining lights.

"That's quite all right, Senator. I don't want there to be any confusion about the program. I should point out that Bertha also automatically scans any text for key words. Documents can then be sorted or retrieved by analysts according to key words, subject, location of device, data, and time of collection. We have an instantaneous library of intelligence information, courtesy of every consumer nation of Western technology."

"A great idea," Falcone offered, not quite scoffing. "But could you tell us how DECIMAL DEWEY—you know, one day I'm going to give you a goddamned gold star for whoever sits around thinking up code names out there. How do you plan to get these magical chips into the machines of the target countries?"

"Well, as you know, we are basically talking about China and the Soviet Union. Both countries have had an absolute aversion to technology that facilitates the distribution of information. Both of them have finally recognized that they can't compete with the West by controlling information so tightly. If they buy any copying system from the West—American, European, or Japanese—that system will have the implanted chip."

"What if they build their own?"

"It's a problem, but not insurmountable. Copying machines are in constant need of repair. We've got agents in key target countries, graduates of their own trade schools, who need less than ten minutes' access to a machine to repair it to our satisfaction."

"Sounds like a variation of what the Soviets did to us a few years ago." Falcone still bristled at the stupidity of allowing typewriters destined for use in the U.S. embassy in Moscow to be stored temporarily in Soviet warehouses. Within a matter of a few hours Soviet technicians had been able to insert, under the space bar, a sophisticated device that electronically recorded which keys were being touched by the embassy secretaries; the device then transmitted the data to receiving stations in Moscow. The Russians were reading our mail before we were.

"Indeed it is, Mr. Chairman," Oberdorf replied. "No good deed should go unpunished."

There had been an uproar within the intelligence community when the typewriter bugs had been discovered. The State Department, ever the object of contempt for its indifference to the most basic security precautions, had been even more embarrassed when it was revealed that the Soviets, declaring that they lacked the ability to pour concrete on site, provided precast concrete for the construction of the new U.S. embassy in Moscow. They loaded up the steel beams and walls of the embassy building with so many bugs that, as Falcone once remarked to Oberdorf, "the man from Orkin would have died of old age if he tried to remove them." The entire building had had to be demolished. The only salvation from a monumental act of State Department negligence was that the Soviets were not allowed to move into their impenetrable embassy on Mount Alto, the second highest point in Washington, until the United States assumed occupancy of a new embassy in Moscow. Falcone secretly hoped that day would never come.

"Incidentally," Oberdorf said, "the second program to discuss is a variation of the first."

"GLOWWORM?" Falcone asked, shaking his head.

"Yes, sir. It's a remarkable breakthrough we've achieved in

electromagnetic technology. We've got the ability to track our agents anywhere—under ground, under water, anywhere."

"The equivalent of tagging pigeons," Falcone observed.

"Exactly. The primary purpose is to protect CIA and other intelligence officers assigned to certain dangerous posts where they might be kidnapped. We can mount a rescue effort within a matter of hours."

Stan Thurston, from North Carolina, raised his hand. "Mr. Chairman, I have to attend an Appropriations Committee markup. Could I ask a question out of turn before I leave?"

Glancing at the other nine members, Falcone observed that there was no objection. He nodded to Thurston.

"Why wouldn't the kidnappers suspect that you might use such a device and just torture their captive until he disclosed its existence and location?"

"Senator, no system is foolproof. We've anticipated that. First of all, we install the device on our agents without their knowledge during routine physical exams before their assignment overseas. Tooth fillings and crowns are the easiest places, but we've become more sophisticated with our fiber optics. Second, we use a cover device—watch, ring, gold chain, belt, or shoe heel—that the agent is told about. He is advised to disclose its existence if he is ever taken hostage and threatened with physical abuse or torture. That should be enough to throw off his kidnappers for a while. It buys us a few hours or days. We hope it's enough to save his life. But no system can guarantee his safety."

Falcone listened with fascination. America was said to be in a scientific decline, but there seemed to be few limits to U.S. imagination and capabilities. He glanced briefly around the dais. What was equally astonishing to him was that no one bothered to ask the most obvious question: How were these devices implanted without the agents' knowledge?

Falcone knew. He and Vice Chairman Christy had been briefed privately by the director.

The answer was hypnosis. The Agency had started to get into the mind-bending business of parapsychology. During the 1950s and 1960s, the CIA had conducted a covert research program known as MKULTRA to explore the psychic/distorting powers of LSD, mescaline, and other exotic drugs. Part of the program involved the use of hypnosis to see if researchers could implant certain commands that would trigger specific actions or reactions in a posthypnotic state. They were looking for a prototypical "Manchurian candidate," one who might be programmed to wipe out the darkest parts of his own memory or maybe even another's life. Whether they ever found him remains a secret, because all the MKULTRA records were destroyed before Senate investigators could put their hands on them.

But the CIA's interest in mind manipulation had never been erased. And that, Falcone thought as he looked at his colleagues, was a matter worthy of investigation. One that he intended to lead . . .

The last of the six black programs that Oberdorf discussed was a satellite laser system for detecting submarines. Given the alarming production rates of Soviet submarines, and the fact that they could dive 2,000 meters and travel in excess of 80 knots, this project appeared to have the greatest potential. But there was a problem. As Oberdorf explained it, the system had to be used sparingly because it relied on solar power, which had to be stored until it reached sufficient strength to power the laser. A search of a wide area required more power. So did a demand for greater detail on a specific target. "We have something of a bureaucratic struggle on our hands at the moment, Mr. Chairman," Oberdorf explained.

"Such as?"

"The Agency would like to use the system to study the technical characteristics of the new submarines, a longer operation against a single target. The Navy, with the support of the Joint Chiefs, wants to use it for greater ocean surveillance, which requires short operations over broad areas. We simply haven't reached the point where we can do both. We're trying to work this one out, but the President probably will have to cut the knot."

Falcone thanked Oberdorf for his presentation. As Oberdorf stood, Falcone held up his right hand, palm forward, and said, "There is one thing that I'm unclear on. The program you called HONEST BROKER—exactly what did you mean by the reference to Israel and its role in one of our black programs?"

Oberdorf turned to look at Atkins, signaling that he should respond.

"Actually, Mr. Chairman, it's sort of the other way around,"

Atkins said. "As you know, Israel has established its own vigorous satellite program and has developed a twenty-four-hour, all-weather capability to observe the entire Middle East. In fact, in January the Israelis began giving us all of their photo reconnaissance to supplement our own."

"What do you mean, 'supplement our own,' General?" A touch of anger crept into his question. "What in hell does 'supplement' mean?"

Atkins's eyes shifted quickly to Oberdorf, whose expression remained unperturbed.

"Mr. Chairman, if you'll permit me to explain," he said.

"Indeed. Explain is precisely what I want you to do."

"As you know, we are still getting over a rocky time with our space program. The Challenger explosion set us back nearly five years. Then we lost four of our most sophisticated satellites when the Titan missiles malfunctioned. After we signed the INF and START treaties with the Soviets, our ability to monitor global activities was stressed—actually *stretched*—beyond tolerable limits. We had to put Moonscape and Trover in geosynchronous orbit right over the Bear. The Chinese have been modernizing rapidly and have been accelerating their long-range missile tests, and we've been tasked to keep a twenty-four-hour watch on them. Add ocean surveillance to the drug interdiction demands of Congress and you'll find we're stretched too thin. We can't do it all."

"If I read you right," said Falcone, "you're telling us that the United States delegated responsibilities to the Israelis to monitor the Middle East. Is that right?"

"Mr. Chairman," Joshua Stock broke in, "I think you're being a bit unfair to Director Oberdorf. The Agency has asked for greater satellite capability, but the Defense Department—and, I might add, Congress—has turned it down because of budget constraints. Frankly, I don't think it's a bad idea to have our allies share a little bit of the burden."

Falcone, responding to Stock, kept his eyes riveted on Oberdorf. "Let me say to my friend from Florida that it's not a question of sharing the burden. It's a question of maintaining the integrity of our intelligence. Director Oberdorf, am I correct in my belief that for years the Israelis wanted total access to our photo reconnaissance in the Middle East?"

"Yes."

"And we provided intelligence to them on our terms, not theirs. Correct?"

"Right."

"We wanted to be in the position of determining whether any of the countries were making covert plans to prepare for war so we could help avert it."

"Yes, sir."

"And while we wanted to protect our allies the Israelis, we did not want to give them information that might enable them to launch a preemptive strike against key Arab facilities or personnel."

Oberdorf nodded in agreement.

"Now, if I understand what you're telling me, the Israelis will be taking the overhead pictures of the Middle East and then sharing the photos with us."

"In a timely fashion, yes, sir. But their photos are supplemental to our own."

Once again Stock interrupted Falcone. "Sean, with all due respect, I think you're missing the point here. We're in trouble and we've got a friend who's able and willing to help. It's a partnership, and a damn good one."

Falcone returned again to the deputy director. "Director Oberdorf, can the photography be doctored? Can it be altered so as to include or exclude information?"

"It would be difficult to do so."

"Difficult, but not impossible. As a matter of fact, I recall that several years ago, the United States was called upon to provide the Iranians with some overhead shots of the Iraqis. That was intended as a gesture of good will to a bunch of thugs who we thought would help get our hostages back."

Oberdorf sat stiffly now behind the witness table, a slight flush creeping up his throat.

"Tell me, Director Oberdorf. Did we give them accurate information, or did we fudge it a little?"

"Under those circumstances, we tried to give them as little as possible."

"Exactly. My point is, and I say this to my colleagues as well as to the witnesses, I would rather have no intelligence than bad or altered intelligence.

"One final point. General Atkins, you mentioned, ever so briefly, something about a joint SDI project with Israel. I'm not familiar with that. Could you explain it in a bit more detail?"

Before Atkins could respond, Stock intervened. "Mr. Chairman, I believe that is not an intelligence project but one that's within the jurisdiction of the Armed Services Committee. It is highly compartmentalized. It would be wholly inappropriate to discuss that program here."

Falcone stared momentarily at the man who had been his friend since their college days. Stock was right. There were rules, procedures, compartments, a minefield of deception to negotiate in order to find the facts. The veil of secrecy necessarily had many layers.

"The senator's point is well taken," he finally said. "I now yield to the vice chairman for any questions he might have."

Falcone failed to hear much of the remaining dialogue that morning. He continued to brood about what he had heard. Stock might be right, at least technically. Something was going on that he did not like. His first thought was that perhaps he was upset at being openly challenged by his friend. But there was something more. There was something of a tight smugness in Stock's tone, a detectable edge of superiority, of knowledge, of position. It troubled Falcone. He did not expect deference. But he did not expect defiance either.

8

AHMED JOOMA TROTTED down the steep stone stairway that began at the upper end of Thirty-sixth Street. He had heard another Georgetown student call this "the *Exorcist* staircase." When he had tried to look up the word in his Arabic-English dictionary, he had not been able to make much sense of it. He had finally asked his cousin Mustafa, who, as usual, had chided him for his ignorance. "A movie," Mustafa had told him. "A stupid American movie. They made it here in Georgetown. The stairs were in a famous scene. It is not important."

Ahmed still did not understand, but he did not like to ask Mustafa questions, especially when they were not important. Mustafa often said that: not important. *You are not important. That is what he means, looking down from his twenty-five years to my twenty-two years like a father scolding a son.*

The stairway, which clung to the side of a brick building, ended at Canal Road, on the edge of Washington's two Georgetowns, the university and the neighborhood. What the Americans called the rush hour was ending, but the cars still crawled along here near the bridge over the Potomac, and Ahmed twisted between them, running lightly in his red-and-white Adidas. He wore a blue headband around his thick black hair, which all but hid a pair of earphones. The wires snaked down the front of his white Hoya T-shirt to the Walkman clipped to his red shorts. *Mustafa thinks I'm listening to an English-language tape.* Ahmed smiled, his pace picking up the beat of "Wild, Wild Life."

A bearded, dirty-faced beggar was walking along the side of Canal Road, holding a white Styrofoam cup up to the windows of the cars. As Ahmed passed him, he turned his cup toward Ahmed, who responded by making his right hand into a fist, then wiggling the middle finger. A woman driver glared at Ahmed, gave him the same gesture, and waved a dollar bill to summon the beggar to her open window.

Ahmed ran down a ramp that led to a path along the eastern side of the Chesapeake & Ohio Canal. He headed south to a bridge that arched over the canal near Milepost 0, crossed the bridge, and turned north on the towpath, where muleteams once trod, pulling the canal boats. From here to about Milepost 2 the towpath was crowded, a stretch of pebbly ground worn down by joggers, mothers with babies in strollers, impatient bike riders, and walkers who seemed oblivious and out of place in city clothes. After Milepost 2 it had fewer people, and Ahmed liked that.

Three days a week, as the day was ending, he took the same route for his ten-mile run to Milepost 5 and back. Mustafa approved of Ahmed's runs as training, a way to keep his body ready for the mission, whatever it might be. *Always the mission. Always hinting he knew of the mission.* So far the mission had consisted of getting into the United States on an Egyptian passport, enrolling in Georgetown University as a cover, meeting with other false-passport Libyans living around Washington, and waiting. Now, after five weeks, at last they seemed to be getting ready for action.

Through a contact in the District of Columbia government, Mustafa had obtained a storm-sewer map and the floor plan of the Israeli embassy. "You'd better learn to run fast," Mustafa had said this morning, laughing at Ahmed. "Soon the Jews will be chasing you." Tonight would be the first meeting to plan the mission.

Running made Ahmed feel free, conscious of his body only by the touch of his feet on the path, by the passage of breath into his lungs. He was running well, keeping his legs pumping to the tempo of his pulse. He smiled at a black woman who was jogging toward him. She smiled back, and as she passed him, Ahmed turned his head. For a moment he watched her long black legs and the edge of her yellow shorts fluttering over the bared roundness of her hips. *Perhaps today I will see the dark-haired woman.*

This was a good day. He felt that he could control his mind as he controlled his body. He could empty his mind so that he felt himself hovering, looking down upon himself running along the towpath, looking down and imagining that today he would talk to her again, see her smile, which would make him wonder if her smile and her words were friendly . . . or something more. Today. If she was there today, he would find out if she would meet with him, make love with him. As the spires of Georgetown University disappeared around a bend, he quickened his pace.

The song "God Bless America," broadcast through a speaker recessed in the high ceiling, sounded scratched and warped. The tall woman winced as she completed fifteen minutes of stretching exercises on the heavily padded floor. Thank God T. M. Lin's classes were over. Otherwise the volume would be high enough to shatter a case of wineglasses, and Lin would be leading the song with the enthusiasm of a college cheerleader.

Cheerleader—a great description of the little man. Power; speed; God and country. That's what Lin preached. He was the best product ever exported by Taiwan. A million-dollar salesman. He sold the art of self-defense and all the personally designed and patented equipment to keep you from being separated from your senses. Copying the selling techniques of South Korea's Jhoon Rhee (and siphoning off much of his clientele), Lin now owned twelve tae-kwon-do centers, and he flitted from one to another, supervising the instruction of thousands of students, among them Cabinet officials, politicians, and lobbyists.

But more than self-defense, Lin sold America, land of liberty and opportunity. Thinking about this, her torso flexed, her head now touching her knee, the woman wondered whether Lin was working for the Taiwanese government. He had access to and influence with the powerful. And a noble cause to promote: the goodness of America. There were plenty of buyers in the marketplace. It was something worth checking out at some point. But not today.

Rachel Yeager had only another twenty minutes to practice her spin kicks against the three-hundred-pound fiber-filled bag that hung on a chain in a corner of the large gymnasium. Leaping effortlessly, then whipping her body in a 180-degree arc, she smashed her left heel high against the bag, sending it swinging backward. As the bag swung back, in a lightning-fast move she flicked her left hand, which she held horizontal with the floor, hard against it, then drove the heel of her right hand, fingers locked together and slightly flexed, deep into the bag. She was fighting an imaginary enemy. Had the enemy been real, and unskilled, he would have suffered a broken neck.

Not satisfied with her speed and precision, Rachel repeated the movements again and again, alternating kicks from left and right, using her forearms and elbows, moving as if she were under attack by not one assailant but two or three. Beads of sweat broke out along her hairline. She was breathing and perspiring heavily now, her face flushed. The taste of salt on her lips seemed to excite her, pushing her, forcing her to concentrate the energy of every movement into a death-dealing blow. She worked in silence, emitting no spine-chilling yells to terrify—or alert—her victims. She was able to visualize every movement in her mind, milliseconds before acting, calling upon an imaginary scream to focus the unleashed power into a laserlike intensity. In her mind she imagined the scream as the sound of a knife blade on a grinding wheel.

Several students at the other end of the room watched her with admiration, marveling at her grace and power. The loose jacket and full cotton pants concealed the shape of her trim, long-muscled body. But one of the men had seen her shopping one day in a Connecticut Avenue grocery store. She had worn a tight skirt that looked painted on her sculpted body, its hemline revealing perfectly shaped calves. He thought then and he thought now, *She has the legs of a dancer.*

Abruptly she finished at the bag and walked rapidly to the women's locker room. At her locker she slipped out of the jacket, baggy pants, and panties. She wore no bra. Her glistening body was supple and deeply tanned. The two touches of white—crescents on

her firm breasts, a narrow band across her buttocks and groin—
seemed like adornments on her dark, rippling skin.

Rachel showered quickly, wrapped herself in a white towel,
and returned to her locker. She opened a small blue duffel, looked
around to make sure she was alone, dropped the towel, and pulled
on panties, red running shorts, and a red sleeveless shirt. Then she
dressed in what she had worn to the gym: silky black slacks, a loose-
fitting white blouse, and white running shoes.

She slipped out a side entrance and walked to her car, a black
Acura with District of Columbia plates. A few steps from the car,
while reaching into her handbag for her keys, she pressed a button
on what looked like a garage-door opener. The device checked the
locks, ignition system, and sensors on the undercarriage. A faint
beep told her that no one had entered the car or placed a bomb in or
on it.

After unlocking the car and slipping into the driver's seat, she
looked around again and checked her rearview mirror. When she
saw that the gym's small parking lot was empty, she opened the
glove compartment and removed a small leather purse. Placing it on
the seat next to her, she slipped out a .22-caliber semiautomatic
Beretta in a black holster, which she swiftly strapped on her right
ankle.

The gym was on Arlington Boulevard, about two miles from the
Key Bridge, which crossed the Potomac between Rosslyn, Virginia,
and Georgetown. She drove down the boulevard, through the glitter
and glass of Rosslyn's cluster of office buildings, and crossed into
Georgetown, bearing left at the foot of Thirty-sixth Street.

The beggar was working the northbound lanes now. Her passenger window was already rolled down. When he approached, she
dropped two quarters into his Styrofoam cup, then drove up Canal
Road, staying in the left lane to make the turn onto MacArthur
Boulevard, which paralleled the Chesapeake & Ohio Canal.

She entered a stream of cars flowing toward Chain Bridge, the
next crossing of the Potomac. Most cars stayed on the left and
crossed the bridge. She continued on MacArthur, speeding up in the
sparser traffic. Through the slope of trees climbing from the Potomac she could see the stark white lines of the Bluffs, Michael
Rorbach's palisade home. From a balcony there a few months ago,
she realized, she had looked through the skeletons of trees at the

river and the canal and Rorbach had told her a little about the history of the canal. The double vision—looking up at what she had looked down from—momentarily amazed her. She knew Washington basically from maps, not experience.

She glanced at her watch, which was large-faced, bristling with knobs, and bound to her wrist by a wide silver band. "Not at all like a woman's watch," her father had said in that tired voice he had often used on her. She smiled, remembering that.

She was near Lock Six now. Canal boats, Rorbach had told her, made their way through a series of locks that had been operated by men who lived in stone houses along the canal. She had gone to the canal herself a couple of times and enjoyed running along the towpath. So when the assignment had come, she had been pleased at the coincidence: She knew the layout of the canal, and the profile on the subject of the assignment showed that he ran regularly along the towpath. It was a useful habit to fit into the assignment plan.

Rachel pulled into one of the empty spaces in a small parking area at Lock Six. There were two other cars, a mud-splattered old VW van with a rooftop canoe rack and a Volvo station wagon. Rachel unstrapped the holster, slipped out of her blouse and slacks, replaced the holstered gun in the glove compartment, and reached into the duffel. She donned a black wig, using the rearview mirror to guide her. Then she placed a flowered blue scarf around her neck, drawing one side lightly through the other in a slack overhand knot.

She got out of the car, locked it, pocketed the keys, and fixed the detector under a fender by a magnetic attachment. A path led down to the whitewashed stone lockhouse and the massive wooden gates of the lock, a nonworking relic. A modern plank bridge spanned the canal. Rachel crossed it and began running south toward Milestone 5.

At Milestone 4, Ahmed started looking for the dark-haired woman. He was glad she was not an American. She was a German, he thought, from her name and accent. She was older than he by a few years; he knew that. And she had given him no more than a smile and a few words as, slowing his pace to hers, he had run alongside her. He had not seen her often—what, three times? four?

—but he had sensed that she had an interest in him, had taken note of him.

He had almost told her his true name when she asked. But after making a slip that he had covered up before she could notice, he had given her the name on his Egyptian passport. Mustafa had trained him well. He had not told Mustafa about the dark-haired woman. *Why should I? He would have something to scold me about, something— There she is!*

"Greta!" he called to her, waving with one hand, dropping the earphones to his throat with the other hand. "We run different ways today. Too bad."

Smiling, she stopped and, waiting for him, scanned the towpath. On this stretch of the canal, she knew, she could see half a mile in either direction. She saw no one. A canoe—she assumed it was from the VW rack—passed her, ruffling the muddy canal water. The muscular paddler and his passenger, a red-haired, mini-skirted teenager, paid no heed to anyone on the towpath as they languidly passed.

Ahmed stopped in front of the dark-haired woman and boldly swept his eyes over her body, pausing in his examination first at her breasts and then at the place where her marvelous thighs vanished under her shorts. She reached out and cupped her warm left hand under his chin. "Look up here," she said. "I have a face."

"A—a most beautiful face," he stammered.

"We must talk about your manners," she said, taking his right hand in her left hand and leading him to the river side of the towpath and then down a steep bank. "Would you like to talk to me?"

She steadied him as he clambered down after her. "Manners?" he asked, frantically trying to remember the word's meaning. At the bottom of the bank was a thicket of trees, rotting logs, and brambles. Beyond, the Potomac braided through flood channels, making slim forested islets of riverside lowland.

They walked down a path leading to the river. Near the river's edge, out of sight and sound of the towpath, she motioned him to a fallen sycamore. He sat down and she stood before him. He reached up to pull her toward him, but she sidestepped his outstretched hands and walked behind him, slipping the scarf from her throat. The river's surging waters filled the silence. He turned to look at her, but she placed her left hand firmly on his left shoulder and with her right hand gently turned his head. When he was again facing forward, she took her hands away for a moment and he sat absolutely still. What had been desire and impulse was becoming lust and anger. *The beautiful woman is toying with me, toying with my manhood. I will have her. Here. Show her—*

As he started to stand, she passed the scarf over his head, pulled it tight, and knotted it. He got to his feet, but she pressed down, her hands squeezing his throat. He tried to raise his hands. She slashed her stiffened right hand down on his throat, smashing his larynx and extinguishing what was his last breath. She struck once more and stepped back, and Ahmed's body fell into the sycamore's shadow.

9

Moscow, June 29

Adjacent to anatoly
Voronsky's working office was a new and specially constructed
"room within a room." Following Edward Lee Howard's defection to
the Soviet Union and his disclosure that the CIA had developed
techniques that could practically monitor the Soviet leaders' heart-
beats, the KGB went into a near frenzy. General Viktor Borovlev,
then head of counterintelligence, ordered his top technicians to design and construct a room that would be hermetically sealed, absolutely impenetrable to the Soviet Union's enemies.

Mikhail Gorbachev in turn insisted that he had to have easy
access to the facility and that it should not be a tomb in the bowels
of the Kremlin. After some negotiation with the KGB's technical
division, Gorbachev agreed to a compromise. The KGB completely
remodeled the large library and reading room on the top floor of the
Kremlin, constructing a separate room that was elevated nearly a
foot and a half from the existing floor.

The entire new room was shielded with a thick lead exterior
and multiple layers of acoustically baffled interior walls. A series of
rotating electronic beams encapsulated the room, destroying any

external electrical intrusions. Additionally, the room was guarded twenty-four hours a day, and while it was in use four technicians monitored a sophisticated, highly sensitive receiver to determine the existence of any irregular electropulse activity.

Inside, the room was dominated by a birch conference table large enough to accommodate the President's Security Council. Several modernistic chairs imported from Sweden were set against the walls for key staff members.

Today only seven men entered what they called the Vremya Room—the "show-and-tell-time" room.

Voronsky welcomed his Council: Yuri Borisovich Volokov, the Defense Minister; Dmitri Matrosov, the head of Soviet military intelligence (the GRU); Georgi Markovich Vysochenko, the man about to be designated ambassador to Israel; Nikolai Semenovich Truskin, the Foreign Minister; General Viktor Borovlev, chairman of the Soviet Committee for State Security (the KGB); and Borovlev's favorite deputy and protégé, Gennadi Dmitrevich Dyukov.

After inquiring about his companions' health and weekend endeavors, Voronsky told a few jokes, hoping to put them in a good mood. Then he turned to General Borovlev.

A large-boned man, Borovlev possessed a wide face with flat features. His thick gray hair was slicked back from a high, sloping forehead that might have provoked the interest of curious anthropologists. In most people, however, he simply instilled fear. Borovlev had a nasty habit of splashing himself with cheap cologne, which gave the impression that he had just emerged from the dreadful barbershop next to the GUM department store, where the proletariat searched in vain for quality products. In a closed room—even one as large as the Vremya—the odor was quite overwhelming. But no one dared to suggest that he change his brand of cologne or the habit itself.

After finishing his cup of strong coffee, Borovlev began his presentation by saying, "I suggest, comrades, that we think of the Israelis not as the people of a nation but simply as Jews. On our chessboard, the Jews are among our pieces, as they are among the pieces of our opponents. But in the game we are beginning, we can move the opponents' Jews as well as our own."

Borovlev reviewed the events that had set up his game plan. "President Hollendale has devised a scheme to circumvent the ABM treaty. You recall that Ronald Reagan tried to do the same thing by reinterpreting the terms of the treaty. The Senate refused to permit such a patent distortion." Here Borovlev allowed himself a chuckle, as if to insinuate that the Senate had unwittingly done the KGB's work. "Hollendale is cleverer than Reagan, but he deceives only the Americans, not the Soviet Union.

"The United States is in the funding stage of its defense budget," Borovlev continued. He prided himself on his knowledge of the arcane ways of the enemy. The Cold War might be over, but the United States for him was no friend, and therefore remained an enemy. He also believed that he and his KGB would gain more influence by showing an ability to go beyond mere intelligence-gathering to supplying sophisticated analyses of U.S. economic and political problems. "The Pentagon is eager to receive the next level of funding for what it calls the SUNDANCER program. But the Pentagon has trouble getting anyone to listen these days. Ordinarily its generals would be opposing the scheme that President Hollendale has devised with the Israelis, but there is no other way to save what remains of the SDI program. Besides, the scheme gives the Pentagon a chance to hand a defeat to the Secretary of State, who is opposed to SUNDANCER."

"Why is he opposed?" Georgi Vysochenko asked.

"It's all quite byzantine. He believes it gives Israel too much leverage over the United States in negotiating a peace plan with the Palestinians. Time is also pressing for the Israeli regime. Soon there will be an election. The United States needs to have the arrangement made by then to help the so-called Labor Party win."

"You have done well in explaining what the Americans want," President Voronsky interjected. "How does this pertain to our interests?"

"We must look at another part of the board, Comrade Secretary," Borovlev answered, refusing to refer to President Voronsky as anything but the General Secretary of the Communist Party. "The Americans, particularly the American left, support the release of our Jews to Israel, although as a matter of fact, the joke is on Israel, because the United States has reduced the funding to help settle these people in Israel.

"As you know, Comrade Secretary, the Israelis grabbed at our invitation to reestablish diplomatic relations and to institute direct flights from Moscow to Tel Aviv. The counterintelligence chief in Mossad, the one we call *Canaan,* has been sending us some SUN-DANCER technological information in exchange for more Jews and settlement money, which we are funneling through Ptor Kornienko. *Canaan* believes that he is outwitting us because we are increasing what has become a valuable export: Jews."

"What are his motives?" Vysochenko asked.

"As far as we can judge, his motives are twofold. First, he wants more Jews to increase Israel's population relative to the Arabs, who continue to breed like rabbits. Whatever intelligence he provides us, he thinks he can get more than enough in return with the Jews he hopes to receive. For him it's a zero-sum game. Whatever Israel loses in the trade now, it will acquire later by virtue of what the Israelis call the brain gain. Second, he has lost faith in the United States as an ally. There are two other strategic alliances available to Israel—Germany and the Soviet Union. No Jew will ever trust the Germans. Besides, he believes that the Soviet Union will be the dominant military power of the future." Here Borovlev could not suppress a smile.

"He doesn't sound quite as blind as you've made him out to be," taunted Nikolai Truskin.

"Canaan is only half blind," Borovlev responded.

Truskin saw an opportunity to tweak Borovlev, who did not excel at repartee. "What is the expression—'In the land of the blind, the one-eyed man is king'?"

Borovlev sensed that he was losing the force of his presentation. "Perhaps, Comrade Truskin, I should have said that like most Israelis, *Canaan* suffers from nearsightedness. Whether he has one eye or two, he cannot see beyond the borders of his tiny country. Because we export Jews, the Americans have lifted the Jackson-Vanik embargo, which denied us the status of a favored trading partner. We get trade credits from the United States. We get SUN-DANCER from Israel. They get our Jews. We get rid of a problem—the targets of Pamyat's pogroms. Finally, there is the endgame—BURAQ."

"Chairman Borovlev," Truskin said with obvious impatience, "I must say that whatever the original conceptual merits of your program, the world has changed more radically than any of us could have predicted. I fail to see how BURAQ is now relevant to our—"

"Relevant, Comrade Truskin? Relevant?" Borovlev erupted from his chair and moved to a large global map fixed to the wall. "For years our goal was to pull West Germany out of NATO into *our* sphere, *our* alliance. We wanted German productivity and efficiency to be the engine to drive the Soviet economy." He paused, then looked directly at President Voronsky. "But Gorbachev, Yeltsin, and their happy band of counterrevolutionary thinkers achieved quite the opposite with their *glasnost* and *perestroika*. They gave us not prosperity but a bowlful of dust, the remnants of the Soviet empire." Borovlev used an aluminum pointer to touch Poland, Hungary, Czechoslovakia, East Germany. "The Germans are reunified, and they are now using the cheap labor of our departed allies to make themselves even more prosperous. And what happened to the Baltics? To Azerbaijan? To—"

"Come, Viktor," interrupted Dmitri Matrosov mockingly, "we know all of this. There were miscalculations on the part of many. Even the KGB cannot claim infallibility. What has this to do with BURAQ?"

"Everything, my good friend," Borovlev said with utter insincerity. "Everything. What is the greatest resource we have to offer the world? Our missiles? Mink? Sable? Vodka?" He paused again, surveying the faces at the table. "No, my colleagues. Oil. Natural gas. And where is our greatest competition? Here," Borovlev said, tapping hard at the map, pointing to the Persian Gulf.

"We are not Komsomol students, Comrade Borovlev. Enough. Get to the point." Truskin turned to Voronsky with a look of exasperation. To the outside world, Nikolai Truskin always presented a graceful, deferential manner, one that was quintessentially diplomatic. But in private he enjoyed bare-knuckle exchanges, particularly with Borovlev, whose ideas he considered moronic.

The Soviet President's face remained impassive, so that none of those present could determine who among them was the most persuasive or influential. It was his custom to wait several days after such a meeting before announcing a policy decision, thereby creating the impression that he had arrived at a decision independently. No one, of course, believed such was the case, but the procedure allowed everyone to save face. And when an issue was of marginal importance, Voronsky would do precisely the opposite of what his perceived favorite adviser had recommended—a pretense he struck so that he could maintain that they were all equals. All equally valued. All equally wise. None, of course, as wise as the President.

Moving his pointer to the eastern edge of the Mediterranean, Borovlev continued his lecture, buoyed by Voronsky's silence and Truskin's anger. "Our Foreign Minister said the world has changed radically. True. But to quote a long-dead German, there are two things that cannot change: history and geography. As long as there is an Israel, the Arabs have a common enemy to hate. It has been in our interest to promote the cause of the Palestinians, knowing that Israel's resistance will continue. Thus we have preserved Arab hatred for the Jews and their American benefactors."

"So what are you saying?" Matrosov asked.

"It is time for new thinking that serves our needs. As long as the United States retains an interest in the Middle East, the moderate states—those who want Arab customs and American dollars—continue to supply oil at foolish prices. Remove Israel and the Americans are gone."

"Yes, and you would remove the Arabs as well as the Israelis!" Truskin hissed. "There would be a holocaust that would burn up the oil fields along with millions of people."

"A possibility, Comrade Truskin, but not an inevitability."

Truskin would not relent. "Mr. President, the chairman's plan is absurd. Assume that all the Arab oil wells are destroyed. They could be back in operation within a few months—"

Borovlev cut Truskin off before he could finish. "Nonsense, gentlemen. We have more than sixty billion barrels of proven reserves. American oil companies—ARCO, Texaco, Chevron—are already developing deep drilling techniques for us and new oil fields in eastern Siberia. They want a stable supply of energy, and they want us to succeed. Besides . . ." Borovlev paused as he surveyed the faces at the table. "If the Israelis use nuclear weapons, there will be no rebuilding of oil wells within a few months."

"So you believe," Voronsky interjected, "that either the Arabs will invite us in to protect them from the Israelis or the war will force Japan and Western Europe to turn to us for their oil and gas?"

"Precisely, Comrade Secretary. Without oil, Japan will be on its knees, a toy without batteries. In Germany, we need only to stir the Greens. Release some updated figures on Chernobyl. The antinuclear wave will shut down the Germans' existing nuclear plants."

"President Voronsky," Truskin stated, chopping the air with his right hand, "this is not new thinking at all. This will take us back to the Cold War, maybe even a hot one!"

Borovlev exploded. "No, my new-age friend, this is not a return to the Cold War. This is a matter of our survival!" He paused, fixing each man at the table with a withering glare. "No vast Soviet armies are involved. No Soviet nuclear weapons. The United States is not even involved. We are only going to help Israel do what some Israelis already want to do. Where is the risk of a Cold War? Weigh the very limited action I propose against the coal strikes in the Ukraine, the sight of unfed Russian children, the bread lines, the riots that are tearing us apart . . ."

"And if BURAQ proceeds and there is war and Israel should win that war?" Nikolai Truskin asked.

"If, if. Comrade Truskin, you are always paralyzed by a thousand doubts. If they should win, there will be no Arab oil fields left. As the Americans like to say, 'Heads we win, tails they lose.' BURAQ is the key to *perestroika.*"

"And what about the Americans?" Dmitri Matrosov asked, thinking he had exposed a serious miscalculation by Borovlev. "They still have forces stationed in Saudi Arabia."

Contempt moved across Borovlev's face. Then he flashed a cold, mirthless smile. He could not comprehend the hopeless naïveté of the men who were supposed to guide the Soviet Union into the future. "There are only a few thousand soldiers left. Most Americans are now opposed to their being there. So if they are caught in the crossfire of a holy war, what will President Hollendale or Congress do? Declare war? Order a retaliatory strike against Israel?"

Borovlev knew he was not far from silencing his critics. "Gentlemen, in a few years several Arab nations will have nuclear weapons. In five they'll be able to send them anywhere—*anywhere*—in the world. Need I remind you that Islamic fundamentalism is eating away at our republics like a cancer?" Borovlev squeezed the thick fingers of both hands into fists. "We have the opportunity to rescue our country from disaster. History—our children—will never forgive us if we fail to act."

Borovlev's reach for drama struck Voronsky as pathetic, but

when he looked at the faces around the table, he could see that the general had won some converts.

Borovlev telescoped his pointer, reducing it to the size of a fountain pen, slipped it into his coat pocket, and returned to his chair with a broad, triumphant smile. "And now," he said, "I'd like my principal deputy, Comrade Dyukov, to give you an update and explain why I believe it is imperative that we move more quickly to the final phase of BURAQ."

Voronsky had never liked General Borovlev, whom he considered a dangerous and duplicitous man. He understood Borovlev's motivations and limitations, however. He could anticipate his stratagems and try to counter them. Dyukov was more puzzling and troublesome to him.

The old were said to be chained to the past; they wore blinders to their graves. Perhaps so. But it was a mistake to assume that the young were more open or enlightened.

Dyukov had all the surface appearances of a truly modern—indeed, Western—man. He was fluent in English, French, and German. He wore Savile Row suits, French-cuff shirts, and Italian shoes. He moved easily among the upper reaches of the political and journalistic establishment in Washington and New York. ABC's *Nightline* frequently asked him to appear to offer insights into the nuances of Soviet statements and actions.

But the clothes, the culture, the linguistic glibness were pretense, camouflage. Dyukov was the one who had organized the attack last year on the Central House of Writers in Moscow. Then the police had used only megaphones and clubs, but they had warned the Jewish intellectuals that they would come back the next time with Kalashnikovs. No, Dyukov had a cold heart—the kind Voronsky pretended to have. Perhaps that's why Voronsky disliked him so.

Before Dyukov could begin his briefing, Voronsky decided to shift ground.

"Comrade Dyukov, before you tell us about BURAQ, please tell us more about Vyacheslav Kamamenov's defection. The reports I have seen are pathetic."

A flash of fear swept across Dyukov's face, as though he were a young animal caught in the glare of headlights.

"Yes, comrade," Dmitri Matrosov agreed. The bullfrog of a

man was suddenly alert and energized. "How could you have permitted such a breach of security?"

Dyukov, clearly flustered, turned to General Borovlev, his eyes pleading for assistance. He tried to recapture his composure. "First, I must remind you, Comrade Matrosov, that *I* did not allow a breach in security. I am not responsible for the oversight of every member of the Academy of Sciences. Second—"

"Enough, Dyukov," Voronsky said. "I don't want excuses. I want to know the facts. How was Kamamenov able to walk out of the restaurant Trois Mousquetaires in Geneva into the arms of the Americans? How long had he been working for them? What information was he given access to? Was he polygraphed upon his return from America? I'm told he was not. Why not?"

As Dyukov stammered his replies, Yuri Volokov, the Defense Minister, voiced his concerns about what he called an unforgivable act of stupidity. Finally Voronsky, seeing that General Borovlev and his young deputy were for the moment in disarray, said, "I would suggest, gentlemen, that a damage assessment be completed by our counterintelligence people immediately. I want it before the next scheduled briefing of the council. After that we'll be in a better position to know whether we should proceed with BURAQ."

Borovlev could see that there was no sentiment in the Vremya Room for any further discussion.

10

Washington, July 5

THE MADISON IS A QUI-
etly elegant hotel that offers a small lobby and a sense of familiarity
even to its first-time guests. It is usually the preferred hotel of
visiting dignitaries.

Joshua Stock had agreed to meet Yitzhak Rafiah there for
breakfast. Rafiah had been Israel's ambassador to the United States.
A few months ago he had been assigned to serve in France, where
increasingly blatant anti-Israeli actions had been taken by the government. His unexpected appearance in Washington struck Stock as
ominous. When Rafiah had called him shortly after dinner the previous evening, the urgency in his voice had told Stock that he was not
the bearer of good tidings.

When Stock entered the hotel, Rafiah was seated in a large
leather chair in a small waiting area just to the left of the glass
double doors. He quickly folded the New York *Times* under his arm
and stood to greet Stock. The two men embraced in the European
fashion, exchanged voluble greetings, and then walked toward the
dining room.

Rafiah was tall and scholarly-looking. Like many tall men who are not athletic, he stooped, walking with his shoulders hunched forward. His walk gave him something of a humble appearance, which helped to compensate for his reputed intellectual arrogance—a reputation that was deserved. He was one of Israel's most brilliant diplomats, as well as a historian and linguist, and respect was immediately his wherever he was assigned—Washington, London, Bonn, Tokyo, and now Paris.

Stock had met him three years before, during Rafiah's tenure in Washington. The relationship quickly became one of scholar and prized student. They viewed Israel through the same lens. There could be no peace in the Middle East until the Arab nations realized that Israel could not be defeated militarily. Israel could not be defeated militarily if the United States remained constant and unswerving in support. Any talk of making concessions to moderate Arabs only invited more war, more terrorism. In their view, moderate Arabs were revolutionaries who were out of ammunition.

Although their friendship was close, Rafiah had asked Stock for nothing more than his insights on American policies, and Stock had never volunteered information that could be regarded, even remotely, as confidential or secret. Not until three months ago. After his meeting with Polanski.

In a routine CIA briefing, the Intelligence Committee had been told that the United States had been putting quiet diplomatic pressure on Sweden not to continue with a scheduled shipment of missiles to Iraq. But the Swedes had shrugged off American displeasure and gone ahead. The briefing officer said that a U.S. satellite had spotted the ship being loaded in Stockholm. The briefing was more concerned with the performance specifications of U.S. satellites than with the destination of the missiles. But Stock, as Polanski had requested him to do, passed the word to Rafiah.

Several days later, on an inside page of the *Post*, he saw a short article about a Swedish ship exploding and sinking in the North Atlantic. "Three members of the crew died in the explosion," the wire service story said. "The rest were picked up in lifeboats the following day. Swedish shipping officials later said that the ship had been carrying volatile chemicals."

The next time Stock talked to his friend, an exuberant Rafiah told him what had happened. Israeli saboteurs had got aboard the ship and exchanged several of its fire extinguishers for explosive devices that looked like fire extinguishers. The devices were set off by timers. "The beautiful part," Rafiah said, "was that all the evidence went to the bottom. But the Swedes know. They know."

And the CIA, Stock had wondered, *does the CIA know?* But nothing had happened. There had been no repercussions, except in his conscience, of the deaths of three strangers.

Jean-Pierre, the maitre d', gushed an effusive welcome to Rafiah and Stock. "Mr. Ambassador. Good to have you with us again. You're looking wonderful," he said, bowing his head deferentially. "And you, Senator Stock. It's been too long since you were last here." He led the men to a corner table opposite the entrance. The table was very nearly a private booth in an open room.

As Jean-Pierre seated them, Stock glanced diagonally across the room. He saw Lars Mumsen sipping coffee, dutifully taking notes as a young man leaned across the table, speaking in what appeared to be hushed tones. Mumsen was a thin-lipped, heavy-faced journalist with skin that had never welcomed the sun. What little hair he had was white, combed in wisps, straight back. Aristocratic in manner, sarcastic in tone, he wrote to a conservative audience. He attacked arms control and Israel with equal fervor. While virulently conservative in philosophy, he gave no quarter to conservatives, including Ronald Reagan, who had flirted with détentists and Zionists. Ironically, although he had attacked Eric Hollendale's liberalism during his campaign for the presidency, Mumsen now glowingly praised his "even-handed peace proposals" for the Middle East as being "wise, moderate, and responsible." He had elevated Hollendale to a "statesman, a remarkable departure from a long, undistinguished line of crass and cowardly politicians."

Stock's eyes did not linger on Mumsen. He turned instead to Rafiah, exchanged talk about their respective families and Rafiah's assignment to Paris, then took a cursory conversational trip around the global trouble spots until their breakfast orders were taken.

Rafiah expressed his gratitude for Stock's assistance and dedication to Israel, emphasizing how appreciative Israel's leaders were. The use of the past tense signaled that Stock was going to be asked to give again.

"Joshua," Rafiah said, dropping his voice to a whisper, "we are always eager to reciprocate, as you know. Our intelligence people recently scored a remarkable breakthrough. We were able to place one of our people inside Soviet intelligence. He disclosed some truly remarkable information about their military modernization programs."

Rafiah paused while the waiter served their breakfast and poured more coffee. "More important than the Soviets' programs, however, is the United States' problem," he continued when they were alone again. "Joshua, I have tried for weeks now not to involve you in this. My special friends in the State Department have proved useless. The pressure on me is increasing. I don't want to risk your position on the committee by making too many requests of you. But I have no one else to turn to. Our relationship is in peril. You . . . the United States has an informant, an asset, a mole, whatever you want to call him, somewhere in our intelligence network. Perhaps in our government. I don't know."

Stock went pale. "You're sure? A mole in the Mossad? Impossible, Yitzhak! We would never—"

Rafiah's stony gaze cut Stock off in midsentence. The set of his jaw, the intensity of his eyes, told Stock that it was not impossible. "No, it's true. He's been bought, corrupted. I'm told he's reporting directly to Moscow. Everything, Joshua. *Everything.* Unless we can determine who he is, well . . . You know there are some in President Hollendale's administration who would turn this against us. Who would impair, even break, our special relationship. That would be a tragedy for you. It would be a death sentence for Israel."

"You're certain?"

Grim-faced, Rafiah nodded.

"A double?"

"Precisely, Joshua. He's feeding the Soviets highly classified information. SUNDANCER technology, I'm told."

"How long?"

"More than a year."

"Maybe our people know about his loyalties and are using him strictly for disinformation."

"It's possible. But I'm told that the information he is giving the Soviets has been consistently valuable."

"Does your source know who the asset is?"

"Unfortunately, he does not." Rafiah worked a small portion of his eggs Benedict onto his fork, expertly consumed it, then drank deeply from his coffee cup.

Stock pondered the implications of what the ambassador was saying. "I'll pass the information on to the Agency," he said, trying to sound convincing. "I'm sure they'll be grateful . . ."

"No!" Rafiah snapped. He reached across the table to touch Stock's hand. The occupancy and the noise level in the dining room had increased considerably. No one seemed to take notice of the ambassador's voice, which he immediately lowered. "No, Joshua. We both know the CIA is incapable of keeping its own secrets. We can't afford to have it compromise ours. If your Agency is alerted, then it may very well take action that will compromise my source."

Stock stared at Rafiah in puzzlement. "I don't understand why you're telling me this. What is it you want me to do?"

"A simple thing. Just find out the name of the Israeli who is working for the CIA. We will handle the matter from there."

"Yitzhak!" Exasperation was in Stock's voice now. "It's impossible. First of all, there is no way in hell I can find out the name of one of our assets, if in fact we have one. That's just not the kind of information I have access to. It's probably so secret that not more than half a dozen people in the entire Agency know his identity, including the director. Second, you're asking me not to reveal to our people the fact that we've got a traitor stuffed somewhere in the Mossad who's compromising our national security interests. You're asking me to identify the man without discussing the problem with the Agency. It just can't be done. Furthermore, I don't think it would be proper, even if it could."

"Proper? You want to debate moral niceties?" Rafiah slipped almost mockingly into a scholarly pose, placing his knife and fork on the side of his plate and folding his hands under his chin. Stock's face started to flush. "Those incompetents out at Langley have an agent in Israel who is being milked like a goat by the Soviets. Every drop of information that he gives to Moscow compromises Israel's security—fills the bucket not with milk, Joshua, but with Israel's blood. We can't allow that to continue. We need his name. We solve America's problem and ours."

The waiter came to the table to pour more coffee. Rafiah waved him off. "Enough. Thank you. Bring me the check, please."

Stock could feel a lump swelling at the back of his throat. He was confused. *The Soviets had penetrated the Mossad with the same man planted by the CIA. Just what in hell were we doing spying on Israel? And why hadn't Harry Polanski told him everything?*

His thoughts were in turmoil. He had nothing in writing from either Polanski or the President. He had passed classified information to a foreign nation. Three men had died as a direct result. What game was being played? Had Polanski set him up, used him as some kind of fall guy?

After a long silence, Stock's mind finally settled. *Both the Administration and the Israelis believed that a mole had penetrated the Mossad. But was he under American or Soviet control? There was only one way to find out the answer. Only one thing was certain. He was not going to go to Polanski.*

He looked at Rafiah, shaking his head. "I don't know if I can help. But yes, I'll try."

Stock followed Rafiah out of the dining room, his eyes fixed straight ahead. He did not want Lars Mumsen to see his face at that moment.

11

THE TRAIN RIDE TO NEW
York was something of a lark for Stock, a last-minute whim. Maybe
it was just a case of flying jitters. More than four hundred people
had died in two separate air crashes that week. Or maybe he just
needed more time to think about what he was going to say to Michael Rorbach later that evening.

It had been more than seven years since Stock had ridden the
Metroliner. He had forgotten the sheer luxury of wide leather seats,
without seat belts, and the challenge of tightrope walking to the
dining car to pick up a sandwich and a beer, then balancing the
paper carton in one hand while sliding the other along the upper
baggage compartment as the train rocked along the rails.

He had caught the two o'clock train. In little more than three
hours he would be in downtown Manhattan. It didn't take much
longer than flying, then fighting traffic from La Guardia Airport all
the way in to the New York Hilton. Three hours spent in semi-
reverie, swaying back and forth as if he were in a hammock, watching clouds gather, merge into billowy animals, then separate into
indistinguishable cotton fluff.

This romantic vision was shattered as the backsides of Baltimore, Wilmington, and Trenton passed in a blur. Old tires, doorless refrigerators, broken furniture, trash of every sort, raked the banks of the countryside. The graffiti of the poor, the desperate, the don't-give-a-damns. It angered him to see the contempt that people heaped upon the land. But as he stared vacantly out the window, everything within him—his mind, his heart, his guts, his very being—was filled with a vague, disparate, indefinable sense of clutter and debris.

The subject of his address to the group of Wall Street investment bankers was as familiar as his phone number. The faces of the guests were even more so. A "Stock" speech, his friends invariably called it: a few jokes; a condemnation of legislative efforts to reregulate the engine driving the wheels of capitalism; select quotes from the writings of conservative economist Milton Friedman; an inspirational call to his listeners to redouble their moral and financial commitment to our only friend and ally in the Middle East. No formal speech was ever prepared. No mental rehearsal was ever needed.

Stock exited gracefully from the ballroom of the New York Hilton to sustained and standing applause. He was escorted out a side door, whisked through the high-ceilinged hotel entrance, and ushered into a black stretch limousine parked near the corner of Fifty-third Street and Sixth Avenue. He loosened his black bow tie and slipped off the jacket of his tuxedo. For the next hour he rode in silence, with no need to pay attention to the route taken by the silent, robotic chauffeur.

In spite of the relaxing train ride that afternoon, Stock felt fatigued. He dozed, slipping in and out of a dreamy consciousness until he heard the crunch of gravel under the tires of the limousine. He snapped awake as the car entered the palatial grounds of Michael Rorbach's country home in northeastern New Jersey.

The mansion was more than a mile away from the main gate. In the darkness Stock could see only the outline of the magnificent, soaring oak trees that lined the long, curving driveway. He knew by heart precisely where the glorious gardens and flower beds were spread on the green and weedless lawns of the nine-hundred-acre farm. In the distance, the stables for thirty thoroughbreds looked like the small row houses of a century-old village against the nearly full moon.

Indirect lights were focused on the massive Corinthian columns of the mansion, giving it a mystical quality, as if it were alive and glowed from within. It was 11:30 P.M., and it was clear from the darkened first floor that Rorbach had retired long before. Rorbach had once told Stock that there were three things every successful man must have: a chauffeured limousine, a transoceanic jet, and an English butler. Rorbach had all three, plus reinforcements.

One of his butlers, a particularly chilly specimen named Jarrell, greeted Stock with stilted affection and escorted him to the guest quarters, a separate house consisting of five rooms, an entertainment center, a sauna, and a Jacuzzi. Stock poured himself a large vodka and tonic and slipped into the Jacuzzi for fifteen minutes while watching the late news on a huge television screen. He hoped it would relax him. He knew Rorbach would be up at dawn and would expect him for breakfast by seven o'clock. But sleep eluded him for much of the night.

"And how are we this morning, Joshua?"

Michael Rorbach was a shade under six feet, but looked taller because of his erect bearing. He watched his weight, exercised regularly, and generally wore dark double-breasted suits that accentuated his flat stomach. Today he was dressed in pleated brown slacks, a white open-necked sport shirt, and a tan cotton cardigan sweater. A solid gold Cartier watch was the only jewelry he ever wore.

Rorbach, who had emigrated to the United States from Israel in 1962, was rumored to be worth nearly two billion dollars. His lifestyle reflected his enormous wealth. Weekends were spent here, hosting social events and fund-raising parties for special federal officials. The Vice President of the United States was a close friend and frequent guest.

But Rorbach was not given to wanton self-indulgence. In his mind, everything existed for a reason, even his success. He gave millions to art, charitable institutions, and social causes. Not a week passed without at least a hundred requests for donations flooding his foundation's mail. More than a quarter of these requests were answered with checks within thirty days. But while Rorbach's name regularly appeared in the newspaper as a patron of the arts, he never attended the opulent galas or splashy celebrations frequented by the social elite.

"Heard reports about your speech last night," he said now.

"Bad news travels that fast?"

"No, no. A good speech, Joshua, a good speech. They liked what you had to say. Bob Jamison, the dinner chairman, called me this morning. He thinks you should be President."

"Funny, Cleo was saying the same thing just the other day. She thinks we need a home with a tennis court and off-street parking."

Amid the banter, two white-coated house servants brought in dishes of sliced melon, eggs, juice, croissants, hot coffee.

Rorbach was characteristically buoyant. Why not? He possessed health, wealth, and the unshakable belief that no problem was beyond solution, no person beyond manipulation or persuasion. "According to the *Times* this morning, Hollendale is talking about a new arms deal with Jordan," he said, plunging into a new subject. "Upgraded F-16s, Phoenix missiles, Sidewinders, the works. I don't understand the man. We beat him on the last deal he offered to the Saudis, and now he's back for more. The man's an idiot. Certifiable."

"We were lucky on that, Michael," said Stock. "The White House totally mishandled it. The Saudis helped by implying that the price of oil would not be reduced unless the sale went through. The one thing Americans resent more than Israeli political victories is blatant Arab blackmail. We know we're going to be screwed. We just don't like being told that we are—particularly after what we went through for the Saudis. But this one may be harder. Jordan appears ready to climb over the fence and officially recognize Israel."

"Words," Rorbach replied with a snort. "They'll say anything. Remember how King Hussein sold out to Saddam after he invaded Kuwait? The spineless bastards can't be trusted."

"Maybe not. But they're very shaky about Syria emerging as the major Arab power in the Middle East. The Israelis are pretty much out of southern Lebanon. The Jordanians have got to move or be viewed as completely impotent. They'll need to be seen as having leverage with the United States. Probably they'll call for a magnanimous recognition of Israeli security and unconditional negotiations on the legitimate grievances of the Palestinians. If Israel overplays this one . . ."

"What do you think Congress will do?"

"Don't know. The sale is news to me."

"Hollendale never breathed a word about it?"

"Maybe it's just another trial balloon." The image of Hollendale and Polanski in the Oval Office quickly flooded Stock's thoughts. Guilt tugged at him.

"We're counting on you as our point man, Joshua. By Monday morning we will have thousands of calls and telegrams in every office. Hollendale is just going to have to learn that he has to deal with us *before* he cuts deals with Hussein, not after."

Stock picked at his food in silence. Rorbach expected an affirmation of his confident assessment that Hollendale would be defeated. When none came, he stared curiously at his guest.

"You look thin, Joshua. Everything okay with Cleo and the girls?"

"Fine, Michael. Fine. Just working more and enjoying it a little less." Stock had an empty, ineffable hollowness in his voice that betrayed his assurances. He took a deep breath, then exhaled slowly. "I met with Yitzhak on Wednesday."

"I know."

Stock looked directly at Rorbach now, embarrassed that his surprise seemed so obvious. "No sparrow falls without notice?" he said trying to recover his composure.

"Yitzhak would be amused that you think him a sparrow. A hawk, maybe. Hardly a sparrow," Rorbach said, smiling in a vain attempt to lift Stock's frown. "He called me and said he'd be leaving for Paris in two weeks. Said you two had breakfast. He's very high on you, your work."

"Did he tell you what he wants me to do?"

"Unfortunately, Joshua, unlike some members of the Intelligence Committee, I do not have a secure phone. No. He simply said that your insight and support continue to prove invaluable to Israeli security. Nothing more." Rorbach rose from the breakfast table and motioned for Stock to follow him to his private den.

The room was resplendently paneled in dark rosewood, with floor-to-ceiling bookshelves. Chagall and Kandinsky oils adorned the walls. Brocaded green silk drapes shielded the morning sun.

Stock had the sudden feeling that he had entered a confessional. He slid into a low, deep-seated leather chair while Rorbach sat on the edge of an eighteenth-century French desk, the top of which was inlaid with mother-of-pearl.

"He's asked me to get information that even I don't have access to," Stock blurted with exasperation.

"Did you explain this to him?"

"As emphatically as possible."

"Yitzhak wouldn't ask unless it was critical."

"Michael, it's always critical. This time it's goddamned crazy. I'm in over my head already. My career in the Senate is on the line."

Stock saw Rorbach stiffen like a schoolmaster just insulted by a student. Their easy familiarity turned cold, stony.

"What do you think will happen to your career when your constituents find out about your girlfriend?"

In the shadows Stock's face colored. "You . . . you said you would protect me"—his voice cracked—"on that."

"Protect you? I said I would keep that New York incident out of the papers. And I did. At the cost of owing some powerful people some favors, I might add." Rorbach took a step toward Stock's chair, leaned forward, braced himself on the arms of the chair, and shouted in Stock's face. "I also told you to break it off. My God! Are you still seeing her?"

While Stock had been having dinner with Elise in a Greenwich Village restaurant, he had recognized a New York *Examiner* reporter at a nearby table. The reporter left immediately after they did and followed them, Joshua believed, to the Plaza Athénée, where they were spending the weekend. In a panic, at three o'clock that morning Joshua had called Rorbach.

"I'm speaking to you," Rorbach shouted again. "Are you still seeing her?"

"I've got to handle it with some diplomacy. The last thing I want is for her to go public."

Rorbach stood back, looking down at Stock. "Listen, my friend. I've managed to put a plug on this story for over two months. The reporter who turned in the item is demanding to know from his editors why it hasn't run. The *Examiner* has never been known to spike an item like that. Whether you like it or not, the private affairs

of public men are legitimate stories, particularly if the woman involved is a Libyan."

"Libyan? That's bullshit, David. She's French Moroccan."

"That's what she says. So what? Do you believe it'll make a
difference to Cleo and your kids? To your Florida constituents?
They'll bounce you out of the Senate, and then how will you help
us?" His voice suddenly lowered. "Take my advice, Joshua: terminate it."

Stock sighed again, a deep, raspy sigh. Rorbach's voice was
hard. Final.

Stock pulled himself up from the chair. "Okay, Michael, I'll
end it." He waited for Rorbach to ask whether he would honor
Yitzhak's request, but his host now again sat motionless on the edge
of his desk.

Stock turned and walked from the room. Without looking back,
he said, "I told Yitzhak I'd try to get the information. But this is the
last time, Michael."

12

Sean FALCONE CROSSED
the Fourteenth Street Bridge, turned onto the George Washington
Parkway, and headed north. Along the parkway, the trees' fresh
green leaves trembled in a warm breeze. Wildflowers sprinkled the
greensward. Traffic was so light and the morning so gloriously sunny
that when a car passed him, the driver smiled and Falcone smiled
back. He looked at his watch. He had allowed too much time for the
drive. He slowed down and pulled into a turnoff.

Falcone got out of the car, stretched, and walked to the edge of
the asphalt. The National Park Service landscapers may not have
created the view, but they had framed it beautifully by some deft
pruning of the trees on the steep slopes of the riverbank. He looked
down on the Potomac, gray and sparkling, and realized how rarely
he gave himself a moment to savor the beauty of Washington.

Turning away from the view, he walked back to the car. He got
in, leaned back, and closed his eyes, not to rest but to think. The
view of the river faded, replaced now with the vivid recollection of
yesterday's meeting with a troubled friend.

"I can't tell you more, Sean. You have to trust me."

"I trust you, Josh. You know that. But this is a big request. A very big one. And it puzzles me."

"I've told you all I can. My source is very well connected to the Mossad."

"So why doesn't the Mossad just work with the Agency on this?"

"You know the answer to that," Stock said. He sounded angry. *"Ever since Pollard, the U.S. intelligence community has been cool to the Mossad. If they asked the CIA directly, the CIA would suspect some plot. It's Israel-bashing time in Washington."*

"You're wrong. Our relations with Israeli intelligence are as strong as ever." Falcone started to say more but checked himself. *"Okay. For you. Not for the Mossad—for you. I'll give it a try. I'll call Bickford right away and try to set something up for tomorrow."*

Now it was tomorrow, and Falcone was looking at the familiar small brown exit sign with the white letters: CIA FHWA. It still amused him that an agency so dedicated to deception and secrecy would boldly declare its location. The FHWA—Federal Highway Administration—recalled the time when those letters were the code for the CIA's headquarters. Perhaps it was better to be open about that which could not be concealed. But of course it was a deception in itself to suggest that the CIA was located in one place. The Agency was much like the Roman bird Rumor, which had an eye hidden under every feather. The headquarters—the campus, as it was called—was at Langley, Virginia, but there were countless offices spread throughout Rosslyn and Crystal City in Arlington, Virginia, and still more across the river in Washington.

An armed guard at the main gate checked his name against a list on a clipboard and gave him a visitor's pass. He drove to one of the VIP parking slots in front of a long, seven-story building that could still be called modern thirty years after its construction.

Carl Benson, the congressional liaison officer, greeted Falcone at the foot of the stone staircase and escorted him away from the computerized checkpoint in the large, marbled entranceway. Almost by habit, Falcone glanced to the right to count the number of stars etched into the east wall. The stars indicated the number of agents who had died in service. There were fifty-three. One had been added since he was here just three weeks ago. John Harrington, a junior officer assigned to Ethiopia, had been brutally tortured, then castrated and allowed to bleed to death. His cover had been blown by yet another Agency defector. The director of the Central Intelligence Agency had received Harrington's testicles in the mail, COD to Langley.

Over the stars there was a Biblical quote: "Know the Truth, and the Truth shall make ye free." An ironic inspirational message for this agency, Falcone thought.

Stepping off the elevator on the seventh floor, he turned right and entered the director's private dining room. A circular table with a white tablecloth occupied the center of the room, which overlooked a wooded Virginia hillside.

Just as Benson pointed Falcone toward a chair, the director, a short, compact man with dark brown hair, walked brusquely into the room. Jack Bickford had been a protégé of Bill Casey's, and yet he was Casey's complete opposite in appearance and attitude. Casey was a character of fictional proportions. Tall and rangy as an old moose, he dressed in ill-fitting blue pinstriped suits, stooped with age, and had a mouthful of oversized teeth that aggravated a habit of mumbling so one could never be quite sure of what he had said. Friends and critics alike were fond of quipping that Casey had a built-in voice scrambler.

Falcone and the director exchanged pleasantries and spoke briefly about a headline story in the Washington *Post* that reported that German Chancellor Manfred von Seybold had demanded that the United States remove all nuclear-capable aircraft from German soil.

"Does that surprise you, Jack?" asked Falcone.

"Hell, no. I've been warning President Hollendale for nearly a year that this was coming."

"You know that Congress is now going to beat von Seybold to the punch and pull the remaining troops out of Germany before he tells us to. Which means a de facto neutral Germany. Why is he doing it?"

"Everyone has always underestimated von Seybold. He's a

clever bastard who appears to be stumbling around cow pastures. Right now he's playing up to the left-wing Greens."

"Yeah, but he's got the Christian Democrats with him on this, too."

"Exactly. But for a different reason. They know that a unified Germany can't remain neutral *and* without nuclear weapons for very long. Pressure is going to build among the German people to rearm. Within five years, even the Social Democrats will vote to support Germany's 'nuclear defensive needs.' " Bickford shook his head in exasperation.

The talk shifted to Falcone's assessment of the Agency's budgetary problems with the Appropriations Committee. Finally, choosing his words carefully, Falcone looked at Bickford and said, "Jack, I need a special favor. I've never asked for one before."

The director was just starting to eat his dropped eggs and did not look up from his plate. Then he sipped from his coffee cup, all the while acting as if Falcone had commented on the weather outside. At last he looked directly at Falcone, remaining silent. It was a technique that many in the intelligence world employed. Wait and watch. Wait and listen. Silence eventually will provoke action or words.

"I've been told by a very reliable source that we've got an important asset in Israel . . ."

Bickford said nothing.

"Frankly, I think it's a serious mistake for us to be penetrating friendly intelligence services. We are just begging for trouble. Retaliation. It's bad enough for our FBI to have to deal with the Soviets, the Chinese, and God knows how many of their trade associations without having to contend with our friends. It's crazy, Jack. Crazy!"

Still Bickford remained silent.

"But that's a matter I'm going to raise hell about at another time—and not too long from now." Falcone paused. "I have reason to believe that the man I'm asking about is a double agent for the Soviet Union, that we've been feeding off a good deal of misinformation. That our calculations about Syria's activities in Lebanon may be the product of that deception."

"That's interesting, Sean," the director said almost nonchalantly, ignoring Falcone's implied threat to hold hearings on the CIA's intelligence activities in friendly countries. "First of all, we don't make a habit of covertly collecting intelligence from our friends."

Falcone noted how careful Bickford was not to use the term "spying on." No doubt if the conversation was being recorded, "covertly collecting intelligence" sounded a hell of a lot more benign than "spying on."

"I don't have to tell you how explosive things are in the Middle East right now. Arab terrorists. Jewish terrorists. Religious fanatics. *Intifada.* Syrians and Lebanese slaughtering each other in Beirut. Iran is arming to the teeth. It's a tinderbox that could go off at any second. Any intelligence we can get may just help save thousands of lives." Bickford paused, the muscles in his clenched jaw twitching perceptibly. "Maybe millions."

Now it was Falcone who said nothing.

"We're not engaged in a morality play. We can't always draw the fine lines of the ethicists on Capitol Hill, who are the first ones to burn us every time we miss something." Bickford caught himself. He was still bitter over the criticism the Agency had received for not learning about Japan's research and development program in laser weaponry until it had been officially announced by a spokesman for Prime Minister Kirosutama.

"In any event, as you say, it's something we should talk about another time. Now, with respect to this double agent of yours—"

"Come on, Jack. Don't play games with me. He's not *mine.*"

"Okay, okay. Sorry. I shouldn't take it out on you. I don't buy it. We've had the man vetted, polygraphed, checked, and double-checked inside and out like a turkey before Thanksgiving. There's no sign he is anything but genuine and committed to the United States. He has given us damn good information. He actually prevented the PLO from kidnapping one of our military officers during a visit to Haifa. You would have thought Israel would have known about that one."

"My source is extremely reliable, Jack."

"Care to tell me the source?"

"I will. But not just yet." Falcone had promised Stock that he would not disclose where he had gotten the information. The Hollendale administration had not attempted to hide its displeasure over recent Israeli military activities in southern Lebanon, and

Stock feared that the Agency would reject any challenge to one of its assets if it saw an Israeli shadow behind the information.

"Well, what would you like us to do? We'll run another check on him, if you'd like, although I don't think it will be productive."

"I'd like that, Jack. But I'd like a full briefing on how the man was recruited, who recruited him, his background, his activities— the works."

The director gave Falcone his full attention. He sat upright, somewhat tense. "Sean, that is an extraordinary request. You know we can't discuss sources and methods with Congress." A tone of exasperation seeped into Bickford's voice. "Besides, that information is so compartmentalized, less than a handful of people within the Agency even know the man exists."

Falcone had anticipated the director's response. Ordinarily he would have backed off. In fact, ordinarily he never would have approached Bickford with such a request. But he had never seen his best friend so agitated as he had been yesterday. Joshua had been edgy, almost angry.

"I told you I was asking a special favor."

Bickford looked directly into Falcone's eyes. They suddenly seemed very gray and sad. In a city and a government filled with treachery and betrayal, there was no one he would trust more than Falcone. Even after what the North Vietnamese had done to him, he hadn't broken. There was no danger of a leak from this man's lips.

"If it were up to me, Sean, the answer would be an unqualified yes. There aren't many heroes left in this country, and I don't mind telling you, you're one of mine. I have absolute confidence in you. But this is one decision that's beyond my rank. I'll have to speak directly with the President on this one."

Bickford took a final gulp of coffee, then pushed back from the table, signaling that the breakfast meeting was over.

13

Jack Bickford's Ltd and backup security wagon, which had maintained radio contact with the White House since leaving Langley, were waved through the security blockade at the southwest gate of the White House. Bickford was greeted with a driving sheet of rain as he stepped from his air-conditioned sedan. He jumped quickly under the protective green-and-white-striped awning that vaulted from the entrance to the basement level of the southwest wing of the presidential mansion.

Bickford waved at the security guard who sat behind a semicircular desk, turned left, and entered a small elevator that carried him to the first floor. Turning left again, he slipped into Butch Naylor's office. Naylor was sitting at attention—a custom he shared with General Kastenmayer, Bickford thought. He was flipping through an eight-inch stack of classified reports.

"Hiya, Butch," Bickford said cheerily.

Peering over black half-moon glasses, Naylor tried not to show surprise that Bickford had arranged an unscheduled meeting with the President. "All clear for you in there. He bumped the majority leader to get you in." Naylor never let anyone within the range of his voice forget that he was an inside player, a man who knew what others did not know. He was tempted to try to get a hint from Bickford about the purpose of the meeting. But Naylor's power was based on knowing what was going on; he never disclosed a lack of knowledge about anything. As he often did, he covered his puzzlement with banter. "One question before you enter the holy of holies, Director. What in hell is going on out at your shop? This report on the Panamanian guerrillas is bullshit."

"Yeah. I've got a couple of Air Force colonels on loan working on this one. I should have known better. I'll put Admiral Lynch on it right away."

Naylor slipped his glasses off. "*Sheet,* Jack. You know damn well that the Navy can't tell a periscope from a proctoscope."

Bickford laughed at Naylor. The two men, locked into a life of analytic tension, enjoyed ribbing each other.

"How'd your morning briefing with the President go?"

"The Iceman," Naylor said, winking, "is in a good mood today. Don't understand it. We're losing our ass in Honduras, Costa Rica, and Pakistan, but he's not losing any sleep over it."

"That's what you and I are hired for. We're his worry beads," Bickford said. Glancing at his watch, he signaled that he was running late for his meeting with Hollendale, but he quickly reminded Naylor of their weekend dinner plans. "Don't forget. Cocktails at seven. Dinner at eight. Tell Anne it's formal. Black tie and jeans. And bring your own chopsticks. We're having sushi."

Bickford's air of lightheartedness masked the tension that tugged at him whenever he met with the President. Some twelve years earlier, Bickford had been pulled from the practice of law by Bill Casey, one of his senior partners. Virtually from the day he passed the New York bar exam, Bickford was given responsibility for the preparation and trial of complex security law cases that were beyond the abilities of the law firm's more experienced members. He possessed an eye that missed no detail and a memory that forgot nothing. But it was his analytic power that captured Casey's attention, his intuitive ability to grasp the full scope of seemingly unrelated points and find in them a pattern.

When Casey was named director of central intelligence, he asked Bickford to follow him to Washington. After spending five years in the analysis division, Bickford was named deputy director. Three years later, he was named director by Hollendale's predecessor. Because Bickford had worked assiduously to build and maintain good relations with congressional leaders, Hollendale decided to keep him as DCI. Hollendale needed every bridge he could get to the prima donnas on Capitol Hill. But the relationship between the two men was not close; rather, it was formal, businesslike, and covered by a patina of mutual respect.

Bickford respected Hollendale's political skills and his ability to gorge himself with information, digest it, and shape his policies in a way that gave coherency to his foreign and domestic goals. But lately he had detected something that disturbed him. The President's popularity was breeding an overconfidence, an arrogance, inside the White House. Hollendale was becoming increasingly frustrated with members of Congress, with the slowness of the legislative process. He wanted action; they gave him endless debate, delay. He wanted courage; they talked compromise. At the national security meetings Bickford attended, more and more time was devoted to denouncing congressional meddling and devising ways to circumvent Congress's attempts to restrain the President's power.

What worried Bickford even more was that Hollendale had surrounded himself with people who would one day get him in trouble. Clayton Skillings, his chief of staff, had poisoned relations with the Hill. The White House press corps no longer trusted the President's press secretary. But Polanski was the biggest problem. He was too close to Hollendale. Polanski's job was to run the FBI, but he was determined to control the country's policy-making apparatus. He was always slipping in to see Hollendale in the Oval Office or, more frequently, at the President's hideaway in the Old Executive Building, scheming to cut down or ridicule the State Department and the CIA.

Bickford had no love for bureaucracies: They were cumbersome and slow, and they frustrated presidents. But they existed to ensure that presidents had the benefit of a wide range of analyses and views. Bold action could guarantee headlines, excite editorial commentators. But headlines were rarely the prudent way to make progress—a fact that Polanski conveniently overlooked.

Bickford was tempted to resign as DCI before some scandal blew up in the President's face—and before Polanski tried to shift the blame for it to the Agency, as he no doubt would. And yet Bickford hesitated. Resigning, he rationalized, would only strengthen Polanski's hand, exposing the President, and the presidency, to even greater danger. Or was it really just his ego at stake? he wondered.

He passed through the reception room. Several congressmen chatted among themselves with Rotarian amiability as they awaited some ceremonial meeting to be held in the Roosevelt Room. An attractive White House aide, dressed in a lightweight pleated suit, escorted Bickford with crisp efficiency to the Oval Office.

"Good morning, Mr. President," Bickford offered with what appeared to be genuine enthusiasm.

"Come in, Jack. Come in," Hollendale said, shaking Bickford's hand while throwing his arm around his shoulder. "As I said on the phone, my door is always open. All you have to do is call. And I'll drop anything to see you, because I know it has to be important."

Bickford knew that the President did not like unscheduled events of any kind, especially meetings requested by Bickford. They always meant trouble, secret trouble.

"Now, Jack. What seems to be the problem?" Hollendale asked, with just enough stress on *seems* to imply that Bickford did not know a real problem from an imaginary one.

"I had a visit yesterday from Senator Falcone," Bickford began. "He—"

"And what did our war hero want?" Hollendale asked.

"He requested a briefing on a very delicate subject. He wants to know about a major asset we have in Israel."

"Goddamn!" Hollendale shouted. He stood and banged a knee against the English butler's tray that stood next to a deep-cushioned chair. "Goddamn." He took a step toward the fireplace and turned back to Bickford. "And what did you tell him?"

"I told him I had to get permission for such a request directly from you."

"Why didn't you just tell him it was no dice? Why the hell did you have to drag me into this?"

"Into what, Mr. President?" Bickford asked sharply.

"Into the whole Israel mess," Hollendale quickly responded. *"Anything* about Israel is a problem. Goddammit, Jack. If word gets out that we have a man—"

"Senator Falcone has never been a leaker, Mr. President. I would trust him with just about anything."

"And I wouldn't trust him or anyone else on the Hill, Jack. I know those prima donnas better than you do." He hesitated for a moment, as if he were changing the subject. "What specifically would you have to tell him?"

"A standard briefing: background information without full disclosure. The asset's bona fides, a general idea about what he has been doing for us."

"You will have to name the . . . intelligence service?"

"Yes. To comply with the senator's request, I think that will be necessary."

"Did he tell you why he wants this?"

"Yes. He said he had information that our asset has been doubled."

"Damn. Did he give you the source?"

"No."

"Do you have any suspects?"

"Yes, Mr. President. Only a guess, sir. But I wonder if he's running with something from the defector's story, possibly through a leak in the intelligence community."

"You haven't briefed the Intelligence Committee on the defector?"

"No, sir. As you know, we are still evaluating him."

"So you're suggesting that someone leaked defector material to Falcone?"

"It's a possibility, sir."

"You said you suspect that it's out of the intelligence community. You mean the Defense Intelligence Agency, don't you?"

"A *distinct* possibility, Mr. President."

Hollendale walked to his desk, sat down, picked up a pencil, and for several seconds tapped it rhythmically. "I've got to do some thinking, Jack. There's more here than meets even your eye. Go out and talk shop with Naylor for a half-hour or so. I'll call you in when I've made up my mind."

As soon as Bickford left the Oval Office, Hollendale ordered his secretary to put through a call to Polanski on his scramble phone.

"Harry!" Hollendale roared through the phone. He seemed to believe that scrambling called for extra volume. "Get your ass over here. Wait—on second thought, stay put. I don't want anyone to see you come in." He paused. "You sure this phone is safe?"

"They don't make them safer, Mr. President. What's the problem?"

"Harry, I need your advice. Jack Bickford was just here, and—"

"Oh? And what did the Priest want?" Polanski sniffed.

"He's had a request from Senator Falcone for a briefing about a friend who's working in the Holy Land."

"Falcone!" Polanski shouted. "Can't be. He's got to be bearding for his buddy Stock."

"Stock? Harry, what in hell's this all about?"

"Mr. President, this is one of those cases where I think it's better . . . that you not get involved in the details."

"Details hell, Harry," Hollendale snapped. "I'm the President, remember? I'm supposed to know the ambassador to New Guinea's wife's name and who's on the White House tennis court every hour, but not what the FBI is doing with a senator?"

Polanski hesitated, letting the silence absorb Hollendale's growing anger. "Mr. President, I'd rather discuss this with you in private."

"You're the one who said these phones are safe."

"All right . . . Basically, as you know, I always thought Stock was too close to the Israelis. But I persuaded him that he should get even closer, keep us apprised of their interests. At the right time, we tag something. Follow it like a salmon on the way to its spawning grounds. With luck, it could take us right to *Canaan*. Stock agreed to help."

"So what you're saying is that Stock reneged? Double-crossed you?"

Polanski didn't miss Hollendale's point that Stock had double-crossed *him*. He knew the rules. He'd be the one standing on the deck of the ship if it ever went down.

Hollendale could hear Polanski breathing. *He's not fancy*, Hollendale thought. *But he's smart. Street smart.* Polanski had started off as a cop, a third-generation Chicago cop: night classes at the University of Chicago, a hitch in the Marines, then the Bureau. He had done some delicate work for the Nixon White House, stayed publicly clean, and risen in the ranks of the Bureau. After William Sessions retired, Hollendale's recruiters recommended Polanski for director because he could be presented to the public as a tough-on-crime symbol, a career cop who knew his way around Washington. As director of the FBI he was supposed to be a public, nonpartisan figure. In reality, he spent much of his time serving Hollendale as a secret, tight-lipped adviser.

"As I see it," Polanski said, "you have two choices. You can haul in Stock and threaten to cancel SUNDANCER if he doesn't tell Falcone to forget about getting the identity of the asset. If Stock goes along, we're back to square one, although we have Falcone and Bickford wondering what the hell is going on. Well, that kind of open-ended mystery happens all the time. So what, we tell them. If we've got to tell them anything at all."

"You said two choices," Hollendale cut in. "I like this one already. We can pull him right back onto the reservation."

"There's a down side to this one, Mr. President," Polanski replied. "Stock has an erratic streak—more than usual lately, according to what I hear. If he does balk and we do carry through the threat to cancel the program, we stand the chance of having mud thrown back at us. We wind up with nothing. Or worse than nothing."

"You've made your point, Harry. What's choice number two?"

"Through the Bickford-Falcone loop we could give him the wrong name. I should say *identity*. Sometimes there isn't a real name known to anyone. Then, when he plays that wrong identity back to his friends, something interesting might happen for us. But . . ."

"But there's a down side. Right, Harry?"

"Worse than a down side—an impossibility. Bickford is such a straight arrow he wouldn't give Falcone the wrong identity, even if you ordered him to. He'd resign and probably wind up telling Congress why. You know how goddamned righteous he is with those clowns on the Hill. Bickford would never go for a setup that puts him in violation of the oversight laws. So we—"

"Harry, if you knew the two choices wouldn't work, why mention them? Why waste my time? For God's sake!"

"Mr. President. I know I'm not the only one you listen to. If I hadn't told you what could go wrong with those two choices, if some asshole like Naylor had suggested one of them, you might have taken it. The further you stay away from this, the better. I think the best thing to do is let Bickford brief Falcone. And then see how it falls."

"Jesus, Harry! Won't that jeopardize our guy?"

"Not necessarily. Assuming our friends take any action, they'll probably arrest him. Maybe expel him. They won't want to make a public stink about it. If they do, we can always trade Pollard for him if necessary. It's more important to find *Canaan* than protect our man."

Hollendale remained silent, pondering Polanski's logic.

"Second, I think Bickford should give the same briefing to Naylor, but before he gives it to Falcone."

"Naylor? But you just said—"

"Right. I think he's an asshole. But he is a power nut, too. He loves to know things. So let him have the brief. Most important, it would seem kosher to Bickford that Naylor, as your national security adviser, gets the brief. If there is a leak of this, as we expect there to be, you have a witness on your side. Now, you know damn well that Naylor will look wonderful with his war record on display up there before a congressional committee investigating—what will they call it? Leakgate?" Polanski could not suppress a laugh. "In the meantime, I think you'd better leave the rest of this to me and Naylor. The less you know, the better." The director wanted his gesture to sound heroic, patriotic. He knew Hollendale wouldn't have it any other way.

"I've got to admire you, Harry. You do look ahead. Okay, I'll tell Bickford to give the briefs. Thanks, Harry."

"Any time, Mr. President. Any time."

Hollendale hung up and pressed a button on his desk console. "Tell Bickford to come in here."

14

Washington, July 18

SENATORS LIVE BY TRA-
dition and protocol, Bickford thought as he glanced around the
small Intelligence Committee conference room. Madison and Jefferson might not understand all of the arcane testimony given in the
nearby hearing room. But they would feel at home here in the
civility suggested by the well-made straight-backed chairs and the
long, highly polished table. Bickford, a cabinetmaker by avocation,
believed that good furniture was enduring and timeless. On the
cream walls were two paintings, a modern rendering of Faneuil Hall
with Boston traffic whirling past the statue of Sam Adams and a
misty pointillist painting of the Golden Gate Bridge. He was standing in front of the Faneuil Hall painting when Falcone entered the
room.

"What does your analytic mind think about the painting,
Jack?" Falcone asked.

"First, that it hangs here because the chairman of the Intelligence Committee is from Massachusetts," Bickford said, turning his
head to look toward the senator. He could see the Golden Gate over
Falcone's right shoulder. "Just as the bridge is here because the vice

chairman is from California." He turned back to the Faneuil Hall painting.

"There's a certain kind of wit behind this painting," Bickford continued. "Poor old Sam Adams standing there on his pedestal. He started a revolution, and now he can't get across the street. Did you pick this painting for its aesthetic value—which, I think, is considerable—or because Sam was one of our first secret agents?"

"I wish I could tell you I was that smart," Falcone replied. "I didn't remember Adams's underground career until one of our staffers reminded me. No. The prosaic answer is, I chose it because I liked it, and because I admire the work of Benjamin Thompson. He was the architect who brought the hall back to life, just as he did Union Station here."

"I assumed that a constituent had painted it."

"Wrong assumption, Director. When I get a decent painting from a constituent, I make damn sure that it's hung in a place where it can be seen."

"What about the other painting, Senator? Is it meant to reflect the abstract doings in this room?"

Falcone shook his head. "When I look at that painting long enough, Jack, I get memories. Two men I knew in Vietnam jumped off that bridge." He turned to look at it for a moment, then motioned Bickford to a chair at the end of the table. "I guess we should get down to business."

Falcone opened the jaws of his cavernous briefcase, a battered brown lump of leather that he had carried since law school. Following a habit he had developed in this room, he took out a yellow, lined notepad, tore off several pages, and placed them on the table. He knew that not even the impressions of the words he wrote in this room could leave it, and being parsimonious, he did not want to sacrifice an entire pad every time he got a briefing in the Intelligence Committee's secure suite. He pulled a black ballpoint pen from his inside suit pocket. On the side of the pen in tiny silver letters were the words *United States Senate*.

"Okay, Jack. What have you got?"

Bickford carried nothing. He had habits for this room, too. If a briefing called for any visual aids, such as satellite imagery, he brought along a specialist with the necessary equipment. What Bickford felt about this place had been well expressed by an antilittering sign he had seen in a national park: LEAVE ONLY YOUR FOOTPRINTS.

Falcone was not surprised to see Bickford speak without notes. He knew from experience that the director did not talk from the top of his head. He worked from a script, a briefing document that he had memorized and deposited in a CIA safe. Thus there would be a CIA record of the briefing. The only record of any questions Falcone asked would be whatever he jotted down in Bickford's presence. There were no hidden recording devices in the conference room.

"We have developed an extremely reliable asset for supplying us information centered on, but not exclusive to, the Middle East. I use the term *asset* advisedly, because by some definitions he would be considered an agent. But since an agent works under and is tasked by a case officer, we don't use the term *agent* for the man we call *Peg Blazer.*"

Falcone wrote down "asset *Peg Blazer,*" then looked up. He was about to ask a question when Bickford said, "I'd appreciate it, Senator, if you would hold your questions until I finish the brief, which will be short." Bickford did not like to have his carefully controlled presentation interrupted. Falcone nodded his assent, and he continued.

"*Peg Blazer* is too independent to be an operational agent. We consider him a fragile asset; he could easily be destroyed if we pressed him. He is something of a political asset, not unlike a defector in a pre-escape mode. He wants to supply us with information that he believes will help us, or information that will hurt the politicians he disagrees with within his country. He sees himself as a patriot rather than a traitor.

"However, like an operational agent, he was, in a sense, recruited. He was in this country, at Lackland Air Force Base in Texas, in 1978, under the foreign pilot training program. He was assigned to Lackland for advanced F-15 flight training. At that time he was a captain in his country's Air Force.

"We had no intention of recruiting him. But thanks to a misadventure—and some initiative by Air Force intelligence—we were able to give him some extraordinary help. We let him know that someday we would appreciate reciprocity.

"That is what we are now getting. When he first started voluntarily supplying us with intelligence, we suspected a plant. We managed to give him certain tests that convinced us of his sincerity. He has provided us with several important intelligence leads. We rate him currently as our best resource in the area of Middle Eastern military and political information. And that is about it, Senator," Bickford said. *The first question,* he told himself, *will be "What country is he from?"*

"A nicely sanitized brief, Jack," Falcone said, smiling and leaning back from the pile of papers in front of him. "Now for a little more. What country is he from?"

"Israel," Bickford said, allowing himself a smile.

"If I had been going to bet . . . ," Falcone began, then shifted to another question. "Never mind. Just how did you recruit him? I've heard enough of your defector evaluations to know what 'a misadventure' and 'some initiative' might mean. What did you manage to get on him?"

"It was all somewhat fortuitous, Senator. Just before his training cycle ended at Lackland, he borrowed a U.S. pilot's car, drove into town, had a few too many beers, and, on the way back to his quarters on the base, hit and killed a pedestrian. The Air Force MPs responded. That was about 1 A.M. They confined him to quarters until their boss, the duty adjutant officer, decided what to do.

"Luckily for us, the duty officer kicked the case upstairs to the base commander, who had it presented to him next morning, just when he happened to be having a meeting with an officer from the Air Force Special Activities Center. The center runs some Air Force–oriented activities for the Defense Intelligence Agency. This particular officer had been loaned to Langley at one time in his career and had an appreciation of the situation.

"He volunteered to take the case off the base commander's hands. The commander readily agreed. The intelligence officer quickly established the facts of the accident. The dead pedestrian was an illegal Mexican who was drunk himself and who had walked into the road just when the Israeli came around the corner. The Mexican worked as a dishwasher in the officers' club. He had no known kin in the United States.

"The intelligence officer flashed some papers at the hospital morgue, hired a civilian undertaker to claim the body, and, with an okay from the Air Force liaison to Langley, contacted our resident at the U.S. embassy in Mexico City. He arranged for the body to be transferred to an invented cousin in Mexico and had him buried—with an appropriate Catholic ceremony, I might add—in a Mexican cemetery. Case closed."

"But for the Israeli, I assume, case opened," Falcone said.

"Assumption correct. The friendly Air Force officer and one of our Middle East case officers had a couple of long talks with the Israeli. He knew that if the Israeli Government heard about the case his career was over—not necessarily because he had gotten drunk or had accidentally killed a man, but because the Israelis would assume that we would do something like what we did. So he went along with our suggestion: He would be a sleeper. If at some time in the future we needed a favor, he would comply."

"That's all?" Falcone asked.

"At that time, yes. We saw no need to actually *run* him. It wasn't worth the risk. Israel was giving us plenty of intelligence. We treated Israel as a friendly nation and went by the rules. Then came Pollard," Bickford added, referring to Jonathan Pollard, the U.S. Navy intelligence analyst who worked as a spy for Israel. "As part of the bush-beating to find out what damage Pollard had caused, we gently activated *Peg Blazer* and asked him for an assessment. We got that—and quite a bit more.

"When we activated him, he was a thirty-six-year-old lieutenant colonel assigned by the Israeli Air Force to the Mossad. His Air Force career was behind him and they were making him into an intelligence officer. He spoke Arabic, and although Israel-born and a Jew, he had enough Arab blood to pass as a Palestinian on operations. He traveled a bit and was run loosely enough for us to make contact with him now and then.

"The Pollard affair upset him. He felt that the Mossad people who set up that operation were crazy and were risking the special relationship between Israel and the United States. He began giving us valuable information."

"Care to give me any examples?"

"I'd rather not. I have only sketchy knowledge of the actual material, and for me to find out more would be difficult and perhaps a bit risky for our asset."

"Fair enough. But what about the report I heard? That he is a double agent?"

"Impossible. Absolutely impossible. I would stake my reputation on it, and I do not say that often, as you know. As a matter of fact, Senator, he has been giving us certain information that . . . Well, let me repeat. I am satisfied that he is genuine."

Bickford, the model briefer, never faltered. The unended phrase "certain information that . . ." hung in the air.

"What do you mean by 'certain information,' Jack?"

"Let me put it this way: We believe that *Peg Blazer* is on the verge of giving us information about a *real* double agent. Your inquiry about him, coincidentally, comes at a very delicate moment."

"Are you suggesting that my inquiry was designed to hurt or expose *Peg Blazer?*" Falcone sharply asked.

"If *you* trust your source, Sean, *I* must trust your source. And I do. I also know that none of this information will go beyond you. I know that you know the rules. But if I may step a way off the record for a moment . . ." He glanced at the sheets of paper. Falcone put down his pen. Bickford continued, "If this is from the Defense Intelligence Agency, Sean, then I do *not* trust your source, and I respectfully suggest that you should not either."

When Bickford had briefed Butch Naylor yesterday, Naylor had seemed to draw on his experience as an Air Force general to try, to no avail, to get specific examples of the material that *Peg Blazer* had delivered. "Specs on Soviet weapons systems? Syrian order of battle?" Naylor had asked. This was exactly the kind of straight military information that the DIA saw as vital and the CIA saw as mere military bean-counting. Bickford suspected that Naylor's source, and Falcone's, was some Third World general who had picked up something by torturing an insurgent, inflated the information, and slipped it to a gullible DIA operative who had inflated it some more. Bickford had not made any remarks about the DIA to Naylor, however.

"Not to worry, Jack," Falcone said. "My source is not from the DIA." He resisted adding that although the DIA might be more extreme than the CIA in assessing threats to the United States, it had sometimes been a hell of a lot more accurate.

In effect the meeting had ended. But the two men continued to talk about intelligence matters in general. Then Bickford rose from his chair, said goodbye, left the room, and walked down the corridor, where a uniformed guard checked him out and opened the door.

Falcone gathered his notes and placed them into a manila folder he took from his briefcase. He then sealed the folder with a strip of red transparent tape. Carrying his briefcase in his left hand, he walked toward another room at the end of the second-floor corridor. He pressed a series of numbers on an electronic lock, and the door snapped open.

He entered a warren of corridors and work cubicles whose six-foot walls ended well below the high ceiling. Many of the cubicles held committee staff workers laboring over reports and analyses. Their working papers were all highly classified and would never leave the complex of committee offices.

Falcone walked past the last of the cubicles to the door of a room designed to accommodate all the classified information obtained by the committee. Opening the door, he registered with a clerk whose desk was near the entrance. Beyond the clerk was a section of the room devoted to the individual safes that were assigned to each member of the committee. Falcone twisted the combination dial on his safe four times, opened the door, placed the sealed folder inside, closed the safe, and spun the dial.

The next day, on the floor of the Senate, Falcone walked over to Joshua Stock's desk, and while a colleague ardently declaimed on the pressing need for more hydroelectric dams in Alaska, he leaned down to speak to Stock.

"I got a brief from Bickford on that Middle Eastern fellow," Falcone said.

Stock nervously looked around and started to rise from the seat behind his desk. "Not here," he whispered. "Let's go someplace where we can talk about it."

"No. Got to run," Falcone said. "Anyway, there's nothing to talk about. I'm satisfied that the asset is okay." He started to turn away to walk up the aisle.

"Wait!" Stock said, grabbing Falcone's left forearm. "Who is this asset? What's his name?"

Falcone stopped, spun around, and looked down at Stock. His expression quickly changed from anger to puzzlement. "There's no *name*, for God's sake. What would you want with a name, anyway?

Just tell your sources that they didn't know what they were talking about."

"I . . . I can't do that, Sean."

"Yes, you can. You can just tell them that everything is all right. Period," Falcone said, his tone irritable.

"No," Stock said. "Everything is not all right." But Falcone, already on his way up the aisle, could not hear what he had said.

It always amazed Falcone that the nicest homes in Georgetown had the worst parking. You had a crawl space of a driveway if you were lucky, or a two-bay garage. Many homeowners were fiercely protective of their neighboring streets, feeling somehow inadequate for not being able to buy annex space for a car. A visitor trying to park in Georgetown moved cautiously from street to street, like a sea captain negotiating a shallow channel. You saw all the BMWs and Jags parked sardine-tight next to one another and realized that space was the most important distinction, the one true commodity in Georgetown.

If that was so, Joshua Stock had done well for himself. He had a Queen Anne house on Q Street that looked positively expansive compared to the cramped brick townhouses surrounding him. It struck Falcone that the Gothic homes were always the most impressive in Georgetown, since their owners had an excuse, with such a style, to cram as much excess onto the exterior as possible, creating the illusion of having more space. Even more impressive was the wrought iron fence that stretched down to the sidewalk. Having the edges of his property so clearly marked further distinguished Stock from his neighbors. From the bargeboards along the eaves to the intoxicating honeysuckle bushes lining the yard, Stock's home breathed prominence.

Falcone circled Q and R streets several times looking for a place to park. He was tempted to park illegally and display the senatorial license plate that gave him such a privilege on Capitol Hill. He only felt such urges to display his prominence trivially when he was around the wealthy, to remind them that money and power were not always synonymous. As if to quiet his insecurity, a spot immediately displayed itself and he settled his car into it with satisfying anonymity.

Falcone rounded two street corners to Stock's home and was announced with ground-level halogens once he arrived at the entrance gate. The Filipino maid greeted him on the cross-gabled front porch. She had an apologetic look. Stock's two daughters, Jessica and Jennette, were loudly denying the fact that bedtime had descended on them or was likely to in the near future.

Over drinks one night after a late Senate session, Stock had expressed doubts about the wisdom of starting a family so late in his life. It had been Cleo, twenty years younger than Stock, who had insisted.

Falcone could hear Cleo shushing the children wearily. Joshua, ever the arbiter, promised them a trip to Chuck E. Cheese's amusement center in exchange for good behavior. Falcone was tempted to greet the children but decided his presence would only give them more of an excuse not to go to sleep.

Coming down the stairs, Cleo began to chide Joshua for spoiling the kids but suspended her complaint when she saw Falcone. "Sean!" she exclaimed. Her southern trill echoed pleasantly off the high foyer ceiling. Falcone kissed her before her greeting had fully disappeared from his hearing.

"No one told me before I had children that the terrible twos would last five years," she complained.

"You should know nothing happens quickly in a political town," Falcone observed.

"We're in it for the long haul with those two," Stock agreed.

"Oh, please. You're the one negotiating with them like they were swing votes on some budget proposal."

"Every constituent has a favorite issue," Stock said dryly. "I'm just trying to meet the needs of some future voters." He winked at Falcone as he steered his friend into the living room.

"You'd better stay in politics a long time, hon," Cleo warned her husband. "Because right now you're looking at two votes for the price of one."

Stock seemed amused by Cleo's taunts, though there was an underlying dissatisfaction in his manner that indicated he was growing impatient. Reclining on the sofa, Falcone was briefly reassured when Cleo leaned comfortably up against her husband. Joshua responded dutifully and draped his arm around her, though his display of affection seemed strangely unemotional.

Falcone wondered whether his friend's forced enthusiasm was related to work pressures or to some personal problem. He had felt bad for being so short with Stock on the Senate floor, and in following up had inadvertently found himself a required guest for dinner. He realized now that Stock and Cleo needed time together and promised himself he would make this an early evening for his friends' sake.

In the past, Falcone had always felt a mixture of relief and anxiety whenever he visited Joshua and Cleo. He usually ate dinner alone in his apartment, a necessary retreat for him from the day's busy schedule. Dinner with the Stocks was one exception he enjoyed making. He took vicarious pleasure in the participatory demands of a family, the insular comfort of shared love. Ever since Vietnam, he had refused to entertain thoughts about starting another family and keeping a home. Increasingly, though, he was reminded about the intimacy he was missing in his life when he measured it against that of his happily married colleagues. Hemingway's famous line about what might have been between Jake and Lady Brett had become Falcone's favorite respite from too much needless pondering: "Isn't it pretty to think so?"

When the maid announced that dinner was ready, Falcone eagerly abandoned his brooding in favor of sustenance. The dining room was lit with a curious combination of metallic sconces on the walls and two French lamps on a Gustav Stickley table that housed the silverware. As always, the meal was delicious. By the time the pheasant-wing appetizers were cleared, Falcone had boasted of his intentions to treat Joshua and Cleo to a home-cooked meal they would remember.

"We still remember the last time you cooked for us," Joshua replied. "It was a combination Italian and Alaskan dish—frozen pizza. Though I believe it was burned by the time you served it."

"Singed, hon, not burned," Cleo corrected.

"I did that on purpose, though," Falcone said. "If I let on what a good cook I was, you'd never have me over again."

That was the tone of the evening—superficial banter that hovered just above the strained exchanges Falcone had first encountered tonight.

After they exhausted the topics of conversation that Cleo could take part in, Stock went back to his long-shared history with Falcone. "Remember the *Zephyr*, Sean?" He was referring to the sailboat he had had as a young man, the one he and Falcone had sailed off the Florida coast one summer, matching cans and markers against the purple and red dots on their flimsy nautical map. "Remember, Sean?" Stock repeated. He had such an earnest look that for a moment Falcone saw that carefree, innocent time in their youth.

Falcone thought that his friend was about to remind him of that magical day when Falcone had fallen in love. It was a time that he didn't want to talk about right then. "Sure, I remember," he said. "You said something like 'prepare to jibe,' and the next thing I knew I was floating in the water with a dent in my head from the swinging boom."

"You were a terrible sailor," Stock said with satisfaction. He looked to Cleo for confirmation that this was believable or readily apparent if one simply observed Falcone today. Cleo nodded but seemed more concerned that he was on his fourth scotch since dinner started.

"Let me tell you," Falcone said, winking at Cleo, "I'm a hell of a lot better sailor today than Joshua is a storyteller."

"I don't know." Cleo laughed. "He's been telling some pretty tall ones lately."

Falcone glanced quickly at Cleo to determine if there was any hidden meaning in her words. He found none. A few moments later, he said his goodbyes. Joshua pressed him to share a nightcap before he left, but Falcone declined good-naturedly. Cleo thanked him for being so considerate and went on up to bed.

"Everything okay?" Falcone asked, pausing at the heavy oak door.

"I'm sorry I seemed so frantic today," Stock said. "Everything's fine. If anything were wrong, you'd be the first to know."

Falcone walked back to his car, wondering if he was ever the first to know anything.

"Shall I get the ambassador now, sir?"

"Yes, Jarrell, he usually eats lunch at his office. I'm quite sure he's in Paris today."

Michael Rorbach vigorously toweled his hair dry, then stepped into the terry-cloth robe Jarrell held for him. He had just completed his daily workout. Twenty minutes on a stationary bike, ten minutes on his Universal weight machine, capped with fifty laps in the swimming pool that ran parallel to his large mirrored exercise room. He was a fitness addict, oddly narcissistic about his appearance, since he was something of a recluse, shunning virtually all public events.

He remembered reading that a man could have fame or riches but not both. *Well, leave the fame for others,* Rorbach thought as he drank from a large glass of chilled orange juice. Fame meant attention. Attention drew the paparazzi, society reporters. And just behind, the IRS and other snoopers. *Give me wealth.* Money was the key to America. It opened every door of influence. Or rather, it opened his door to everyone of influence. Because everyone came to him, asked for his support, on his turf, on his terms.

Rorbach stabbed the pieces of pineapple and melon that Jarrell had prepared for his breakfast. He felt his face grow warm in the sun, donned a pair of Zeitz sunglasses, then glanced across the expanse of his estate. Nearby a flock of Canada geese floated on the pond, which looked as if it had been set on fire by the morning sun.

Jarrell stepped out onto the slate-floored patio and plugged a phone into an outside jack. "He's on the line, sir."

"Good morning—afternoon, Yitzhak. I know how busy you must be. I won't keep you. Just checking to make sure that you received the book."

"Yes, Michael. It arrived today. You know I'm not fond of mysteries, but I'm looking forward to reading this one. In fact, I've already started it. Fascinating."

"Wonderful. I know it won't take you long to finish. I know that others will be anxious to read it when you do."

"Of course."

"Well, Yitzhak, let me know when you plan to visit again. Or perhaps we can have dinner when I get to Paris next week. And give my love to Rachmella. She's a lovely lady. You have much to be proud of."

"Goodbye, Michael," Rafiah said softly, hanging up the receiver.

15

YITZHAK RAFIAH CARE-
fully nurtured the image of a man who never acted in the grip of
emotion. He had a well-earned reputation for viewing a crisis merely
as a problem that happened to be bigger than ordinary problems.
While others might panic and rant when a crisis hove into view,
Rafiah quietly explored ways to divert it. When he did become
angry, he tried to make the anger work for him.

He did that now, as he read for the third time a Jerusalem *Post*
story about an Israeli Air Force colonel who had been blown up in a
car bomb in Tel Aviv.

Colonel Nathan Mizrahi was killed instantly. Air Force officials
identified him as an analyst assigned to the office of the Air
Force chief of staff . . . Three hours after the explosion, authorities arrested three young men, ranging in age from twenty
to twenty-five. Police described them as Palestinians involved
in the uprisings in the West Bank and Gaza . . . The car was
parked in an alley behind Colonel Mizrahi's apartment house.
Authorities said that the walls of the alley confined the explo-

sion. The bomb was believed to have been remote-controlled, police said.

What the story did not say was that the bombing had the signature of the Mossad. In 1988, Rafiah remembered, three PLO operatives were killed in a car bombing in Limassol, Cyprus. Rafiah had reason to know about that bombing. It, too, had been remote-controlled. They had called it surgical. Exactly enough explosives to do the job, detonated where a retaining wall blocked off the blast.

He looked closely at a photograph of Mizrahi's car. As in the Limassol bombing, the doors had been blown open but were still on their hinges; the roof had almost disappeared. In both bombings, Rafiah reasoned, the bomb, designed to explode upward, had been placed under the driver's seat.

The words came back to Rafiah, the horrible words told to him between sobs. From the waist down, everything was gone. Fragments of flesh and bone had been blasted like shrapnel into metal and leather. And blood. Blood had sprayed with such force that it was first a mist, hovering in the acrid air, and then a red dew settling upon the twisted metal, upon the shirt and arms and hands and face, the face with that look of surprise . . .

Why? he had asked then. *Why did they do this?* And there had been a reason, one as old as blood vengeance: *lex talionis;* an eye for an eye. Kill a PLO agent in retaliation for what he did to us. He looked again at the photograph of Colonel Mizrahi's car. Now he again asked himself why. What had Mizrahi done? What had he truly done? But this time there was no one here to answer.

The secure phone on his desk rang. *Secure?* he thought. *Perhaps against the PLO it's secure. But not against the Mossad. Well, let them hear this one.* The phone line went from his desk to a scrambler in an embassy communications room, where the call was transmitted in bursts on a reserved frequency to the Foreign Ministry in Jerusalem. From there it was relayed to Avi Nesher's office in Tel Aviv.

"Nesher here," said a high-pitched rendering of Nesher's deep voice. "Good to hear from you, Yitzhak."

"I doubt that, Avi. I saw the *Post* today. Unfortunate what happened to the young colonel. You told me it would only be a matter of cutting him out of the information loop. Do you realize what this will do to my friend? I must go to the Prime Minister on this. It jeopardizes our relations with the U.S."

"Trust me when I say it came as a total shock to me," Nesher said.

"Trust you, Avi?" Rafiah said, exasperated. "If I trust you, then it means there is someone in the Mossad I cannot trust. If you did not betray me, then someone must have betrayed you. There must be a rotten fish in the Mossad, and the Prime Minister should know about it."

"We have been friends for many years, Yitzhak," Nesher said, a tone of pleading entering his distorted voice. "Please do not call the PM about this. Let me come to Paris and discuss this in person. Give me that."

"I told you I was *going* to the PM," Rafiah said. "I'd be on my way today if it weren't Friday. And I *am* giving you something. I am giving you this warning call. I will be meeting with the PM. If he wants to call you in, that will be his decision. I consider this gravely serious, Avi. Gravely serious. Goodbye."

Rafiah replaced the phone in its niche in the console, pressed a button, and spoke into another phone. "Deborah, book me on a flight to Tel Aviv Sunday morning. Call the PM's office. Arrange for a gravely serious meeting on Monday evening. They know what those words mean. I will return Tuesday. Make the usual arrangements with security and so forth. Now get me Senator Stock." He glanced at his watch. "Yes. In his office. The private number."

In Washington, Joshua Stock picked up a beige phone that was not connected through the Senate switchboard. He had been expecting the call ever since breakfast, when he saw the three-paragraph story on page B-5 of the Washington *Post.* The headline read:

CAR BOMB KILLS ISRAELI OFFICER;

3 WEST BANK YOUTHS HELD

But what had set his heart racing was the reference to Colonel Mizrahi's having been a former pilot in the Israeli Air Force. The same sense of foreboding that had touched him the night he had been called to the White House three months ago engulfed him now. He knew intuitively that the Israeli's death had been the result of no random act of Arab violence.

Without introducing himself, Rafiah said, "I am calling you about an unfortunate incident. I assure you, my friend, that this was not my doing. I'm going to take up the matter with the proper authorities on Monday."

"Be careful, Yitzhak. There may be more to this than you are seeing at this moment," Stock said. He was looking down at a pink message slip on which was written, "Call Senator Falcone. Urgent!!!"

"There are times, Joshua, when being careful can be dangerous. That incident is a symptom of a disease. There is indeed more to this than either one of us is seeing."

"What do you advise me to do?" Stock asked. He crumpled the message slip and started to drop it into the wastepaper basket under his desk, but then began smoothing it on his desktop.

"Say nothing. Do nothing. Nothing at all. This has not ended as you or I wished. Goodbye."

16

THE CHIEF OF AVI NESHER'S
security detail, a disarmingly slim man with an even more disarmingly angelic face, stood up when Nesher stormed out of his office.
"Stay here," Nesher ordered. The security man did as he was told,
resuming his post in a gray metal chair in the small, bleak anteroom
outside Nesher's office. Several times in the last few months Nesher
had made it quite clear that there were times when he was not to be
accompanied by any security man. This was clearly one of those
times.

Nesher's office was on the top floor of a three-story office building, which municipal records identified as an electrical power company substation. A chain-link fence ran the length of the front of the
building, whose entrance was at the end of a short sidewalk leading
from the fence's locked gate. A sign warned DANGER HIGH VOLTAGE
KEEP AWAY. The sign was rarely read, for there were few passersby
on the block-long dead-end street. A two-meter-high concrete barrier
barred road traffic.

Many of the people who entered and left the building did so as
Nesher now did. He walked down three flights of stairs to an under-

ground parking garage, unlocked a door, and entered a tunnel that
ended at another door. Nesher unlocked this door and emerged in
the restricted stacks of the library of Tel Aviv University. The door
that shut quietly behind him was labeled STAFF ONLY. He ascended a
spiral staircase to the first floor of the library and walked out the
main entrance. Making his way across the campus by entering and
exiting buildings, he once doubled back to make sure none of the
security escorts had disobeyed his orders.

A few blocks from the campus he found the restaurant where
he occasionally had lunch. A phone was attached to the wall near
the restrooms.

Ordinarily it was Ptor Kornienko who would arrange to meet
Nesher in Paris. In case of an emergency, Nesher was to call the
Raphael Hotel and ask to speak with a man called Renald Fouché.
In the event Nesher requested reservations less than forty-eight
hours from the time of his call, Kornienko would be notified in a
coded message returned to Nesher almost immediately.

Nesher followed the procedure and was surprised to find the
call returned to him at the restaurant within ten minutes. "Good
morning. *[Stand by for word-code message]* Your book *[a meeting to-
night]* has arrived. You may pick it up after five *[at seven]*. We are
glad to be of service *[Café l'Orangerie]*."

Six hours later Nesher arrived at the Charles de Gaulle Airport, passed easily through customs with false papers describing
him as an Austrian art dealer, and stepped quickly onto the moving
belts enveloped by glass tubes that looked like giant straws emanat-
ing from a punch bowl. A cab took him to Île St.-Louis, where he
spent half an hour strolling through one of the quaint galleries.
From there he proceeded to the Montparnasse Tower, the tallest
office building in Europe. On the fifty-sixth floor he sat at the restaurant bar, sipping wine. He picked out all of Paris's major landmarks
—the Louvre, Sacré-Coeur, Nôtre-Dame, the Eiffel Tower, the Bois
de Vincennes, Orly Airport . . . From the tower he took the métro
to the Trocadero Gardens and walked to the Guimet Museum. Finally he hailed a cab to Montmartre, where he found Café
l'Orangerie on the Boulevard de Clichy.

Although Nesher, as the Mossad's counterintelligence chief,

could easily explain slipping off to Paris occasionally, any meeting with Ptor Kornienko was risky. The French intelligence service, Gurrat, would be keeping Kornienko under surveillance. And it occurred to Nesher that the Mossad itself, operating out of the Israeli embassy in Paris, might have an interest in a Russian who purported to be a member of the Soviet Academy of Sciences.

The safety of their meeting depended on their respective skills in avoiding surveillance. Nesher's worst nightmare was that a photograph of him and Kornienko would end up in the Mossad's files. He would have to claim that Kornienko was a double agent. Then his superiors would demand to know exactly what he was getting from Kornienko. Nesher could imagine the lie upon lie that would be necessary, a shaky structure that might intrigue him but that would infuriate a top operative like Kornienko. And Nesher did not have to dwell on the fate of Colonel Nathan Mizrahi to remind himself just how dangerous the world of a double agent could be.

Kornienko was seated at a table in the back of the café. He appeared to be in his late fifties. At their very first meeting, Nesher had noticed something strange about Kornienko—his face seemed to be too slender for the rest of his body. It was almost as if he selected clothes that were deliberately too large for him and wore padding underneath, perhaps some kind of protective shield. And that ill-fitting toupee did not quite match the color of the neatly trimmed beard. Nesher wondered whether Kornienko wanted to appear to be a brilliant but disheveled Soviet academician or it was just a poor disguise that he wore for these meetings and later discarded.

Tonight Kornienko wore a dark, nondescript suit, white shirt, and brown tie. As always, his eyes were obscured by lightly tinted glasses. He was not, Nesher noted, someone who would attract much attention in a Paris café.

Nesher sat at the table and waved away a waiter who was approaching him.

"You were not followed?" Kornienko asked, already knowing the answer.

"My friend, believe me. The French are good, but not good enough to give me any worries. It may, however, have been a good drill for them. I made them think that they lost me because of what they did, not what I did."

"And the Mossad?"

Nesher dismissed the notion with another wave of his hand. It was clear that he was impatient tonight.

Initially the two men spoke in Hebrew; one was a foreign visitor, perhaps, the other his Parisian friend or relative who worked nearby. Then Nesher summoned the waiter and asked for a beer. Kornienko was drinking coffee. Nesher, thinking of their four prior meetings, had never seen Kornienko drink alcohol of any kind.

"I'm glad to see you, Avi. The streets of Tel Aviv are becoming dangerous," Kornienko said. "Terrorists, car bombs—very dangerous."

"I know that perhaps even better than you do, Ptor." There was sarcasm in Nesher's voice. He paused and took a long pull on his glass of beer. "Why, Ptor? Why did Mizrahi have to die? You said he had to be identified, not terminated."

"Be careful about accusations, Avi," Kornienko said in a low, calm voice. "We had nothing to do with his death. According to the intelligence reports I've seen, it was either the work of the fundamentalist group in the Gaza, the Hamas, or that of the so-called United National Leadership of the Uprising. That group looks to the Iranians for leadership. You remember that after the Gaza incident, they pledged to kill five Israelis in reprisal for each Palestinian fatality."

Nesher's anger slackened somewhat. He knew about these groups. He had read every leaflet that called for the liquidation of Israelis and their Palestinian collaborators. He seethed at the notion of the *intifada* being seen as anything but terrorism. "I have seen similar reports. But Mizrahi's death came rather soon after we identified him."

"Coincidences are rare in our business, but not impossible."

"Perhaps so. We'll soon know. Our director has ordered a full investigation."

"They will find nothing extraordinary, I trust," Kornienko said with noticeable apprehension.

"No. I personally sanitized his files. Nothing incriminating will be found."

Nesher mentioned nothing about Rafiah's threat to go to the Prime Minister. But Kornienko knew about the subject of the call.

The Soviet embassy in Paris could not hear Nesher's words, but they had little difficulty in hearing Rafiah's.

Kornienko steered the conversation around to other matters. There was no point in further discussion of what had happened. But Nesher was not satisfied with Kornienko's easy denials. The bombing—the car sandwiched between concrete walls to confine the explosion—had all the hallmarks of a Mossad operation. The Palestinians were not interested in concealing their handiwork; they were always eager to claim credit for killing Jews. No, someone was playing games, and Nesher didn't like the way the cards were being cut. He suspected that Kornienko had in fact ordered Mizrahi's death. But he knew he could do little about it. Wittingly or not, he had been one of the executioners.

Nesher finished his beer. The meeting was over. It had been a complete waste, unproductive and unprofessional.

Kornienko had agreed to the meeting because he needed to know whether Nesher was going to hold steady. He got what he went for. Throughout the night, cables rattled to and from Moscow. Then came the final message from the Soviet counterintelligence chief, Cyril Metrinko: PROTECT BURAQ AT ALL COSTS. ULTIMATE ACTIONS SANCTIONED.

Ptor Kornienko knew that more people would have to die.

17

As YITZHAK RAFIAH moved quickly through the lobby of the Royal Monceau Hotel, he smiled and acknowledged several guests he had met earlier in the evening. He had spent a boring night with boring men at a boring banquet. The American Chamber of Commerce in Paris had hosted a tribute to America's new ambassador to France, Alton Fedder. Fedder was the heir to a fortune accumulated by his father in the timber business. He had neither experience nor wisdom in diplomatic affairs. He was young, rich, and a major contributor to President Hollendale's campaign. His versatility with French consisted of a five-week Berlitz course.

The Americans are so stupid about diplomacy, Rafiah thought as he left the hotel, avoiding the large revolving doors that his security men had cautioned him against. The French loved to hold others in contempt. The Americans seemed to enjoy making it easy for them. Just once, he would like to see some American President insist that his ambassadors be fluent in the language of the country they were assigned to. An ambassador would not even have to know the history and customs of the country, just the language.

Rafiah was an eminently civil and social man, but he had some difficulty suffering those he considered visibly incompetent. There was no doubt in his mind about the category in which Ambassador Fedder fell.

To the gathering of three hundred people, Fedder had given something akin to a pep rally speech. He praised President Hollendale's leadership. He urged those in the audience to redouble their efforts to compete with their European counterparts. He expressed sympathy for the obstacles they faced in doing business abroad, implicitly criticizing Congress for failing to repeal the Foreign Anti-Corruption Act, which prohibited American businesses from giving bribes to procure contracts. He closed with a message that he failed to carry off in French: "Give us a level playing field and we will not only compete but prevail."

Rafiah shook his head at the very thought of Fedder. Another wasted evening away from his lovely wife. Rafiah had wanted to spend his last night in Paris with her before leaving for Israel in the morning. They could have had a quiet dinner together, maybe even called their son in Haifa and their daughter in Washington. Such a waste.

Rafiah was outside now, flanked by four dark-haired, very serious-looking men who scanned the Avenue Hoche with cold, unblinking eyes. Traffic was moderately light this evening. Nonetheless, you could see the tension in their faces, in their bodies, coiled tight to spring into action at the slightest sign of danger. Bombings had increased in Paris. The Red Army faction had begun operating with seeming impunity. There had been twenty-three terrorist attacks so far in this wave. Eighty-three victims.

Rafiah was worried, too. He was meeting with Israeli Prime Minister Gerstel on Monday. A private meeting, just the two of them. Rafiah was not sure now how he would explain how he had let Nesher bully him into getting information from Joshua Stock. Or Nesher's duplicity—stupidity—which may have jeopardized Israel's relations with its only foul-weather friend.

As Rafiah was about to enter the black Citröen sedan that had pulled up in front of the hotel, a sudden explosion fifty feet to his left nearly knocked him over. A large green trash barrel lifted straight up in the air and went careening clear across the street.

In almost one fluid motion three of the security men drew their nine-millimeter handguns, gripped them with two hands, and dropped into a firing crouch. The fourth man grabbed Rafiah and was about to shove him into the Citröen when a high-speed motorcycle carrying two men in black helmets and leather jackets came roaring from the right. The explosion had temporarily deafened Rafiah and his men, who didn't hear it. As the motorcycle came within forty feet of them, the passenger raised an automatic weapon to his shoulder and began firing.

The first shot struck a security man dead center in his chest, punching him backward. The next hit Rafiah in the right shoulder and spun him around. One of the next shots caught Rafiah in the lower back. The final one entered the back of his head, ripping away a portion of his skull.

It happened so quickly, so quietly, that the other security men were not even aware that Rafiah had been hit when they were cut down by the gunman. One of them tried to shoot at the figures on the motorcycle, but he was already falling backward and managed only to knock out several lights that illuminated the hotel's marquee. In less than eight seconds from the time of the explosion, four men lay dead on the Avenue Hoche. Another was bleeding profusely from the shoulder, back, and head. Life was leaking out of Yitzhak Rafiah. He was barely breathing.

18

FOR SENATOR JOSHUA
Stock, lying on his bed in his Georgetown home, a nightmare was
ending and a dream was about to begin. He had given Yitzhak
Rafiah what he wanted. Israel had apparently responded with swift
justice. He had not answered Sean's call. Later—it could wait until
later. Sean, like him, would just have to remain in the dark. He
would tell Sean it was one of those intelligence operations that
would never be fully explained.

But all that was in the past. He was free of them. Free.

And now there was Elise. He could hear the dryer droning
softly in the bathroom. She was drying that long dark hair that fell
about her face and shoulders in soft, full waves . . . Ever since he
had met her, day and night, he had thought about her body, the full
breasts, the long tapered legs of a dancer.

Never before had he taken such a risk. Afternoons at the Madi-
son. The trip to New York. Rorbach, he supposed, had been right.
No matter what her nationality, Elise potentially could destroy him.
He was a husband, a father, a family man—reliable, trustworthy.
But what Rorbach did not know was that tonight was the end. To-

night, in many ways, he would return to his true self; he would go back to where he and his career had been before that night at the French embassy, and, he thought with a smile, before Rafiah.

In the past five days he had seen Elise many times. His two daughters had been invited to visit their grandparents in Florida, and Cleo was off with her friend Charlene to the Golden Door in California, to climb mountains, eat goat cheese, and massage her spirit.

He would tell Elise in the morning that the affair was over. And if she resisted, or threatened him with blackmail, Stock knew what he would do. *Counterthreat. Tell her that she would be hearing from the FBI. Warn her that she'd be kicked out of the country—or into jail . . .*

She slipped silently into the bed and hovered above him. Her nude body glistened with a perfumed lubricant that she rubbed on him, beginning at his neck and continuing down his body. She was leaning forward now, her dark hair nearly enveloping her face. She might have been a hooded monk in prayer. Her breasts, round and full as ripe melons, began to sway as she rocked back and forth.

Stock's face was flushed. He could feel sweat start to trickle from his hairline down his temples. He could not see Elise clearly; he could only feel her warmth engulfing him. His eyes seemed to be covered with film, giving him the sensation of looking up through lakewater at an object floating above him.

He felt strangely relaxed tonight. The drink Elise had poured for him had been strong. He had never felt quite so intoxicated. Visually, everything had turned liquid and soft. He felt as if he were standing in front of a carnival mirror, looking at a reflection that was so foolishly distorted that he began to laugh. The rock album that was playing on his tape deck suddenly seemed too loud. He thought he could actually see notes coming from the large Marantz speakers in the corners of the bedroom. The music achieved a clarity he had never heard before. It was perfectly clear. He could hear the drum-beat growing louder, insistent, aggressive, primal. He could not tell whether it was his heart pounding inside its bone cage. The song's lyrics mystically seemed to synchronize with the pressure that was building inside him.

Stock had the vague sensation that someone else was in the room watching them. Perhaps it was merely the shadow of guilt lurking there. His wife, his children, his parents. He didn't care. The candlelight flickered, casting eerie, dancing silhouettes against the ceiling. He might have been in a cave, lit and warmed by a campfire, performing a ritualistic act in the presence of savages. It didn't matter. It didn't matter.

Elise quickened her movements, rising, then plunging like a hawk attacking its victim. She whispered obscenities to him, words he had never heard from a woman. Words that flattered, that pleaded, that brought him to a pitch of maddening excitement. Her voice and the music became indistinguishable.

Suddenly he felt something sharp bite into his throat. He looked up in panic. Elise had arched backward, and, with her elbows locked, held her leather-gloved hands nearly against his ears. She lifted herself up from him and then brought her full weight down through her arms and shoulders.

Not much pressure was required. The razor-like wire sliced through Stock's larynx as if it were passing through warm butter. The steel cut all the way to his spinal cord, sending blood spurting upward, covering Elise's face, turning it into a crimson mask of horror.

There was a sickening sucking noise as Stock's lungs struggled for oxygen. Instead they filled with carbon dioxide. He tried to scream. More blood gurgled out of his throat. He tried to fight back. But even as his body jerked spasmodically, he could not move his arms or legs.

He wanted to believe that it was all just a dream, that Cleo would wake him, save him from this horrible nightmare. That tomorrow he would be eating breakfast with Jessica and Jennett before going to work. *Please, God,* his mind begged, *please let me live!*

His silent scream for life went unanswered. His chest kept heaving, futilely seeking air. Blood pumped out of the severed artery, soaking his ears and running down the backs of his shoulders, still in spasm.

Stock felt himself falling, tumbling into a dark void. The light from the candle seemed no more than a distant star in a depthless galaxy. His eyes widened, searching for death or God, then went cold. As the last vision in his mind faded, Stock saw himself looking up through water that had turned into a sheet of ice.

PART II

"The bread of deceit is sweet to a man; but afterwards his mouth shall be filled with gravel."

—Proverbs 20:17

19

Sean Falcone angrily cursed the telephone. It sounded like a fire bell ringing in his head. He reached across the bed and fumbled for the receiver.

He was only vaguely aware that he was alone. His friend Tina, a flight attendant with TWA, must have left for the airport. She had to be at Kennedy in New York by 8 A.M. and then leave for Rome. She had had an unexpected layover in Washington, and Falcone had taken her to dinner at Positano's, his favorite restaurant, in Bethesda, Maryland.

He could not remember her waking him to say goodbye. Maybe she was calling him now, just to show off her stamina, as she was given to doing after they made love for what always seemed like hours to Falcone.

He lifted the receiver off the cradle, expecting to hear Tina's voice, which usually seemed to carry a hint of laughter.

"Hello, Senator?" The voice, familiar to Falcone, was tense, anxious, shaky.

Falcone's disappointment caused him to turn surly. "Who the hell is calling?" His head was pounding. He promised himself that he would stop drinking those incendiary milk punches that Tina loved to make.

"Bob Gibbs," said the voice over the phone.

Robert L. Gibbs was the Senate sergeant at arms, the man responsible for keeping the machinery of the United States Senate running and for attending to the needs of individual senators. If they needed transportation anywhere, he arranged it. If they wanted to use a special room at the Capitol to entertain constituents, he authorized it. If they wanted their tickets fixed with the D.C. Metropolitan Police, no problem.

"What is it, Bob?" Falcone asked, toning down the edge in his voice.

"A big problem, Senator. It's Senator Stock . . . I don't know how to say this other than to tell you flat out. He's dead."

"What?" Falcone shouted, fully awake now. He swept aside the bedsheet and nearly vaulted to a sitting position on the side of the bed. The sunlight streaming through the vertical blinds revealed the scars on his wide back and shoulders. The skin around them was smooth, hairless, yellow. "How?"

"Murdered. His throat was cut. A wire or something. It's a pretty bad scene. I'm here at the house. If you can come over, maybe you can be of some help."

"Jesus Christ. Where's Cleo? Have you—"

"She's in California. I spoke with her just before I called you. I've got a C-20 picking her up. The kids are in Florida. Joshua's folks are bringing them back tonight. It's a mess, Senator, I gotta tell you. It's a real frigging mess."

Falcone hung up, then swung quickly off the bed and into the bathroom. He lived in a two-bedroom apartment on the fourteenth floor of a condominium in Crystal City, Virginia, across the Potomac from Washington. The rooms were neatly and efficiently decorated. The walls were covered with a tan, textured, imitation suede paper, framed by a gold wood overlay. There were no family photographs or paintings on the walls. Two white sofas and a Barcelona chair were the only pieces of furniture in the living room. It was the home of a man who lived alone and spent little time there. There were a few plants, no flowers. Everything was in place—books, magazines, records, tapes. The room, the entire apartment, had the orderliness of an ascetic or a military man. There was not a hint of the casual luxury and comfort that one would expect from a person who took pleasure in his home.

Of course, Falcone never considered it his home. He used the second bedroom as a study, a place where he retreated each night to tap away at the keyboard of an IBM computer, which provided most of his evening companionship in Washington. On the desk rested a sepia photograph of a pretty blond woman and a young towheaded boy. They were leaning against a car that was more than twenty-five years old.

Inside the shower, Falcone let the hot stream of water run off his head, hoping it would stop the pain that had been amplified into a migraine by the news of Joshua's death—his murder.

Ten minutes later he was driving his 1965 Ford Mustang out of the condominium's underground parking garage. He turned right onto Route 1 North, started across the Fourteenth Street Bridge, and then swung down the exit ramp that put him on the George Washington Parkway. Within minutes his polo shirt was soaked through with perspiration. It was only ten o'clock, but already the sun hung like a murderous eye in a gray-yellow sky that would turn an ominous black in a few hours and bring afternoon thundershowers. On days like this, Falcone wished he had yielded to practicality and installed an air conditioner in his Mustang. But he wanted to maintain the car just as it had been when he bought it more than twenty-five years ago. It was the one thing in his life that he would not allow time to change.

He crossed over the Key Bridge, followed M Street to Wisconsin, and turned right onto Q Street. He parked more than three blocks away, knowing that by now he would not be able to park near the house. The police would have the block sealed off to alarmed neighbors, curious students, pestering reporters, and pure sensation-seekers.

Falcone could barely break through the line of people held back by the police. Their cruisers had cordoned off access to the block between Twenty-eighth and Twenty-ninth streets. An ambulance, its revolving red dome screaming tragedy, was parked directly in front of the three-story townhouse. A television reporter was standing on the corner of the street conducting an interview with the young man who had called the police.

Falcone showed his Senate identification to a bull of a man

stationed at the foot of the outside stairs and said that he had been asked to come. The man looked at the card, then at Falcone, and without speaking motioned with his head for Falcone to go in.

Someone in the crowd shouted, "Senator Falcone! Hey, Senator Falcone! What can you tell us?" Falcone never looked back.

Inside, he worked his way past a flurry of anonymous people until he reached the living room. Bob Gibbs was sitting on the sofa talking with a black man in a dark blue suit. The man seemed overdressed for the occasion. Perhaps he was planning to go to a funeral, Falcone thought.

Gibbs spotted Falcone and heaved himself up from the sofa. He was a large man who usually concealed his excess weight with well-tailored suits that he picked up during senatorial junkets to Seoul and Hong Kong. Today, in slacks and a short-sleeved shirt, he appeared to be the beefy ex–football player he was.

"Senator Falcone," he said, extending a paw of a hand. His face was pale; his voice cracked. "This is Detective Clarke from the D.C. police." Falcone shook hands with the detective, looking into brown eyes that were cool and noncommittal.

"I understand that you were a close friend of Mr. Stock's."

"*Senator* Stock's," Falcone said. "Yes. Yes, I am." He heard himself and realized that he did not want to accept the past tense. A chair was pulled up for him. Clarke sank back onto the sofa.

"We were hoping you could help us with the investigation, give us some background on Mr. Stock's habits, acquaintances, possible enemies. Someone with a motive to kill him—an angry constituent, possibly a jealous mistress . . ."

"Mistress?" Falcone's voice flared up unexpectedly. "Why do you say that, Detective?"

"Sex, Senator Falcone. Sex. There is a mess lying in the middle of the bed upstairs." Clarke spoke calmly, ignoring Falcone's agitation. "I recognize not only blood when I see it, but—what shall I call it for you, dried seminal fluid? It's caked all over him. Mrs. Stock's in California. We found the remains of what appear to be marijuana joints in an ashtray beside the bed. Sensimillia sticks. Maybe coke. I understand that you were once the attorney general in your state. What conclusion would you draw?"

"Marijuana? Christ, the only thing Joshua smoked was cigarettes. Maybe a cigar. And he never drank anything stronger than white wine."

"Maybe you were not as close as you thought," Clarke said with a touch of malice. "Incidentally, do you know Maria Christiani, the maid?"

"Yeah. She's an illegal." Falcone waited for an insinuation about lawmakers who break the law. None came. "Is she a suspect?"

Clarke made little effort to hide his sullenness. It was the kind that slaves once reserved for their plantation owners. Washington, D.C., capital of the United States, heartbeat of the nation's ideals, home of the hallowed Constitution, was the last plantation. A city of more than 600,000 people, 70 percent of them black, whose only representative in the United States Congress was a nonvoting delegate. A political gelding. A eunuch, some satirist said, sent off to participate in an orgy. The "owners" concerned themselves with the fancy art museums, the Kennedy Center, restoration of the Willard Hotel or the old post office building, parking tickets they wanted fixed. But they were oblivious or indifferent to all the black faces that belonged to people who were there to serve them. Blacks were killing each other, out of rage, because of the summer's heat, through drug-fueled desperation, or because of just plain viciousness. No one seemed to care. If you picked up the Metro section of the Washington *Post* (rarely the first page), you'd find four or five dead on any given day. Violence slithered through all the rundown hovels that mushroomed just beyond the perimeter of Capitol Hill: white America's Versailles Palace, a place of barricaded privilege.

Only when the violence touched them or threatened them did the masters on the Hill show concern. They did nothing constructive, of course, just threatened future appropriations for the city, or made veiled racist comments about the competence of local government. Well, now one of the feudal barons was about to be shoved into a refrigerated filing cabinet at the D.C. morgue. Now, suddenly, the violence was a matter of great national importance. The sergeant at arms. A senator. Networks. Clarke had been wrung dry of sympathy. His eyes smoldered with cynicism, like damp leaves that would not burn and would not stop smoking.

"Not really, Senator. Being an illegal doesn't make her a criminal. She had the weekend off but came early this morning to pick up a dress she had forgotten. She saw Stock's car parked across the street. When she entered the house, she smelled a pretty bad odor. Someone had turned off the air conditioner last night. Apparently, whoever it was wanted to make sure Stock didn't go unnoticed for too long. When Maria yelled up to Stock, he didn't answer. She found his body and vomited all over the upstairs hall floor. Then she ran out into the street, screaming for help."

"Maybe she vomited last night," Falcone said.

"No, that's fresh. The body is not. Besides, she was sleeping with her boyfriend last night. We checked it out."

The questions continued inconclusively in a semiformal matter for the next few minutes. No, Falcone did not know of any girl-friend. No, Joshua's marriage was not on the rocks. Perhaps he had succumbed to a one-night erotic impulse. Yes, maybe midlife crisis was upon him. No, Joshua didn't have any enemies.

Finally, Falcone asked if he could see Joshua's body. He wanted to verify for himself that his friend was dead, that there would be no more laughter between them.

He was prepared to see death up close in its most violent form. He had seen it hundreds of times before, as a Ranger in Vietnam and as Massachusetts's chief prosecutor for six years. Men cut in half by frag grenades and Viet Cong mines, intestines hanging out like sausages; babies beaten blue and stuffed into ovens by parents who claimed that they were inspired by God to purge the world of sin . . .

He moved past a policeman who stood at the foot of the stairs. It occurred to him that in all the times he had been to Joshua's home, he had never been upstairs, inside the bedroom. A cluster of men moved about methodically, gathering fibers and fingerprints, snapping photographs, collecting things in little bottles and plastic envelopes. Even with the air conditioner on high, the stench nearly overcame Falcone, sticking to the back of his throat like some foul phlegm that he could not clear out. He coughed roughly, then in-stinctively closed his mouth and tried not to inhale.

On the bed, Joshua's body was stretched out as if on a rack, a body so drained of life that it might have belonged to a leper. His arms and legs had been tied to the bedposts with monogrammed towels. His mouth was locked open and his bloodshot eyes pro-truded, as if a scream were still trapped somewhere in a ragged throat. Rigor mortis had stiffened his body, giving it the look of a wax mannequin.

Falcone stared at Joshua for what seemed to be minutes, becoming an impediment to the man with the camera, who was searching for a variety of angles from the corner of the room. The others went about their business, dusting, picking, measuring, oblivious to his presence. Strangers had moved into this place of secrets and were callously foraging through every possible intimacy ever shared here. For them, the dead had no right to privacy.

Clarke and Bob Gibbs had climbed the stairs and were standing behind Falcone.

"Quite a crucifixion," Clarke said.

Falcone couldn't tell whether Clarke was mocking his dead friend. He didn't acknowledge the comment.

Clarke motioned to Falcone and Gibbs to follow him downstairs to the family room. The two men exchanged quizzical glances as they trudged behind him. Falcone felt a sense of foreboding. Each step down seemed to bring him closer to perdition.

Clarke inserted a cassette into a VCR on a shelf below a twenty-seven-inch Sony television screen. The lights were flicked off. Falcone's stomach was tied in a knot of anxiety. Suddenly Joshua's nude body appeared on the screen. Falcone had not realized how rail-thin his friend had become. He was sitting on the side of the bed. Shadows cast by flickering candlelight danced across his face. A woman's sultry, coaxing voice could be heard over the eerie guitar punctuated by a hypnotic drumbeat that filled the room.

A woman moved into view, her back to the camera. She appeared tall, lithe, with perfectly sculpted buttocks and long tapered legs. She went out of focus and the camera seemed to whirl around the room, pointing at the ceiling, the floor, the tousled bed. She was apparently changing the camera from one location to another. Finally the bed came into focus again and she reappeared, her back still toward the camera. Her body was so erotically beautiful that for a shameful moment Falcone forgot the horror he had just seen. His shame instantly turned to anger. He felt like some trench-coated voyeur sitting in a cheap moviehouse on Fourteenth Street, where in some twisted fantasy men masturbated their afternoons away. "For Christ's sake, Clarke, stop the film," he snapped, restraining the urge to smash the detective's face.

But it continued. In flickering semishadows, Joshua and the woman moved over the bed, where the woman mounted Joshua, then began to rock slowly back and forth. The whispers were barely audible over the driving beat of the music . . .

The last image on the tape was Joshua's glassy eyes.

Gibbs and Falcone pushed past the men in the hallway and moved quickly down the stairs and away from the gathering crowd and the sea of TV cameras. Falcone refused the shouted calls for a comment. Gibbs shielded him as if he were a blocking guard.

Once at his car, Falcone looked at Gibbs. "You were right, Bob."

"About what?"

"It's a real frigging mess."

President Eric Hollendale was horseback riding at Camp David with his wife, Cornelia, when he learned about Stock's murder. A Secret Service agent accompanying him signaled him to stop. The agent had been radioed the news of Stock's murder. He relayed the scant details to the President and urgently suggested that the Hollendales return to the lodge. Hollendale had grumpily complied. He knew that in the days after the murder of any public official the Secret Service was especially nervous.

It took two infuriating hours for the President to reach Harry Polanski, who was off in his sixty-foot Magnum speedboat on Chesapeake Bay. "Get over to the Oval Office," the President ordered, infuriated that Polanski, in his high-speed isolation, had not even heard about Stock's murder.

Now it was shortly after 6 P.M. In the Oval Office, both men were agitated about events that seemed destined to rob them of any hope of respite from their eighteen-hour-a-day jobs. But Polanski had immediately noticed that Hollendale was more than agitated. It was the first time in the years they had known each other that the director had seen the President rattled, scared. There was a thinness to his voice when he spoke, as if it were a strip of plastic veneer about to split under the slightest pressure.

"Harry," the President began, fingering a single sheet of paper that contained a wire service story about Stock's death, "what in hell happened?"

Polanski stared momentarily at the paper in Hollendale's trembling hands, pursed his lips, and shook his head. "At this point, we don't know much more than what the Associated Press has reported. My men have been in touch with the D.C. police, but they don't have much to go on. They've got a videocassette of Stock's drug and sex orgy with a woman, who is probably the one who slashed his throat, but she is not identifiable in the film. When we get a copy of the cassette, I can run it by our experts and try to get a make on her. At this stage, the local police aren't about to back off from the investigation unless we tell them that we have exclusive jurisdiction on what they feel is a brutal and kinky murder."

"It's kinky all right," Hollendale said. "And . . . and what about the timing, Harry? Is this tied to the other matter? The guy who was killed in Israel?"

"I can't answer that at this time," Polanski replied in his best bureaucratese. "That is also out of our jurisdiction. I don't believe it should be of concern to our government at this time."

"Oh, for Christ's sake, Harry. Don't talk to me like I'm a goddamned congressional committee. There's *got* to be a connection. And it could hurt us, hurt us bad. You know that damn well. Why doesn't the FBI have jurisdiction over Stock's murder? Isn't it enough that he was a United States senator? Isn't killing a senator a federal crime?"

The President moved off the large sofa and walked toward the French windows that overlooked the Rose Garden. A hummingbird, its wings whirring invisibly, paused a few feet from the window and then darted away as if it had been fired from a slingshot. Hollendale sipped hot coffee from a bone china cup that carried the presidential seal. He turned back to face Polanski.

"It is a federal crime, and we do have jurisdiction," Polanski said. "But we've got a hell of a problem, Mr. President. If I turn my people loose on this one, they'll do a real thorough job. Maybe *too* thorough. They'll look at every stone as if it were the Hope Diamond. That might cause . . ." Polanski hesitated, withholding just in time words that he realized might one day prove unfortunate. Seemingly relieved by his caution, he continued. "That might cause more problems than necessary."

"Can't you control the scope of the investigation? Your own agents?" Hollendale asked almost derisively.

"Not a chance. If I tried to put the clamps on this, it would be in the early edition of Philip Dake's column in the Washington *Post*. I've got as many whistle-blowers as I do agents, and I think they've all got a hot line wired into Dake's ass."

"Well," Hollendale snapped irritably, "why not let the Washington P.D. handle the investigation? We'll both be writing our memoirs before they solve anything."

"That's my inclination, but it's not so easy. Stock was on the Intelligence Committee. The press will want to know if there is any evidence of a security breach that has compromised classified information. The Senate Intelligence Committee is gonna want to know, too. The only good news there is that Sean Falcone was close to Stock, and he won't be inclined to believe the worst about his buddy. And besides, Falcone may have some explaining of his own to do. He was the guy asking the CIA for information, and the next thing anybody knows, the Israeli source is blown up. No, I wouldn't worry about Falcone. Don't figure on him for any trouble."

"I've already heard from Bickford on the Israeli thing," Hollendale said. "He's jumping mad about that bombing. He wants an internal inquiry to find out who told who what. An inquiry, of course, by his boys."

"Just stall him for now. He can't ask *you* any questions, and he can't mess around with a domestic investigation. That's my turf."

"Well, what about the press?" There was a slight rattle of the cup against the saucer. The President set his coffee down on the glass-smooth surface of his large mahogany desk.

"I think we can say that we are coordinating the investigation with the D.C. police, leaving the homicide to them and the national security parts to us. Who knows, maybe the Washington *Post*, which is always bashing us for trying to trample on home rule, will praise it as a fair division of labor."

Hollendale was not satisfied. He leaned against the back of his leather chair, groping in the momentary silence for some plausible solution to the problem that was mushrooming in his mind. In a tone of critical exasperation, he said, "I thought you were watching Stock, Harry."

The director answered calmly, without apology, "We were. Not a twenty-four-hour surveillance, but his home and office were both wired. I reviewed the tapes before coming over. There's nothing that would surprise you. He was a careful man on the phone. We don't have any idea of how he met the woman who killed him. She could be a twisted hooker from Fourteenth Street, or a dopehead who was turning Stock on, or his mistress."

"An assassin?" the President asked, in a way that suggested he hoped for a negative reply.

"Maybe. It's possible that Stock was hit by a foreign intelligence service. The question is, whose? Syria? Libya? Russia? Pick one. The problem is, if we are going to find out, we've got to start asking questions, and the more we ask, the more we get asked about why we want to know."

A long silence followed.

"What do you think would happen if the story ever got out about what Stock was really doing?"

"Mr. President," Polanski responded, keeping his response formal, "I don't even want to *think* about it. The country can't afford another scandal that has any White House fingerprints."

Hollendale looked hard into Polanski's eyes and said, "So what you're saying, Harry, is that we are better off leaving this as the unfortunate culmination of one man's private perversion."

"As long as we can, Mr. President. As long as we can."

20

FALCONE DROVE MIND-
lessly along Rock Creek Parkway. He had planned to slip out of
Washington today. He had wanted to drive up to Gettysburg and
climb up Little Round Top, tracing the steps of Longstreet and
Chamberlain. Joshua Chamberlain, a long-dead military hero of his.
Now another Joshua was dead, this one no hero. Just his friend.

A short distance past the Kennedy Center he veered right onto
the Theodore Roosevelt Bridge, crossed the Potomac, then headed
north on the George Washington Parkway. After thirty minutes he
reached the Great Falls of the Potomac. He parked near the Visitors'
Center, got out of the car, and walked to a pile of boulders near the
river. Climbing the boulders, he watched the torrents of white water
blasting against unyielding rocks in a thunderous, ageless overture.
He paced a flat stretch of rock, and he softly cursed.

Then he drove back to his apartment in Crystal City. He
poured himself one drink—Jack Daniel's, straight—and then another. Stripping off his shirt, he stepped outside, onto his balcony
and into the heat. He loved it up there, up on the high ground,
where he could watch a constant flow of motion—planes landing and

taking off at National Airport, cars speeding along the parkway below, boats cruising the Potomac, trains rattling their cargo on groaning rails. The movement and noise were a benediction to him, an affirmation of vitality. To be is to be in motion.

That was what had always fascinated him about Joshua—his perpetual energy, his absolute compulsion to see and touch everything. They had met during the summer of their junior year in college at a boys' camp in New Hampshire. Falcone, an all-American halfback on the Syracuse University football team, had been hired as an assistant to the athletic director of Camp Kowonki, where rich parents dumped their sons for eight weeks of a little discipline and a great deal of communing with nature.

An image of Joshua formed in Falcone's mind. He was sitting beside a campfire, strumming a guitar and singing bawdy lyrics to a small group of campers. Tall and wiry, he was smiling that slow, easy smile that was so engaging and attractive. The boys were huddled in blankets against a cluster of rocks that leaned near the edge of the lake. Light was dancing in their eyes, as much from Joshua's lyrics as from the campfire. They were happy, mostly because he treated them as special, allowed them to enter his world of music and laughter, but also, of course, because it was after curfew.

Joshua invited Falcone to join his coterie of rule-breakers. A friendship was struck immediately, although the two of them had little in common.

Falcone, half Irish, half Italian, was raised in the streets of Boston's North End. With a name like Sean, that was no easy accomplishment. During much of his first twelve years he was the victim of beatings at the hands of older boys. "Get your mick ass out of here, Falcone, or we'll kick it out!" they would yell, and someone would lodge a foot in his stomach or club him behind an ear. "Yeah, try Dorchester. You'll be right at home with all the Jews and niggers." Then a final punch for good measure.

Sean begged his father to move, but Sonny Falcone would have none of it. "Where will you run to?" he would ask with a smile. "To the Irish? What happens when they turn on you for being a wop? Or ask you to kiss their Blarney Stone? Sean, you're going to have to learn to defend yourself. The only way your enemies will become your friends is to learn to respect you. To fear you."

When Sean was six years old, Sonny introduced him to Friday

night fights at a rundown place called the Chateau. There he saw young locals or old clubhouse fighters pound each other senseless before jeering, beer-drinking crowds. When he was eight, his father bought him a membership in the YMCA, where he learned to swim, play basketball, and box. By the time he was twelve, Sean stood five-foot-nine and weighed 150 pounds. His coach at the Y told Sonny that his son had a killer's instinct in the ring. Sonny seemed proud.

And Sonny proved right. Never again did his son come home a beaten boy.

Falcone not only excelled in sports—he won letters in football, basketball, and baseball in high school—but was an honor student as well. Syracuse offered him a full athletic scholarship. He took it, and by the end of his junior year he was captain of both the football and the boxing teams and the recipient of a coveted research fellowship in mathematics.

Joshua, by contrast, had never had to face adversity of any kind. His family owned a chain of drugstores in Florida. He lived and played in a wealthy and safe neighborhood in Fort Lauderdale. He had been given whatever money could buy: private tutoring, music lessons, trips abroad, a Harvard education, and, of course, the inevitable trust fund, which provided him with a monthly income that exceeded Falcone's yearly scholarship.

Different as their backgrounds were, an indefinable bond fused their friendship. Joshua taught Sean how to water-ski, paddle a canoe, and play the guitar. Sean introduced Joshua to the fundamentals of boxing, teaching him how to counter a straight right hand to his head with a short left cross to an opponent's jaw. They shared a golden summer, nearly completing their contractual obligation to the camp. One night Joshua took a group of six boys skinny-dipping after taps had blown. The director of the camp, having ignored prior complaints from jealous counselors, concluded that Joshua was impairing the moral development of his campers and fired him. Sean quit in protest, and the two of them headed off to Florida, where they spent the balance of the summer in bonded friendship.

After that summer, they never saw each other again, until they were sworn in together in the United States Senate. Stock had gone on to graduate work at Wharton, and Falcone had gone to Boston College Law School. Stock went into business. Falcone went to Vietnam as an Army Ranger.

Sweating profusely in the 105-degree heat, Falcone now stepped back into his air-conditioned apartment and closed the heavy glass doors, muffling the roar of the jet aircraft that continued to take off and land every ninety seconds. He poured another drink, a tall one this time. He turned on his stereo set and slipped in a tape cassette: Kenny G's Duotones. He never tired of hearing a saxophone played sweetly.

The saxophone had always been his favorite. He could see the sounds in his mind. Dark birds scattering, soaring, diving in perfect formation, roaming over the skies, suddenly reappearing and lighting upon a perch as if they had been there all along. Freedom, seemingly chaotic, anarchistic, yet in reality restrained, tethered. So much grace and discipline. Not like the mindless shrieking of electric guitars, the mayhem of asexual rockers beheading animals while prancing in leather pants, filling stadiums with psychosis posing as art.

He eased down onto one of his living room couches and lay there for a long time listening to the music. He remembered that when his father had been young he had played a saxophone. Well, at least there was a broken one in the attic of the house on Hanover Street. Falcone had promised himself that one day he would have it fixed so his father could play for him. It was one of the few promises he had failed to keep.

The room went into a slow spin, as if it were a giant record and Falcone could only lie there, helpless against its gathering momentum. He felt consciousness slip into a world of different sounds, sounds that were no longer musical.

Northwest of Da Nang. The air is thick with noise: the crackling rattle of M-16 rifle fire, the slower ka-chung *of heavier automatic weapons, the crunch of an exploding mine. Men screaming, "Medic, medic!" His patrol under attack. Three dead, four wounded. PFC Kelsey Baker is dragged in from the perimeter. His legs are gone. A Medivac helicopter is near; the flat thump of the rotor blades announces its approach. It settles down like a giant grasshopper. The landing zone is hot, under heavy fire.*

A medic jumps from the chopper, head tucked, a hand on his helmet. Suddenly the pilot is hit by a burst from a machine gun.

He is slammed forward against the controls. The chopper lurches to its side. Falcone can see it all happening in slow motion. He starts to scream, "Down! Down!" The corpsman, unable to hear anything above the roar of the chopper, does not see the large rotor blades coming at him like a guillotine. In an instant he is decapitated. Blood spews from his arteries like an uncapped geyser. Thump. Thump. Thump. *The blades pound the air, blowing dirt, rocks, mud, blood, until the copilot is able to gain control.*

Falcone is on his feet, running in a low crouch, screaming, firing his M-16 blindly into a tree line. He is in a rage.

He bends down to give aid to the medic. He reaches to gather the boy's head as if he can physically reunite it with his body. Surgeons can do miracles. Sew up arteries. Transplant organs. Brains. Doctors, next to God. Do anything, anything . . .

His heart is pumping wildly now, his throat dry. Sweat is pouring down his face. He finally manages to work the head back onto the soldier's shoulders. The helicopter blades continue to thump away.

Two men are trying to grab Falcone by the shoulders and pull him away. "Jesus, Captain!" they scream. "We've got to move. Others are going to die. Christ, Falcone, what are you doing? You can't—"

Falcone shrugs them off, continuing his task. Perfect, *he thinks,* perfect. If we can just load him into the chopper, this way—*he cradles the boy's head against his shoulders*—he'll be okay.

Falcone wipes the blood from his patient's face. He is so young, so handsome, just a baby . . .

Falcone begins to scream now, uncontrollably, as he stares into the pale bloodless face of . . . Joshua! Jaw open, eyes bulging, protesting the fall of the guillotine.

Falcone bolted up, shaken by the screams that still echoed in his mind. The sofa cushions were soaked with perspiration. He thought that his heart had been injected with amphetamines, that it was pounding so hard it might rupture.

He took several deep breaths, trying to force his pulse to slow.

He scanned the room. He was in his apartment. Safe. No VC, no mines, no Hueys . . .

Outside, a commercial helicopter swept past, not more than fifty yards away. The whipping of its rotary blades only faintly resembled the powerful, hypnotic thump of the Hueys in Falcone's dream.

21

AT 5:45 A.M. THE WASH-
ington *Post* arrived at the door of Falcone's apartment. The automatic timer on the coffee machine had gone off five minutes earlier.
The aroma of coffee filled the kitchen as the early sun began to filter
through the slatted drapes in the living room. The story in the *Post*
was all that Falcone had feared. Headline type normally reserved for
declarations of war screamed SENATOR STOCK MURDERED. In slightly
smaller print, the subheading declared *Sex, Drugs Linked to Ritualistic Slaying*. A three-column photograph of Stock, next to one of his
house, filled the center of the page, just above the fold.

There was other news of tragedy. A tornado had ripped
through St. Louis, killing four. An East Los Angeles gang had fired
grenades from a passing truck into a police station, killing six officers and injuring ten others. A mud slide in Chile had wiped out an
entire town; the unofficial count of the dead ran into the hundreds.

If Falcone had turned from the front page to the international
news section, he would have seen the report of the assassination
attempt on Israel's ambassador to France. But the murder of Senator
Joshua Stock was the news of the day. Hollendale could have or-

dered an invasion of Cuba and not forced Joshua Stock off the front page for the next week.

Falcone, his head pounding from too much bourbon, drank three cups of coffee, showered, took the elevator down to his car, and headed for the Hart Senate Office Building. As he drove across the Rochambeau Bridge, he felt a vague sense of anger. Over the years he had succeeded in repressing memories of Vietnam. He had even refused to visit the Vietnam Memorial, for fear that seeing the names of all the men who were lost—whom he had lost—in battle would bring back the nightmares. Seeing Joshua yesterday had released the latch to the dark hole where he had locked away the experiences of another lifetime.

Years ago, images had floated down in his sleep, like flares swinging silently on parachutes in the night, freezing the landscape in an eerie phosphorous glow that announced the coming of hell. Sometimes he would wake, nearly naked, drowning in sweat, screams echoing in his mind. Night after night he had relived the firefights that had erupted between his unit and the North Vietnamese, watched the limbs of his men being ripped away by RPGs, bouncing Betty Claymores, .50-caliber bullets. Bagging up the bodies was the part they never prepared you for—stuffing eighteen-year-old boys into green body bags. They were out in the asshole of the world, defending freedom, duty, honor, country.

I pledge allegiance . . . one nation under God . . . Where was God when the night came, when the silence was so loud it became a sound, when the night wind carried the smell of coming death, when the hot metal came racing at them from a thousand focal points like a comet storm in a black galaxy? Why did the God of mercy abandon them when they were doing his work?

Falcone never found the answers to his questions. Still, he held on to his faith, an irreducible belief that God would return to reclaim his children. Until the summer of 1968. That's when Falcone's world changed forever. In the Calcutta Room . . .

As he entered the underground garage, Falcone dropped his visor, displaying a blue plate that read S-48, "48" indicating his seniority in the Senate. It was an unnecessary gesture. Every Capitol Hill police officer recognized him and his car. But Falcone wanted no

favoritism shown over security precautions. He let every officer
know that anyone who failed to check each car entering a Senate
parking facility would be collecting an unemployment check the
next day.

A uniformed guard, his right hand extended with a flat palm—
the gesture of an MP, Falcone remembered—waved him down the
ramp. Falcone eased over the speed bump at its base, swung over to
the right side of the garage, then turned left. The garage was virtually empty at that hour. He proceeded to a space marked S-67.
Joshua's slot was empty. Two spaces away, Falcone saw a red 911
Porsche. Peter McCloskey was in the office. Falcone waved to the
Capitol Police security officer on duty as he entered the Hart Building and stepped onto the elevator marked "For Senators Only."
When its grooved steel doors opened onto the seventh floor, he
stepped off with legs that were heavier and less steady than he
would have liked. Too much Jack Daniel's, too little sleep.

He glanced over the balcony into the huge atrium, which was
filled with a monstrous Calder sculpture, the gift of some great
humanitarian. The sight of it never failed to anger him. Take $140
million in taxes, construct a nine-story building of marble and glass,
then fill the core with twenty tons of black-coated steel that looked
as if it were cut out of the bowels of a World War II aircraft carrier.
Then, just for good measure, hang a mobile with three prongs that
looked like Texas-sized surfboards from the glass roof so that it
blocked out most of the sunlight—and you have the Senate's monument to art. Calder or not, it reminded Falcone of a primitive war
memorial that belonged, if anywhere, in a parking lot at Soldier's
Field in Chicago.

He turned away and walked down the open corridor toward
Joshua Stock's office. It was 7 A.M., two hours before life would
blink awake in the Hart Building. Most offices would not be open
yet. But he knew that Joshua's would.

Falcone pushed through the double glass doors and entered a
darkened room. The receptionist had not arrived yet. A bundle of
newspapers and the first of what would be the day's three mail
deliveries lay stacked on her desk. A clear line of sight ran from the
reception room all the way to the rear of the building, where
Joshua's office was located. Falcone could see that the lights were on
and a man was pacing around inside. Peter McCloskey, Stock's ad-

ministrative assistant, was holding a telephone with a long extension cord. He saw Falcone approaching and cradled the receiver against his ear with his shoulder, motioning for Falcone to come in.

McCloskey was a tall, thin man with straight, closely cropped brown hair that had just started to thin. He wore tortoise-shell glasses that rested on a strong, slightly turned-up nose. He was wearing a white shirt, dark tie, and gray slacks that were held up by a pair of red suspenders. He looked like a recruiting partner for an accounting firm or a law firm. It was obvious that he was talking to a reporter—one, Falcone surmised, who worked for a Florida newspaper.

With a flick of his hand, McCloskey motioned for Falcone to sit on the red leather couch, but Falcone preferred to wander on his own around Stock's office. He perused the books in the bookcase that filled the entire west wall of the office. It looked like a small library at the University of Tel Aviv. *Abandonment of the Jews, The New Anti-Semitism, Alive at Auschwitz . . .*

Two abstract paintings hung over the couch. Both were of the Old City of Jerusalem. The sixteen-foot wall behind Stock's desk was covered with plaques and awards from the Anti-Defamation League of B'nai B'rith and the United Jewish Appeal. Photos of Joshua with Prime Minister Gerstel, Shimon Peres, Abba Eban, Moshe Arens, and Teddy Kollek gave testimony to his access to Israel's highest officials.

Most senators lined their walls with books—leather-bound law books, novels, biographies, historical treatises. The handsome multicolored jackets were supposed to serve as a statement of the possessor's scholarship, character, and diversity of interests. They were there to impress and to intimidate, a badge of honor, a shield of armor that forewarned a constituent or reporter that the senator was no intellectual lightweight. Most of the books were sent courtesy of the publisher. Most of them were never read.

Stock was an exception. He felt no need to display his intelligence. His was a working library, filled with dog-eared reference materials that documented his fiercely held convictions about Israel, about the need for Jews never to have to wander in the desert again. There were to be no more pharaohs, no more Hitlers, no more ovens. The Jews finally had a homeland, one that deserved to be supported by Americans and defended by Israelis.

McCloskey finally hung up the phone and slumped into a deep leather chair. "Bastards," he snapped. "Those vultures want more details about Joshua's private life. Was he a cokehead? A womanizer? The papers are getting a ton of crank calls alleging that he participated in every orgy south of Jacksonville. Jesus!"

"I was at Joshua's place yesterday, Peter. It was a pretty bad scene. The police have a video of Joshua in bed with a woman. Drugs were involved. We both know something was wrong. But he never offered to talk about it, and I never pried. I assumed there was trouble in paradise."

"Joshua and Cleo? An understatement. She threatened to leave him last year. You know how obsessed he had become with Israel. It was consuming him and driving her all the way to the Wailing Wall. He was going fifteen, sixteen hours a day, then banging on the doors of every group from Manhattan to Monterey on weekends to raise money for Israel. Cleo played the role of model wife, but she was miserable. I know. I got the phone calls every Sunday."

"Peter, I never understood Joshua's obsession with Israel. If he had been Jewish, it might have made some sense," Falcone said, his eyes sweeping across the paintings and bookcases. "But there was something frantic, something desperate about him the last few months. Something else was pushing him over the edge. Was it money? Drugs?"

"No," McCloskey replied. "Joshua was making a ton of dough in the market. As for drugs, the highest Joshua ever got was on the caffeine in Diet Coke."

"Any new people that he was associating with? Anyone you had any doubts about?"

"Not that I can think of."

Falcone glanced at the mess on Joshua's desk. He remembered that McCloskey had once straightened it out and Joshua had refused to talk to him for nearly a week. The desktop looked chaotic, but Joshua always claimed that he knew where every note and doodle was.

"What about travel?"

"Well, he made more frequent trips to New York in the past six months—the standard fund-raising stuff. Some for Israel, some for him."

"Women?"

"None that I am aware of. Where the hell would he find the time, anyway?"

"He found it Saturday night," Falcone said. He sighed, walked to the couch, and sat down. "If you don't object, Peter, I'd like to look through Joshua's desk. I want to help find his killer, and frankly, judging by what I've seen from the D.C. police so far, I'm not confident that they really give a damn."

"How about the FBI?"

"I'm sure they'll be in on it soon. The counterintelligence people will be checking for security breaches. You know—blackmail, extortion. Ties to organized crime or foreign intelligence services."

"Jesus," McCloskey said. "That pit bull of a director would like nothing better than to offer Joshua up as a scapegoat to Hollendale right now." There was a pause while McCloskey ran through the implications of what he had just said. It was going to be tough for him and the other members of Stock's staff to find work in Washington—or out of it. The name Joshua Stock was not going to look like a gold star on their résumés now. His final act had obliterated a lifetime of accomplishment. They had bathed in the glow of his prominence, with the promise of lucrative private employment always just over the horizon. Now they were left to float amid the debris of his scandalous death.

"Sure. Go ahead and look," McCloskey said, speaking slowly, his gaze fixed on the wall behind Falcone. "The desk is unlocked. He kept the key to his closet in the tray of the middle drawer. I'm going down to the take-out to get some coffee. Want one?"

"Black, no sugar. And Peter—take your time."

Falcone knew that within hours Joshua's desk would be emptied by the police or the FBI, the contents swept into cardboard boxes or plastic bags and carted off to a lab to be scrutinized by professionals looking for clues to his past activities: notes, telephone numbers, names, old letters, datebooks, calendars, articles jammed randomly into red, blue, and green manila files whose colors carried no discernible significance. He knew that McCloskey would begin the slow process of removing all the plaques, photos, and cartoon sketches that adorned the walls, packing them up or parceling them out to staff members as mementos. The books would be boxed, the plaques and pictures stacked. All of it, every last remnant of

Joshua's political life, would be sealed in cardboard and left for Cleo to dispose of.

Time: Falcone didn't have much of it to waste. Another forty-five minutes and the staff would be making their funereal way to the office. Detective Clarke. The FBI. In a matter of days Florida's governor, who had been threatening to run against Joshua next year, would probably appoint himself to serve out the remainder of the senator's term. Under ordinary circumstances the governor might have considered appointing Cleo. But scandal stains those who are closest and most innocent.

Falcone had no idea what he was looking for. The inside of the desk was characteristically disheveled. Paper clips, elastic bands, old pencils, and dried-up pens were strewn around the middle drawer. In the left-hand drawers were stacks of personal stationery; a dozen or more photographs, none of them with a woman, that obviously didn't merit a frame or a place on the wall; a dish full of lapel pins that constituents expected Joshua to wear when they held their annual conventions in Washington, most of them emblazoned with an orange, a palm tree, or the sun. In the bottom drawer was a small shoeshine kit and a packaged Izod polo shirt with a small tag attached, another gift from a constituent.

Falcone took the key from the desk and opened the closet. More chaos. Two sets of skis and boots, luggage, two large boxes containing the various manuscript drafts of a book Joshua had written on the religious roots of anti-Semitism. The book had not burdened the shelves of many bookstores. A crude money tree made of dollar bills, a gift from Lenny, the masseur in the Senate gym. Three leather purses and an oxblood briefcase, purchased in Pusan, South Korea, during a trip Falcone and Joshua had made last year. At the rear of the closet hung two dark suits.

Feeling like a pickpocket, Falcone impulsively started to go through the pockets of the suits. Nothing in the first one. Then he felt something in the inside chest pocket of the second. Papers. There were three separate sheets. Receipts from hotels: two in New York, the Plaza Athénée and the Ritz-Carlton, the third from the Hilton Hotel in Baltimore. They had all been paid in cash.

Falcone, wanting to write down the dates and amounts, snapped up a piece of paper from Joshua's desk. The half-crumpled paper was a pink message slip on which was written "Call Senator

Falcone. Urgent!!!" For a moment, startled to see his name, Falcone stared at the slip. Then he remembered. An angry Jack Bickford had called him, telling him to check the Washington *Post*'s international section. Bickford had said, "You've been curious, Mr. Chairman. Now there's a dead cat. Now I'm curious." After agreeing to meet with Bickford to discuss the matter, Falcone had placed a call to Joshua. But Joshua had never returned his call.

Falcone put the slip in his shirt pocket, where he usually put message slips, opened the desk drawer, took out a piece of stationery, and wrote down the information from the hotel bills. The significance of what he was copying eluded him. He simply thought it strange that Joshua had stuffed cash receipts into a suit pocket in a dark corner of his closet.

As Falcone closed the closet door, he turned toward Joshua's desk, noticing for the first time the computer terminal, which seemed to be staring at him like an angry eye, a witness to his trespass. Joshua had used the computer for everything: access to the wire services, the Library of Congress, a research service in Alexandria, Virginia. He typed in interoffice memos, drafts of speeches, schedules, birthdays of prominent constituents and friends. *Maybe he even managed his stock portfolios here,* Falcone ventured. *Maybe . . .*

A knock on the office door startled Falcone. "Coffee's here," McCloskey said as he entered the room. He offered a slight bow as he handed Falcone a Styrofoam cup that was steaming. "At your service."

"Peter," Falcone said as he sipped, "Joshua was a notorious notetaker." Again Falcone found it odd to be speaking in the past tense. "He used to brag to me about the journal he was keeping for his next book. He threatened to expose all of my irreverent comments. I used to kid him that the truth would be treated as fiction, but it was probably the only way he'd ever write a best seller. I almost demanded half of the advance and royalties."

McCloskey nodded.

"How do I get into the computer? What's the code?"

"You can't. That's the one thing Joshua wouldn't give me."

Without the access code, whatever information Joshua had entered was as good as buried in Fort Knox. Most codes were simple—a four- or five-letter word that had some personal significance. Some thing that was not obvious and yet could not be forgotten. A childhood nickname. A relative's name. A mythological character. A Biblical hero.

Falcone surveyed the office intently, looking for some clue in the midst of all the clutter, knowing that he would probably never see this place again in all of its splendid disorder. He scanned the inscriptions on the photographs, the book titles, the plaques, some of which were in Hebrew. Nothing leaped out at him. The credenza behind Joshua's desk was stacked with old newspapers, a collection of the magazine sections of the Sunday New York *Times.* A photograph of Cleo and the kids adorned its center, while a foot-high pair of hands, touching each other at their index fingers, sat as an ornamental paperweight on the credenza's right side.

Nothing stuck out.

Falcone, hearing the sound of voices in the outer office, finished his coffee in two long gulps. He did not want to be part of the scene of mourning. Joshua's staff did not need a stranger in their midst. He put down his cup, thanked McCloskey, shook his hand, and left through the side door.

Within five minutes Falcone had entered the Russell Senate Office Building. He had a suite of eight rooms on the second floor, overlooking the Union Station plaza. He loved the Russell Building for all the reasons he disliked the Hart Building. It was old and rich in tradition. Teapot Dome, McCarthy, Watergate, Iran/contra—political scandals had been dragged into the magnificent high-ceilinged, Corinthian-columned Caucus Room on the third floor and exposed to the world. There was an enduring solidity to this structure, a stateliness that spoke of history and preserved a sense of privacy behind plaster walls and seven-foot-tall, solid mahogany doors.

The Hart Building's interior consisted of Plexiglas walls that revealed stacks of papers, books, art posters, a host of oddities, the personal idiosyncrasies and work habits of staff members—including a miniature basketball hoop in Senator Dobin's office. It reminded Falcone of those watches that contain no coverplate under the crystal but expose all of the wheels, springs, and screws. Revelation without purpose or grace.

Falcone slipped through the last door along the west side of the hall, an entrance that he used often to avoid meeting unwelcome visitors. He entered a large room that smelled of leather and polished wood. A football sat on the mantel above the fireplace; it was now a mere decoration. The football was old, but the inscriptions were still legible. Paintings by Massachusetts artists adorned the walls, which were eggshell white. A corner table contained the only photograph in the room, a shot of Falcone stepping off an Air Force transport plane at Wiesbaden, West Germany. He looked thin, haggard, and old beyond his thirty-three years. President Nixon was reaching to shake his hand.

The solid oak desk was burdened with nothing more than a calendar and a telephone. Two overstuffed leather chairs sat like bookends against a glass coffee table held up by a chunk of driftwood that had been rubbed a smooth silver by Atlantic tides and a merciless sun.

Falcone stood at the window and looked out at a perfect Washington day, with a blue, cloud-brushed sky and the green rolling lawns of Capitol Hill, meadows in a city. He thought suddenly of Clarke and the dirty, murderous city that Clarke, as a homicide detective, knew. No wonder he was so bitter. That city, that D.C. of drugs and murders and want, was so different from this blessed city on a hill. And the people of this city—so often they were not what they seemed.

Politics is a life of artifice. You become, through press releases and self-promotions, a figment of the public's imagination. A man of conviction, principle, strength. The successful legislator, one who makes the Washington establishment take note and yet does not forget his roots.

From the new legislator's day of arrival in Washington, almost his every move is made with the intent of creating and reinforcing an image, one of instant visibility and success. Each legislative initiative is weighed not simply on its merits but according to whether it will promote the legislator's interests in his home state. No weaknesses, no vulnerabilities, are permitted to show through the varnish —for while they might reveal a human dimension, they also invite challenges from ambitious opponents. The myth has to be created, then maintained. Senators remain imprisoned behind a thick wall of glass that gives the appearance of openness—like the interior of the

Hart Building—but never lets anyone in. The insulation is absolute. The Senate has a collegial, back-slapping clubbiness. Deference and charm are all. But there is an Orwellian quality to it. "My good friend" or "distinguished colleague" frequently means "my political enemy" or "fellow stonehead."

Not that friendship between members is insincere. Rather, it is not as deep as it appears. Talk always lingers on the surface. Feelings of inadequacy, despair, emptiness, heartaches, are never shared. Image is all. Senators are the hollow men, filled with facts, studies, statistics, reports, proposals, travel schedules—everything but time enough for genuine concern.

Joshua had been a lifeline for Falcone. With him, Falcone had been able to take off the mask that he wore in public to talk about momentary despairs, about the aimlessness of what they were doing, about the absolute cowardice of individual senators, about broken dreams and false hopes. About the need to get out, to actually do something instead of carrying a title, parading around the Senate floor in a blue suit, begging lobbyists for political contributions, and spending weekends flying home to reinforce the image of accessibility, just so he could come back for another six years.

Falcone could hear himself saying to Joshua, "Don't you ever feel time leaking through your fingers? You could be home with Cleo and the kids instead of listening to that asshole Drexler filibuster until he can get his way on some nutty amendment that doesn't amount to a marshmallow in a microwave."

Joshua always listened. Whatever his private doubts, he always had a glint of optimism in his eyes. He reminded Falcone about the power to influence the lives of millions, to breathe life into their dreams, to lift them up. Sure, the process was slow, almost paralytic. Yes, much of what they had to do was shallow, phony. But would Falcone want to be a fat-cat lawyer, negotiating mergers so some greedy bastard could make $50 million instead of $30 million? Falcone could still hear Joshua's words: "There is no other job in the world that can match the excitement of shaping world events. No checking account can pay you for the satisfaction that you get from helping people achieve a better life." Joshua was always willing to give Falcone what he needed—renewal, reaffirmation. He had what Falcone did not, a sense of completeness, undiminished idealism, a burnished hope that he could alter and shape events, a spiritual reservoir that kept him vigorous and filled with laughter and jokes.

Or so it seemed.

Perhaps Joshua had had his own mirror to hold up to others. Maybe he had been a better actor than the others, who lived in a Potemkin village of gregarious, fulsome, happy family men. Perhaps . . . no. Falcone knew better.

He had sensed a change in Joshua. It was vague and indefinable. It was signaled by little things: a sudden wistfulness in his eyes one day; an unconscious furrowing of his brow; an uncharacteristic edge in his voice; his starting to smoke again. But the little changes were never persistent, never worth mentioning.

Besides, Falcone now bitterly told himself, lately he had been too busy to talk to Joshua on more than a superficial level. He had been working on a book, an account of his war experiences. A publisher had contracted with him to write an "honest book," but Falcone was not sure he could disclose his dirty little secret: He had never felt more exhilarated than when he was in combat, when adrenaline was pumping so hard he thought his heart would burst, when every skill, every animal instinct, was stretched to the edge of sanity. There was no satisfaction he had ever known that would equal the thump of his heart beating in triumph after a firefight, when he was riding on the very wings of death, looking into the chasm of hell—and this moment was the moment when he had felt most alive. That was the book he wanted to write, the one he knew he would not write.

It seemed that it had been that way since childhood. Odd experiences, a sad thought striking him in the midst of happiness. Feeling a darkness inside when the sun was brightest. Unable to enjoy a moment because he knew it would not last. Was it the Irish blood in his veins, a Celtic morbidity? Did blood have anything to do with it? Was it more that we never stop trying to play to the applause of our parents? Do they ever let us go?

"Sean, whatever you do, don't ever touch that. Understand? You'll hurt yourself. Bad. You understand?"

The boy nodded his acknowledgment as his father, Sonny, ran

off with a package he was delivering to poor Mrs. Cataldo, a widow confined to a wheelchair in her home.

When Sonny came out, he found Sean crouched against the door, crying in pain. A strange smell filled the car. Temptation had proved irresistible. Sean, fascinated by the magic of the 1940 Packard's cigarette lighter, had pressed it, while red hot, against his thumb. The lighter had cut into his skin like a branding iron, leaving it black, with deep ridges that crusted white.

Sonny Falcone wanted to spank Sean for disobeying him, but although he was a hot-tempered man capable of volatile mood shifts, he never struck his son. Not once.

Sonny owned a butcher shop on Walden Street in Boston's North End. He and his brother, Tony, and sister, Vivian, were second-generation Sicilians. Their father had emigrated from the port town of Messina in 1902, worked as a tailor in New York, then moved to Boston with his young family in 1929, at the beginning of the Great Depression. There was no market for Caesar Falcone's skills; people sewed their own clothes. So Sonny and Tony worked odd jobs in shoeshine parlors, gas stations. Vivian cooked in soup halls. Sonny joined the Army and worked in a kitchen at Fort Dix in New Jersey. He sent his monthly pay of twenty-nine dollars home.

When he left the Army, he decided to open a butcher shop. He had picked up the idea—his brother called it the *strange* idea—in the Army. Less than a year after his discharge, he did something else strange: He married an outsider. Her name was Claire O'Connor, and she was a blue-eyed blonde from South Boston. They met at a dance hall called the Chateau in the summer of 1937. Sonny was making extra money by playing alto sax in a pickup band. He could not stop looking at her face. She had cheeks the color of apples. Over Papa Falcone's objections, they were married a month after they met.

When World War II started in Europe, Sonny worried about being called back into the Army. Then came the draft, and new worries. But they were not taking married men yet. And then, in March 1940, Sonny had another reason to be relieved. He became a father.

Claire's relatives and friends said the boy's face was the very map of Ireland. She insisted on the name Sean. Sonny finally relented, though Caesar maintained a gloomy silence, his dark eyes a smoldering rebuke to his son. Sicilian men were supposed to be in charge. Family honor was at stake. But Claire Falcone proved stronger than Sicilian pride.

During the war, business boomed in Boston. The shipyards were working furiously, hammering steel into warships. Sailors flooded the streets. Americans were locked into the cause of preserving world freedom. Jazz was big. Money was flowing.

At first meat rationing threatened Sonny's business. The WASP rationing board members made sure that their society pals on Beacon Hill got all the meat they could eat, Sonny told Claire, and there was damn little left for Eyetalian butchers in Little Italy. So Sonny bought meat on the black market. He made sure he got good merchandise cheap, marked it up enough to undercut the wholesalers who sold to restaurants, and became one of the most prosperous butchers in the North End.

Sean did not see much of his father, then or after the war years. Sonny went to the slaughterhouse every day before sunrise to pick out the beef carcasses and big birds that would hang on hooks in his walk-in, steel-doored freezer. He rarely slept more than four hours a night. He continued to play in the band, shoot pool at Donatelli's, and roll dice at Constantino's. Sometimes he would go directly to work from the gambling tables.

He was not a big man, but he was wiry and surprisingly supple. He had large forearms and hands with fingers as thick as bananas. He was fighter, too. He once knocked out a much larger man who later became a bodyguard for the gangster Tony Gambino.

Falcone did not remember much of those early years—images and smells, mostly. He remembered his father spreading sawdust on the pine floors of the shop each day, the two rotating ceiling fans, the strips of flypaper hanging over the cutting blocks and display counters, and a cash register that curiously always rang up "No Sale." He could still hear the high-pitched scream of the saws, the thud of the cleavers, the unmistakable ring of blades running against a sharpener. He knew the insides of every animal—thin-sliced veal, marbled beef—and he knew the mysteries of knockwurst, Italian sausage, chicken livers, hamburger, sheep's tongue. He knew how an order was cut and weighed and wrapped in vanilla-colored paper, right in front of the customers, who never worried about fingers on the scales, not in Sonny's market. Sean used to laugh at the sign that hung in the front window. It had been painted in awkward block letters by his father: SONNY'S—A GREAT PLACE TO MEAT.

He remembered his Uncle Tony and Aunt Vivian arguing constantly and openly in front of customers. No one took offense. Everyone knew the Falcones worked hard and slept little. Besides, it was that way with Sicilians.

Mostly, Falcone remembered how angry he had been.

22

FALCONE WAS SEVERAL minutes into his awakening ritual—the coffee-making, the shower, the shave—when grief and anger suddenly swept over him. The routine of everyday life was trying to . . . trying to deceive, distract. He was grasping for a phrase that had once consoled him. Lincoln—his letter to the woman who lost her sons in the war. Lather still on half his face, Falcone walked to the bookshelf in his study and took down *The War Years,* a volume in Carl Sandburg's biography. There it was: "How weak and fruitless must be any words of mine which should attempt to beguile you from the grief . . ." Beguile. That was what routine tried to do at times like this.

Walking back to the bathroom, he stopped. On his desk, in a plain black frame, was the photograph of Karen and Kyle. It served as both tribute and torture. He had insisted on preserving that photograph and an oil painting she had once done. He turned to the wall over his bed and looked at the painting of a young man sitting on a stool, a brown jacket draped across his shoulders. He wore a collarless striped shirt underneath. One foot rested on the rung of the stool, the other hung casually down. He was holding a wineglass in his right hand. An empty bottle stood near the base of the stool, and a white sheet was draped decoratively behind him. The rest of the canvas was covered by what looked like a deep indigo curtain, whose heavy folds turned purple in a suffused light. What fascinated Falcone was why Karen had chosen to omit any discernible features on the man's face, which was as blank as the white sheet behind him.

Was the young man her fantasy? An anonymous visitor who provided conversation during the hours that Falcone left her alone while he studied the law? Or had she painted Falcone himself, his featureless face symbolic of his impenetrability? Perhaps he was the enigma who came home one day and told her that he had decided to join the Army, just like that, with no consultation, no attempt to persuade. A *fait accompli.*

Falcone had a vague recollection of sitting in a kitchen chair in their basement apartment in Back Bay in 1965, trying to explain what had prompted his action. "Now let's discuss what it means." Karen had been stunned into silence. She kept her head turned away as he spoke and busied herself with preparing the evening meal. Kyle was in the playpen in his bedroom, demanding attention.

Falcone said his decision was not impulsive. He had been thinking about serving his country for at least three months before graduation. He was not ready to stuff his life into an attaché case and climb some law firm's legal and social ladder into partnership. He needed to give something back, to do what Kennedy had said about doing something for his country.

It sounded pathetic and platitudinous even to him. Oh, there were some patriotic stirrings in his heart, to be sure. But what he needed was a raw physical challenge. There was no football in law school, no boxing ring in which to spill blood. He needed to unleash some of the violence that flowed in his veins. Falcone did not fully understand what made him feel this way, and he was even less able to articulate his feelings. He was educated, civilized. Yet there was a primordial urge to clash and dominate—the instinct of a ram fighting for territory.

In his bathroom, shaving, forgetting, remembering, he wondered if the war inside him would ever end.

Shaved, shirt and trousers on, he resumed his routine. He padded to the apartment door in stocking feet, a coffee mug in his hand. He opened the door and picked up the *Post*. Then again he felt the rage.

The first day's *Post* article on Stock's murder had been basically a police story told by policemen and put together by *Post* reporters, rewrite men, and editors, who were well acquainted with murder. There were even scorekeepers: Stock's was the one hundred and ninety-eighth murder since January 1, and the homicide rate was running slightly ahead of last year's, which had set new records.

Now, as Falcone stood in the doorway, what he was reading, his hands shaking, his mind full of anger, was what newspapers called a second-day story—an after-event story with enough angles and adjectives to keep that event alive. In Washington, an event that generated a good second-day story was destined for sustained coverage, day after day, week after week, until it evolved into an affair and then into the highest possible category: scandal, usually attended by a cavalcade of congressional investigations and its own distinctive label. Teapot Dome. Watergate. Iran/contra.

The *Post* specialist in creating and nurturing such stories was Philip Dake, a Pulitzer Prize–winning reporter whose by-line over an article stamped it as potentially momentous, a nominee for the scandal hall of fame.

Falcone sat at the table in his small kitchen and reread the story, not only as Stock's friend but as a working politician skilled in the craft of reading between the lines of newspaper articles. As usual, the headline—two lines, boxed in five columns—oversold the story:

FBI PROBING LOSS OF U.S. SECRETS,

DRUG LINKS IN STOCK "ASSASSINATION"

In newspaper headline code, Falcone knew, the quotation marks around "Assassination" could mean either that the FBI had given the murder that label or that assassination was one of the matters that Philip Dake's sources were speculating about. The sources were also speculating about whether "an intelligence loss is involved in Stock's death." Dake's story went on to say that "after two days' delay" the FBI had "launched a major investigation" into the murder. "Stock may have been a target of assassins operating for a foreign intelligence service. Investigators are also concerned about the presence of drugs at the murder scene. They speculate that Stock may have had a serious drug abuse problem which was being exploited by foreign intelligence services."

Dake had a reputation for never being farther than ten feet from a phone, day or night. Falcone went into his study, took his phone diary from his desk, and looked up Dake's home number.

He had never called Dake before, but like most influential senators, he had been buttonholed by the reporter at social events and in Senate corridors. As chairman of the Senate Intelligence Committee, he had been a prime target for Dake. The reporter never gave up trying to get information out of Falcone, and Falcone never gave any away.

Dake answered on the second ring.

"This is Senator Falcone. How in God's name could you write this about a man who was a great senator and a patriot? You are disgracing a man, ruining his reputation, hurting his family. And you don't know all the facts."

"What makes you say that, Senator?" Dake asked in an unexpectedly soft voice.

"I know Joshua, and he was no drug abuser or leaker."

"That is not what my sources say. Drugs were found—"

"I'd say you've got some bad sources."

"There's no such thing as a bad source, Senator." Dake's quiet, almost academic tone was a counterpoint to Falcone's anger. "Some sources are better than others, that's all." He paused. There was no response from Falcone, so he went on. "Remember the phrase 'a thousand points of light'? I didn't know what in hell it meant at the time, but it had a nice ring to it. That sort of describes how I work. Some are bright, some are dim, but they come from everywhere."

"Forget it," Falcone snapped. "You are what you are."

"And you, Senator?"

The question momentarily shook Falcone. It was a question he had often asked himself. After a moment he replied, "I'm not interested in philosophy, Dake."

"How about the truth?"

"Not the kind you dish out."

"I never knowingly print a lie, Senator. I never write anything I do not believe. In fact, I almost always know more than I write, believe more than I write. As a journalist, I am a conservative."

"Once again, Dake, I'm not interested in a philosophical discussion. That story is a pack of lies."

"Do you know how many senators went to the scene of the murder?" Dake asked. Before Falcone could respond, he continued. "Exactly one. You. You saw the blood, the video. You did not read about the video in my story, did you?" This time Dake waited for an answer.

"No. Not in the first-day story, either. I suppose I have your bosses to thank for that."

"You have me to thank, Senator, if thanks are in order. The police reporter had it in the first stuff he phoned in to the rewrite man. The night city editor called me—because of something I had been working on, unconnected to this. He told me about the video, and I suggested that he keep it out. He listened to reason."

"From what I've heard about you, Dake, more than reason was involved. You probably had something on the city editor."

Dake spoke slowly, his voice almost a whisper. "That's not fair. I may write things that people don't like. But I do not blackmail people. I do not make threats."

"Sorry," Falcone said, surprised at the words. "I suppose I should thank you, about the video. And I do."

"There is a lot more to this than a killing, Senator. We both know that. You went there. You went there to find out for yourself."

"I went there because he was my friend."

"And to find out who did it. And why," Dake persisted. "I think we ought to talk. Off the record. By whatever ground rules you set down. I suggest not in your office. Your place or mine?"

The question startled Falcone. When he had called, he had had no intention to meet with Dake. But now, in a flash, he decided that the reporter was right. Falcone had started trying to find out why Stock had been murdered. *Why?* Not who—not yet who. Perhaps Dake could help. At that moment, Falcone could think of no one else who could help.

"I have a full morning," he replied. "There are the eulogies. I guess they'll be short," he added bitterly. "And a lunch I can't get out of. I'll come to your place tonight."

"I'm in McLean. I'll have my secretary give yours the directions."

"I'll be there at eight-thirty," Falcone said. "Goodbye."

23

Washington, July 24

Dᴀʏ ᴏʀ ɴɪɢʜᴛ, ᴅᴀᴋᴇ never stopped thinking about what he did for a living. He did not merely write newspaper stories. He protected them, or their parts. Even when he was playing the piano he let a story, or the problems of the story, float through his mind. The best stories, he thought now as he sat at his piano, never seemed to begin or end. They flowed like a theme that a composer almost could not control. And when the composer finally did manage to place the theme into a piece that was fit for a public performance, he knew something his audience would never know: *There was much more there.*

From where he sat, Dake could look through a pair of glass doors to a walled garden. He was in his mid-forties, of medium height, with dark wavy hair, a strong square jaw, and lips that somehow hinted of amusement, as if he were always on the verge of a smile. Now, with that half-smile on his lips, he felt his eyes drawn from the newly arrived crape myrtle and roses to the hydrangeas, exploding in large bursts of white, pink, and blue. *That was no sex murder. Stock was assassinated.*

He had been practicing Beethoven's *Tempest* Sonata the way his teacher had instructed: with heartbreaking ardor. He bore down heavily on the last torrent of notes, stood, and drew the drapes on his garden. He wanted no distractions during his talk with Falcone.

In front of the piano were two beige settees with a low mahogany table between them. On the rare occasions when Dake played for friends, the settees were rearranged for the audience's front row. Three straight-backed chairs stood along one of the bookshelved walls. Dake placed a chair between the piano and the low table, then walked the length of the room to an oak rolltop desk and sat before it in an oak swivel chair. Taking from his pocket a key ring linked by a gold chain to a clip on the belt of his jeans, he unlocked the desk and rolled up the top.

The chair and desk had belonged to his father when he was the editor of a North Carolina weekly. His father would not recognize the interior of his old desk. The pigeonholes and shelves had been removed so a computer could be installed. Dake clicked a switch and slid out a keyboard from a niche where galleys of the Galston *Times* had once been stacked. With a few swift strokes he called up his file on the Stock murder. *Why did the FBI stall on this?*

He scanned the file, glanced at his watch, and pulled a spiral-bound stenographer's notebook from one of the side drawers. He plucked a pencil from a black mug stamped *CBS Nightwatch,* jotted down a few words, turned off the computer, closed the desk, and went to a cabinet recessed amid the bookshelves. Opening the door and using the same key chain, he unlocked a two-drawer file cabinet. From the top drawer he took a file folder marked *Falcone, Sean.* The folder, much thinner than the others in the drawer, contained several newspaper and magazine clippings, two computer printouts, and a stack of several three-by-five cards clipped together. Dake removed the clip, looked through the index cards, wrote a few words in his notebook, and methodically repeated all the motions involved in the simple act of examining some index cards. *What the hell is it that Falcone knows? And what does he want to know?*

Ever since Falcone had called, Dake had been uneasy. Usually when a politician called he was after something, although, of course, it was rarely a direct request. The smart politician never offered a deal or anything resembling one. Instead he presented his wishes as a shared quest, often legitimately. Falcone did not play games with the media. He avoided media exposure beyond the amount that automatically came with his job as chairman of the Senate Intelligence Committee. He rarely granted interviews. He was not known to talk to reporters or to aggrandize himself with phony media moves. He stayed off TV talk shows unless he saw his presence as a way to mute someone who was selling a line that he opposed. The only time Dake had spent more than few minutes with Falcone was on an ABC *Nightline* show on which Dake had promoted his latest book on U.S. covert operations, *Deeds of Deception*. Falcone had found a couple of inaccuracies in the book and had displayed them with all the skill and ardor of the tough prosecutor he had once been. Dake inwardly winced as he remembered one other time, when Falcone had called in a rage over a story he had written exposing a CIA covert action. *He practically accused me of murder. Now, to call me and agree to talk to me, here. Why?*

Dake admitted to himself that although he liked what he knew about Falcone, trusting politicians was not a safe practice for an investigative reporter.

Distrust politicians: It was a rule born of experience. Each election year brought a new crop of representatives and senators to Washington—new pennies, all bright and shiny with idealism, out to fulfill dreams or campaign promises that were hopelessly inflated. They rushed about, studying rules, lobbying for committee assignments, accepting office space that failed to measure up to their perceived self-importance. They plowed through the blizzard of résumés from job-seekers, culling out the mediocre and the threadbare. High on the list of important staff positions would be press secretary, to be filled by a hack who had to possess the personality of a circus barker, a puffery expert who could shamelessly call an acorn an oak tree, a media manipulator who could make his boss an overnight Washington sensation.

The Washington press corps watched the circus-barker routine with cynicism and amusement. How long would it take these dewy-eyed, ambitious innocents to discover that the road to success was paved with back-slapping, back-scratching, ass-kissing acceptance of a system that they had campaigned against but now had to live with? Power came with seniority. Seniority was purchased with campaign money. Money carried its dues. There were no shortcuts. It took time, patience, and accommodation. Those who understood the rules got along. Those who fought them got isolated headlines and little else. They would be provocateurs but never power brokers.

Washington reporters might pretend that they were merely voyeurs of an obscene process, but they were part of it. They traded off it. At the beginning of each new congressional session they would pick out those who had the potential to be national figures. Potential meant looks, intelligence, savvy, and ambition. The politicians with those attributes were the politicians whom the reporters watched, captured in profiles, and chronicled. They picked favorites, turned to them as sources, and then invariably described them as "thoughtful," "highly respected," or "talented." Members of Congress who enjoyed favorable mention by the press received most of the invitations to appear on nationally televised programs. Those who appeared on nationally televised programs became the requisite guests at Washington social festivities. And from all this they drew more power. The Washington power game was, like the city itself, a circle.

Dake saw it more as a carousel, with painted horses that moved predictably up and down to a monotonously raucous calliope. He did not watch it, and he refused to ride it. He began with the premise that ambitious men and women were the least reliable sources for the truth. It was not that they were dishonest or given to falsehoods. Rather, they could not afford to be completely honest about themselves or their colleagues. Their words were always guarded when they agreed to be quoted on the record. And when they wanted to go off the record—or, worse, "on background"—they usually had an ulterior motive.

Dake always found it more productive to deal with those who constituted Washington's permanent bureaucracy—those anonymous men and women who sat endlessly at computer terminals or wearily shuffled the tons of paperwork generated by the policymakers. They were drones whose labors went unnoticed or unappreciated. Dake considered them gold mines. He befriended and cultivated them, learned about their backgrounds, talked philosophy with them. Philosophy was important. They cared about government policy.

He knew that some of them bore grudges or had less than the public interest in mind when they divulged information. But he always had multiple sources, and he sifted their stories like a panhandler searching for precious metals. He checked, double-checked, and checked again. When he knew he had a story, he wrote it in a way that protected his sources. Readers knew that his stories were factual and authentic, but they were left to marvel at how Dake got them.

Dake did not turn to high-level executives or elected officials until he had done his investigative homework. At that point they had two choices: to confirm the story or to decline comment. They could not afford to lie to or mislead him. The only time he trusted politicians was when they had nowhere to go but to the truth.

Ever since Falcone had become chairman of the Senate Intelligence Committee, he had refused to answer Dake's calls. Dake did not carry any animosity. Falcone had not slighted him; he had refused to talk to any reporters about intelligence matters. Fair enough. But it is a short road that has no turns. Now Falcone was calling Dake. Either the senator was in trouble or he had information he wanted to share. Dake sensed it was trouble.

He walked out of what he called the music room, closed the tall oak doors behind him, and crossed the entrance hall to the living room opposite. The room was about the same size as the music room, but it did not have doors. He stepped down two steps and opened a cabinet next to the fireplace. Behind the cabinet was a wet bar. He checked the ice cube trays in the small refrigerator. The maid had filled them before she left, just as he knew she would. But it was worth a check. He reached into a lower cabinet for a bottle of Jack Daniel's. He knew that bourbon was Falcone's favorite liquor. Only today had he learned the favorite brand; the bartender at the Monocle—one of Capitol Hill's popular watering holes—had told him.

Dake switched on a floor lamp behind one of the two leather chairs near the bar. Then he returned to the hall and went up the stairs two at a time. Five doors bordered the second-floor landing. Entering the small bathroom, he pulled a blue hand towel from a shelf by the door and placed it on a rack next to the sink. He left the bathroom light on and the door ajar. Then he took two steps to another door, which he unlocked. He touched a switch that flicked on a battery of recessed overhead fluorescent lights. The room was long and narrow. Along one wall were a dozen two-drawer filing cabinets. Above them were shelves full of books, stacks of photocopied papers, slipcases full of documents, and piles of publications. Along the other wall were two computer workstations and three four-drawer file cabinets with steel rods running through their handles. At the tops of the rods were padlocked hasps.

Two narrow tables ran the length of the room. At each were four office chairs. At times as many as three people worked here, doing research and cross-filing data for Dake's books and newspaper stories.

To the discerning eye of any Capitol Hill veteran, Dake's walls lacked something usually found on the walls of the power players: the honorary college degrees and the look-at-me-with-the-powerful-people photographs. But if Dake were to hang what he had really won, his walls would be adorned with the scalps of the politically powerful.

For more than a decade virtually every major news story involving an abuse of position or power had been broken by Dake. Although his specialty was penetrating the veil of secrecy that shielded America's intelligence operations, he would, as if to make nothing more than a parenthetical point, expose the bizarre lifestyles of prominent actors and authors as well. He had written three books, all best sellers, and was rumored to be working on a new project—an exposé of the United States Senate.

Dake walked to a cabinet at the end of the room and unlocked it. Stacked on three shelves were hardback and paperback copies of his books. He took out a paperback copy of *Deeds of Deception*, found a black felt-tip pen in a workstation, and wrote something on the title page for Falcone, then signed his name. He glanced around the room, walked to the door, switched off the lights, and locked the door behind him.

The next door was not locked. The overhead lights in this room bathed a small gym: weights and pulleys in a black steel frame, a rowing machine next to a green mat, a punching bag, a stationary bicycle. Dake put the book on the mat, mounted the bicycle, set the dial to "moderate 5 difficult 25," and clicked on the tiny television set clamped to the handlebars. For the next thirty minutes, at a speed averaging nineteen miles per hour, he watched the ABC evening news.

At 8:02 he was in the shower in the bedroom suite he shared with his current girlfriend, a twenty-nine-year-old graduate of the University of Maryland. With her degree in journalism and a phone call from Dake she had gotten a job as a deputy assistant press secretary, or gopher, on the staff of the Senate Foreign Relations Committee. At the moment she was spending a week visiting her family on the Eastern Shore. Dake was not sorry that she was not there to be introduced to Falcone.

Fifteen minutes before Falcone was to arrive, Dake was again at the piano, again playing Beethoven's *Tempest* Sonata the way his teacher had instructed.

Falcone, driving through the fading light of this hot July day, sensed but did not see the green splendor rippling past the open windows of his car. He was on the George Washington Parkway, watching for the Spout Run turnoff and having second thoughts about talking to Dake.

He secretly respected Dake's intellectual thoroughness. But he looked on the reporter's professed search for the truth as a phony moralism wrapped in a pious declaration of the public's right to know. For Falcone, much of Dake's work was little more than aiding and abetting the enemy. Damn it, there were bounds, lines to be drawn, moral distinctions to be made. The First Amendment did not guarantee the American people the right to know everything, particularly not as soon as there was something to know. Diplomacy could not always be conducted openly. Ends were not always achieved in public forums.

Although Falcone frequently seethed with anger over Dake's ability to obtain and disclose classified information, on only one occasion before had he called him. Dake had disclosed a plan by the Sultan of Oman to assist in an assassination plot against Adeeb Miari, a man so ruthless that he was considered an equal to Abu Nidal, the notorious hijacker and hostage-taker. The CIA had provided the Sultan with intelligence information that helped to establish the location of several of Adeeb Miari's camps. An unsuccessful attack was launched on one of them by a group that the CIA had trained several years earlier. Dake spread the story on page one, not only informing the American people of the CIA's role but putting the Sultan on Miari's hit list.

Falcone's words had been brief, his message understated: "You are protected in what you print, but I think that you've done an enormous disservice to the country."

Dake feigned surprise. "Really? How so?"

"Because the Sultan is a dead man."

"Maybe he should have thought longer about the consequences before he caved in to the crazies at the Agency."

Falcone wanted to correct him; the incident had occurred on the Sultan's initiative, not the Agency's. But Falcone could never tell how much Dake actually knew about the operations he exposed. The reporter had a favorite technique of writing only part of a major story and then waiting for the calls to flood in. Some callers confirmed what he knew and added new pieces of information. Others contradicted his story and unintentionally opened up new avenues for exploration. Dake played the role of ingenue masterfully, acting as if he were stumbling along in desperate need of assistance in order to get the story straight.

Dake never used a recorder in front of people he interviewed. Occasionally he would pull out a notebook and, with a naïve expression on his face, deliberately mispronounce the name of a highly classified program. An unsuspecting source would often correct him; the professionals would maintain a stoic silence. It didn't matter either way; Dake always got the answer he wanted.

As Falcone drove along Spout Run, he forced himself to recall Joshua's exact words that day at lunch. He created a picture in his mind, reconstituting his friend's face, hair, eyes, gestures, phrases, tone of voice. Joshua fidgeting with his briefcase. Joshua referring to his sources, predicting disaster for the United States if his information was correct. Joshua having difficulty in looking directly into Falcone's eyes. Everything about him now seemed wrong. He had seemed unusually worried. He had been pressing Falcone to do something that was certain to meet with objections from the Agency.

At the time, Falcone had not suspected that Joshua was being anything but cautious. Both men had been discussing how Castro had once doubled almost every American agent who was working in Cuba and thus gained access to our most classified files. The Cubans were reading our mail right under our noses, and we never suspected them. It was only after Major Florentino Aspillaga defected that we learned how lax and foolish we had been. The Intelligence Committee members were outraged when they learned of this counterintelligence failure. Falcone thought Joshua's concerns were entirely reasonable. He did not want another scandal during his chairmanship of the committee.

Falcone drove to the end of the block-long cul-de-sac and parked at the curb in front of the steep slope on which Dake's home was perched. He was halfway up the stone steps when the door opened and Dake jovially called down to him, "They're steep, but you get used to them." He wondered how many thousands of times Dake had said those words to climbing guests.

The reporter came out to the small porch, greeted Falcone, and followed him through the door. Falcone turned left, but Dake touched his arm and directed him to the right. "I thought we'd meet here. I call it the music room," he said, ushering his guest through the open doors and over to one of the settees.

Dake sat in the straight-backed chair and began talking amiably about the room, his preoccupation with the piano, the remodeling he had done on the house. He was in the middle of an anecdote about how he had once coaxed the director of the National Symphony into playing the piano for him when Falcone interrupted him.

"Let's get down to business, Dake," he said. "I don't need to be charmed." He stood abruptly and took a step to the side of Dake's chair. "And I know all about interrogation techniques. See? Now I'm looking down on *you.*"

Dake laughed. "Well, at least call me Phil. When you say Dake like that, it makes me feel like an enlisted man under your command." He stood, went to the glass doors, and opened the drapes. "I guess you know about this, too."

"Sure. Don't let the bastard be distracted." Falcone looked through the doors. "Nice garden."

"How about a drink?" Dake asked.

"Maybe later. I think we should talk now."

Dake nodded and sat on one of the settees. Falcone sat down opposite him, leaned forward, and said, "All the way over, I wondered about talking to you. All this"—his hand took in the open drapes, the straight-backed chair—"makes me wonder even more. I'm in no mood for games."

"Come off it, Senator. I've seen you in action. And I've heard about you in a courtroom. You know how to bear down on people, how to make them talk. It's all in the technique. Don't forget, I have to work without subpoenas or staff investigators. Charm, as you call it, is part of getting people to feel safe. Do you feel safe?"

"Perhaps."

"Well, why don't you start by telling me what I know already? No secrets. No inside information. Just tell the public story of Senator Stock's death."

"As . . . as you know," Falcone began, surprised at his hesitation, "we . . . Joshua and I were friends. Not just the kind of friends that you make in politics, in the Senate. But real friends, who went back a ways in time."

He stood again and went to the glass doors. Looking out on the deepening shadows in the garden, he spoke more softly, as if he were addressing his reflection in the glass.

"I saw him, saw his body. I saw that goddamned video. And thanks for that, thanks for letting that one by. Maybe that's why . . . maybe your doing that is why I am here. Anyway, I saw it. And I *knew*. I knew that something was wrong—awfully wrong." He turned and looked at Dake directly. "That wasn't Joshua. Something happened to the real Joshua, and this was somebody else. It wasn't what that goddamned D.C. cop thought it was."

"Clarke?" Dake asked. He continued without waiting for an answer. "He's not that bad, Senator. I've known him a long time. He tries to stay sane by being angry. He told me once about tracking down a kid who had shot two women in some kind of drug deal that went wrong. He emptied an Uzi into them—mostly into their heads. When Clarke found him, later that same night, the kid was in his house, asleep. Clarke told me about it and asked me how that kid could be sleeping. He hated the kid more for that than for the murders."

"Have you talked to him lately?"

"Day before yesterday."

"He told you about the FBI coming in?"

"I don't discuss my work, Senator."

"Okay. Okay." Falcone realized he was sounding impatient. He paused. "What I'm really asking is what you think about the FBI's dragging its feet and then coming in." He returned to the settee and sat down. Leaning back, he realized that for the first time since he arrived, he felt relaxed.

"What I thought at first," Dake replied, "was that the FBI stayed out because the murder was too messy for it. Then I had another idea: The FBI stayed out to give the D.C. cops a chance to screw up the investigation. The D.C. police's murder-solving record is profoundly dismal. Then, when I heard the FBI had come in, I had another thought: The Bureau realized that by staying out of the case, it was making the murder look like something it *wanted* to stay away from. By at least going through the motions, it would look as if it was doing what it was supposed to do. And that would give the FBI control—always important in an investigation."

"That's just about what I made of it," Falcone said, obviously surprised that Dake agreed with his assessment. "But of course it also means that someone told the FBI—someone told Polanski to get into it. And of course that someone had to be Butch Naylor, acting for the President. Or the President himself."

"So the White House is somehow in this," Dake said. It was a statement, not a question.

"I didn't say that."

"But you thought it. Why?" The tempo of Dake's voice changed. This was the moment, he knew. This was when Falcone would either say something or pull back.

"I don't know, Dake."

"Phil."

"All right, *Phil.* I don't know. But I want to find out."

Falcone made an instantaneous decision, the kind he had had to make in combat. This conversation was like combat; it was a duel, of something more than wits. Falcone knew he could either hold out and keep it a game, or he could begin to cooperate. It would still be a duel, man-to-man combat. But it might accomplish something.

"White House," Dake said. "What is it that makes you think the White House is involved in this?"

"I don't know that, either. I only know something that Joshua said, something that came back to me when I was trying to make sense of this, trying to find an explanation."

Falcone waited for Dake to ask him what Joshua had said. But the reporter did not speak.

"It was in April. He called me and came to my office. He was upset, very upset. I said something about his smoking again—he hadn't smoked in years. He said, 'There is one thing I want to tell you, Sean. And only you.' Those were his exact words."

Falcone paused, but again Dake did not speak.

"But, goddamn it, he didn't tell me anything." Falcone thrust his head toward Dake. "That's the truth."

"Let's go back over this," Dake said softly. He moved slightly, so that he was directly opposite Falcone. "He came to you upset, he said he wanted to tell you something, and then he said nothing?"

"That's right. All he said was that he was working on something."

"Working on something. That's all? Working on something?"

"Yes."

"No hint? Nothing about anything to do with the Intelligence Committee?"

"I remember asking him that. I was mad for a moment. I remember that. I said, 'Is this committee business?' And he said no."

"Why were you mad?"

"Well, he knew damn well that committee business cannot be discussed in an unsecure situation."

"And he said it wasn't? He said that what he was doing had nothing to do with the committee?"

"Yes. And he gave me a date. I remember that, too. He said that I should remember it." Falcone nodded his head and continued, speaking faster. "So *that* is what he told me. Only the date. April 15."

"Do you know of any significance to that date?"

Falcone went on as if he had not heard Dake. "That was all. 'Remember the date.' And one thing more—his computer. He gave me the impression that the information was in his computer."

"And no significance to the date?" Dake repeated.

"None that I know of."

"Have you been to his office?"

Falcone described his visit—except for finding the papers in the suit pocket—and recalled his conversation with McCloskey about the computer and its unknown password.

"Nobody from the FBI has been there yet?"

"McCloskey would have called me if they had come today. No. No FBI visit to the office yet."

"You've got to get back there tomorrow morning. First thing. Don't use the telephone. Tell McCloskey not to tell the FBI about the computer unless they ask. Can you trust him to do that?"

"Absolutely. Besides, he's out of a job and he's going to do whatever any senator wants. Shall I ask him to try to get into the computer?"

"No. Those things are tricky, Senator. You do it wrong and the security program will wipe out everything on the disk. Let it be for a while. Let me talk to some hackers I know. I'll find out what I can about bypassing a password. Meanwhile, we've got work to do."

"We?"

"I thought that was the idea. Would you like that drink now?" Dake stood and headed toward the hall.

Falcone hesitated, then followed Dake across the hall and into the living room. The reporter held up the Jack Daniel's bottle and smiled. Falcone nodded and almost smiled back. He sat in one of the leather chairs. Dake poured a generous amount of the bourbon into a glass, added a splash of water and two ice cubes, handed the glass to Falcone, then reached into the back of the refrigerator, took out a can of Pabst Blue Ribbon, zipped it open, and raised it in a silent toast. Falcone moved his glass almost imperceptibly.

Dake settled in the other chair. "Tomorrow morning, first thing," he began, "tell McCloskey you want a copy of Senator Stock's schedule for the past four months and the next three months. Maybe for openers we'll get an idea about April 15."

Falcone took a sip of his drink. "I'll do that. But I keep what I find to myself."

"Is that open to negotiation?"

"Agreed. We can talk—like this, with no notes, no recordings, no story—until we decide what happens next. I am doing this for Joshua, you know. Joshua and his family. Not for you."

"That's fine with me, Senator. I want to know what happened. Just like you, I don't think that things are as they seem. At least we agree on something. Nothing is ever as it appears to be."

"Meaning?" Falcone asked. He took another sip and contemplated Dake across the rim of the glass.

"Meaning that Joshua Stock was involved in something that made him feel guilty, something that may have killed him."

"I didn't say he was feeling guilty about anything, Dake."

"*Phil*, Senator, please. I mean no harm to your friend's memory. I am only following a method that I have learned from long experience."

"And what is that?" Falcone asked, adding an almost whispered "Phil."

"Start with the proposition that he *was* guilty."

"That may be your proposition. It certainly isn't mine."

"Don't get mad, Senator. It does no good. Just remember, if you begin with that proposition, you now have to prove he was innocent. Presumed guilty is where I always start."

Both men sensed that the talk had ended. After a few minutes of polite conversation, Falcone got up and walked to the door. "I'll let myself out," he said. He descended the stairs to the street in silence, letting Dake's comment hang in the night air, which was sweet with the perfume of the flowers that graced the rock wall surrounding the front of the house.

When Falcone arrived back at his apartment, he stepped out onto the balcony, slipped into a casual chair, and propped his feet up on the table where he frequently ate his meals. He was uneasy about having gone to Phil Dake's home. Maybe he should have gone to the FBI instead.

He dismissed the thought almost as soon as it entered his mind. He could just hear Harry Polanski: "No, Senator, I'm sorry. The matter's under investigation. Any congressional interference would only complicate matters, jeopardize the investigation and prosecution of Senator Stock's killer."

Oh, sure. The FBI would investigate. Just as it had investigated the Pan Am Flight 103 bombing. It had put the whole goddamned plane back together, piece by piece, identified the exact size and shape of the luggage that had contained the *plastique* and where it had been in the cargo hold. After we'd spent three years and a couple of zillion dollars, no terrorist stood in the dock on trial for mass murder.

Well, he wasn't going to wait years to come up with a goose egg. He couldn't answer the questions alone. He believed that Dake could get him closer to the truth than the FBI could, and in half the time.

But it had been too easy. Dake always worked solo. Other people might have different motivations, objectives. Dake only wanted the story—what he called the truth, Falcone thought bitterly —and he didn't give a damn who perished in newsprint. He didn't need Falcone; he could get the story on his own. It might take him longer, but he'd get it. And yet he hadn't offered any resistance to Falcone's proposal. Hell, he was the one who had suggested a division of labor.

Dake wanted the story, all right. But he wanted something more, something he didn't have—a line into the Senate Intelligence Committee. That's the way he operated. Get another source, another piece of gold. Hold it up to the sunlight. Bite into it. See if it's real or hollow. *Well, all he'll get out of me is fool's gold,* Falcone promised himself.

He stared out at the runways, marked by a string of blue lights that guided planes in from the night. Planes took off and landed in slow motion, big-bellied birds lifting, landing, with the gentleness that day never allowed. A stroboscopic pulse sent a thin white light across the balcony. In the distance, beyond the airport and the basin of the Potomac River, the line where the landscape broke and the heavens began was impossible for Falcone to discern. The blackness was sprinkled with diamond-hard lights, as if a shower of stars had fallen on a distant beach and were blinking in the sand until morning came and robbed them of life.

As Falcone sipped from a glass of bourbon, he felt a sense of loneliness settling onto him. He preferred to say that he was alone, never that he was lonely. It was a lie that he masked with activity, motion, not stopping long enough to reflect on the emptiness that had taken root inside him and spread like a cancer, hollowing out his emotions.

He finished his bourbon and went inside. Then he poured another and lay back on his king-size bed. He snapped the radio on. The disc jockey announced that a sixties tune was next—Simon and Garfunkel's "Old Friends." The song released a flood of emotions. His thoughts drifted, carried on the music's melodic waves to a different time . . .

The voice, high-pitched, nasal, and singsong, came to him with remarkable clarity. He thought he could reach out and touch her. In his mind, she had large almond-shaped eyes, long black hair, and a lithe body discreetly covered with a white dress slit high up the side. Hanoi Hannah. How he hated her.

"LBJ has betrayed you. He has lied to you and the American people, and you are asked to die for him. The American people must be told the truth. You must be willing to fight for the truth, not to die needlessly for lies. Your parents, your wives, your girlfriends, want you home. They want peace. Help end this terrible, unjust war. Everyone can be home by Thanksgiving. Help end the war . . ."

The words were sometimes different, but the message was always the same. Only the holiday and season of their departure date changed. How long had it been since he had heard Hannah's voice? So false, so mocking in its professed sincerity. And yet how he looked forward to its regularity. It always made him angry, and it was anger that sustained him, helped him resist betraying his fellow prisoners.

He knew the North Vietnamese's tactics, how they planned to break him. Establish a routine, change it, reestablish it for varying durations. Reward, denial. Pleasure, pain. He was confined to a twelve-by-twelve-foot cell, his bed just a few two-by-fours nailed together to form a plank that rested on two sawhorses. Each day a gong would sound at 5 A.M.: his morning wake-up call. He'd empty his bowels into a slop bucket, which he would later carry to a dump. Mornings would be used for interrogation, beatings, or idleness.

Lunch was the first meal of the day. It was soup—cabbage, mustard, or pumpkin—and a slice of bread. On odd days cantaloupe was substituted for the soup. Hannah would entertain the men with readings from antiwar books and speeches, then play popular American music.

From noon to 2:30 Falcone and the others were allowed to nap. Another gong broke their rest. Dinner, a piece of bread and soup, was served between five and six o'clock. Hannah was back with them at nine, just to tuck them in with some warm thoughts. Lights out—actually, it was a single naked bulb—was at ten.

Some days—and this was the only thing that was unpredictable—they would be interrogated. The Bug was a short, muscular man with narrow eyes and fat hands. He and his sadistic friend, Prick, played rough. They enjoyed inflicting pain. Their methods were crude and not particularly effective. Cigarettes and tea were standard fare for cooperation. Prick beat at least one POW every day just to emphasize the cost of noncooperation. In truth, cooperation was incidental to the need to satisfy his blood lust.

Frenchie, who was thought to be fluent in English but spoke only in French, played the debonair good cop. How he suffered to see the prisoners tormented so needlessly! He winced with every deprivation, every blow.

"Captain, would you like to be released? We are willing to make an exception in your special circumstances."

The death of his family was surely special.

"Stick it, slant."

"The doctor says you're in bad shape."

"I need a second opinion."

Frenchie was exasperated. For months he went through the

same routine, with similar failure, again and again. But he was patient. He sensed that Falcone was weakening. He had prepared a letter addressed to the New York Herald Tribune, *confessing Falcone's war crimes, expressing regret to the innocent Vietnamese people, and condemning the immoral imperialist aggression of the United States.*

He handed the pen to Falcone. Falcone hesitated. Two words, just two words, and he would be on a plane home, out of this hellhole. Maybe it was a lie. Maybe Karen and Kyle were still alive. Why shouldn't he sign? Twelve others had already been released.

But there were some who had been there longer than he had: Tyler Jackson, Conrad Moore, John McConnel . . . In a moment of rage, he took the pen and snapped it in two, then knocked his chair over.

"They taught you too well," Frenchie said, obviously disappointed, outwardly calm. He had come close. He would come closer.

The Bug was less generous. "Things will go bad for you."

Both men left the interrogation room, and Falcone was returned to his cell. A rifle butt thrust between his shoulder blades sent him sprawling on the floor. He struggled to his feet. He needed air. The stink in his cell cloyed in his lungs. The small hole cut near the top of the cell's wall for ventilation let no air in, no smell out.

A week passed. Nothing happened—just the daily routine and sultry, seductive, infuriating Hannah. Then the Bug came and took him to what Falcone and the others called the Calcutta Room.

After breaking Falcone's left arm, the Bug pulled both of his arms behind his back, bound them, and then tied his neck between his legs. He left him there for a week, untying him once, sometimes twice, a day, then binding him up again. Falcone had no chance for illicit communication with the other prisoners, no exercise, no baths, no light, and only half-rations. He began to hallucinate.

At one point Frenchie came to him, and Falcone actually signed a confession. He could later claim that it was done under duress; the shaky and illegible handwriting would be proof enough. But he felt shame and guilt that for the first time in his life his will had been dominated, his spirit broken. He had be-

trayed no one, but honor shone less brightly for him. He had reached a breaking point, crossed a threshold that he had thought impossible to cross. At first he reacted with despondency. He remained completely uncommunicative. Finally he sustained his rage and told Frenchie, Bug, and Prick that they'd have to kill him before they'd break him again.

Falcone's anger and courage fired the spirits of the other prisoners. They devised ingenious means to communicate. They sucked the air out of a cup, wrapped a T-shirt around it, and placed it next to the concrete wall so they could pick up a whisper, and they developed tapping codes. They swore at their captors, taunting them.

Frenchie decided that Falcone had been too impetuous and that "for the good of the camp" he should spend the remainder of his imprisonment in solitary confinement.

Falcone stopped measuring time. Days went unnumbered, hours uncounted. Months no longer mattered. He knew seasons, of course. The bitter cold left him shivering in his cell, uncontrollably at times. The furnace heat of summer caused him to become feverish, often delirious, and pushed him from hallucination to the edge of death. He slept fitfully. Dreamed. Woke in the claustrophobic darkness and did not know whether he was trapped inside the dimensionless walls of his nightmares. He held on to the borders of sanity by constructing elaborate castles in his mind, diagramming rooms, rooms within rooms, each filled with music, walls hung with paintings he produced with the fine and precise strokes of his imagination . . .

Impetuous—the same word Karen had used in an argument after he told her he had joined the Army.

But it was more than that, he knew. He was destined from the beginning to run along the knife's edge, to see how far he could go without falling, or, falling, how far he could drop without dying. Death was his destiny, so why not defy it if he could, taunt it, dare it to take him? He was going to drive full-force right into the heart of mortality—not like his father, who, chewed up by cancer, melted like a candle in a slow, painful slide into extinction.

The Calcutta Room gave him time, so much time, for self-examination, self-knowledge. He knew in his heart that more compelling even than his love for his family was the love of danger, a readiness to die for the feel of adrenaline rushing through his *veins. It was pure hedonism that fueled him. He was an addict, a junkie, who had betrayed his family in the name of patriotism.* Betrayal. *The word hung in his mind like a faint, ineradicable hologram that only he could see, when he allowed a stillness to take him . . .*

"Old friends sat on a park bench . . ." The lyrics tugged at him, pulling his thoughts back to his meeting with Philip Dake. His mind had wandered for less than three minutes. It seemed like three days. The past's ghosts had floated by him in their upward flight, dark birds released from a long captivity.

Falcone rubbed his fingers against his temples. A dull throbbing eased momentarily, then returned. He sat up on his bed and stretched his neck left and right, trying to loosen the knots that had gathered in his shoulders. Then he went to the bathroom, took several aspirins, stretched out on the bed again, and stared at the ceiling for a long time.

Outside, he could hear the sounds of distant traffic, but they were muffled, as if filtered through a sheet of gauze. Finally he fell into a long, dreamless sleep.

24

THE SUN'S FADING LIGHT filtered through the slats of the window's venetian blind. Viktor Borovlev loved his high-ceilinged office, which was on the third floor of the KGB's headquarters at 2 Dzerzhinsky Square. He had refused the opportunity to move his official quarters into the sleek steel-and-glass edifice on the outskirts of Moscow, in the suburban district of Yasenevo. The long, low lines of that building, which now housed the First Chief Directorate—the foreign intelligence service— looked too much like the CIA's headquarters in Langley, Virginia. Rumor had it that Nikita Khrushchev had approved the design as a finger in the eye of America, to taunt the Americans by implying nothing was safe from the KGB, not even the blueprints of their secret agency's headquarters.

Borovlev, however, felt no need to taunt the Americans. The modern building smacked too much of a bureaucrat's notion of cost efficiency—all those small cubbyholes, with their computers and spread sheets. They were breeding more bureaucrats out there. What good was efficiency without results?

Here, among the oriental carpets, the mahogany-paneled walls, the velvet-covered sofas, there was a sense of history. Here the very word *Lubyanka* sent a message, a chill. Here, one imagined, there was still blood on the walls of the interrogation rooms. And everyone knew that an image was worth more than a thousand efficiency reports.

A church bell in the distance wagged its mournful tongue. It told him that it was seven o'clock. But it told him much more. Mikhail Gorbachev had permitted organized religion to raise its ugly head in the Soviet Union, and General Secretary Voronsky had broken his pledge to suppress it. The Council for Religious Affairs had permitted more than twenty thousand churches to open their doors. Borovlev's secret reports indicated that more than a hundred and five million citizens believed in a divinity. There were only twenty million members of the Communist Party, and that many Bibles were now in circulation. It was just a question of time before the believers voted the Communists out of office. Like the trade unionists had in Poland! Like the mobs had in Czechoslovakia. Like . . .

He did not understand how Voronsky could be so blind and timid. Militarily, the Soviet Union was still the strongest nation in the world. But its empire had crumbled. There were coal strikes. Riots. Secession by the Baltics. Russian ethnics deprived of voting rights. Ukrainian thugs marauding around, armed to the teeth. And all the while, Voronsky kept imitating Gorbachev, turning a photogenic cheek, sympathizing with people's complaints, sending trade ministry officials off to Harrod's in London to purchase soap and panty hose! Anger spread through Borovlev like a poison. Voronsky had deceived him. He had worn wolf's clothing, hiding a sheep inside. Before he assumed office, he had approved BURAQ. Now he was backtracking like Kennedy had done in the Bay of Pigs.

Borovlev stood up from his large ornate desk, a czarist heirloom whose broad surface he had had inlaid with a hammer-and-sickle design, and walked to the window behind his chair, pushing aside its tasseled curtains and raising the blind. From there he looked down at a large bronze statue in the square in Marx Prospekt. It was of Dzerzhinsky—"Iron Feliks"—who had once held the avenging sword of the Bolshevik Revolution in his hands, purging hundreds of thousands of dissenters, traitors, in a campaign of terror. He had once been the feared head of the secret police, the

Cheka. Now he was a forgotten hero. Now he was nothing more than a target for pigeon shit . . .

Borovlev stared vacantly at the activity in the square for a few moments and then lowered the blind. He returned to his chair and opened the slim file that weighed on him like a stone. It was the final damage assessment report on Vyacheslav Kamamenov's defection to the United States.

The earlier reports to the Security Council had been inadequate, inconclusive. This one was no better. Swiss cheese had fewer holes. There was nothing but meaningless, evasive words to cover their stupid asses. Kamamenov walked away from a restaurant. No prior signs of discontent. No marital problems. No alcohol. "Yes, and no polygraph either," Borovlev muttered. That was a clear violation of the rules. And why did no one think it significant that two days before his defection, Kamamenov was observed praying in a church? A Communist scientist in a church! *"Su kin sin,"* Borovlev cursed, slamming the file back on the desk.

But what did they expect? Mikhail Gorbachev and his crony Vladimir Kryuchkov had systematically dismantled the power—and destroyed the quality—of the KGB. They had removed its domestic surveillance responsibilities. They had caved in to the yellow dogs in the Supreme Soviet who demanded the creation of a legislative oversight committee for the KGB—just like those in the United States Congress!

At first Borovlev had threatened to resign from the KGB rather than permit such an outrage. But he knew it would have been a futile gesture. At that time Gorbachev was very popular with the Soviet people and the media. Besides, KGB Chairman Krychukov would have selected some gelding to replace him. So Borovlev had decided to yield, remembering an old maxim: "There is one thing worse than having one's wish go unfulfilled, which is to have it fulfilled too completely."

He would give them information, all right. They complained about a drought. They would soon complain about a flood. He would give them so much detail that they would drown in the trivia. Yes, oversight was an accurate word for those who thought they would know about the KGB.

Borovlev picked up the receiver of one of the eight telephones on his desk. It was a direct line to the favorite of his six deputies. He asked him to stop by before he left for the evening.

Ten minutes later, he heard a knock on his door. "Come," he said.

The door was opened by Gennadi Dmitrevich Dyukov, who stood nearly at attention until Borovlev motioned him to a high-backed couch in a sitting area to the right of his desk.

"Comrade Dyukov, this report is worthless. It speaks of nothing but one stupidity after another." While Borovlev's tone was fatherly, there was an edge to his voice that the younger man found unsettling.

"Yes, Chairman."

"It minimizes the damage Kamamenov can do—has done—to our security. We both know that he has intimate knowledge of our new weapons programs, our negotiating strategies, the names of agents operating under diplomatic cover in Geneva."

Dyukov nodded, not sure exactly where the chairman was heading.

"And he knows what we have been getting on the SUN-DANCER program. He knows about *Canaan.*"

"But there is absolutely no way he could know his identity," Dyukov protested.

"True. But looking back now, do you think it was more than coincidental that within days of his defection, we were suddenly told that the Americans had penetrated the Mossad?" Borovlev's manner was no longer fatherly.

Confusion suddenly appeared in Dyukov's eyes. "Per—perhaps, sir."

"I ordered Ptor Kornienko to find the mole if he existed and arrange for his elimination."

"Yes, sir."

"But I said nothing about a United States senator. Or the Israeli ambassador."

Dyukov's face grew red. "He—"

"He?" Borovlev shouted.

"Colonel Cyril Metrinko, chief of our Foreign Counterintelligence Department—"

"Decided on his own to kill . . . ?"

"Once Yitzhak Rafiah threatened to go to the Israeli Prime

Minister, there seemed to be no other choice," Dyukov said plaintively. "Metrinko said that he thought you would approve."

"No other choice?" Borovlev shouted, throwing the file at Dyukov. "No other choice? You listen to me. It's one thing that we keep certain matters from the General Secretary. But it is another that you, Metrinko, or anyone else makes decisions that are mine to make! *I'm* running this service, not the Pamyat! Do you understand me?"

Borovlev's face looked like a blowfish, ready to explode. He rose from his embroidered wingback chair and turned away from his deputy. Going to the window, he stared out again into the square. "You are foolish, Comrade Dyukov. Foolish. Now there is another American senator we have to contend with. And this time, I don't want you to do anything without my express approval. Do you understand?"

Dyukov's jaw muscles began to twitch. He gritted his teeth, fighting back the impulse to explain his actions further. Silence was better, he assured himself.

Borovlev opened the door to his private bathroom, ran hot water into the sink, then lathered his face with thick shaving cream. He held up a straight-edged razor against the light, as if to see whether the blade needed sharpening. Deciding that it was adequate, he began to shave. It was common for him to do so before leaving for the evening. Shaving seemed to reinvigorate him for whatever he did in the nighttime. No one seemed to know what that was. Dyukov sat in silence, watching each stroke of the blade as if it were a guillotine slicing his own neck.

Finished, Borovlev splashed his face, first with hot water, then with cold. He uncapped a bottle of his favorite cologne, poured the liquid into the palm of his left hand, then clasped both hands together and rubbed them vigorously over his large Slavic face. Even from where Dyukov sat, he could smell the chairman. The whores at the Metropole had better taste in toiletries.

Walking slowly toward his deputy, Borovlev reached into his pocket. It was an innocent gesture, but at that moment it seemed quite ominous. He extracted an unfiltered cigarette from a crumpled pack and offered it to Dyukov. *Truce*, he was saying. "We are going to have to move ahead with BURAQ."

"But Comrade Chairman," Dyukov said, drawing smoke into

his lungs, then exhaling, "President—General Secretary Voronsky is adamantly opposed."

"*Today* he is opposed, Gennadi. But soon he will change. His strategy has been to purchase time with constituents by negotiating these meaningless agreements with the United States. But he buys retail and sells wholesale . . . He wants a chemical weapons agreement with the United States. He shall have it. But he will have to pay for it. It will be what the Americans call a cost-plus contract." Borovlev's lips cracked into a wintry smile. He walked over to his desk, gathered up a stack of folders, and stuffed them into a worn leather briefcase. The meeting was over.

As Dyukov left the room, Borovlev could not ignore something he had seen in his deputy's eyes. Shame? Guilt? Fear? Perhaps he had been too harsh with him. But doubt continued to nibble away at him as he snapped off the office lights and closed the door. Dyukov was too smart to have been so dumb.

25

FALCONE AGAIN FOUND McCloskey at work early in Stock's private office. A glance showed that not much had been done since Falcone's previous visit. He could almost feel the reluctance in the air, the feeling that if nothing here was changed, then somehow Joshua would be back and all would be as it had been before.

Falcone knew that feeling. He remembered how, after an action, after the body bags had been sent to the morgue crew, he had had to write the letters and then take care of what the Army called the personal effects. If you wrapped up the trinkets and the stack of letters and the photographs and sent them home to what the Army called the next of kin, if you did all that, then the kid was dead, totally dead. So you kept putting off the ordeal.

McCloskey greeted Falcone with the news that the FBI had just called. "They're sending over two agents to interview the staff," he said. "I'm supposed to begin lining them up for the interviews, beginning at ten." McCloskey looked at his watch. "In an hour and a half I'm in an FBI file."

Falcone explained that it was important for McCloskey not to mention anything about Joshua's computer unless he was specifically asked about it. In due course, Falcone would tell the FBI about Joshua's diary, but he didn't want to run the risk of having the contents destroyed. McCloskey agreed.

"I have another request," Falcone said. He asked for copies of Stock's schedule, phone logs, and personal correspondence for the past four months.

"Done," McCloskey replied. Falcone inwardly winced at his sudden burst of obsequious behavior.

"How far ahead was he scheduled?"

"About . . . Let's see. I'd say there are some appointments that go into October."

"I'd like a copy of those, too."

"It'll be spotty. Some appointments are just jottings."

"Fine," Falcone said. "That will be fine." He was impatient to get out of this office. He started to leave, then stopped and turned to McCloskey. "How are *you* doing?"

"I think I'm going home, into the family business. Retail sales."

"Before you pack your bags," Falcone said, "talk to me. And about my requests—they are confidential."

"Certainly, Senator," McCloskey replied. He smiled a faint smile. "And I will take you up on that talk."

Around the time the FBI agents arrived at Joshua Stock's suite of offices, Falcone was in the hearing room of the Senate Intelligence Committee, wishing that he could start doing what he did best: interrogating witnesses. Interrogation, as he had reminded Dake, was a Falcone specialty.

His technique was that of a classic prosecutor. His manner exuded strength, sharpness, seriousness. Usually his neck would thicken as his voice expanded, filling a hearing room. A witness could never tell whether Falcone would be sympathetic or hostile, and therefore could not anticipate what answers he wanted. Most witnesses quickly learned that they should come well prepared and play no word games. Falcone was the pit bull among the show dogs of the Senate.

But today he was unable to play prosecutor. The script had

already been written. The actors had their parts. Familiar roles would be played. A chemical weapons agreement was about to be signed by President Hollendale and Soviet President Anatoly Voronsky. Everyone knew there was no way in hell to verify it.

How could we distinguish an ordinary fertilizer or chemical plant from a weapons-producing facility? How many plants did the Soviets have? How did we know? Could they covertly manufacture and stock chemical or biological weapons? Would on-site inspection be sufficient to detect and discourage cheating? How many inspectors would it take, realistically? Were we willing to let that many Soviet scientists—meaning intelligence agents—roam around the United States, demanding without advance notice the right to inspect any American chemical plant?

These questions were the thrust of Falcone's brief opening statement, which set as a duty of the Intelligence Committee a need to satisfy itself that the treaty was "adequately verifiable." Falcone had difficulty masking his contempt for the phrase, which he thought to be so soft and malleable as to be meaningless. But he knew that the gas attack in Gaza last April had made his questions virtually irrelevant. The public wanted an agreement, and nothing he could say was going to stop them from getting one.

Falcone gaveled the committee to order as he sipped quickly from a cup of steaming black coffee that an aide had just placed in front of him. He welcomed the witnesses, turned to the vice chairman, John Christy, for his opening remarks, and then called on Jack Bickford, the DCI.

Bickford began his statement with cool professionalism. He was customarily articulate and unflappable. Falcone settled in for a long morning of testimony. He heard words, technical, arcane words, words familiar to the priesthood, but they floated past his consciousness. His thoughts were elsewhere.

Dake's questions would not leave him. Why did the FBI wait to join the investigation? Had it finally been ordered in? Was this an honest investigation or some part of a cover-up? What could Hollendale be covering up?

And where had Polanski been? How had he been reined in? Joshua had not been one of Polanski's favorite senators, but surely Polanski would not allow his personal feelings to interfere with an investigation. Polanski was paranoid about security breaches.

Joshua's murder, particularly if drugs were involved, raised this possibility. If any classified information had been compromised, was Hollendale reluctant to find out because it might have some impact on this agreement? Could the Russians be involved?

Falcone continued to turn over the endless possibilities. Maybe it was just a case of Bureau incompetence. Maybe. Somehow, he did not think so. But a logical explanation eluded him. At some point, he was going to find out from Polanski himself.

A loud, piercing buzzer interrupted his thoughts. At the rear of the room, a light showed over the numeral 10 on the clock, indicating that a roll-call vote had just begun. Falcone allowed Bickford to complete his remarks, expressed his regret at interrupting the hearing, and declared a recess so that members could ride the subway cars to the Senate floor to cast their votes.

It was a meaningless quorum call, a morning check to see how many senators were present. No one wanted to miss the vote. Records are important. World War III would have to wait.

After the last witness of the long day, after the last phone call, after a sandwich from the Senate cafeteria, after most of the people in the Russell Building had gone home on this Friday night, Sean Falcone sat alone in his office, staring at a yellow pad on his cluttered desktop. He had not told Dake about Joshua's request for information about the CIA's asset in the Middle East, code-named *Peg Blazer*. But Falcone believed that somehow this was behind the secrets of Joshua's increasingly secretive life.

There had been no way to tell Dake about *Peg Blazer* legally. Even here, in the security of his own office, Falcone did not want to commit the code name to paper. He wrote the initials PB on the pad and drew a circle around the letters.

So who knows what? Falcone asked himself as he looked down at the circle. *Joshua knew we had a valuable asset.* He drew a line from the circle and made a box around Joshua's name. *I learned the code name of PB.* Another line, ending in a box around Falcone's name. *The CIA—Bickford—knew and told me.* Three more lines, one more name. *The Mossad—I don't know. Yet.* Another word, no line. *The Israeli killed by the car bomb? I assumed it was* Peg Blazer.

Another box, another line. *Name. Who knew the name?* One line. *Who wanted to know the name?* No line.

The diagram on the yellow pad remained unconnected.

Falcone took off his reading glasses, rubbed his eyes, and stood. He walked to the window behind his desk and looked outside. Two elderly women were walking past the large water fountain in the center of the Union Station park in the rapidly disappearing light. By the time they reached the sidewalk on C Street, the light was gone and the fountain glowed like a mystical gold-and-red jewel in the darkness.

Falcone walked back to his desk, sat down, and resumed staring at the yellow pad.

Name. Joshua asked me to find out the name. It would have been more typical, in an intelligence matter like this, to speak of an anonymous asset. "Who is the asset?" Joshua asked when I came back from my talk with Bickford. "What's his name?" Joshua was after an identity. Why? Who would want it? He drew a dotted line from the Mossad to Joshua.

Israeli, car bomb. The Israeli officer killed by the car bomb was Peg Blazer. *Bickford's call left no doubt about that. He must be doing the same thing I'm doing—looking for a connection. The unanswered phone call, that crumpled telephone slip on Joshua's desk. I wanted to talk to Joshua about the car bombing. Joshua never answered.*

Joshua. Always championing Israel. That business at the hearing about SDI. He wrote the three letters at the bottom of the sheet but did not draw any lines. *I'll need to check. Assume that the Mossad killed* Peg Blazer; *how could they get the information? Even if he helped them, Joshua could not have helped them much. He did not have the name. I didn't have the name, only identifying characteristics. If someone had that information, someone in Israeli intelligence, he could easily establish the identity of* Peg Blazer. *But I did not give that information to anyone. My notes on the Bickford briefing are locked up in the committee safe.*

The knock on his office door startled him. He had been so focused on the puzzle in front of him that he had lost all track of time.

Tim O'Brien, a man whose large forehead seemed to be fixed in a permanent frown, was always the last to leave and locked up the office. "Got a minute for the bearer of bad tidings?" he said now.

"Sure." Falcone looked up, relieved for the break from his dreary task. O'Brien had been with him since the time he had run for attorney general in Massachusetts. He was the majordomo of Falcone's office, responsible for counting pencils, charting legislation, and giving psychological counseling to all the Type A personalities on Falcone's staff, which meant most of them.

"Things are going to hell back home. You've become the Invisible Man. The folks never see you."

"You mean the folks or the staff, Tim?" Falcone could feel anger flaring up. "You know, the staff treats me like Robo Cop, some mechanical zombie they program for eighteen hours a day, rushing around, smiling, shaking hands, cutting ribbons, speaking to high schools, service clubs—they never let up! I'm not exactly slacking off down here." Falcone flung the pencil he was holding across his desk.

"Sean, you spend all of your time on the Intelligence Committee. You can't tell anyone what you're doing down there, so they think you're not doing anything. Even if they knew better, they wouldn't give a damn."

"Yeah, I know. While America sleeps," Falcone shot back.

"Look, you can count every jumpsuit Muammar Qaddafi's got stuffed in his closet, but my job is to count votes back home, and I'm telling you, it doesn't look good. Morale is down back there, and it's lower than whale shit right here."

"What's the *staff's* problem?"

"They don't think you're going to run again."

"Why? Because I missed the vote yesterday to authorize the production of sterile screwworms to sell to Africa? Or a sense-of-the-Senate resolution on National Honeybee Day? Dammit, Tim, that stuff's a stupid waste of time!"

"Nah. You just don't seem interested much in legislating. Your people've got a sense you're going to bail out."

"What do you think?"

"I'm not taking any second mortgages."

"Great vote of confidence."

"Come on, Sean. No games. You'd been off the track long before Stock died. By the way, I know what you're up to, and my advice is to leave it alone. Stay out of his office. Let the FBI or the cops handle it. It's a goddamned tar baby, and you're going to get dirty."

Falcone stared at O'Brien for a long time, knowing that he was sincere, that he was right. "Tim, I've never walked away from a buddy, wounded or dead. I can't leave Joshua out there."

O'Brien nodded and let a deep sigh escape from his lungs. "I know. I know."

26

Fort Lauderdale, July 27

USUALLY A SENATOR'S
funeral is something of a major event. Flags around Capitol Hill are
flown at half-staff. Official proceedings are suspended. An Air Force
plane is requisitioned to fly Senate colleagues to the deceased's
home state to attend the service. No matter how loathsome a man
might be in his dealings with others, senatorial courtesy usually
compels at least a dozen colleagues to attend. Let a scandal touch a
senator's death, however, and any association with him is treated
like a contagious disease: keep your distance.

Back in Washington, the Capitol Hill flags were at half-staff for
Senator Joshua Stock. The Senate had at least done that. But little
else had been done publicly to memorialize the dead man. The usual
solemn elegies and lamentations from colleagues had not echoed in
the Senate chamber. Only Sean Falcone had entered a eulogy about
Stock in the *Congressional Record.* In death, Joshua Stock had become a nonperson, a nonsenator. Except here.

As soon as the D.C. police had released Joshua's body, it had
been flown to Fort Lauderdale for burial in the family plot. Although
the Senate had recessed on Friday, no formal delegation traveled to

Florida to attend the funeral. This was at the request of Joshua's
father, who had wished to spare the family, and the Senate, embarrassment. Today's memorial service was to be private, but Carlton
Stock had hoped that the Senate his son had served would be unofficially represented.

Only four senators had come. One of the four who entered the
small chapel on Laurel Street one by one was Sean Falcone. He
glared at the reporters milling around outside the chapel, then
turned his face away from them. They had ignored the family's
request for privacy. But at least they could not enter.

A minicam from WKIX was drawn up in front of the chapel. A
cameraman and a reporter with a microphone were lining up a shot
before a short, hastily erected pole on which a flag, at half-staff,
hung limp. The humidity threatened to reach at least ninety-eight
percent. The reporter spoke a few words into the microphone, and
the van's roof-mounted dish antenna moved. It looked to Falcone
like a giant obscene ear, cocked to pick up a vagrant, unguarded cry.

As he entered, he saw Cleo and the children getting out of a
limousine. The reporters rushed up to the car door, and the widow
and her daughters brushed by the pack, heads down. The children
hid their faces behind their hands.

Next Joshua's two sisters and brother arrived in rented sedans
and escorted their mother and father through the chapel's dark oak
doors. Carlton Stock was a fastidiously trim man who watched his
diet. Not tall, he was flawlessly dressed in a dark blue suit whose
herringbone weave was barely visible, a starched white shirt, and a
three-pointed handkerchief in the breast pocket of his suit. He was a
proud man whose grief had not yet been overtaken by shame.

His voice was strong as the minister led the mourners through
the various prayers. Falcone joined in the chanting drone.

"Friends of Joshua Stock, take joy in his life, comfort in his
death," the minister said. "We do not disappear. Could it be said
that the child disappears from the remembrance of his parents?
That we here, the living, do not cherish in everlasting memory those
we love but no longer see?

"Joshua, as we all know, was a great friend of Israel. According
to the Jewish religion, the blossom that has fallen from the tree of
human life flowers and blooms again in the human heart. And so it
seems fitting today that in the spirit of this ecumenical service we

should recite the words that sometimes precede the Kaddish: 'At the rising of the sun and at its going down, we remember them. At the blowing of the wind and in the chill of winter, we remember them . . .' "

With a clarity that astonished him, Falcone did remember. What he remembered was the last time he had seen Carlton Stock and his wife. The whole family had attended Joshua's swearing-in ceremony in the Senate. Joshua had invited Falcone to join them all for lunch in the Senate dining room. Carlton Stock had held forth, telling not just his table but everyone in the dining room about his son the senator and his son's friend the senator. Then he had begun a long, rambling story about the summer that Joshua had brought Sean home.

Now, in the fifth row of this sleek, air-conditioned chapel, Falcone sat between Senators Sam Magee (who looked as if he might soon doze off) and John Christy. Once again, this time softly and sadly, Carlton Stock was speaking about his son. Falcone did not want to listen. He wanted to remember.

He tried to turn his mind away from the present, as he had just turned his face away from the reporters. He hated the present. Hated Joshua's stained memory. Hated hearing the words that were trying to wash that stain away. Hated funerals. Since returning from Vietnam, Falcone had refused to go to funerals. He had known enough death. He had even missed the last rites of his wife and son. Strangely, he was grateful that he had been in a prison camp at the time.

" 'At the blueness of the skies and in the warmth of the summer, we remember them . . .' "

The last time Falcone had been to Fort Lauderdale was in 1961. He had boarded an Eastern flight in Boston. Joshua had been in the seat next to him. A smile started to creep across Falcone's features, momentarily easing the creases etched in his forehead.

He could see that summer so clearly now: he and Joshua drinking martinis in the Elbow Room and Omar's Tent, lying on the beach, sailing, driving to Miami, watching jai alai, getting brown during the day and drunk at night. Falcone had wanted the summer to last forever.

It was all quite by accident, but Falcone concluded that heaven had orchestrated it. They were sailing *Zephyr*, Carlton Stock's forty-foot ketch, about five miles offshore. A steady wind was blowing, and Falcone felt as if they were not even touching the water. His hair was blowing straight back; the sun kissed his face with its sensuous warmth. He closed his eyes and imagined that the *Zephyr*'s mainsail was the wing of a giant sea gull, transporting him into the clouds that billowed in the afternoon sky.

"Boat ho!" Joshua yelled, breaking Sean's reverie. He looked up, shielding his eyes until he could find his sunglasses.

She was standing on the deck of a thirty-foot Chris-Craft inboard that had gone dead in the water. She wore a white bikini, and her long hair was so light in the sun that it appeared almost silver. She waved to them with remarkable calm and good cheer. Her smile lit up a sun-darkened face. It was dazzling. Falcone could feel his heart jump in his chest.

Joshua circled her boat once before dropping his jib and mainsail. They sat bobbing gently in the green waves, ten feet from her boat. She tossed Falcone her line, and he pulled the Chris-Craft alongside. He reached out and clasped her right hand with his left as she jumped aboard. It was a moment frozen in his mind even now. Her hand was wet and slippery with tanning oil. But her grip was firm—not from panic, Falcone decided at that moment, but firm with self-confidence, expressing a love of adventure, a willingness to engage life fully and without fear. They clasped hands for a moment only, but an electricity surged through Falcone, fusing his entire being with this stranger in a graceful pas de deux. And he knew that he was going to love her.

Introductions were quick, as the three of them laughed. Joshua broke open the beer. They flipped off the tops in celebration of her distress and their rescue. Her name was Karena Sommers. She preferred just Karen. She lived in Minnesota and was visiting relatives for the month of August. With one more year of college at Wellesley, she planned a career of teaching mathematics.

Joshua told her that they were escaped convicts, had stolen the yacht, and were on their way to Havana to join Fidel Castro's army. She could come along or swim for shore.

Karen laughed at Joshua's preposterous lie but volunteered to accompany them. Falcone was sure she would have gone to Cuba. After consuming more beer, they gave up their flight to Havana and, with the speedboat in tow, made their way slowly back to shore.

That night they had dinner together at an Italian restaurant called Michelangelo's. Falcone could not take his eyes away from Karen. He was drunk on her laughter, her unbridled spirit.

The three of them became inseparable. They sailed, sunbathed, sang songs, made sand castles, lolled in the warm surf, spoke of disappointments and dreams, and allowed a special kind of love to fill them, knowing that summer would end too soon.

Falcone was smitten. Joshua never competed with his friend for Karen's attention or affection. He knew from the moment that they saw Karen that Sean wanted her. His friendship with Sean was the most important thing in his life, and he had no intention of jeopardizing it.

Then why did he do it? Why did he risk his career, my career, our friendship, for a name? Falcone tried to turn away from his thoughts. He knew that he had to go to Joshua's safe, to check it. *Betrayal. The worst of all words.* He tried to concentrate on what Carlton Stock was saying: "A good man, a good father . . ."

It was Falcone's mother who came first to mind: tall, blond, aloof, protective. As a child he had not known what her relatives meant when they told him that his face, like his mother's, was a map of Ireland. He had known she was beautiful, and, yes, her cheeks *were* the color of apples.

His father, Sonny, was short and dark, and everything about him was Old Country. He was a passionate man, in a strangely inconsistent way. Outwardly he was warm and gregarious, full of dance and music. But within the family there was no passion, only a cold discipline that demanded self-denial, work, and achievement. Sonny insisted on a strict moral code for his two sons. In the seventeen years before his mother died, Falcone saw his parents embrace only once, at a dance at the Elks Club annual banquet. He was twelve at the time. *Love* was a word that Sean and his brother could not use. "*Love* is a girls' expression," his father said at the dinner table one evening. "Boys say *like,* not *love.*" Sonny said this with neither meanness nor malice. It was a statement of fact, not open to question. Sean had glanced at his mother, looking for a hint of contradiction. But there was none.

And just as love was unutterable, so was the expression of fear.

———

After the ceremony, Falcone talked for a few minutes with Carlton Stock and expressed his grief to each member of the family, one by one. Cleo, her face covered with a veil, was trying to carry herself with a regal elegance. She succeeded until she saw Falcone. Then she broke, collapsing into his arms.

"Cleo," Falcone whispered as he felt her tears hot against his neck, "I'm going to find the people who did this to Joshua. I promise you." Then he hugged Joshua's daughters and left the chapel.

The other three senators were planning to spend the recess in their home states, so after a somber cab ride to the airport, they went their own ways. Back at Washington's National Airport, Falcone located his Mustang in the area restricted to members of Congress and Supreme Court justices. He got into his car and pulled out of the lot for the short drive to his apartment—a short drive, but not so short that there was no time for thinking about the present and the past. What had the minister said? "In much wisdom is much grief." Is it wise to remember? To lurk in the past, avoid the present?

When Falcone had returned from Vietnam, he had been carried like a laurel-wreathed athlete on a wave of adulation. For what? Surviving a prison camp? Had heroism come to mere survival?

He never liked the hero label, but it stuck. It carried him to the office of state attorney general and then into the Senate. It granted him instant status in Washington, wiping away the advantages that many of his colleagues had gained through seniority.

Falcone's motivations remained unclear to him even as he took his oath of office. Of course he wanted to serve his country. But, he asked himself, did his commitment to public service spring from a deeply buried burning desire for revenge against Congress, the liberal press, and the left-wing loonies who had burned the American flag while he and thousands of others were eating bullets and white-hot schrapnel? Was it the need to make good on a pledge that he had repeated like a litany in his hellhole cell: that he would never let America abandon its soldiers again?

Whatever moral anxieties he turned over in moments of solitude, they were of little concern to others. Conservatives welcomed him eagerly to their ranks. They put him on the lecture circuit, holding him up as a shining model for Americans to respect and emulate. Initially he basked in the floodlights of their praise, and

privately relished declarations that he was bound for the White
House while he publicly dismissed the notion as unlikely. But he
learned soon enough that past heroics, while giving him instant
political status, could not sustain it. Causes came in packages, and
packages were to be taken whole, like a dose of castor oil. All or
nothing.

Falcone found the social agenda of the right too bitter to swallow. He was not a born-again Christian. He had lost God on the
battlefield. He did not believe that prayers in schools were the salvation of our souls or our country. He could not bash gays or condemn
women to carrying the babies of rapists.

More troubling to him was the conservatives' chest-pounding
eagerness to send men into battle zones—Beirut, Panama, the Persian Gulf—without regard to whether the American people would
back them. He was willing to support people who were fighting for
freedom, but not with American troops, not unless there was a clear
consensus for the decision. He believed there should be no more
cannon fodder, no more deceptions. If the cause was worth fighting
for, make Congress and the American people go on record. There
should be no backing out when blood was on the line.

As doubts began to flock around Falcone, enthusiasm for his
political future cooled. His star, while high in the Washington firma-
ment, was no longer rising. Increasingly he was seen as a maverick,
and he gained wider popular appeal while losing political influence.

It was hard for him to determine whether his falling political
stock was the result of his disenchantment with politics as practiced
or of practicing politicians' disenchantment with him. Falcone found
remarkable similarities in the mind-numbing insanities of fighting a
war and the banalities of making laws. In Vietnam he had been
ordered to run like a robot from point to point, because his superiors
were seized with the mad notion that survival demanded taking
some strategic location. Usually it was a frigging pimple on the map.
He would lose fifteen men in the process, only to abandon the spot a
week later for another point, decreed more strategic than the last,
and begin all over again. Motion. Movement. Forward thrust. Lat-
eral slide. Strategic retreat. None of it made much sense.

Not much of what he was doing now made any more sense.
Budget and trade deficits climbed. Defense budgets dropped. German and Japanese economic power increased. Alliances shifted.

Drugs and AIDS spread like cancer. And all his somber, blue-suited colleagues could offer was some foolish amendment to a meaningless feel-good resolution, or a commission comprised of yesterday's patricians to solve a problem they were too cowardly to tackle themselves. Motion that led nowhere. Talk. Delay. Strategic retreat.

Perhaps that's what Dake had picked up on. Perhaps he had sensed that Falcone was unlike many of the others. Perhaps he saw Falcone drifting outside the orbit of political play-making, not seeming to care anymore.

Falcone reached over to snap on the radio. He swung onto Route 1, heading toward Crystal City. Then, hardly thinking, he kept going, past Crystal City, past the Pentagon. He crossed the Potomac on the Arlington Memorial Bridge and pulled up at the Lincoln Memorial, behind a bus full of Indiana high school students. Walking up the broad stairs, he felt his heart quicken. The glowing marble, which symbolized the political courage of another age, at this moment seemed out of proportion to the timidity and temporizing that Falcone witnessed every day of his political life.

That's what had driven Bob Hogate out of the Senate last year. When Falcone had asked him why he was leaving, Hogate had said, "Remember how when you first came here, everyone kept coming up to you with a plate of horseshit and asked you to eat it? And you did, smiling all the time?"

Falcone had laughed at Hogate's Missouri brand of humor.

"And then," Hogate continued more seriously, "remember how you asked for seconds? Well, Sean, I've just come to the point where I can't ask for seconds anymore."

Falcone got back into his car and headed for his apartment. A few minutes later, as he passed the Pentagon, slipped up the ramp onto Route 1, and drove along Crystal Drive toward his underground parking spot, he thought again about Hogate's remark. Maybe that was it. Maybe what he had been thinking was showing in his face. Horseshit. He couldn't ask for seconds anymore.

Maybe that's what Dake had seen.

27

FALCONE ARRIVED AT his office at 8:30 and told his secretary, Alice Moresi, to forget that he was in the building. At 9:05 he called Edward Fulwood, chief of the Intelligence Committee staff. Fulwood answered on the second ring.

"Ed. I'm going to the Hole to do some work. Give me about half an hour. Then I want to meet with you there."

"Okay," Fulwood answered. "Is there anything you want me to check out?"

"Certainly nothing that I can say on the phone," Falcone replied in a scolding voice. "I'll tell you over there."

Falcone descended a flight of broad stairs to the first floor, left the building, walked briskly along Constitution Avenue to the Hart Building, and entered a suite of offices on the second floor, where he greeted a uniformed guard. The guard, genuinely pleased to see him, waved him through the large glass doors. Falcone passed the reception room where he had met with Bickford and stopped at a door that snapped open after he pressed a series of numbers on an electronic lock. Behind him he could hear Ed Fulwood entering the suite, but he did not turn to speak. He nodded to three committee staff workers hunched over papers in their work cubicles and hurried on to the vaultlike classified information room—the Hole.

After registering with a clerk stationed near the entrance to the room, he went to the wall dotted with the individual safes assigned to members of the committee. He twisted the combination dial on his safe four times, opened it, and took out the manila folder that contained his *Peg Blazer* notes. The red transparent tape that sealed the folder looked intact. He put on his glasses, held the folder under an overhead light, and turned it to dispel the shadows. He could clearly see a hairline cut and a very slight misalignment between the edges of the sliced tape.

He sat down at a nearby table and closely examined the tape. There was no doubt. He opened the folder. The notes on the yellow pages looked like they were arranged the way he had put them in. If he had not suspected that the seal had been broken, he might never have noticed the cut. There was a stack of similarly sealed folders in his safe. Careful as he was, he knew that when he slit the tape with a fingernail he would not have seen it.

I did what Dake said to do: I presumed guilt. The suspicion had come to him during the previous night. He had thought about the other yellow page, the one with the lines leading to PB. No lines led to the Mossad. But if one did . . . It meant that Joshua had been tasked (he had instinctively used intelligence jargon) to get the name. And the only way Joshua could have gotten it was from these yellow pages, the briefing notes on *Peg Blazer.*

But that was impossible. Or was it? Falcone had slept fitfully, awaking just after dawn. Then he remembered. When Joshua was assigned to the committee, Falcone had shown him around the Hole. When they came to the array of safes, Joshua had said he could never remember combinations and always had to write them down somewhere. Falcone had sternly warned him not to write the number down. But the committee's security officer, a retired Marine major named Joe Lipton, had solved the problem for senators like Joshua (and Falcone): They could submit a four-digit number, and if it was technically feasible as a combination, he cranked it into their safe. "I use the two numbers of my birth year and the last two numbers of my office suite," Falcone had said, and Joshua had decided to do the same. *Presume guilt.*

Fulwood appeared in the doorway. He saw the expression on Falcone's face and prudently did not speak.

Falcone looked up and saw him. "You're early," he said, motioning Fulwood to a seat at the table.

"I saw you come in. I was right behind you. What's up?"

"Two matters," Falcone said wearily. "One's history. And the other"— he tapped the folder—"is so new I don't know what to do about it."

"How about starting with the history?" Fulwood said. He was a tall, broad black man with an angular face, gray-tinged, short-cropped hair, and unblinking eyes. He wore a light gray suit so impeccably tailored that the left sleeve at first glance did not seem empty. He had lost his left arm to a VC hand grenade.

"There's a black program, something to do with SDI. It involves Israel. Know anything about it?"

"Oh, one of those *black* programs," Fulwood said, a quick, tight smile playing across his face. It was an old joke between them. "That sounds like the program that was mentioned when the staff received a briefing on SDI projects about a month ago."

"What about me, the chairman of this goddamned committee? Aren't you forgetting something? I was never briefed on that."

"Well, we assumed that you knew about it, that you had been briefed on it in the past. The only new question is about the money. The funding still hasn't been agreed on. The Pentagon is still negotiating with the Israelis about the size and scope of the program. And the test."

"Test? What test?"

"All I know is that a test was mentioned by the briefing officer. We got no more on it, because it is sensitively code-named, and as I understand it, it is confined to Armed Services."

"But you know the code name, right?"

"I have friends on the Armed Services Committee. Just like you."

"Do you know the code name?"

"If you tried SUNDANCER, you just might be right."

"What else might I just happen to find out?"

"I'm told that it involves some kind of field test."

"When and where is this field test?"

"To my knowledge, Senator, no definite decision has been made."

"Any other news on this?"

"Pertinent to the committee?" Fulwood asked with a new note of caution in his voice.

Falcone nodded.

"It's . . . it has to do with Senator Stock."

Falcone involuntarily slammed his right fist on the table. Two women sitting across the room looked up. Fulwood tried not to show a reaction.

"We gave a detailed brief on this to Senator Stock, at his request. He said he had a double interest because of his membership on Armed Services. I got the impression that he wanted to try out our briefing against briefings he got there."

"You can get a date on this special briefing?"

"Certainly. It was all by the numbers, logged and so forth. Why?"

"I'm not prepared to answer that yet," Falcone replied. *Presume guilt.* He hesitated for a moment, not quite sure whether he should draw Fulwood into the picture forming in his mind.

"Has the FBI talked to anyone on the staff about Senator Stock?" Falcone asked.

"Not that I know of," Fulwood said, the note of caution still in his voice. "Senator, what the hell is this all about?"

"Ed, do you trust me?"

"Certainly, Senator. More than any other guy on the Hill. Maybe in this town."

"Okay. I am going to say something. Think about what I say. If you agree, fine. If you disagree, also fine. But if you do agree, I must ask you to forget what I am about to say. Okay?"

Fulwood gave Falcone another tight smile. "Sounds complicated enough to be intriguing. Start talking."

"If the FBI does ask you about Senator Stock, do not volunteer anything about this black project. I'm not asking you to lie. If they bring it up, tell them the truth. But don't volunteer."

Fulwood did not immediately answer.

"In response to what I assume you're thinking, Ed, I am not trying to cover anything up. As you will see when I take up the next item of business," Falcone said, pointing to the manila folder.

"Okay. No volunteered information. And as a bonus, Senator, I will pass the word that if the Bureau boys come here, I am the only one on the staff who is to talk to them."

"Thanks, Ed. Now for this." Falcone hefted the file folder. "A couple of weeks ago—I can give you the exact date—I got a special, extremely sensitive briefing by Bickford. It was one-on-one, here in the Hole. I followed the routine and put my notes in this folder, sealed it with the standard red tape, and put it in my safe." He pointed to the cut on the tape. "Don't touch it. I'm going to get Lipton to do a thorough security check on this. There may be fingerprints."

"Stock's?"

Falcone could not mask his surprise. "Why do you say that?" he asked.

"Just a hunch. Lipton and I, sometimes we check the logs," Fulwood said, nodding his head toward the door. "We noticed that lately Senator Stock had been coming in here a lot. Mostly on weekends. Well, you know Lipton. He's paranoid about security. He muttered something about 'senatorial Pollard.' He felt that Stock might be another Pollard, stealing stuff for Israel. He wanted to make something out of his suspicions with hidden cameras, tails, that sort of stuff. I told him to lay off until I got a chance to talk to you. Then, when Stock was killed, I figured there was another reason to talk to you. I planned to try to see you today. I figured we'd try to keep it in the family until we had our own damage assessment."

"I guess we'd better get Lipton in here," Falcone said.

Shortly before four o'clock, Falcone, Fulwood, and Lipton met in the Hole. They sat around the same table that Falcone and Fulwood had used in the morning.

"Okay, Joe," Falcone said, turning to Lipton. "What have you got?"

"Stock's fingerprints on your folder and on your notes. And, to top it off, the faint impressions of a ballpoint pen on your notes. It's obvious from them that he copied your notes."

"Who did the fingerprinting?" Falcone asked.

"I did," Lipton replied, looking at Fulwood.

"We decided to keep it in the family," Fulwood said to Falcone. "Okay?"

"Okay," Falcone replied. He assumed that Fulwood had not told Lipton about his request to keep the FBI in the dark about Stock. What the FBI called "liaison services," including FBI fingerprint files and the FBI forensic laboratory, were available, on call, to the committee, but Falcone had used them warily in the past. The staff knew that he preferred to keep the Bureau out of committee business. Lipton welcomed this approach. He was used to working on his own, which happened to be the way he liked to work.

Lipton nodded and continued as if his report had not been interrupted. "From a security standpoint, this is a bell-ringer, Senator. We have to assume extensive compromising of committee information. I certainly can see from what is in your folder that the material there is highly sensitive. We must assume that *someone*— and there may be more than one person—had a pipeline into the committee through Stock."

"What are your recommendations?" Falcone asked.

"I have three preliminary suggestions. One, that this specific breach of security be reported immediately to Director Bickford, whose agency is most immediately concerned. Two, that a damage assessment be done, starting with the assumption that Senator Stock had been doing this"— he made a sweeping gesture with his right hand—"during his entire tenure on the committee. The assessment would be based on an examination of logs showing Senator Stock's use of this room, and on an examination of the contents of the safes of the other members of the committee. Three, that our findings be confidentially reported to the FBI, with the suggestion that they may have a bearing on the investigation into Senator Stock's murder."

"Let's take them one at a time, Joe," Falcone said. "First, I'm telling Bickford. I'll handle that personally, since it is my responsibility. I'll try to do it in private, not as an official report from the committee to the Agency. Second, let's keep the damage control tightly held. I don't—"

"How tightly held, Senator? No disclosure?"

"No disclosure to anyone. You have my specific permission to open the other senators' safes, without prior notification, and dust the contents for Senator Stock's fingerprints. Do you want that in writing?"

"Not necessary, Senator. 'Tightly held' to me means I don't talk to anyone, don't interview anyone, don't do anything but snoop around on my own."

"Exactly. You must assume that no one has a need to know anything about this at this time," Falcone said, his glance taking in both Fulwood and Lipton. "Now, recommendation number three— the FBI." He paused and looked at the two men again. "I have reasons to want to keep the FBI uninvolved with committee business. Will you trust me on this, Joe?"

Lipton nodded but did not speak.

"I promise you this: Within twenty-four hours after you give me your damage assessment, I will personally pass it on to Polanski himself. Okay?"

"Accepted, Senator. You can expect a preliminary assessment by next Thursday."

Falcone ended the meeting by rising and going to his safe. He opened it, replaced the folder, and, turning to Lipton, pointed to the open safe. "Start with me," he said. He left the room wondering how he would keep his promises to notify Bickford and Polanski. Before he did that, he wanted more information. And he knew where to get it.

"Damn it, Colby, you've got to help me on this one," Falcone told the chairman of the Armed Services Committee. They were sitting in a booth at the rear of the Monocle, a haven for staffers and lobbyists. Occasionally senators who were looking for more than food would stop by and move through the patrons as if they were noblemen in search of vassals.

It was close to seven o'clock. The noise coming from the bar, on a level two steps higher than the restaurant section, told Falcone that the mating game was moving into high gear. Loud laughter, male and female, punctuated a steadily rising hum. Liquor was flowing. Ties were loosened. Primness was forgotten. The semidarkness softened the daytime's anxieties and blemishes. Everyone looked appealing in the shadow beyond the bar's fluorescent lights. An easy sexual languor was unfolding like a panther arising from sleep.

Falcone had picked the Monocle because it was a three-minute walk from the Russell Building. That was important, because Colby

Sugarman had a couple of steel rods in his hips and Falcone didn't want to add to his burdens. Sugarman enjoyed a bourbon or two. Sometimes three. Falcone wanted to make the meeting as easy as possible for him. The two could have shared a drink in Falcone's office, but it was too quiet there, and it was unprotected from the ears of foreign intelligence services. They could have gone into the Hole, but there was no bourbon there. The Monocle was perfect for what Falcone needed.

Nick Selimos, the maitre d', set them up with two rounds, the first one on the house. Halfway into the second, Falcone dropped his pretense at small talk. He was speaking in a normal tone, but he could barely hear his own voice. Sugarman, a crusty former Air Force fighter pilot with more crevices in his face than a dried-up riverbed, had a perforated eardrum. He cocked his head, turning his right ear toward Falcone. "Speak up, you young bastard. Can't hear a friggin' thing you're saying." Sugarman swore like a pirate; he was the only man in public life who felt free enough to swear on and off the Senate floor. Every time he cussed, his approval rating back home in Wyoming climbed another point.

"I said, I need your help. I know that the Pentagon has a project under way with the Israelis." Falcone scribbled SUN-DANCER on his napkin and showed it to Sugarman. Then he pulled the napkin back and shredded it, stuffing the strips into his coat pocket. "We've got the intelligence part of it. You've got the military part."

Sugarman nodded and said, "Yup. And it's held tighter'n a teenybopper's butt." He leaned forward and added in a hoarse whisper, "I'm breaking the rules, Sean, and they'll have what's left of my broken ass if you breathe a word about this program."

Falcone feigned hurt. Sugarman dropped his voice to a conspiratorial tone. "The Israelis are carrying on the testing for the anti–tactical ballistic missile defense system. You know that. Theoretically, that's so they'll be protected against a preemptive launch of a chemical or nuclear missile by one of the Arab states. But we're using that as a cover to conduct some facets of the testing for our SDI program—outside the laboratory."

"Jesus, Colby. You mean outside the law. You know Congress confined all research and development to the laboratory."

"Hold on, Sean. It's not all that clear. The U.S. can't test anything in space, but there's nothing to prevent any of our allies from doing it."

"Colby, that's bullshit coming straight out of those ten-penny lawyers at Justice."

"Maybe. But in any event, Hollendale authorized the project himself."

"Without a finding?" Falcone was incredulous.

"He doesn't need one. It's a secret activity but not a covert intelligence operation."

"That's a cute distinction, Colby. But Hollendale had to get authority to carry out the program. Who did he notify on the Hill?"

"He told me," Sugarman said. "I don't know who else." He took a long draft of his bourbon and coughed. "The program is in two parts," he said. "Research and lab testing here, and we've got a small amount of money that's been allocated for some field testing by the Israelis."

"How small?"

"A hundred and twenty-five million."

"For a small test? Why wasn't our committee prebriefed on this?"

"Come off it, Sean. You've got some loonies on that committee you couldn't trust with the car keys. This is one we simply cannot spread around. If it leaked, it would cause an uproar in Israel and the Soviet Union, not to mention in our own Congress."

"You mean we're letting the Israelis build the beginnings of an SDI program under the guise of another program, the antiballistic missile system we're giving them?"

"You've got it."

"So we're having them build an infrastructure for our SDI program. And we'll probably have to buy the whole thing back from them."

"You've got that right, too," Sugarman said. "But better them than the Japanese. There's no doubt in my mind that the Japanese have a very vigorous SDI program under way."

"This is getting complicated, Colby. Publicly, Hollendale has cut the SDI program back so far that it's on a life-support system. I've been calling it the strategically dead initiative. And privately he has this Israeli deal going—a program my committee doesn't know about."

"Be satisfied with a bureaucratic explanation, Sean. There are two parts to this. You got the signals collection part, the satellite photograph collection component, which is categorized as an intelligence program. The other part, which has to do with a defensive operational capability, belongs in Armed Services." Sugarman smiled and reached across the table to jab Falcone's arm. "So why don't we let it go at that—goddamned bureaucracy—and enjoy our drinks?"

"Because, Colby, I think that this project is somehow tied to Joshua's murder. Right now all I've got is a bunch of unconnected dots that I can't link together. But my gut tells me that Joshua was wired into that project. He was doing something with it, and got snuffed for it."

"From what I heard, he was doing the sniffing," Sugarman snapped, swallowing his bourbon in one long gulp.

"That's bullshit, Colby. He was doing a lot of things I never knew about, but dope wasn't one of them. Christ, he was my best friend."

Sugarman stared at Falcone for a long time. He felt a bond with the younger man. Falcone did not want anything for himself and he did not fear any man alive. Sugarman liked that. In his late seventies, depressed by the loss of his wife of forty years and in constant pain from his war wounds, he was preparing to retire from public life. He felt better about leaving the Senate because Falcone was there to carry his legacy.

"Joshua knew more about this than he had a right to," Falcone said, his voice sharpened by anger.

"Well, if he did, I sure as hell didn't tell him. Sean, I've got to go. I'm doing a debate on *Nightline* tonight with your liberal buddy Franklin. That sonofabitch is either the dumbest or the weakest man I know." Sugarman slid out from the booth with a low groan, which he tried to conceal with an exaggerated spring to his feet.

"Something I've never understood, Sean," he added.

"What's that, Mr. Chairman?" Falcone said with mock formality as he stood, signaling to Nick for the check.

"How a state like Massachusetts can send both a man like you and an asshole like Franklin to the Senate."

Falcone, flattered by the compliment, shrugged his shoulders noncommittally.

"I'll tell you one thing, son," Sugarman said, lifting his cane, a slow smile creeping across his leathery face like a desert sunset. "He's no Benjamin!"

As Sugarman turned, Falcone caught for a fleeting moment, in the tilt of his head, a glimpse of his robust spirit. Falcone's mind was drawn to the huge painting that hung in the reception room of Sugarman's office. It showed the senator perhaps fifteen years younger, tall, still rugged, jut-jawed, with white hair swept back from a tanned face. His cobalt blue eyes were laughing, and a fluff of white chest hair crept up over the pearl buttons of his blue denim shirt. He had his legs crossed, his jeans riding up to reveal the hand-tooled black cowboy boots that were his trademark, and the dramatic Grand Teton mountains in the background. The man in the painting was as vivid and sturdy as those mountains, alive and inanimate at once, defying God himself to cut another in his mold. As Falcone stared at Sugarman, the image broke and fled from his mind. Sugarman now stood, not quite steadily, still defiant, ready to shove his cane into the eye of the devil he planned to meet.

Back in his office a few minutes later, Falcone reflected on the significance of what Sugarman had told him. The plan was a brilliant stroke by Hollendale. The Intelligence Committee had several members who were strong supporters of Israel but pathological in their opposition to developing space weapons. In contrast, the members of the Armed Services Committee were unanimous in their desire to help Israel develop a defense against an Arab missile attack and also hoped that the emerging technology might later be used in America's SDI program. Hollendale knew he could trust Colby Sugarman with the knowledge that Israel would be doing the Lord's work, using an openly authorized program as a cover for the covert one.

Falcone had no doubts about Sugarman's claim that he had not discussed the project with Stock. But Joshua had been the chairman of the Armed Services subcommittee on strategic systems, which had authority over the program that had spawned the Israeli testing idea. He had been in charge of authorizing the "white" project. It was possible that he did not know about the black one. Yet he did know.

Certainly Hollendale would not have wanted him to know. But perhaps the Israelis had wanted him to know. And how did *they* find out? Was Joshua only one spy among many?

Falcone began speculating about the black testing program. Perhaps it would be worthwhile to backtrack to find out whether Joshua had been a secret advocate of it in the White House . . . *No. We all advocate. That's not the point. The point is espionage.*

It would be so easy to be a senatorial spy.

In the men's room of the Armed Services Committee office suite, Falcone recalled, there was a poster showing Soviet troops in Red Square. The legend along the bottom said, "Come visit us before we come visit you." There were senators on that committee even now who would nuke Red Square before breakfast on any given day.

But while they were worrying about Soviet espionage, along came Joshua. Just how good a friend was he? Drugs, the woman. Spying. Fingering a guy who blew up in a car . . . There was so much that his friend had not told him, so much that he had to find out.

28

IT TOOK RACHEL YEAGER nineteen hours, with delays, to fly back from Israel. She arrived at Washington's National Airport on the last Trump shuttle out of La Guardia.

She was bone-weary, too exhausted even to consider going into the Israeli embassy the next day. It was more than physical exhaustion. She felt soul-dead. She was tired of all the killings. There were too many of them. They kept coming in dark waves. And with every stroke, every killing, the water turned darker, colder, bloodier. Her violence had only begotten more violence. Now it had spread. And now it had struck at home once again.

She slept fitfully during the night, just on the edge of consciousness. She tossed in her bed repeatedly, trying each time to readjust her pillows in a way that might bless her with a few hours of sleep. "Please," she mumbled. "Please . . ."

At the very moment her prayers seemed about to be granted, the phone rang. It shrieked four times, five. It would not go away. She turned over and glanced at the digital clock on the headboard.

It read 10:00. Ordinarily, that was a civilized time for someone to call. But today it was cruel.

When she picked up the phone, she heard a man's voice. She recognized it as Zev Ben Ami's; he was the chief intelligence officer at the embassy.

"Rachel," he said, only half apologetically, "I know you're not scheduled to come in today. But something has come up, and I think we'll need your assistance."

Rachel blinked several times, not sure exactly what he meant. *What could have come up?* she wondered. *What kind of assistance? No more killing—please, no more.* "Zev, I've been up all night. Can't it wait until tomorrow?"

"I'm sorry, Rachel. Ambassador Dimcha called me. It's his request. Why don't you sleep for a few more hours and then come in shortly after lunch?"

"Okay." She sighed. "Okay." She pushed the disconnect button on the phone, set her alarm for 1 P.M., then took the phone off the hook. It seemed to take forever for the angry, protesting alert bell to fade away.

At two o'clock Rachel sat in Ambassador Shlomo Dimcha's office. Dimcha, one of Israel's most distinguished foreign service officers, was a short and slightly portly man who had an inexplicable penchant for double-breasted suits. Finely tailored suits, Rachel noted, but no craftsman could alter the lines to make him look taller or less round.

"Rachel," Dimcha began pleasantly, "this morning the State Department called to advise me that a Senator Sean Falcone has requested an invitation to the dinner Secretary Shanahan is hosting tonight for our Foreign Minister."

So? Rachel thought, remaining silent.

"Falcone is not considered to be particularly friendly toward Israel."

Rachel nodded, not knowing what this had to do with her. There must be a lot of senators like Falcone, neither friend nor foe.

"He was, however, close to Joshua Stock—perhaps you knew that."

Rachel shook her head. "No, Stock never mentioned his name to me."

"He has asked to take Stock's place for the evening. It strikes me as being quite curious. I realize how exhausted you must be from your trip, and I am truly sorry about the tragedy that has touched you—we all are—but I think it's important that you get close to Senator Falcone."

Rachel stiffened visibly in her chair. *What in hell does Dimcha mean by that? Spy on him? Seduce him? Or . . .*

Dimcha, seeing Rachel's reaction to his choice of words, quickly added, "I mean find out what he's up to, why the sudden interest in tonight's dinner."

Rachel was angry that she had been given no time to rest or grieve. She was not completely reassured as to exactly what Dimcha had in mind, or why in the world he had chosen her, but after staring into his dark eyes, she finally agreed. "Yes, Mr. Ambassador" was all she could bring herself to say.

Later that afternoon, she opened a file drawer marked *Political Leaders—Senate* and thumbed through the tabs until she came to the name she was looking for. The manila folder contained two single-spaced, typewritten pages.

SECRET

Subject: Falcone, Sean

BIOGRAPHY AND EVALUATION

Born in Boston, Massachusetts, March 1, 1940. Father, Italian; mother, Irish. Both deceased. Education in public schools. Graduated Syracuse University, 1962. Outstanding in football and boxing. Married Karena Sommers; one child, Kyle. Graduated Boston College Law School, 1965. Joined Army, June 1965: OCS, Fort Benning; Ranger School, Fort Benning. Began tour of duty Vietnam 1967.

On June 4, 1967, subject's unit was decimated by VC forces. He was severely wounded, taken prisoner, denied immediate medical treatment. Moved from various prison camps south of Lao Cai until sent in 1968 to camp outside Hanoi normally reserved by VC for pilots shot down in the north.

During imprisonment, served as inspirational leader of other prisoners. Developed codes for communication. Rejected request to pose with American actress who campaigned against the war. Beaten and placed in solitary confinement for most of the remainder of his imprisonment.

Wife and son killed in bizarre automobile accident in 1968. Subject refused early release for medical and humanitarian reasons.

Released with 22 surviving prisoners on September 24, 1973. Treated at military hospital in Wiesbaden, West Germany. Returned to USA October 1973.

POLITICAL AFFILIATION AND ACTIVITIES

Republican. Ran as law-and-order candidate for attorney general in Masachuetts, 1976.

Frowning and mumbling a curse against clerks, Rachel picked up a pen, corrected the spelling of the state name, and resumed reading.

Elected by surprising margin of 63 percent to 37 percent in an unusually liberal state. Prosecuted top members of Anthony DeVitale's gang. In 1980, elected to U.S. Senate after refusing to accept political action committee funds. Strong supporter of Ronald Reagan and George Bush. Considered conservative on defense, foreign policy, and economic issues; liberal on social.

While personally congenial and affable, subject does not socialize often. Avoids formal banquets and dinners. Dates infrequently. Drinks moderately.

FOREIGN TRAVELS

U.S.S.R., China, Germany, South Korea, Japan, England, France, Italy, Bahrain, Oman, Egypt, El Salvador.

ASSESSMENT

While generally pro-Israel, subject cannot be counted on as an unqualified friend. Political popularity insulates him against pressure. He is a close friend of Joshua Stock's, but Stock is unable to influence him. Open to persuasion.

PSYCHOLOGICAL PROFILE AND EVALUATION

See file #19700632—classified. Codeword: *Saturn.*

Preparation had always been the key to Rachel Yeager's success. Surprises were for amateurs. Tonight's assignment was only a social event, but Rachel knew that the Foreign Minister expected perfection, even at the dinner table. It would be her responsibility—at least part of her responsibility—to make certain that she was properly briefed on the guests she was likely to talk with. Falcone would be the most important guest at the minister's table.

Rachel glanced at her watch. It was 5:05, and she had to fight traffic to her apartment at the Colonnades on New Mexico Avenue, shower, dress, and be at the State Department by 7:00. She closed the folder. The psychological evaluation could wait. It would be interesting one day to read what the Rorschach boys in the Mossad's psychological unit had to say about Falcone, but she'd had enough for tonight.

In going over Joshua Stock's schedule, Falcone had winced when he had seen the State Department dinner for the Israeli Foreign Minister, Etan Narkiss. Falcone hated formal dinners. He inevitably wore a dark suit, rather than formal attire, to the few he did attend. Stock had been a more typical Washingtonian. Resplendent in the most fashionable tuxedo, he had appeared at a calendarful of receptions and dinners.

Falcone was sure that Stock would have gone to this one, if only to mingle with Israelis and other diplomats and, he thought bitterly, maybe to get in a little spying on the side. With this thought echoing in his mind, he told Alice Moresi to call the State Department protocol office and say that he would like to attend the dinner in Senator Stock's place. It was a request that he knew would not be refused.

The State Department, an eight-story, flat-roofed building, had never struck Falcone as particularly imposing—not in the daylight, at least. But tonight, as he turned the corner of C Street, the structure took on an unusual elegance, the floodlights casting its stone into alternating patches of light and darkness. Dark-windowed limousines moved rapidly up the curved driveway, discharged their passengers in front of the tall glass doors, and glided off to make room for others.

As Falcone walked up the driveway, a battery of television

cameras and glaring lights assaulted his eyes. He could hear muffled whispers of surprise as the network journalists assigned to cover the dinner caught sight of him.

Once, when a reporter had asked him about his habit of declining invitations to official dinners, Falcone had snapped, "They don't want my conversation, they want my vote. Besides, I rather enjoy the pleasure of my own company." It was the type of remark that was guaranteed to be quoted, one that would add to his image of forthright eccentricity. More and more he was seen as a recluse, a man who needed to repair to the solitary confinement of his self.

Washington, while ultimately a political city, is very much a social one. Public appearances are important, certainly in defining the people of influence. This show of self does not merely mean attending the flashy galas and benefits at the Kennedy Center and in hotel ballrooms, events that make the Style section of the Washington *Post*. These extravaganzas merely provide an affirmation of one's social desirability. They serve as window dressing, a display for the bureaucrats and worker bees who cough their way through the smog of morning traffic and during their coffee breaks read with envy about the life enjoyed by the beautiful people.

Influence is truly calibrated at the dinners in private homes, held by hosts and hostesses who want to celebrate their proximity to power. Falcone had attended such dinners during his first term. But he soon wearied of them. The circle of insiders was small and tightly woven—an obligatory Cabinet member or ambassador, a long-toothed congressman or a brand-new "golden couple," an art gallery director, a respected columnist alert for a subtle hint of headlines in the making. There was a richness about the setting—the expensive homes, catering by Ridgewell's, fine wine and champagne, cultivated conversations. But wealth was not flaunted. Indeed, any deliberate display would be considered tacky or *nouveau riche*. What annoyed Falcone was the aroma of arrogance that permeated those carpeted rooms, the notion that those in attendance were the high priests of a special cult, that the fate of their countrymen was tied up in their very thoughts.

Maybe it was. Maybe that was where the deals were cut between the Cabinet secretary and the Senate chairman, where a major story or editorial in the *Post* or the *Times* was born, where secrets slipped through wineglasses into word processors. Maybe the congressional hearings, the debates, and even the votes were the window dressing for the American people, just like the galas were for all the bureaucrats. That thought bothered the hell out of Falcone.

The eighth floor of the State Department, a suite of ten diplomatic reception rooms, was as elegant as the building's exterior was modest. The entire floor had been transformed from bland and tiresome modernity into the breathtaking neoclassicism of the eighteenth century. Falcone passed through a long receiving line outside the John Quincy Adams state dining room, where masterpieces by cabinetmakers—Chippendale, Hepplewhite, Sheraton—clustered beneath portraits of Jefferson, Franklin, Jay, Washington, and Adams.

Falcone greeted Secretary of State George Shanahan and Israeli Foreign Minister Narkiss, approached a tuxedoed waiter holding a large silver tray of cocktails as if it were an ashtray, and was handed a bourbon and water. He sipped the drink while peering around a room infused with the sounds of rising voices, clinking glasses, and noticeable gaiety. A string quartet floated among the guests, playing first Mozart concertos and then themes from popular Broadway musicals. Falcone spotted familiar faces from the congressional staff and the diplomatic corps. Reed Barrington III, the U.S. ambassador to Israel, was there. Falcone had met him once before, in El Salvador, and had formed an immediate and deep dislike for him. He was certain that Barrington held him in just as low regard but was much more adept in concealing his emotions.

The ceiling lights flashed on and off, the signal to proceed to dinner. Falcone picked up a small envelope containing the number of his table. He—*Joshua,* he thought; *not me, Joshua*—was at table one, the table designated for the guest of honor. Falcone finished his drink and entered the dining room. His eyes immediately moved to the fluted scagliola columns, which soared to a plaster ceiling decorated with gilded moldings radiant in the light. Eight cut-glass chandeliers hung like an emperor's jewels from gold-braid chains.

Falcone waited until the other guests arrived before taking his seat. Walking quickly around the table, he read the names on the engraved cards at each table setting. He was to sit opposite the Secretary of State and the Israeli Foreign Minister. To his right was Adelaine Brewster, the widow of the diplomat David Brewster, an aristocratic woman who devoted her considerable talents to the arts.

A Russian émigré comedian, the president and chairman of the National Geographic Society, and Mrs. Narkiss made up the remaining two sides of the table. After they entered and took their seats, the chair to Falcone's left remained empty. The name tag read *Rachel Yeager*. It meant nothing to him.

Rachel Yeager's appearance a few moments later, after the arrival of the guest of honor, was a breach of protocol, but no one seemed to care. She slipped into her chair with quiet apologies to the Foreign Minister: "Car problems," she said. It sounded implausible to Falcone, not because mechanical malfunctions were unknown in Washington but because he could not visualize this elegantly dressed woman driving herself to the State Department, or anywhere, for that matter. She was wearing a light blue silk dress that no doubt had a designer label and a five-figure price tag. The cut of the dress, tapering off wide shoulders to a V, drew attention to her taut breasts. Her honey-blond hair was pulled back into a neat ponytail. A gold herringbone chain holding a simple diamond was the only jewelry she wore.

Falcone did not focus on her face until she turned to introduce herself. Distracted by the quickness and grace of her movements, he was prepared to be disappointed.

"Hello, I'm Rachel Yeager," she said, shaking his hand with a grip that was unusually firm.

"Sean Falcone." He was unnerved by her beauty, but he tried to remain nonchalant. She looked at him with large sea-green eyes that seemed at once innocent and worldly. He could hear a sudden thrumming in his chest.

A waiter intervened by serving the first course, crab salad piquant. Falcone welcomed the interruption. Momentarily embarrassed, he was prepared to turn away. It took him several seconds to realize that when he looked at Rachel, he saw Karen. When he took her hand, he was transported back to the moment when he had first touched Karen's hand, as she stood on her disabled boat off the shore of Fort Lauderdale. He felt the same strength and self-confidence. The shape of the face, the eyes, the coloring, were nearly identical. His mind—or heart—had to be playing cruel tricks on him.

When the waiter stepped back, Falcone started to speak to her again, but Rachel was chatting with the Russian comedian. Falcone turned to Mrs. Brewster, knowing that he would have to wait until the next course before he could gracefully recapture Rachel's attention.

He felt awkward now, out of place. His refusal to dress in anything but a dark suit at a black-tie affair seemed, even to him, an act of puerile defiance.

Mrs. Brewster was engaging enough. She spoke knowingly of the domestic difficulties facing President Hollendale and the emerging role of the Chinese in commercial satellite launches. She inquired about his recent literary indulgences.

"Actually, I haven't read much," Falcone replied. "I recently read John Mortimer's autobiography. I enjoyed it very much."

"Oh?" Her voice insinuated disapproval.

"*Clinging to the Wreckage.* That's Mortimer's advice to those who find themselves capsized while crossing the English Channel. It struck me as a pretty good credo."

Mrs. Brewster emitted a throaty laugh. "I find him occasionally entertaining," she said.

Falcone felt himself sinking into dangerous conversational territory. During the first embassy banquet he had attended, more than ten years ago, he had found himself sitting next to Margaret Hempstead, who, he had not known, was one of Washington's most prominent socialites. Not knowing quite what to say, Falcone had asked her what she did. She had stared at him coldly. Finally, with acid dripping from every vowel, she said, "Nothing, darling. Absolutely nothing." She refused to acknowledge his presence thereafter, her silence being the most perfect expression of contempt. If Falcone didn't know who she was or what she did, he was hardly worth knowing.

Adelaine Brewster's ego was not nearly as demanding. "Actually, if you have the time—and I'm sure yours is quite limited—I'd recommend *Belles Lettres,*" she said. "It's a wonderful spoof of life inside a publishing house."

Falcone nodded, lamely assuring her that he would obtain a copy, all the while keeping one ear cocked toward Rachel Yeager's conversation with the comedian. He picked up only fragments. "London . . . Jordan . . ." She spoke of travel.

When she finally turned to him, he wanted to ask her about where she had been, but he knew that it would either force her to repeat herself or indicate that he had been eavesdropping. Also, he was on his guard. He assumed that whenever he spoke to a foreign national, even one from a friendly nation, his words were being recorded mentally, if not electronically. He might sound casual, but inwardly he was sifting his words, always aware that everything he said would find its way into an intelligence report. He sized up Miss Rachel Yeager as someone to be wary of. But he also told himself that he could handle her. And what harm was there in being a little flirtatious?

Falcone tried not to pry while doing precisely that. He wanted to know all about her, but there were too many ears, and tongues, around the table. The food continued to come: chicken with shallots and thyme, lemon rice, sautéed red and yellow peppers, and fresh green beans. Rachel indulged in the obligatory conversational waltz, confirming only that she worked at the Israeli embassy. Each time he pressed her for information, she deftly turned the inquiry back to him, giving the appearance of being interested in his life while protecting the privacy of her own.

She was, he realized, no casual Israeli questioner. She was a pro, undoubtedly Mossad. He wondered whether he would have gotten an invitation even if he had not requested one. Israeli intelligence officials certainly knew that he was looking into Joshua's murder. And this Rachel Yeager had been assigned to work him. Well, why not?

Acting like a shy high school sophomore—*don't act too eager,* he told himself—he asked, "May I—may I call you? Dinner?"

She did not answer for several long seconds.

This might be very interesting, Falcone thought, staring at her. *Maybe a pleasant encounter. Or another duel, which might accomplish something.*

Finally Rachel smiled and nodded. "I'm in the book. Well, the embassy is. Ask for Cultural"—a pause—"Affairs."

29

FALCONE OPENED HIS office's hall door to Dake shortly after noon. On a low table between two chairs in front of his desk were two tunafish sandwiches, two apples, and two large Styrofoam cups full of coffee. In a display of his prowess as a host, Falcone had removed the sandwiches from their plastic bags, put them on top, and placed a folded napkin next to each one. As Dake sat down, he removed the covers from the coffee cups with a slight, and unintended, flourish.

"When you say lunch at your office," Dake said, grinning, "you don't mean a catered affair."

Falcone nodded and smiled. "One of my Washington cultural heroes," he said, "was Admiral Hyman Rickover. I read in his biography that when he had the Secretary of the Navy come to his office, he served him cottage cheese, crackers, a very thin soup, and skimmed milk." He gestured to the lunch. "What did you expect? Take-out from the Jockey Club?"

"No. But that I have seen. It's a new status symbol."

"In lawyers' offices, no doubt."

"And in senators' offices. They aren't all like you."

"I should hope not. Shall we get down to business?" Falcone motioned toward a pile of packets containing sugar and cream substitute. Dake shook his head. Like Falcone, he drank his coffee black.

"Why don't you begin?" the reporter suggested, somewhat to Falcone's annoyance. Falcone had been determined to control the meeting, which he saw as a necessary evil, part of a deal he had made reluctantly and with apprehension. He wondered now if dealing with Dake was worth it. Yet to find out why Joshua had been killed he had already broken some rules. And he would probably break some more.

"I got his schedule for four months back and about two months forward. I also decided to fill in for him at a State Department dinner for Etan Narkiss, the Israeli Foreign Minister."

Before Falcone could continue, Dake grinned again and said, "I know."

"But it was a last-minute decision. How . . . ?"

"It's in the Personalities column of today's *Post*. Seems when *you* go to a dinner it's news. You were the only man there not in formal attire, and so forth. But"—the grin vanished—"did you learn anything?"

"Well, except for Narkiss's uttering the proper words of condolence, Joshua was not a topic of conversation. I did, however, get the distinct impression that if the Israelis could have had their choice of a senator to replace Joshua, they would not have picked me."

"Something you said?" Again the Dake grin.

"Oh, Narkiss made the usual seemingly offhand remarks about the Arab arms buildup. Shanahan said nothing. And I said something to the effect that if I lived near well-armed unfriendly neighbors, I would not only trust in God but keep my powder dry."

"Sounds like another one of your cultural heroes—Colby Sugarman. Were any other Israeli events on Senator Stock's schedule?"

Rachel, Falcone involuntarily thought. "My focus," he replied, "has been on Joshua's back schedule. Where he went. Who he saw."

"Have you seen anything that seems unusual?"

"Yes. I am, of course, assuming that he would have tried to hide any contacts that . . . that he could not explain. So I looked for repetitions. Was he doing something, seeing someone, with a frequency that seemed abnormal?"

"And?" Dake asked. He put down his coffee and took a bite of his sandwich.

"What stood out was a series of breakfast meetings with a National Association of Manufacturers representative at the Sheraton Hotel."

Dake nodded. "And?"

"Joshua wouldn't be meeting almost weekly with the NAM. And anyway, the meetings would not be at the Sheraton. They would be at the Hilton, where the NAM holds these tête-à-têtes with senators. I've been to one of them. So has just about every senator. But weekly? There's something phony about it."

They talked for another half-hour, but they did not exchange any more information. Falcone had decided not to tell Dake—or anyone else—about his belief that Stock had been spying for Israel. He wanted to maintain a balanced information trade with Dake, and he was enough of a realist to assume that the reporter had a similar goal in mind.

As soon as Dake left, Falcone made two calls without the aid of Alice. The first was to Bickford's private line to set up a meeting at 6:30 in the Hole. Falcone didn't want to use the telephone to tell Bickford what the talk would be about, but he was sure that Bickford knew.

He felt his pulse quicken as he punched 411 for information, asked for the number for the Israeli embassy, and then made his call.

"Israeli embassy," said a woman's cheery voice. *"Shalom!"* No embassy in Washington answered the phone more quickly or crisply.

"Ms. Yeager, please. Cultural Affairs."

In a moment he heard her voice: a lyrical "Yes?"

"This is Sean Falcone . . ."

"Yes, the man who may or may not—I believe you said maybe —ask me to dinner."

"You're right. I just may. Friday night?"

"Well, of course. Pick me up at seven-thirty."

She gave Falcone her address and managed to speak and laugh for a few more minutes before she said goodbye. She knew the darkness was coming over her mind and she needed not to talk and not to think. Only to remember.

She was tired, so tired. Of the traveling, the waiting at the hospital, the doubts there. She was tired of stalking the corridors, of the pain, of the fear.

She pulled the blinds in her small office and switched off the lights. The window looked out on the walls that made up the fortress called an embassy. She did not want to look at anything. The darkness was so deep in her now, the darkness called vengeance.

She could never free herself from the past, from the hatred others felt for her, not because of who she was but because of what she was.

Everything about Hitler's Third Reich, about the Holocaust, Rachel had known only vicariously, from the fragments her parents had told her of the horror they had witnessed. She had read about the death marches, the mass graves, the gas-filled showers. She could recite the names of all the camps—Buchenwald, Treblinka, Mauthausen, Auschwitz, Bergen-Belsen, Dachau . . . She had learned about the rows of warehouses where the Nazis had stored the clothing of the Jews they had murdered, including thousands of pairs of shoes of every size, even tiny children's shoes, all numbered. They had kept the hair of all the women they had executed, arranged according to color in the warehouses. She had tried to visualize the belching smokestacks of the crematoriums, but her mind was simply incapable of grasping the enormity of malnourished, stick-thin people being shoved into ovens, the ashes of her grandparents being used for fertilizer.

It must have happened. She had seen the tattoos on survivors. But surely it could not happen again, this monumental aberration of the human soul. And surely no one would mean her harm—she was a pretty, popular girl, liked by everyone—or her brother, Moshe. But hatred came, harm came. Once again on German soil.

There were times when Rachel wondered why she had let the desire for revenge so completely dominate her life. Wouldn't it be nice, she asked herself, to have a husband, children, an apartment in Jerusalem? Her thoughts wandered.

At the age of thirty-three, she had known half a dozen lovers.

They had been romantic and playful enough, but she had never considered any of them worthy of being a permanent partner in her life. Perhaps her expectations were too high. Maybe her brother's image was too big for any man to compete with.

Her eyes grew moist whenever she thought of Moshe. He had been a big man, a giant really, especially to his twelve-year-old sister. He was strong and gentle, protective and solicitous of her. She thought him a god, incapable of being destroyed.

Her parents had taken her to Munich in September 1972 to see Moshe bring home a gold medal with the wrestling team. She remembered every detail of the trip. Her father had said that Moshe's participation in what the West Germans called "the Games of Peace and Joy" was an important political statement as well as a personal triumph for Moshe.

The West Germans wanted desperately to repair their reputation for the crimes perpetrated against the Jews—against humanity itself—by Hitler. The Israelis, despite great emotional resistance, decided to participate in the Olympics, not to forgive the Germans or forget their unspeakable barbarity but to remind the world that Israel was capable of rising above hatred for a former enemy, at least for a few weeks. And what better place than in Munich, where Hitler began?

Munich had dressed up for the Twentieth Olympiad in bright, gay colors that exuded a festive spirit. In spite of the rise of European-based terrorist groups, the West German authorities were more paranoid about projecting an image of repression, with police dogs, armed soldiers, barbed wire, than they were about the threat posed by terrorists. On September 5, in the early hours before dawn, a group known as Black September had little difficulty gaining entrance to the Olympic Village, killing two Israelis—the wrestling coach and the weight-lifting champion—and taking nine others hostage.

The West Germans were stunned. The terrorists demanded safe passage to Cairo, where, they promised, they would release the hostages in return for the release of two hundred Arabs being held in Israeli jails. The Germans instead concocted a plan to cut them down as they transferred their hostages from helicopters to a commercial airliner.

The would-be rescue operation was completely bungled. As

soon as the West German snipers opened fire on the Black Septem-
brists, some of whom they initially missed, all of the hostages were
executed. Five of the bodies were burned beyond recognition in the
fire set aboard one of the helicopters by an exploding hand grenade.
In a matter of seconds, Moshe's body had been reduced to little
more than a bag of charred bones and ashes.

Rachel remembered the screams of her parents, their hysteria,
her own cries, tears, disbelief. She remembered watching a televised
memorial service held at the Olympic Stadium the next day, hearing
the somber music, seeing the lowered flags. She remembered the
cameras panning the eighty thousand people in attendance and then
seeing Soviet and Eastern bloc athletes kicking a soccer ball around
while all the world pretended to be in mourning. Her brother had
been slaughtered by Arab terrorists, and the best the Germans could
do was play Beethoven while Russian bastards kicked a soccer ball
on a grassy field!

Even at a young age, she understood the cruel calculations of
the times. Europeans catered to, even paid tribute to, terrorists for
fear of alienating the Arab world. They needed oil to fuel their
prosperity. If a little Israeli blood had to be spilled to ensure the oil
supply, well, so be it.

A brief pause, a prayer, a song. Let the games proceed!

Rachel remembered reading a program booklet that contained
a portion of the Olympic truce written by the Greeks twenty-eight
centuries ago.

> Olympia is a sacred place. Anyone who dares to enter it by
> force of arms commits an offense against the gods. Equally
> guilty is he who has it in his power to avenge a misdeed and
> fails to do so.

She remembered wondering, as Moshe's remains were lowered
into his grave, how much a body weighed without flesh, without
blood. "How much does Moshe's soul weigh?" she had asked her
father, who could not bring himself to speak—just as now, twenty-
one years later, he remained mute in the face of her cries.

And she remembered that she had vowed that day to avenge
Moshe's death.

As usual, a CIA security man accompanied Bickford as far as the anteroom of the Hole. Lipton was on hand to escort the director into the small conference room, where Falcone was sitting at one end of the table. Lipton stood in the doorway until Falcone signaled him to leave. He was not surprised. He had escorted Bickford to dozens of one-on-one meetings with Falcone, and the escort service always ended here.

As soon as Lipton shut the door, Bickford reached into the inside pocket of his suit coat and took out a single sheet of paper folded two times. He sat down, unfolded the paper on the table in front of him, glanced at it, and then slid it across the table to Falcone, who read:

Asset *Peg Blazer*'s death bears Mossad hallmarks. Unable to determine motive for extreme action. Assume betrayal by friendly source, via US or Israel, but betrayal in such cases never before resulted in execution. In meet 5/16, showed no anxiety. *Clock Driver* out of contact. He and we lying low on this unless told otherwise. DIX.

Falcone refolded the paper and handed it back to Bickford, who returned it to his pocket. "Chief-of-station cable. That's about our total knowledge, Senator."

Falcone could almost hear the question Bickford had not asked: *And what do you know about this?* "*Clock Driver* is another asset?"

Bickford nodded. "I am not inclined to talk about him."

"With me," Falcone said.

"With anyone, Senator. Our practice when something like this happens is to do what the cable says: lie low for a while. No moves in-country, or anywhere else if we can help it."

Again the unspoken question seemed to hang in the air.

Falcone finally spoke. "I'll tell you all I know, which isn't much. And I don't know where it fits. I believe it comes down to this, Jack: Joshua Stock may have been the finger man. I assume that he got enough information on *Peg Blazer* for the Mossad to translate *Peg Blazer* into a real name and identity." Falcone took a breath. "It began when Joshua asked me to get information about our asset in the Middle East. He said it was important, that he could tell me nothing more than that he had information, presumably trustworthy information, that the asset was unreliable."

"So you came to me," Bickford said when Falcone paused.

"Yes. I wrote the notes on this table," Falcone said, tapping the highly polished surface. "And I put my notes in my safe. When Joshua asked me about the asset—and he had an air of desperation —I told him I had checked into it and was satisfied that the asset was still on our side."

"You say he seemed desperate, Senator. Anything specific?"

"Yes, he . . . he grabbed me by the arm and asked me the name of the asset. I was shocked. He knew that I could not possibly give him the name, even if I knew it. And he should have known that I wouldn't know it. But he persisted. We were on the Senate floor, in an aisle. I got angry and told him just to tell his sources that everything was all right. And then . . ." Falcone's voice faltered. "And then he said, 'No. Everything is not all right.' When he said that he seemed agitated. No—looking back, I would say frightened. He was frightened."

"Somebody had something on him."

"I don't know about that, Jack. But I do know this: Someone, and it has to have been Joshua, got into my safe, broke the seal on my folder, and copied my notes on *Peg Blazer*. I have just satisfied myself on that."

Bickford was not a man of nervous habits, but he found himself rubbing the thumb of his left hand across his lips. It was a curious gesture, Falcone thought. After this slight pause, Bickford said, "Senator, when I told you about the asset, I told you we believed he was on the verge of giving us some information that we expected to be extremely valuable."

"Yes, Jack. I remember that. And that made me wonder more. Did you get the information?"

"No, Senator. And the assumption is that the asset was silenced in order to keep the information from reaching us."

"Jesus!" Falcone whispered. He placed his hands flat on the table, lowered his head, and spoke so softly that Bickford had to lean forward to hear him. "I had assumed that the Israeli was killed by coincidence or by a screw-up." He raised his head and spoke in a normal tone. "Now you're suggesting that he was killed to stop him from doing something to benefit the United States. That makes Joshua more than a spy. It makes him a willing traitor."

"Whatever he was, now he is dead."

Falcone remained silent.

"Have you informed the FBI about this, Senator?"

"No, not yet. I wanted to speak to you before I did anything else."

"My inclination as of this moment is to keep this tightly held. You and me. Further disclosure will do no one any good and could do harm."

"Agreed, Jack," Falcone said, rising and shaking Bickford's hand. "And I'm sorry."

"You have no need to be sorry. You did nothing wrong."

"I'll have to work that one out for myself, Jack."

30

Dake was alone in his home. For several hours he had been in the second-floor room that a friend had once called the Book Factory. Hunched over the keyboard of one of the computers, he tapped a series of numbers. He was making a computer-to-computer phone call to one of the many electronic databases that can be reached by specially equipped personal computers. CONNECTED appeared on the monitor screen. He tapped some more keys, entering into the remote computer the subscriber name and password that a Pentagon source had given him. In a moment he was in the restricted—but unclassified—database operated by the Defense Advanced Research Projects Agency (DARPA).

Tapping responses to instructions on the screen, he perused the electronic equivalent of folders in a locked filing cabinet in a locked Pentagon office. Occasionally he plucked a paragraph or two from the information cascading down the screen. Through commands made by his fingertips, he retained the information in a computer file named STOCK.SKD.

Dake now had six computer files devoted to Joshua Stock:

STOCK.BIO, with basic biographical information about the sena- tor's life and career; STOCK.MRD, with facts on the murder that Dake had got from Detective George Clarke of the District of Colum- bia Police Department's homicide squad; STOCK.INT, with the rel- atively little information he had obtained about Stock's work on the Senate Intelligence Committee; STOCK.ISR, with Stock's connec- tion to Israeli and Jewish-American organizations; STOCK.FAL, with all the information Dake had obtained from Falcone about his relationship with Stock; and now STOCK.SKD, which was filling with bits and pieces of information about what was and was not on Stock's schedule in the months before his death.

Dake paused for a sip of black coffee. The electronic world was timeless. But for him and other humans in Washington, it was 4:30 A.M.—nearly twenty-four hours, he suddenly realized, since he had begun his legwork on STOCK.SKD.

He had decided first to find out more about the suspiciously frequent references to breakfast meetings at the Washington Shera- ton with a representative of the National Association of Manufactur- ers. He started with a visit to the Washington office of the NAM. It had taken him only five minutes to talk his way past the receptionist and into the office of the director of public affairs, who instantly drew up in her mind a list of reasons why Dake would suddenly be putting the NAM in what she envisioned as the cross hair of a weapon called the Washington *Post*.

After he introduced himself—an introduction that was cer- tainly not necessary for any Washington public relations executive— Dake said in his gentlest voice, "Just to relieve you of any apprehen- sion, my inquiry is not focused on the NAM."

"The thought had not even crossed my mind," the woman said. "Please sit down. Coffee?"

"No, thanks," Dake said. He sat at the edge of the chrome-and- leather chair. He never felt comfortable in the role of celebrity journalist. But sometimes, he had to admit to himself, his status did produce information from the most unlikely sources. "I suppose I could have a researcher do this for me on the phone, Ms. Snyder, but—"

"Nancy. Nancy Snyder."

"Nancy," Dake repeated, smiling. She was tall. She had brown eyes and auburn hair that did not quite go with the eyes—a touch of color to ward off a few gray hairs, he decided. She was about thirty-eight, he estimated. And she kept fit.

"Sometimes, Nancy, I have to go way off on a tangent to find one small fact. As I said, this has nothing directly to do with the NAM. Believe me, your organization probably will not be mentioned in any story growing out of my"—he paused to add a certain timbre to the next word—"investigation."

She did not have a ring on the third finger of her left hand, but that meant nothing these days.

"Well, Mr. Dake, we're here only to help you. What's on your mind?"

He smiled again. "What is really on my mind at this moment has nothing to do with why I came here." He waited a minute but got no response, so he continued. "Someone of influence in town has continually listed on his schedule meetings with an unnamed member of your organization. I have reason to believe that he wrote down NAM to cover up"—her eyes widened at that major Washington phrase, he noticed—"who he was really meeting."

"How fascinating. Would I recognize the name of this man of influence?"

"I'm afraid I can't tell you his name. But—listen, I don't want to keep you from your work." He looked at his watch. "They keep a table for me until one o'clock at Maison Blanche. It's only two blocks from here. But I suppose you're booked solid for lunch for the next two weeks."

"Go save your table. I'll meet you there. But first I have to make a phone call," Nancy Snyder said. Being seen at lunch with Philip Dake at a power restaurant, while not something that could be put on her résumé, was a business matter. And that was the reason she gave her fiancé when she called him to break their lunch date.

Dake did not believe in telling sources exactly what he was working on; for journalists, Washington is a small town, and one never knows where words spoken in confidence will go. But he did believe in describing what he was doing as a kind of exercise in problem solving and then giving his sources some idea of the problem that he was attempting to solve. Sometimes they became not just sources but accomplices in problem solving.

"So, Nancy," he said over coffee, "getting back to the problem,

I have some dates on a schedule, and next to the dates the name of a hotel—the Sheraton—and the words 'NAM meeting.' "

"Well, as I told you, Phil, the NAM does not lease any rooms in the Sheraton. You can, of course, check this out, if you don't—"

"That won't be necessary. Of course I believe you. But where do I go from here?"

"May I make a suggestion?"

"Please do."

"Well, if I were your Mr. X, as you call him, why would I want to keep a record of presumably secret meetings in the first place?"

"You tell me."

"Because this is some kind of *official* schedule, one that a lot of people must see." She smiled what she believed to be a knowing smile. "Such as the schedule of someone at the White House."

"No fair making a guess like that," Dake said, trying to look stunned and a bit contrite. "I've told you all I can."

"Well, suppose I was going to see someone—perhaps a young lady?—in a hotel. I have to put down something. So I put down the NAM. It's safe enough, God knows. Then, just to throw off somebody—somebody like you—suppose I put down the wrong hotel?"

"The Sheraton," Dake said, a touch of irritability in his voice. Valuable time wasted on the pursuit of the obvious. "I already know that the Sheraton's the wrong hotel. You confirmed that the NAM does lease a room for small meetings, but the room's at the Hilton. So Mr. X puts down the wrong hotel. So what? We're back to square one."

"No, don't you see? The Sheraton is the *right* hotel. Mr. X is going to the Sheraton and covering up with the NAM entry on his schedule. Very cleverly, at the cost of a wonderful lunch, you have established that the NAM doesn't use the Sheraton. But that's not the point. Mr. X *is* going there. He knows that he can't change the destination—people see him enter, or a taxi driver or a doorman recognizes him. What he's fibbing about is who he sees at the hotel when he gets there."

Except for using the present tense in referring to Stock, Dake told himself, she had the answer that he had overlooked. "Thanks," he said with a genuine smile. "You've been really helpful."

They both told the usual lies about getting together for lunch again, and Dake walked Nancy back to her office building. Then he

cut across Farragut Square, taking the diagonal sidewalk that provided the best place for looking at the lingering few K Street women
who made a lunchtime picnic ground of the thin lawns of the park.
He crossed K Street and continued east to Fifteenth Street, where he
turned north to the big boxy building in which the *Post* was published. In the lobby, he chatted for a moment with a security guard
who wanted to be an investigative reporter.

Then Dake took the elevator to the editorial floor. In his small
office off the newsroom he checked his mail, tapped a few keys to
handle messages on his computer, and made several phone calls.
Then, for nearly an hour, he kibitzed over the shoulders of young
reporters writing stories against a deadline. His coaching, known in
the newsroom as the Dake Master Class, was considered a blessing
by most young reporters.

As the first edition deadline neared for most of the other people
in the room, Dake bid goodnight to the managing editor, national
news editor, and several others. After taking the elevator to the
lobby and deftly avoiding the security guard, he walked down a
concrete stairway to the corporate garage, where he found the cars
—most of them BMWs, Volvos, and Hondas—of the couple of
dozen *Post* employees deemed worthy of an inside parking spot.
Dake squeezed into his green MG, slipped a cassette into his stereo,
and drove off, a Bach violin sonata wafting through the air-conditioned coolness that soon engulfed him.

When he reached home, he flicked on the answering machine,
which was connected both to his unlisted but well-known number
and to what he thought of as his private line. None of the messages
was worth copying down. *Nothing from her.* Even when someone was
living with him, he was still living alone. He wondered where she
was, how long she would be gone, and whether she would come
back. *She could at least have called. The beginning of the end comes
when you stop being courteous to each other.*

He went into his routine: a workout, a salad and soup, an hour
at the piano, then up to the long, empty room for another session at
the computer, working on the book outline. To check out the Washington Sheraton, he would follow another routine. He had explained
many times to reporters in the Master Class, "Washington is a tight-
ass town in the daytime, full of bureaucrats who keep looking over

their shoulders. But at night and on weekends, the town loosens up, and so do the people at the outposts."

Outposts was a special Dake word that encompassed the many Washington places where a few people worked while all the other people slept or played. He knew the night people—the young military officers who did not yet have the seniority for a steady Pentagon day shift; the State Department officers who had angered their bosses and were being punished with rotten working hours; the cops who liked the nighttime solitude but welcomed an occasional visit from a reporter; the hotel night managers who saw so much, heard so much, and had so few people to talk to.

Dake arrived at the Washington Sheraton at 12:30 A.M. and found the assistant night manager in her office, looking bored. At 2 A.M., when she got her dinner break, he took her a few miles farther north on Connecticut Avenue to a new place, in the guise of a 1930s diner. They talked there over cheeseburgers, french fries, and coffee. Then they talked in her office, now dimly lit. When he left the hotel, he wondered once again how much the MG and the midnight air had to do with it and how much was just being Philip Dake.

Around the time that Dake arrived at the Sheraton, Sean Falcone was on the balcony of his apartment, gazing out at the starlit darkness and, for the first time in a long time, not feeling the dread that darkness so often brought him. He felt the night breezes blowing through his hair. He heard a mockingbird and, not quite sure of bird calls, believed that he had heard a nightingale. He imagined that he could smell lilacs from somewhere far below. *She is so like Karen, so incredibly like Karen.*

She had told him she would be waiting in the lobby of her apartment house on New Mexico Avenue. When he pulled into the driveway, she emerged, moving so quickly that she had opened the passenger door and seated herself while he still was opening his own door and swinging around to get out for her. *Probably,* he thought, *she hates men who open doors for women. Fine.*

"Lovely evening," he said, not knowing what to say. "August usually isn't one of our best months."

"Which is your favorite?"

"October. It's crisp, and sometimes there is a surprise, a touch of summer. We call it Indian summer. I don't know why."

He saw her at the edge of his vision as he twisted the wheel and pulled out onto New Mexico Avenue: her face in profile, her lustrous blond hair flowing onto a flowery blue blouse, her body looking trim in dark silk slacks that rippled in the night air. In that instant he sensed her more than saw her, and the image of gold and blue and black lingered in his mind.

"Lonesome October," she said, turning to look at him.

"Why do you say that?" he asked, again glancing at her, wondering how he looked to her, how his voice sounded.

"At the university, in American studies, we had a book that told about the United States. It was in English, of course, and it had a section about 'the American year,' as if, I suppose, America was so strong that it could *have* a year. The section was divided into months, and each month started off with a poem. I memorized them. October was 'the lonesome October of my most immemorial year.' Edgar Allan Poe."

Her English was flawless mid-Atlantic, neither quite Oxford British nor East Coast upper-class American. Falcone decided not to compliment her on it, sensing that she would take the compliment as a typical American affront to foreigners.

"And August?" he asked.

" 'The leaves fall early this autumn, in wind. The paired butterflys are already yellow with August.' Your unintelligible Ezra Pound."

"A madman. But that 'paired butterflys' business sounds intriguing."

Rachel laughed. "Actually, Pound said they hurt him—reminded him that he was growing older."

"Like I said, the man was crazy."

They did not speak again until Falcone cut across to Cathedral Avenue and then headed south along Foxhall Road.

"Don't think we're going to Georgetown," he said, unexpectedly sounding defensive. They were inching toward Key Bridge in the congealing Friday night traffic.

Although she did not respond, he spoke as if she had. "You said it was my choice. And Georgetown is not what I usually choose." He turned his head and was surprised to meet her eyes. "I picked Arlington. A Vietnamese restaurant." His voice rose slightly, as if he were asking her opinion.

"I will not miss Georgetown," she said. "And Vietnamese is fine with me. Don't worry about choices after you make them. My— my father taught me that."

Falcone's favorite Vietnamese place was the Queen Bee on Wilson Boulevard, in the heart of Clarendon's Little Saigon. Rachel had never been in this part of Arlington, but from the moment she stepped into cool dusk of the Queen Bee she knew she was going to like it. Her premonition seemed inspired by the way Falcone was greeted at the door. He and the manager, a slick-haired Vietnamese man with a mustache, rapidly exchanged words in Vietnamese. The manager's last remark ended with a glance at her. Falcone introduced her, and they then followed the beaming manager to a table near the rear of the restaurant.

"You are well known here, Senator."

"Ghan Nguyen is an old friend."

"Did you know him in Vietnam?"

"No. We met for the first time here." Falcone hesitated, as if he were drawing something up from a dim memory. "He and his wife and four kids and her mother all got out of Vietnam by boat. They were picked up by a Navy ship. Like a lot of Vietnamese, they wound up here. He was a schoolteacher in Vietnam, and when I met him, he was a gardener."

"He must have been surprised that you spoke Vietnamese. Not many of your countrymen learned the language, I understand."

"That's right. Ugly Americans and all that."

"But you bothered to learn."

"It was more or less a necessity."

"How much time did you spend there?"

Falcone picked up his menu and looked at it for a moment before replying. "A long time. Too long." He paused and said, "The grilled shrimp is good. It's served in a garlic fish sauce and—"

"No shrimp, Senator. I don't live kosher, but . . ."

"Sorry," he said, flustered. "I'm sorry." He was relieved when a waitress appeared at the table. "Would you like a drink first?"

She glanced at her menu. "Is the house white wine good?" He nodded. "And for you?"

He looked up at the waitress. "White wine it will be," he said, trying to sound chipper.

They did not speak until the waitress returned and filled their glasses.

"So, Senator, what do you recommend, upon reconsideration?"

"I first of all recommend that you call me Sean and that you recommend that I call you Rachel."

"Done!" she said. "And the food?"

As soon as he picked up his menu, the waitress returned. He could see Nguyen move to get a better view of her performance.

Falcone, speaking in Vietnamese, asked her if she were related to Nguyen. Blushing, she said she was a niece. She rapidly added that she had been a waitress for only a month.

"Did she tell you the expensive special of the night?" Rachel asked.

"No. Just catching me up on family gossip. I haven't even begun to order. She is a new waitress and somewhat on the spot."

"Because you are a special customer?"

"Not exactly. Special to the family."

Seeing that the waitress had not written anything on her pad, Nguyen hurried to the table and spoke sharply to her in Vietnamese. Just as sharply, Falcone intervened.

Nguyen laughed and said in lightly accented English, looking toward Rachel, "He scolds me more like a brother-in-law than like a landlord."

"He owns the restaurant?" she asked, a note of surprise in her voice.

"He is an investor," Nguyen answered. "An investor, he says, in me and my family."

Falcone said something in Vietnamese. Nguyen laughed, spoke a few words, and walked away.

"I told him to go back and check the kitchen. Now, let me try again. Chicken with lemon grass? It's a little like bean sprouts. The sauce is a bit hot."

Rachel nodded and Falcone said to the waitress, *"Ga xao xa."* He slowly went through the rest of the meal with Rachel, recommending and describing a dish and then ordering in Vietnamese. He realized that he was showing off a bit for her, and the thought pleased him.

They cautiously talked about themselves—she more cautiously than he, Falcone thought, even though they were hardly doing more than exchanging résumés. He tried to speak to her as he would speak to any new acquaintance, but he knew that she could hear him weighing his words, engaging her as a potential spy. Part of him stayed on the alert, but again and again, involuntarily (he told himself), his eyes met hers for an instant, and again and again it was she who turned her eyes away. Except once.

Toward the end of the evening, she left the table to go to the ladies' room. When she returned, twisting between the crowded tables, he stared at her, his eyes devouring her. She was breathtakingly beautiful. Her body moved strongly, sensuously, surely. She saw that he was staring at her, and for a moment she boldly stared back.

Now, back at his apartment, sipping a bourbon and feeling slightly light-headed as he looked down into the darkness, he conjured up that vision of Rachel moving through the cool dusk of the Queen Bee. And suddenly, dimly, he saw another vision. A chill rippled along his spine, his heart began pounding, and he felt the cold sweat of fear seeping from his body. The darkness was bringing with it the nameless, shapeless dread he had known when he had watched the videotape of Joshua's final moments.

31

Washington, August 3

FALCONE, IN OLD BLACK sneakers, red shorts, and a sweaty gray T-shirt emblazoned with a faded green *Celtics,* pushed open the thick glass door. Panting, he crossed the broad lobby of his apartment building. Running had become a metaphysical exercise for him. Running was being.

As he was about to ask the receptionist behind the counter whether there were any messages, she leaned her ample upper body across the high marble counter and whispered, "That man"—she tilted her head, agitating a towering pile of bright yellow hair—"will *not* go away." Falcone turned to see Dake asleep in a deep leather chair half hidden behind a pillar.

"Don't worry, Agnes. I know him. But thanks for the extra security."

Falcone walked over to the chair and placed a hand on Dake's shoulder, instantly wakening him.

"You're lucky Agnes didn't call the cops," Falcone said. "She believes her prime mission is to protect me, especially from bad characters."

Dake, fully awake, stood and put on the seersucker jacket

draped over the back of the chair. "I have found, Senator, that the best way to snare a politician is to sit on his doorstep on Saturday morning." He looked around the lobby. "Quite a doorstep."

"For more evidence of my life of corruption, come on up and see my apartment." He lowered his voice to add, "I assume you've got some news."

Falcone and Dake, both apprehensive about eavesdropping humans and machines, kept silent during the elevator ride to Falcone's floor and the walk down the carpeted corridor to his door. Once they were inside, Falcone led the reporter into the small kitchen, turned on the radio, and began making coffee.

With the never-ending melodies of a light-music station playing in the background, Falcone said, "I assume you felt that this couldn't wait until Monday and that you couldn't just tell me about it on the phone."

"Senator—"

"It's about time for Sean, I suppose."

"As I recall . . . Sean, you're the one who said that too many phones in this town are party lines."

"What have you got?"

"Stock was meeting someone regularly at the Sheraton. And it wasn't anybody from the NAM."

"I'm not surprised," Falcone said, half to himself. He still could not fully accept Joshua's double—or was it triple?—life. "How did you find out?"

"Persuasion, persistence, putting it together. That's all it takes," Dake replied, smiling. He sometimes acted cocky around reluctant sources like Falcone to soften them up, to make them realize that he had other ways of finding out what he wanted to know.

He recounted as much as he cared to tell about his early-morning coffee break with the assistant manager of the hotel. "She wouldn't give me a list of people who keep private rooms," he continued. "So I said, 'I can't blame you. But I'm not trying to pry into anyone's private life. I'm looking for private companies, lobbyists. What about them?' And she says, 'Okay. I'll give you a list. But I'll only put ten names on it.' "

"Ten?" Falcone asked. He poured Dake a cup of coffee and one for himself. "Why ten?"

"People are funny. You press them. They're reluctant to talk. Then, all of a sudden, they decide to give you some information, *something*, just to end the transaction. They feel the way you feel about panhandlers or the neighborhood collector for the Red Cross: Give them something so they'll just go away. Sources set some kind of value on what they give—not too much, not too little—and then they open their purse and hand it to you. 'Ten names, you pain in the ass, and not a nickel more.' "

"What do you make of the list?" Falcone asked.

"I checked it out through some databases I have access to. Seven of the names have major Pentagon contracts, which figures. Three didn't show up on the screen at all, so I suppose they are phony fronts for the CIA, the KGB, lobby groups. Who knows? But I filed them away. They may be worth following up someday." He handed the list to Falcone. "As for connections to Stock, I can't make anything out of it." He gave Falcone a few moments, then asked, "What do you think?"

Falcone skimmed the list and said, "There's nothing here that immediately rings a bell." He hoped he sounded convincing, for he had seen a name that did connect with Stock: Tri-Dynamics. For security reasons he instantly decided not to reveal his suspicion to Dake. He began searching his memory for what he knew about Tri-Dynamics, but he realized that if he hesitated another moment, Dake would interpret his pause as an attempt to withhold information, so he said, "Let me run it through some files I have. I'll get back to you."

"Fine," Dake said. He had heard "I'll get back to you" often enough to know that it usually indicated temporizing, holding back. He decided not to press, at least right now. Instead he accepted Falcone's offer of a burned piece of toast, looking around in vain for butter. He spread a paper napkin on the tiny table where they sat, knees almost touching, broke off the least blackened piece of the toast, confined the rain of crumbs to the napkin, and said, "There's a bit more. When I got back to the *Post* after lunch, I found a message to call someone from the White House. When she came on the line she said something about our date to jog along the Potomac this morning. Well, I don't jog. But for her I almost made an exception.

"I met her when she finished, about two hours ago—did I tell you I haven't slept for a while?—and took her into the Watergate restaurant. That was quite a scene. I was dressed so I could pass for a guest, but she had these teeny shorts and a sweaty, see-through T-shirt. Anyway, I had a date with her about a week ago and dropped a hook, looking for anything about Stock. She said she'd sniff around. She had called me at the *Post* from a pay phone, I was glad to learn, and had made up the jogging story. Smart girl."

"Sounds it," Falcone said. "But who is she? What did she have?"

"Slow down, Sean. These things take time. Well, she has a lot, in more ways than one. She's lovely. And a great source. She's the administrative assistant to the NSC's deputy chief of staff. She's not high on the totem. And every time she has a drink with me she's supposed to file a security memo saying she had a meeting with a member of the media. I think I've talked her out of *that*.

"She doesn't give me any real secrets or page one stuff, but like most of them at the NSC, she works late quite a bit, and things are usually looser at night. She gets in and out of the offices enough to get a whiff of what's going on.

"She told me that she had seen but not met 'the senator who was killed'—she has forgotten his name; so much for fame and notoriety. She said he was meeting someone from the NSC at the White House almost on a weekly basis. At night."

"*Weekly*," Falcone said, sounding surprised. "If she's right, that sounds as if he was reporting to someone."

"Right. And senators don't do that, do they?"

"The National Security Council is not exactly a haunt for senators, or anyone else on the Hill, for that matter."

"Well, it intrigued me, too. I assume that he and his contact were meeting at night so he wouldn't be recognized. The only reason she recognized him was because I nudged her memory and she remembered that he was 'the senator who was killed.' I asked her whether he seemed to skulk in. After I defined *skulk* for her, she nodded somewhat dubiously. Then she said, 'The funny thing I noticed about him was that he never looked happy. Always sad.' That was all she could tell me about his visits. I must admit that she doesn't tell me a hell of a lot. I mean, she's not the type who will smuggle secret papers out in her clothes for me."

"Did she say whether his visits were logged in?"

"They were not. Once, when she asked, she was told that the man—the man, not the senator, notice—was only a social visitor."

"That's bullshit," Falcone said. "No one gets in there without being logged. Unless there's a damn good reason."

"Or a damn bad one," Dake replied. "What do you think?"

"Let me take another look at his schedule," Falcone said. "It's in my office safe. I'll get back to you on it." He paused, thinking that he saw a skeptical look on Dake's face, and decided to change the subject. "There's something I'd like you to do for me, if you could."

Dake nodded. "Try me."

"I'd . . . I'd like to see the murder video again. Could you arrange it with your cop friend, Clarke?"

"I suppose so. It would have to be unofficial. May I ask why you want to see that horror show again?"

"You can ask, Phil, but I can't answer. It's an Intelligence Committee matter."

"You could subpoena the tape."

"I know that. But I don't want the rest of the committee in on it at this point, so I have to move unofficially."

"What do I tell Clarke?"

"Tell him what I just told you. He's been around this town long enough to know some questions don't get answers right away."

"I'll talk to him. But, Sean, I thought we were working together. This is a two-way street, you know."

"I can tell you this much: We're working on the same idea."

"Assassination? By a foreign agent?"

"You said it, not me. End of conversation. Let's talk about the Orioles."

When Dake left a few minutes later, Falcone resumed searching his memory for bits of information about Tri-Dynamics.

The company maintained a lavish Washington headquarters at the Bluffs, an exclusive enclave of three-story townhouses perched on a high bluff on the Virginia side of the Potomac. The four townhouses had gone on the market nine or ten years ago at $1 million each. No telling what they were worth now. *Joshua and I were there last spring.*

Falcone opened the door to a room off the kitchen. The door to his study was usually open. He had closed it because of Dake. He unlocked the mahogany rolltop desk, rolled back the scarred wooden cover, opened a wide side drawer, and took out a book that looked like a ledger. Like most politicians, he kept a journal in which he jotted down not his observations on life but practical information: the dates and topics of such mundane but voter-filled events as commencement addresses and ribbon cuttings. And names and more names—constituents, job seekers, professional fund-raisers, consultants, financial contributors, lobbyists.

Eventually, the dates and names got into various files and computer mailing lists in his office. But here was the raw material. He often scribbled a note or a date next to a name. Tri-Dynamics was here somewhere. He found it, and alongside it, the name Michael Rorbach. It had been last spring, a warm, starlit night last spring . . .

A uniformed guard stepped out of a gatehouse and scanned Senator Joshua Stock's invitation. "Okay for you and Mrs. Stock, Senator," the slim, bespectacled black man said. "But this gentleman"—he looked over his glasses toward Falcone in the back seat—"will have to wait here until I get someone inside to verify him."

Joshua began sputtering, but Falcone laughed and stepped into the guardhouse. He identified himself. Within a few minutes he learned that the guard had been an infantry sergeant in Vietnam. When Falcone gave him the name of the chief of the Capitol Hill police and urged him to file an application, the guard smiled and shook his head. He made a quick phone call, and while waiting for a return call, he told Falcone that he and the other guards called the enclave Middle East West. "A lot of Israelis—I see their diplomatic plates—come to visit Mr. Rorbach when he stays here. He comes here regular, from New Jersey," the guard said. "Two doors down is a townhouse owned by some Arab. But I don't see many visitors coming up here to see him. And then there's—"

The phone's ring interrupted him. He lifted the receiver off the wall and said, "Mr. Rorbach says he expresses his regrets and is coming out to escort you in."

In a moment Falcone heard a door open and saw a shaft of light spill out of the townhouse, about fifty yards away. The doorway revealed the figure of a man, who began walking rapidly toward the guardhouse. Silhouetted by the open door, he looked thin.

"Michael Rorbach, Senator," he half shouted while he was still ten yards away. "I'm terribly, terribly sorry."

"That's what I get for crashing your party on someone else's invitation."

"Not at all, Senator. Not at all," Rorbach said, thrusting forth his right hand. He shook Falcone's hand, then gripped his arm and adroitly turned so that they were both aimed toward the open door. "Any friend of Joshua's, et cetera. My apologies."

A young black woman in a maid's uniform met them at the door and offered Falcone a brimming glass on a silver plate.

"Bourbon and water, isn't it, Senator?" Rorbach asked.

"You make guests welcome very quickly, Mr. Rorbach."

"Please make it 'Michael.' How I wish this were a first-name town."

Falcone did not pick up the cue.

Rorbach pressed a button on the wall, and to Falcone's undisguised surprise, the door of a small elevator opened. "A bit like the director's at Langley, no?" Rorbach said, smiling. "Same elevator contractor." They entered, the door closed, and, turning to Falcone, Rorbach laughed and said, "A secure elevator, I am sure."

The elevator stopped at the third floor. They stepped out into a large, starkly white room humming with people and, somewhere, a string quartet. The room opened onto a large balcony that overlooked the Potomac. Against the city lights Falcone could make out the spires of Georgetown University, that odd Gothic touch on a glassy modern skyline. Rorbach led him to Joshua and Cleo, who had joined several others on the balcony. After saying a few words to the Stocks, their host turned back to the room.

"Quite smooth," Falcone said.

"He's a self-made billionaire," Joshua said. "Smoothness comes easy."

"What's he do?"

"He runs—or owns, rather—one of those big companies that make a lot of things nobody's ever heard about. Tri-Dynamics."

"I've heard of it," Falcone said sharply. "And I know you have, too."

Cleo Stock looked at Falcone quizzically, then saw the two men exchange glances. "Shh!" she said. "You're both showing your clubhouse-secrets look. Is Michael Rorbach KGB?"

"You can never fool Cleo," Joshua said. "I never tell her a thing and she thinks she knows everything." He pointed to the river. "We should be talking about how beautiful the Potomac looks tonight."

There had been no more talk about Tri-Dynamics that night. Falcone had meant to speak to Joshua about it, but he never had.

Now he knew, or thought he knew, that Joshua had been secretly and regularly meeting Rorbach, probably on behalf of Israeli intelligence. And Joshua had been secretly and regularly meeting someone employed by the National Security Council. Falcone was sure there was a connection. He was also sure that the connection had somehow been lethal for his friend.

32

P HILIP   DAKE'S   STORY
ran under a four-column headline—

ASSASSINATION, SPY FEARS

SPUR STOCK MURDER PROBE

—on the upper half of the front page of the *Post*'s fat, multisectioned Sunday edition.

The half-hearted FBI investigation into the murder of Senator Joshua Stock has taken a dramatic new turn. Intelligence officials, convinced that espionage is somehow connected with Stock's bizarre slaying, are now sure that agents of a foreign power assassinated Stock.

In the two weeks since Stock's death, the FBI has done little more than give technical assistance to District police. Taking their cue from the federal agents, local homicide detectives at first treated the murder as another of the hundreds of unsolved, drug-related slayings that have plagued the city.

But in the past few days there have been several previously undisclosed developments:

• Stock was "definitely" the victim of an assassination by agents of a foreign government, according to information that has reached the U.S. intelligence community. Previously, the assassination was only speculation. Now investigators are convinced that the killing was the work of one or more assassins.

• The killing was "pure stagecraft," an investigator said. According to a source in the D.C. Police Department, an attempt was made to cover up the assassination by making it appear that Stock was murdered during a drug-and-sex orgy with a still unidentified woman. An international search is on for the woman, who is believed to be of Middle Eastern nationality.

• Indications of assassination and espionage have been strong since the beginning of the investigation. But the FBI is still, in the words of one law enforcement officer, "keeping an arm's length" from the Stock murder investigation. For unstated reasons, the FBI has, for example, declined to assign agents from the crack Division Five counterintelligence squad. In fact, it took the Bureau two days even to enter the case.

• In the weeks preceding his death, Stock had a series of regularly scheduled meetings with an official from the National Security Council. The reason for these meetings is not known, but some investigators believe that there may be a connection between the meetings and the events leading to Stock's death.

• Detective George T. Clarke, who is heading the metropolitan police investigation, has established through D.C. homicide laboratory analysis that Stock did not voluntarily take drugs prior to his death. The drug found in his system was a strong barbiturate, apparently ingested in alcohol. "We believe he was drugged to make it easier to kill him," Clarke said. Such information would have come earlier if the FBI's world-famous forensic lab had been called in immediately.

FBI Director Harry Polanski was not available for comment on these latest disclosures . . .

" 'Not available for comment.' That lying sonofabitch," Polanski said, tossing the front section of the *Post* to the floor. "I was available. I just didn't want to talk to the bastard."

Polanski sat before a desk in a small office in the Executive

Office Building, adjacent to the White House. The office was the same hideaway to which President Nixon had gone in brooding search of solitude, away from White House aides and visitors.

When high-level executives go to their offices on Sundays, they advertise their zeal by wearing recreational costumes that proclaim *I could be having fun, but instead I am working for my country.* President Hollendale wore a short-sleeved green sport shirt, chinos, and scuffed loafers. Polanski wore a short-sleeved red knit shirt, spotless slacks, and a pair of white deck shoes. His arms were muscular and hairy.

"I'm glad we had a chance to talk privately about this," Hollendale said, shifting his gaze from Polanski to the crumpled paper. "But after giving it some thought, I think it looks like a phony story, a trial balloon. It hints a lot, but it doesn't say much. I think you're making more out of it than it's worth."

"I strongly disagree, Mr. President. Dake always writes less than he knows, or thinks he knows. He's spiraling in on this. He's been snooping around some Pentagon computer files, going through DARPA contract awards."

"DARPA?"

"Defense Advanced Research Projects Agency," Polanski replied. The President's ignorance of government acronyms always amazed him. "I have an idea he's looking for connections between Stock and contracts with Israeli companies. He may be on to something. I can feel it. I've got to talk to him, to keep the Stock investigation centered on me and the Bureau. We've got to keep the case away from the Oval Office."

"Use your judgment, Harry. Just don't make this thing any worse than it already is."

"I'll take care of it," Polanski said, rising from the straight-backed chair. He hated this spartan room of ghosts and bad memories. "Will there be anything else, Mr. President?"

"I don't believe so, Harry. Thanks for stopping by." Hollendale extended his right hand across the pristine surface of the desk. "I hope you'll be able to get at least a couple of hours on your boat."

"Not today, Mr. President. I'm going to be busy."

As soon as Polanski reached his seventh-floor office, he summoned the FBI duty officer and ordered him to find Philip Dake.

"Do you want him apprehended, sir?" the agent asked.

"I want you to find him and tell him that I want to see him as soon as possible."

"Today, sir?"

"Yes, goddammit. Today. Right away today."

Forty-six minutes later, the duty officer and two other agents ushered Dake into Polanski's office and silently left. Polanski rose, walked around his desk, and shook Dake's hand. The journalist wore white slacks and a light blue linen jacket over his button-down white shirt, which was open at the neck. He looked like a yacht owner about to interview a prospective captain.

"I would have come without the escort, Harry," he said. Turning, he strode to a couch across from Polanski's desk, sat down, looked around the large room, and took a notebook from a jacket pocket. He opened the notebook, unsheathed a silver ballpoint pen from his shirt pocket, and leaned back against the slowly yielding black leather.

Polanski sat in a matching black leather, chrome-framed chair next to the couch. He put his feet up on a glass table, also framed in chrome. "I read your story," he said. "And I—"

"It would have been a better story if you had returned my calls," Dake interrupted. "And are you talking to me now for publication?" He waved his notebook. "Or did your boys just bring me in for a chat?"

"Let's call it friendly advice, Phil. On background. First of all, you're painting an unfair picture. We're working as hard as hell on Stock's murder. But we are also trying not to alarm anyone or unjustly accuse anyone. We are using all our investigative resources on this. Trust me."

"You're using Division Five?"

"Yes."

"Starting when? Today?"

Polanski laughed. "No comment."

"You were slow getting in, Harry. You can't deny that."

"There are wheels within wheels, Phil. You know that. Other people, other matters."

Before Dake could respond, Polanski lowered his voice and

said, "There's one thing, for instance . . . I shouldn't even be *thinking* about talking to you about this." He leaned toward Dake and, still half whispering, added, "This is totally off the record. We are investigating Sean Falcone."

"What?" Dake exclaimed. "Why? What for?"

"We're pursuing every lead," Polanski said, giving an answer that Dake had first heard as a young police reporter covering the Washington suburbs. He did not believe it then and he certainly did not believe it now.

Polanski slumped back and began talking in his gruff normal voice. He switched to statistics, one of his favorite diversions: the number of overtime hours put in by the agents assigned to the case; the number of background interviews conducted by agents; the number of Bureau offices working on the case.

Dake had never trusted Polanski, and he trusted him even less when he began acting as if he was confiding in Dake. *I'm being fed something,* Dake thought. But he said, "Falcone. Get back to Falcone."

"We happened to discover," Polanski said, "that Falcone had contact with one Michael Rorbach, the president of a company called Tri-Dynamics. Our information is that Tri-Dynamics is an Israeli intelligence front. We believe that it was set up a few years ago, around the time the Israelis began running Pollard. Rorbach was born in Bialystok, which I guess is now part of Poland, but he grew up in Israel and immigrated here, and he's done all right. He's a goddamned billionaire."

"So what? So a senator has contact with a guy with big Israeli connections."

"We don't know what it means yet," Polanski continued, as if he had not heard Dake. "But we're investigating the possibility that Stock and Falcone were leaking information to the Israelis. Stock and Rorbach go back a long way. Check out the campaign finance records on that one."

"What about Falcone and Rorbach?" Dake asked.

"Both Stock and Falcone are pretty cute about meeting with shady characters. But we've pinned them, for instance, at a party last spring at Rorbach's house in Virginia. You've heard of the Bluffs? Those million-buck townhouses? One of Rorbach's places is there. His main estate is in New Jersey. He also has places in Palm Beach and Paris."

"Tri-Dynamics," Dake said. "Tell me more about that."

"You tell me."

"What does that mean?"

"No big deal, Phil. But when a hacker targets the DARPA mainframe, our tech boys know about it. That's all."

"You're tapping my phone."

"Wrong. But we *are* keeping track of the phone numbers used to enter the DARPA computer and ask about Tri-Dynamics."

"Since when?"

"Since we first started wondering about Tri-Dynamics and Stock and Falcone. But I'm not going to tell you any more about that. And I'm not telling you how we monitor hackers trying to log on to Pentagon computers." Polanski again leaned forward and spoke softly. "But I'll tell you this: Your pal Falcone knows all about Tri-Dynamics and the Israeli connection."

"How the hell do you know that?"

"We cooperated with the CIA when one of their guys did a briefing for the Intelligence Committee on Israeli espionage activities in the United States. Tri-Dynamics—well, I guess you know this —has some big U.S. defense contracts."

"Nothing wrong with that," Dake said. "From what I could see on that DARPA computer, Tri-Dynamics is just one of several Israeli companies with Pentagon contracts."

"What's wrong," Polanski said, "is espionage."

"Suspicions of espionage," Dake responded. "Did Falcone and Stock know about the suspicions before they were linked to Rorbach?"

"Absolutely. The CIA briefing was just before the party at the Bluffs."

"So what you're saying—or *not* saying—is that two United States senators, both of them on the Intelligence Committee, might be spying for Israel."

"Maybe not just Israel."

"Maybes don't mean a damn thing, Harry," Dake said, closing his notebook and replacing his pen in his shirt pocket.

"Look, we don't know what the hell Falcone's involvement with Tri-Dynamics and Rorbach means in terms of espionage. I'll admit that. And we don't know what those two buddies Falcone and Stock were up to."

Polanski stood and walked to the window, eyeing the clear sky, wondering if he might just be able to get an hour or two on the boat. He turned to face Dake, who had risen.

"Stock's very dead," Polanski said. "Dead in a way that senators usually don't die. And Falcone's very powerful. You don't move against a senator, living or dead, lightly. So we're low-balling this right now."

"Because the President is putting his relations with the Hill ahead of national security?"

"Negative," Polanski said, scowling at Dake. "The President is not in this loop. We're going slow and cautious because one of our most important national security programs may have been compromised. And we don't want to get the KGB interested in trying to know what we know. A visible FBI counterintelligence investigation could give away a very complex, very important intelligence operation." Polanski paused. "As far as Falcone is concerned, we're using all investigative means," he said. The remark, as the director knew, translated to Dake as *wiretaps.*

When Dake stepped out of Polanski's office, one of the plainclothes security men in the anteroom slipped through the open door and closed it behind him. The other escorted Dake through two other rooms in the director's suite and into a corridor. As they neared the elevator, the escort said, "I will be accompanying you to the visitor clearance area. Another agent will meet you in the courtyard." Dake smiled at the image that sprang to his mind: knights assembling in the courtyard of the castle, checking their lances before going off to fight for God and king.

Officially, the FBI is a responsibility of the Department of Justice. But architecturally, the colossal FBI castle of beige stone dwarfs the old granite Justice building nearby, on Constitution Avenue. FBI headquarters, named after J. Edgar Hoover, is a huge box of a building that fronts on Pennsylvania Avenue, squarely between its budgetary overseers on Capitol Hill and its presidential bosses in the White House.

Hoover had taken a personal interest in the design of the building, and some of his beleaguered personality, Dake thought, could be seen in it: Great, massive blocks were squared around a central courtyard paved in stone. His seemingly contradictory passions for secrecy and publicity were also satisfied by the design. Chambered within the building, like a tomb within a pyramid, was the FBI tour, a favorite sightseeing stop. The tour gave tourists the impression that they were inside the heart of the FBI. It was all so *visible* through walls of windows—here was a lab, there was a shooting range, there was a fingerprint being analyzed, there was a gun collection. But everything on the tour was staged. The real FBI was sealed off from the exhibits that enthralled the tourists. The building and the blazer-costumed guides all seemed so friendly, but that was staged, too. The guides could have worked in Disneyland. The building was not friendly. It was a fortress.

The escorting agent asked Dake for the laminated visitor's pass that had been handed to him when he had entered. The agent inserted the card into a slot in a post next to a turnstile. He then inserted his own card, removed it, and handed Dake's card back. Somewhere there was a computer record showing who had issued the card to Dake that day, when he had passed through the turnstile into the inner building, when he had passed out again, and who had been his escort. If the escort's card had not been inserted at the same time as Dake's, he would not have been able to use his card to get out of headquarters that day. Locked inside, he would be the subject of an immediate interview by internal security operatives.

There was a faint click as the turnstile unlocked. Dake pressed through to a short dark passageway that ended at a large waiting room, deserted except for two agents behind a glassed-in podium that contained an array of consoles and phones. One of them picked up a phone, pressed a button, and spoke a few words. He asked Dake for the card, had him sign the visitor registration book again, and pointed to the courtyard. There, in their dark suits, striped ties, and white shirts, stood the two agents who had picked Dake up. He wondered which one had called him on the phone number he had believed to be absolutely private.

Dake opened one of the glass doors of the visitor clearance room and walked into the dazzling sunlight of the courtyard. The tall one, named Patterson, stepped forward and said, "The car's right out front. We'll take you back home." The shorter one, named

Green, turned and took a step toward a passageway that opened to Pennsylvania Avenue.

"No thanks," Dake said. "I think I'll walk to the *Post* and catch a ride home from a friend there." He had had enough FBI for the day.

"Come on," Patterson said. "We'll give you a lift there." He had been the affable one on the ride to the meeting with Polanski. Green had not said much.

On one of the Oldsmobile's sun visors Dake had spotted a card listing license plates. He had recognized the letters. The State Department assigned diplomatic license plates to embassies with letters designating the countries. FC, known to Division Five as the "fuck communism" plate, was assigned to the Soviet Union. Most of the numbers on the card on the visor started with FC.

"On second thought," Dake said, "I'll hitch a ride. You're probably going in that direction anyway."

Green stopped and turned. "What makes you say that?" he asked.

"The Soviet embassy's only a block from the *Post.*"

Patterson smiled broadly. Neither he nor Green spoke on the walk to the car. The Oldsmobile was a block away, in a legal parking spot. FBI cars were not immune to D.C. parking tickets, which, despite perennial appeals from the U.S. attorney's office, could not be canceled.

Patterson got behind the wheel and Green took the seat next to him. He reached up to the visor, removed the card from the rubber band that held it, and tossed it into the glove compartment. Then he unlocked the right rear passenger door for Dake.

As they pulled into the trickle of Pennsylvania Avenue traffic, Dake asked, "Don't you want to know why the director wanted to see me?"

"No," Green said. "Not in the least. It's none of our business."

"I'm not too sure of that," Dake said. "I think I'm working on the same thing you guys in Division Five are working on."

"Maybe you're right, Mr. Dake," Green said, pausing just long enough to get Dake's full attention. "Maybe you should have walked."

Dake and Patterson laughed, and they drove the rest of the few blocks to the *Post* in silence.

When Dake walked into the newspaper building, he stepped back from the plate glass window and watched the Oldsmobile disappear around the corner. He spoke with one of the security guards for a few minutes, then walked through a door to the mailroom and made his way through the first floor of the building to the loading platform. He hurried down the concrete steps and cut across the truck-filled lot to an alley running between Fifteenth and Sixteenth streets. The alley ended next door to the Soviet embassy. After standing in a shadow for a few minutes, watching for the Oldsmobile, he ran across Sixteenth Street and entered another alley, which took him to Seventeenth Street. There he turned right and walked to the broad-stepped entrance to the National Geographic Society's headquarters, made of gleaming marble.

Tourists wandered around the exhibit-filled lobby. Dake went into the men's room. Between the outer and inner doors, he knew, there was a pay phone. He looked up a number in his notebook and jabbed the push buttons. Three jabbering Cub Scouts pushed past him as Falcone answered the phone.

"This is your friend, the one Agnes wanted to chase. Please, don't mention my name. Remember that big black object on the first floor of my house? Meet me in twenty minutes where it could do its stuff. Got it?"

"I called you and your goddamned answering machine—"

"For Christ's sake, shut up!" Dake shouted. Two newly arrived Cub Scouts stopped and gawked. He waved them through the inner door.

"Do you know where I mean?"

"Yes."

Dake heard the hesitation in Falcone's voice. "Okay. On the *outside*. Understand? On the *outside*."

Dake hung up, made his way through a blue cluster of Cub Scouts, and left the building. He crossed the street and walked a short distance to the back door of the Mayflower Hotel, where he strode through the ornate, block-long lobby and emerged on Connecticut Avenue. The doorman, resplendent in green and gold, gestured imperiously for a cab, which pulled up to the marquee entrance. Dake tipped him. When the cab driver asked, "Where to?" Dake waited until the doorman had closed the door and the open-windowed cab had pulled away. "Kennedy Center," he said.

When he arrived at his destination, Dake took up a post on the marble-slab terrace, one foot on a marble bench, his gaze slowly pivoting from one end of the terrace to the other. He saw Falcone approaching and could see that he was not being followed. He turned his gaze to a lone sculler rhythmically rowing up the Potomac.

Falcone walked directly to him and confronted him, eye to eye. "What the hell is this all about?" he said. "When I read your goddamned story—"

"Hold it right there, Sean. *I'm* the one who should be pissed off."

"What do you mean?" Falcone asked. "And what the hell was that mysterious phone call about?"

Dake took his foot away from the bench, and Falcone sat down. Dake put his foot up again and glared down at the senator. "You knew what Tri-Dynamics was and you pretended to be dumb. In fact, you and Stock were both friends of Rorbach's, who operates that Israeli front. For all I know the two of you were asshole buddies in this thing together. Or in something together." Dake lunged forward, his face near Falcone's. "You've been holding out, deceiving me. You're using me."

Falcone was stunned, but he tried not to show it. "I'm not using you," he said, his voice rising. "I'm only trying to get at the facts. You're the one who's always telling me that things aren't what they appear to be."

Dake turned and sat down next to Falcone. "They aren't," Dake said. "They never are."

"Your story. It's—"

"Let's forget about the story for a minute, Sean. There are other things going on."

"Like what?"

"Like the fact that you're under investigation by the FBI."

"I have a great deal of trouble believing that," Falcone said, surprised at his composure. "Even if it were true, you'd have no way of knowing." As Dake began to speak, Falcone waved him to silence. "The FBI is always interested in picking up whatever it can about the Intelligence Committee. Somebody fed you 'FBI,' and you jumped at it. One of your goddamned 'informed sources.' "

"I never use that hackneyed term," Dake said. "And I never

reveal sources. But for you I'm going to make an exception. The somebody who fed me 'FBI' is named Harry Polanski. I was summoned to his office a couple of hours ago by a couple of Division Five types."

"My God! But why? Polanski hates the media even more than I do."

"You're talking to me."

"That's different."

"How different? You need me, so you talk to me. Polanski needs me, so he talks to me. You both talk to me—or act as if you're talking to me. You're both using me. But Polanski's more obvious about it."

Dake recounted his meeting with Polanski. When Falcone did not respond, he said, "So we have the Tri-Dynamics connection. What about it?"

"Tri-Dynamics connection," Falcone mockingly repeated. "That's what the *Post* will call it. Then will come Tri-Dynamicsgate, or maybe Tri-gate. It's catchier." He sighed theatrically. "I didn't tell you I had heard about Tri-Dynamics because my knowledge about it was classified. I make it a point, as you may have noticed, not to leak information. I take the classification system seriously."

"Sure, I know that, Sean. You're famous for being a stiff about never leaking anything. But the point is that we were supposed to be working together. I tell you about Tri-Dynamics and you don't tell me that you know about it. Not a hint. But when the director of the FBI mentioned Tri-Dynamics and Rorbach to me, I didn't bat an eye. I didn't tell him, 'Oh, sure. I know Stock met with Rorbach once a month in the Sheraton.' I didn't do that because I was working with you. I was holding out on Polanski, and maybe that is a criminal offense, but I wasn't holding out on you."

Falcone sighed again. "I told you why. I don't disclose things I learn at CIA briefings. Besides, Tri-Dynamics wasn't that important an item in the briefing. There was much more on Israeli intelligence activities—information you'd probably call 'interesting.' Besides Pollard."

"Meaning what?"

"Meaning that Tri-Dynamics was mentioned almost as an aside in a section of the briefing that had to do with commercial espionage. One thing about that has leaked already. From the State De-

partment Arabists, I suppose. State has given diplomatic status—
diplomatic status—to more than a hundred Israeli commercial
agents."

Dake laughed. "You are a rare one, Sean. Sometimes I think
you don't even know how the game is played in this town. You don't
even read the *Post. I* broke that commercial agents story. And you're
right, it was a guy in the State Department. But let's get to the main
thing. You *are* under investigation by Polanski's boys. Why?"

"I think that he thinks I know what Joshua was doing."

"What about you and Rorbach?"

"That was bullshit, a red herring. I met Rorbach exactly once.
At the Bluffs. I can give you the date. It was last spring. I spoke
maybe twenty words to him."

"That's it?"

"That's it. I talked to the security guard at the Bluffs more than
I talked to Rorbach."

Dake laughed again. "The security guard knew who you
were?"

"Sure. We talked about Vietnam and—"

"Did it ever occur to you that the security guard could be on
Polanski's salary? Or the CIA's?"

Falcone looked embarrassed. He reached down and removed an
imaginary piece of lint from his jeans. "No," he finally said.

"Okay. Well, let's try this: The FBI's tapping your phone."

"Impossible!" Falcone said indignantly. "They have to get a
warrant from the Attorney General, go to the Intelligence Court. The
procedure—"

"Procedure?" Dake interrupted. "Do you think there's any worrying about procedure when the White House pulls out the stops?"

"Why the White House?" Falcone asked. "I'm no fan of Hollendale's, and vice versa. But . . ."

"Who the hell do you think tells Hollendale what to do? If you
keep an eye on mundane things like White House logs, you'll find
that Hollendale spends more time with the director of the FBI than
he does with his national security adviser."

"You have access to White House logs?"

"Sure. They're basically open. The *Post*'s White House reporters routinely check all the normal run-of-the-mill meetings and appointments and file them. Why?"

"There's a date—a date Joshua gave me. I . . . I have to try to find something. I think it's in his office."

"Sure. But don't tell me about it, right? And watch your back. The FBI has been crawling all over his office. Clarke told me. And by the way, he gave me a copy of the video. For your eyes only, as they say. You can look at it anytime you want."

"Thanks," Falcone said. "Thanks." He sounded distracted. "I'll call you tomorrow to . . . arrange to see it. And—"

"*Don't* call," Dake ordered. "Your phone is tapped. Every call you make and every call you get is going right into the FBI and the White House. If you want to call me, use a pay phone. And speak guardedly. If we have to talk on your phone, arrange for a meeting right here by saying something about music and then mentioning a number. That number plus one is when we meet. You say the Fifth Symphony and we meet here at six A.M. You say you got a dozen new records and we meet here at one P.M. Got it?"

"Got it." Falcone said. But his mind was racing toward tomorrow, and he hardly heard the rest of Dake's conversation.

33

WHAT HAD BEEN JOSHUA Stock's office was now a room, an empty room plucked clean of a life and a past. A decent interval had just about elapsed, and so, in the inexorable ways of the Senate seniority system, another senator would soon be moving from a less exalted office to this one. Cartons marked *J. Stock* stood in the hallway outside the office suite. The Florida state seal that had hung by the door was gone, as was the plaque that had borne Joshua's name. Falcone imagined Cleo or one of the kids opening a box marked *J. Stock* one day and finding the seal and the plaque and then starting to cry.

A young man that Falcone vaguely remembered as a Senate page had suddenly stood at attention when Falcone had entered the suite's reception room. The kid was staking out the office for his boss, the next occupant. Without speaking a word, Falcone had passed through the reception room, past the deserted cubicles where the staff had worked, men and women who were now making the rounds on the Hill, trying to find jobs. He wondered if they could hear the leper's bells hung around their necks by the murder.

Dake was right. Not only had the FBI been here, but so had the movers. He cursed himself for having waited so long.

He opened the desk drawer. Some paper clips, three pennies, a dime. No one would touch the money.

He sat at Joshua's desk and tried to remember what had been here when the room and Joshua were still alive. He twisted the swivel chair around. On the shelf behind the desk had been a parade of photographs: Cleo alone, Cleo and Joshua, the kids growing, frame by frame. And that silly snapshot in a silver frame of Joshua and Falcone at Camp Kowonki. He swung back and placed his hands on the desk. *April 15. "I want you to know the date," Joshua had said. "That's all. Just remember the date."*

He turned his eyes from the desktop to the monitor of the computer on a stand to his right. He had a computer just like this one in his office, a personal computer, not connected to the Senate computer network. He swung around again and reached out to the keyboard, holding his hands above the keys for a moment. Then he switched on the computer.

The monitor screen lit up. In dark green at the upper left of the screen, "Please Log In" appeared.

Falcone assumed that the log-in protocol, log in and initials, would be the same here as on the computer in his office. He typed LOG IN followed by IJS, Joshua's initials. Then on the screen appeared "Enter Password."

This was the moment that Dake had warned him about. Dake had talked with his computer expert and relayed the lore to Falcone: Most systems equipped with password safeguards allow two errors and then automatically shut down. "There's another possibility you have to worry about," Dake had said. "In some systems, you can tell the computer to destroy certain files if someone attempts an unauthorized entry. Make a mistake and *pfft!*—the files go up in smoke. They're beyond recovery, because the security program wipes them clean. It's as if they never existed."

The last sentence echoed in Falcone's mind as he tried the first of the two passwords he had decided on. The expert had said that most passwords were words easily summoned from memory: obscenities, family names, pet names, hobby names.

Falcone had ruled out obscenities. Joshua had no pets or hobbies. Falcone typed CLEO. So that onlookers could not see a password, the letters did not appear on the screen. Even as he typed the last invisible letter he knew he had made a mistake, but he hit the Enter key, which signaled to the computer the end of the password, and he thought, *Too goddamned obvious.*

Error.

"Enter Password," it said again.
One down.
Not since he had been in the prison camp had Falcone's palms sweated like this. He hunched over the keyboard, staring at the keys, willing them to give him the answer. After Cleo's name he had planned on one of the children's names. Which one? Again he thought, *Obvious.* But he sucked a deep breath into his lungs, held it —as if he were going to pull a trigger, he thought—and typed an invisible J. Then ENNETT. Before he typed the final E he stopped and, his fingertips sweaty, reached for the Delete key and wiped out the invisible letters.

He had thought of place names—another possibility, according to Dake's expert. FLORIDA, or FORTL for Fort Lauderdale, or ISRAEL. *Pick one. Any one. What the hell.* This time he did not hesitate. Quickly he typed the invisible letters ISRAEL and hit the enter key.

Error.
Enter Password

Two down.
Falcone stood and massaged the back of his neck. He felt the knots forming in his back, his shoulders, his gut. He looked again at the shelf where the photographs had been lined up. He gazed at the shelf for nearly a minute.

He remembered another warning relayed from Dake: "There's usually a time limit, a *short* time limit. Hesitation is the sign of an intruder. It's like a soldier stuttering when he's asked for the password. Even if you don't blow it on the third try, you may still blow it just by delaying."

They had been counselors at Camp Kowonki. In that snapshot Joshua and he had been standing in front of the mess hall.

He went back to the keyboard, and without sitting down he hovered over it, typing the invisible letters KOWONKI. He banged the Enter key, somehow knowing that he was right.

Logged On

Falcone yelled. It sounded to him like a gleeful *Yooow!*, but the sound frightened the young man in the reception room, who ran in and asked, "Is anything wrong, Senator?"

"Not a thing, son," Falcone replied, his eyes on the screen. "Not a damn thing."

"Full System" replaced the logged-on message. Directly below it appeared

2655360 bytes total memory
1233440 bytes of memory free

Stock had used up about half of the memory in the hard disk of his computer. Falcone had more than a million bytes to search through. He had enough experience on his own computer to conduct a fundamental search, but he knew enough about his quirks to realize that knowledge of his own computer might be of little value in tracking through Stock's. That's why they were called personal computers.

C:\ appeared, and next to this prompt Falcone typed DIR. A list of words appeared.

IJS < DIR >
LOG < DIR >
PRESS < DIR >
QUOTES < DIR >
SPEECH < DIR >
SKED < DIR >
STAFF < DIR >

The computer automatically recorded the time and date when anyone entered it. Falcone was relieved to see that no entry had been recorded since Stock's death. Of course, the time and date entries could be altered, but Falcone assumed that if FBI technicians had entered the computer, they would not have tampered with the files because of their potential evidentiary value. He further assumed that the FBI would eventually examine the computer's contents, so he decided to erase all traces of his own entry when he had finished his exploration.

That would come at the end of his session. Now he looked at the list of directories and decided to ignore those that were clearly professional—PRESS, STAFF, SPEECH, QUOTES. He picked a directory by typing the computer abbreviation for "change directory" and the name of the directory he had selected: \CD\SKED.

In the SKED directory were individual files named for the months. Next to the prompt, which now was SKED, he typed LIST MARCH.

The screen filled with dates and notes about receptions, meetings, speeches, travels. Next to March 8 Falcone read:

8:30	Staff meeting
9:00	Bfast, Sen Din Rm Gleason & 4, Fort L CofC
10:00	Armd Servcs (B-2)
11:00	Open
Noon	Open
1:45	Armd Servcs (B-2, Trident)

The rest of the day, which ended with a Florida Club reception at the Mayflower, looked typical and could be checked. He would ask Colby whether Joshua had been at the Armed Services Committee sessions that day. Colby kept meticulous records about his committee. But what could not be checked was the time listed as open. Falcone scanned a few other days in the SKED directory to confirm his suspicion that the word *open* was rarely used in any of Stock's schedules. Like every other politician in town, Stock had a full schedule, especially when the Senate was in session. There were few open hours in the day.

Falcone called up LOG and scanned it by transferring its files to a word-processing program. Stock apparently had used LOG the way Falcone used his journal. Instead of scribbling in an old ledger book, he had entered notes into this directory. Falcone spent about twenty minutes going through LOG files. But after scrolling through IDEAS and BDAYS (for the birthdays of family, friends, and constituents), he decided that the directory had little of interest for him. When he entered NAMES, he used the computer's search program to look for Rorbach. The computer reported

Search Fail.

Falcone was not surprised. If Stock had been passing secrets to Rorbach, he certainly was not going to keep records of the transactions. Falcone changed directories to the one he had known from the beginning was the most likely to hold information close to Joshua's heart and soul: IJS. He had hesitated to call it up because he feared disappointment and the end of a futile exploration. IJS *was* Joshua, who had been a monogram fanatic. Shirts, sweaters, cufflinks, a gold ring—they were all stamped IJS.

Joshua once had confided to Falcone that the monogram was partially a fabrication. He had no middle initial. He had invented the I, listing his first name as Isaac when asked. In reality, he once told Falcone, his monogram stood for "I, Joshua Stock." Now, changing to the IJS directory, Falcone smiled at the recollection.

There were few files in IJS. Even the thought of looking at CLEO or KIDS or DAD or WILL made Falcone feel like a voyeur. But there, to his heart-thumping amazement, was SEAN. He called it up, convinced that this would be the file that held what he was looking for. But instead of the file, what appeared on the screen was

Enter Password

Falcone was shocked, then momentarily unnerved. To have come this far—and now this. Joshua had inserted another password. No one would be able to retrieve or print the file without knowing and using this extra password. *But Joshua wanted me to see this,* Falcone told himself, half in panic, half in faith. *And he wanted only me to see it.*

Falcone thought first of Kowonki. No. If the first password had had a connection with Sean, then surely this password would, too. If someone managed to get in using Kowonki, then this second password had to be more elusive. *After Kowonki,* he thought, and his memory raced back to other moments. Where else had they been together in their youth? And in his mind's eye the two of them were aboard Carlton Stock's ketch, flying before the wind. Laughing with Joshua then and smiling confidently now, Falcone typed ZEPHYR.

The screen went blank for a terrifying instant, and then the screen filled with Joshua's words to Sean.

Sean: First, a note for you. The original name of this file was BLACK, as in blackmail, black projects, black thoughts. Dramatic, no? Then I changed the name to SEAN because I had a vague, maybe romantic idea that a day would come when I was not here and I would have to tell you about this. I don't mean I feared for my life, or anything *that* dramatic. It just occurred to me that I could wind up like McFarlane or Ollie North or Poindexter: involved in something covert, exposed, put under the glare of the Washington spotlight, examined and cross-examined, perhaps put on trial. And when it was all over no one would really know what happened.

I wrote the following record of a single event so that people would know what happened at that event. I had the idea when I wrote this—on the night of the day it happened—that I might wind up in exile, in prison, or just on some dust heap somewhere, disgraced, despised. No one would want to listen to me then.

After I asked you for the asset's name and after I learned what appeared to have happened, I realized that it was not "people" I owed an explanation to. I owed the explanation to you. So I changed the name of the file to SEAN. But I didn't change anything that I wrote into the computer on the night of April 15.

It is my hope that instead of reading this you'll hear it all from me over too many drinks some night. But if for some reason that is not possible, here is my story of what happened. I intend this as the first installment. I will keep writing into this file until this mess comes to an end.

But messes never do, Falcone said to himself. He turned to look again at the empty shelf. Then he went back to reading what SEAN had to tell him.

My understanding is that not even the DCI knows about this.

I will start at the beginning. I got a call last night (April 14) from Katherine White, President Hollendale's personal secretary. She told me that the President wished to see me at 11 A.M. today. I couldn't figure out why. Was there some national security issue he wanted to discuss? Was it some kind of political meeting? I asked her what the subject of the meeting was to be and what other senators would be present. "I am not aware of the purpose of the meeting," she said in that whispery voice of hers. "And to my knowledge, Senator Stock, no other senators will be present."

I slipped out of an Armed Services Committee meeting around 10:30 and, without telling anyone, drove to the White House. All the way there I was wondering why Hollendale wanted to see me. I waited in an anteroom only a short time before being ushered in to see him.

Surprisingly, the President was alone. He greeted me with that phony affability of his, and after some meaningless chatter that I assume he thought would put me at ease, he suddenly called Harry Polanski into the room. I stood and reached out my hand, which Polanski refused to shake. I knew then that I was going to be the subject of a kangaroo court run by these two.

The President, as is his wont, passed the buck to Polanski, who wasted no time getting to the point: "Senator, information has developed that makes it necessary for us to talk." Then he said something about "a way out of this dilemma."

Before he went any further, Polanski, as if he were following a script, suggested that the rest of the conversation take place in the Situation Room. The change of venue, I think, was dictated by the probability that the President, while perhaps reticent about taping conversations in the Oval Office, knows that the Situation Room has marvelous videotaping and audio-taping equipment.

I trooped down to the Situation Room, with Polanski treating me like a prisoner. As soon as we were seated at a table, an aide pulled Polanski out, saying he had an important phone call. When Polanski returned he began talking. "I have been advised that someone has been feeding the Israelis some high-grade information." He paused, dramatically, I suppose. "Information that was given to the Senate Intelligence Committee. The National Security Agency also has something interesting on this involving Israel."

"And?" I said.

"And our counterintelligence people traced a number of phone calls from your office to the Israeli embassy."

"So?"

"Your calls are clustered around the dates of the Senate's briefings."

I was mad—really mad. "I'm waiting, Polanski."

"Senator," Polanski continued, "we think you've been leaking to the Israelis. We think we can prove it if we have to."

"You're damn right you have to!" I yelled.

Polanski came back at me with sanctimonious calm. "Senator, we are not talking about a court of law. We are prepared to discuss our concerns with the majority leader. It's likely that he might ask the Senate Ethics Committee to investigate the matter."

"And of course," I said, filling in the blanks, "the investigation will be duly leaked to the press. So even if no evidence is found by the committee, I'll be fingered in the newspapers as the prime suspect in a new Israeli spy ring. Suspicion is enough to convict me with my constituents. Is that your game plan?"

Polanski said nothing, confirming my assumption that the conversation was being taped.

"Just so your record is perfectly clear, Mr. Director, are you prepared to tell the Ethics Committee that you either have been running intercepts against the Israelis or wiretapping U.S. senators' offices? That should go over real big in the Washington *Post!*"

Polanski smiled at my attempt to toss the political ball back in his court. "We are prepared, if necessary, to tell the American people exactly what is going on, how our 'special relationship' has been compromised, jeopardized. Perhaps you have forgotten what the reaction was in this country when the public learned about Pollard? Some felt that a life sentence wasn't severe enough." He paused, then finally said, "I think there is a way out of this dilemma, Senator. One that will be helpful to us and to you."

"And what might that be?" I asked, as calmly as I could.

"We have reason to believe that the Soviets have penetrated the Mossad."

"Have we told the Israelis?"

"No. It would be like telling the British while Philby was working for them and spying for the Russkies. The guy who is working for the Soviets in Israel may be so highly placed that our tip to the Israelis would be a tip to him.

"We need to prove it using our own resources, our own asset. We want you to keep on doing what you're doing—giving material to the Israelis. Only we will give you better and better stuff, to make the Israelis believe that you have gone in deeper. We'll—"

"Just one goddamned minute," I said. "I haven't spied for the Israelis, and you know it. Never—never—did I give them classified information."

"Okay. Have it your way. The point is that unless we find out who the Soviets' man is, we may have to cancel some of our programs with the Israelis." Polanski could probably tell from the look on my face that he had finally shocked me. "We'll feed you enough information to establish solid bona fides. They won't object. They'll trust you."

"I have two questions," I said. "One, how do you know there is a Soviet mole in the Mossad? And two, if I go along with this, what then?"

Polanski picked up one of the phones on the console in front of him. A moment later a Navy officer, a commander, walked in and pressed a button somewhere, and a section of a wall rolled back to reveal a screen and what looked like a fancy VCR. The commander inserted a tape in the machine and left the room.

What came on the screen was the interrogation of a defector. He was identified as Vyacheslav Kamamenov, a member of the Soviet Academy of Sciences and the KGB. He defected to us in Geneva, apparently while he was on a mission to improve communications between Moscow and Germany. He said he was a high-ranking official of the Thirteenth Department, which, as you may recall from all those full CIA briefings on the KGB, is responsible for communications between Moscow and foreign residencies.

The video was apparently a CIA show-and-tell for the President. It's a very professional-looking film. Kamamenov, wearing what looks like a blue-and-white running costume, sits in a stark, garishly lighted room, facing the camera. Two CIA interrogators in shirtsleeves have their backs to the camera; one is bald. The video begins with everybody speaking in Russian. Then the Russian fades to a whisper and a woman with a lilting voice gives what seems to be a running translation. It's the usual: "I grew tired of a life of deception, I wish to live in a free nation." Then there's a touch of hard information, just before the end of the video, which lasts about ten minutes: "For some time we have received high-quality material from a highly placed source in Israel. Very recently there has been information about a secret USA project in Israel."

When the video ended, Polanski stood and stretched and yawned. Then suddenly he spun around and leaned over me. He began speaking rapidly, sometimes sputtering, so that a spray of spittle punctuated what he said. I won't give you a complete transcript of the threats and obscenities. Several times he mentioned *Canaan*, which he said was the code name of the Soviet source in the Mossad. He implied that I might even know his identity. I tried not to respond in any way.

Polanski could see that he wasn't getting anywhere with this approach, so he backed off and switched to the good-guy role that he sometimes tries to play. As he returned to his seat, he leaned across the table to pat me on the arm. "The point, Senator, is that we take this defector very seriously. He spoke knowledgeably about our SDI black program, SUNDANCER."

"I know about it," I replied. "And you can be goddamned sure that I did not say one word about it to anyone. Anyway, why should I? The Pentagon is giving Israel information on a lot of our black programs as part of our 'special relationship.' "

"Exactly," Polanski said. "But because we share A, B, and C with Israel, it doesn't mean that A, B, and C are supposed to wind up in the Soviet Union. What we want to find out is how material goes from us to Israel—and then to the Russians."

"So," I said, "you want me to play at being a spy to get the mole to trust me and then do something that will incriminate him. No thanks. This is not something I want to get into. This is a rogue covert operation managed out of the White House. You know the rules, Polanski. There has to be a finding, and the President must notify the chairman and the vice chairman of the intelligence committees or the leadership of the House and Senate."

Polanski showed me a finding, already prepared and dated April 8. "Notice is being withheld until this op is complete. But it will be revealed to the proper congressional representatives at the proper time."

"No," I replied. I guess anger was beginning to show in my voice. "I know the rules. And you should, too. As for—"

Polanski interrupted to say, "You have to have some trust here, Stock. After all, we've trusted you under some very dubious circumstances."

Sean: I was tempted to break off here and not give you the full story. But on second thought I realized that you should know about what follows. Please don't judge me until you have given me a chance to talk to you about this.

"We know," Polanski said, "that you have been having an affair with a foreign national, a woman who we suspect is a courier for an intelligence service."

The sonofabitch tried blackmailing me *twice*, Sean! I told him that the backlash from the Senate would cost him his job.

Polanski acted as if he had not heard a word. "We really have no reason to think that you have been leaking any vital information to her," he said smoothly. Then, going into his bad-cop act again, he put his jutting chin inches from my face and said, "But that is not the way it's going to play in the media. Your little Middle Eastern beauty will even make the front page of the *Post*. Phil Dake will love it. I'm sure you

know goddamned well that the media could get a solid leak—
that information is being passed to Israelis, that it is ending up
in the hands of the Soviets, and that you have a girlfriend who
has an interesting résumé. Any day we want to, we can see to it
that it's all over the press and TV, complete with photos. Any
day we want to."

Please believe me, Sean. I didn't need Polanski to convince me that I had to end the affair. It was stupid of me,
incredibly stupid. All I can say is that she is the most beautiful
woman I have ever known. I told her a little about you. I wish
you could meet her. But I want very much to end this. Nothing
would be served by mentioning her name.

I agreed to do what they asked me to do, Sean. Not because of the woman or anything else. I agreed because I knew
that without my help, the SUNDANCER program and Israel's
security were in deep trouble.

They called in an Air Force colonel in civilian clothes.
Polanski said he would be my "reporting officer" on the National Security Council. I had never seen him before. Polanski
introduced him as James Kammer and said he was a special
assistant to Butch Naylor. I have to believe that this is true.
But I don't really know who he is and who he works for. All I
can assume is that this is a tight White House operation. No
CIA, no State, no DIA. I have no idea where in hell this is
going to go or how it is going to end. All I know is that Naylor
and Polanski are running this operation.

Falcone stood, rubbed his eyes, walked to the window, and
looked down at the sidewalk. Five men, all wearing red-and-white
visored caps, were walking along in two rows. A man in the front
row seemed to be in charge, looking at what Falcone assumed to be
a map. A delegation. The office of some senator—perhaps Senator
Sean Falcone—was about to be visited by a delegation wanting
something started or something stopped. It was all so simple. Three
branches of government. Checks and balances. The Constitution.
Laws. Everything was in check all right, but no one seemed to be in
charge.

He walked back to the computer and resumed reading. Stock
had continued to make entries in the file: arrangements for meetings

with Kammer at the NSC, the request for the asset's name, his disappointment at Falcone's failure to supply it, the desperate certainty that he had helped kill the traitorous mole with a car bomb, the feeling of relief, the dream that somehow there would be an end to the mess that had become his life. The last entry was dated July 20.

> Tomorrow, Sean, I see the woman for the last time. That is finished. I am also going to inform Polanski that my work for them is done. Knowing that you have been a straight arrow since Kowonki days, I realize that my career on the Intelligence Committee is over. And unless I have phenomenal luck with the voters, I'm also probably finished in the Senate. All I hope, Sean, is that in perhaps not too long a time you and I personally can close this one down and put it behind us as if it never happened. Stay tuned.

Falcone shut down the computer, sat for a few minutes at the desk, and then picked up the phone. Senatorial phone-changing procedures being what they are, he assumed that no one, including the FBI, would even know how to find this transitory phone, let alone tap it. He first called Ed Fulwood, chief of the Intelligence Committee staff.

"Ed. This is Sean. I'm in what used to be Joshua Stock's office. Get Lipton, a uniformed security officer, and a dolly of some kind up here right away. We're going to impound a computer. Yes, I know the architect's office has authority over equipment, but this computer has information that even the architect can't see. Now, dammit, get that dolly. I want the computer taken to the Hole and locked up very, very tight. After we take it to the Hole, I want a printout of a file I will name. I want that and the computer itself given the classification level of SCI. Yes, right away."

Falcone took out his wallet, consulted a slip of paper, and called Dake at the *Post*. "You know that big black object you mentioned to me yesterday? I want to meet you where it is. No, not where it *could* be. Today. Listen, to settle an argument, didn't 'Heartbreak Hotel' sell nineteen million records?"

His third call was to the National Security Council. "This is Senator Falcone," he said. "I wish to speak to Butch Naylor. Never

mind that 'hold on' bullshit. I want to speak to him *immediately.*"
He looked at his watch. In thirty-four seconds a brisk voice said,
"Naylor here."

"Sean Falcone, Butch. I must see the President."

Naylor knew enough not to ask why. He rifled through his
infallible memory and could think of only three times Falcone had
made such a request. All three times he had seen the President.

"He's in South Bend, Senator, at an American Truckers' convention address. Then he swings up to Chicago for a big political
dinner. Won't be back to Andrews until after eleven. Give me a sec
to look at his schedule for tomorrow." Falcone drummed his fingers
on the barren desk. Fulwood and Lipton entered, followed by a
uniformed man pushing a cart, followed by the young office tender.
Falcone waved them to the couch across the room. "Here it is,"
Naylor resumed. "How's eleven-fifteen?"

"Fine," Falcone said. "It shouldn't take long. And Butch, you
have a zoomie colonel on your staff named Kammer?"

There was a pause. "I'd . . . I'd have to check."

"Well, you do that, Butch. If he does exist, have him stand by
with you outside the Oval Office at eleven-fifteen tomorrow morning."

Falcone smiled at the thought of double-dealing Butch Naylor
roaring around the White House and the Executive Office Building,
trying to find out what was going on.

"Okay, boys. Take her away," he said, pointing to the computer.

The young man stood and started to say something. He got only
as far as "But Senator—"

"Son," Falcone said, "do you know who I am?"

"Yes, Senator."

"And do you know I am chairman of the Intelligence Committee?"

"Ye—yes, sir."

"And do you know what SCI means?"

"No, Senator Falcone."

"It means sensitive compartmented information. Higher than

top secret." He pointed again to the computer. "That's SCI as of this moment, son. And we're taking it out of here."

At five minutes before eight, Dake opened the door of his house to Falcone.

"You took a big chance, calling me like that. Meeting me here," Dake said.

"I didn't call you. You must have imagined it."

"Okay. You just happened to be driving by."

Falcone stepped into the cool of the house, took off his suit jacket, tossed it on a chair, and loosened his tie. "Do you know what it costs to tail somebody, Phil?"

"Sure. By FBI estimates, about $2,000 a day. They say that just following Soviets in D.C. can cost $30,000 a day."

"Do you know who makes sure the FBI gets all that money?"

"I see your point. But do you believe I'm tapped?"

"If not today, by tomorrow."

Dake led him into the living room. "How about a drink?" he asked, reaching for the Jack Daniel's.

"Fine. A light one." He sat back in one of the leather chairs. "I came to see the video."

"I figured." Dake pointed to a VCR. "It's set up to run."

"Phil, why did Joshua's killer make the tape? And leave it?"

"I asked the same questions. One of the criminal behavior psych boys at the Bureau said that whoever killed Stock wanted him not only dead but totally discredited. Without the tape, his family could have claimed it was a Charlie Manson–type ritualistic murder. This way, there's proof that Stock was balling some chick, doing a little sadomasochism that got out of control."

He handed the remote control to Falcone, took a beer out of the refrigerator, left the room, and closed the door.

Falcone drank half of the drink before he hit play and waited for the appearance of an olive-skinned woman with the legs of a dancer. In a moment she was there on the screen, walking into the scene, her neck hidden by her dark, lustrous hair, her shoulders strong, her hips perfectly formed, her legs long and tapering to slim ankles. Falcone hit the freeze button and stared at the woman's body. He could not see her feet.

He hit play again and then fast forward to a scene he had hoped never to see again. Her hair was swaying rhythmically on her glistening back as she straddled Joshua, her legs pressed against his hips. Then the wire flashed in her hands, Joshua's eyes opened in an awful stare, and she plunged it down into his throat. The swaying quickened.

The camera snapped off. Falcone wondered whether it was operated by another person or by an automatic device she controlled. He imagined her turning from the dead eyes of Joshua to the dead eye of the camera, adjusting it so that it would record what she had done. The camera came on again, and there on the bed, fully exposed, was the writhing body, the gushing blood. The camera whirled as if it had toppled, and Falcone saw a flash of flesh the color of wave-washed sand. He hit freeze. She hovered in a frame as a blur, only part of her body showing. Her left leg and foot were visible as she apparently spun away from the camera.

Falcone poured himself another drink, hit rewind, sat back, and played the video again. When her blurred body appeared, he hit freeze and called Dake. He was in the room in an instant.

"I need you to check someone out for me," Falcone said. "I have an idea."

"What are you looking for?" Dake asked, his eyes fixed on the screen.

"A woman," Falcone said. "The woman who is *that* woman."

34

BUTCH NAYLOR WAS waiting for Falcone when he walked into the small reception room near the West Wing entrance. "Welcome aboard," he said, using the nautical greeting currently in favor in the White House. "It's been a while, Sean." Smiling, he simultaneously clapped Falcone on his left shoulder and grasped his right hand in a strong grip. Naylor was much too friendly. Something was wrong.

Naylor motioned to a chair and asked, "Coffee?"

Falcone glanced at his watch. "I don't think there'll be time, Butch. I'm due in there in a few minutes, assuming the President's schedule isn't out of sync already."

"Well, as a matter of fact," Naylor said, "it is." He made a sweeping motion with his right hand, and a black steward appeared in the open doorway and brought a silver tray into the room. He placed it on the low table in front of Falcone's chair and quickly arranged two porcelain cups, blue napkins, and small plates in front of Falcone and Naylor, who had pulled up a chair opposite Falcone. Naylor took a Danish pastry from the tray, put it on his plate, and offered the plate to Falcone. The steward left the room, closing the door behind him.

"No thanks, Butch. But I'll take some coffee."

Naylor put the plate down and poured them each coffee from a silver urn. He added cream to his, put the creamer back on the tray, and looked up. "The President said you might have some questions that I could answer."

"I don't think so, Butch. I'm here to see the President."

"I know that, Sean. Just like I know that you keep a buttoned lip, especially about Intelligence Committee things."

"Butch, there's nothing for you in this. Relax."

"You said you wanted to know about Colonel Kammer."

"I said I wanted him standing by."

"May I ask why?"

"Because after I talk to the President, he, and possibly I, might want to talk to Kammer."

"About what?"

"Come on, Butch. All this poking round isn't going to get you anything."

"I have a right to know something, Sean. Kammer was on my staff."

"Was?"

"Was. He was transferred, on very short notice."

"Where to? Anchorage?"

"Farther. He was put on the staff of the Air Force attaché in Tokyo."

"Who cut the orders?"

"I've discreetly tried to find out. It seems to track back there." He jutted his jaw in the direction of the Oval Office.

Falcone took a sip of coffee and snatched a piece of the pastry from Naylor's plate. He ate it, took another sip of coffee, and leaned forward to look at Naylor directly. "Butch, you had a fine career in the Air Force. You probably could have wound up Air Force chief of staff, maybe on the Joint Chiefs. But you opted for retirement so you could serve here. Things are going on here that are going to blow up in your face. My advice is for you to get the hell out of this place. And don't ask any more questions about Kammer."

Naylor did not outwardly react. Instead, he changed the subject. They talked for a few minutes about the probable fate of the

Defense Department budget. Then the door opened and an aide Falcone vaguely recognized entered. "I've been asked to escort you to the Situation Room, Senator."

Naylor said his goodbyes and left Falcone and the aide as they headed downstairs. The aide showed Falcone to a seat at the table that dominated the small room, and Falcone looked up at a camera that was partially hidden behind a bubble of dark glass on the wall. He suspected that everything in the room would be videotaped. The aide slipped out. A moment later Polanski walked in and took a seat opposite Falcone.

"I have an appointment with the President," Falcone said, looking toward the door.

"The President has been delayed," Polanski said. "He has asked me to speak to you."

"He's all guts," Falcone said, smiling. He felt in control—an alien on hostile turf, but somehow in control. "Okay. Let's you and I talk about what I wanted to say to the President." He pointed his finger at Polanski. "I know that you and Hollendale contacted Joshua Stock and used him as a source of information and dis-information to the Israelis. You set him up, made him a spy under White House control. And that is why he was killed."

"I don't know what the hell you're talking about," Polanski said, glaring at Falcone. "Your friend was under investigation for spying—*spying*—for the Israelis."

"Spies get arrested, Polanski. By the FBI."

"Bullshit. You know goddamned well that some spies *don't* get arrested, for a lot of reasons."

"You didn't arrest Joshua for two reasons. One, you didn't have anything on him. And two, you wanted to use him."

"We had plenty on him, Senator." Polanski's voice rose, and he sneered the last word. "Stock had been meeting on a regular basis with the Israeli ambassador. After the ambassador went to Paris, your friend continued meeting the head of Tri-Dynamics, an Israeli front outfit. We have photographs, transcripts of phone calls, the works."

"That's not what his memorandum says."

"What memorandum?"

"A memorandum of his meeting in this room with you on April

15. A memorandum that tells how he was set up. And as you god-damned well know, because of your illegal operation he was killed."

Polanski was slumped in his chair, the way he sat at the beginning of hearings, Falcone thought. But when he was on the defensive, he rearranged himself with surprising speed and grace and became a model witness, erect, confident. Polanski went through this metamorphosis now, taking his time about speaking. "Has it occurred to you, Senator, that Stock's memorandum might be a complete fabrication to cover himself?"

Good politicians learn to answer questions by changing the subject. "I came here," Falcone said, "because I wanted to speak to the President about a matter that concerns my committee."

"I speak with the full confidence of the President," Polanski responded. "He is not available."

"All right. You're in this together anyway, so you can tell him what I'm here about. He's as liable as you are. I want an answer to one question: Where is the presidential finding that was supposedly authorized on April 8? The running of Stock as a spy is a covert action as far as I'm concerned, and the President is required *by law* to notify me and the vice chairman of the committee about covert actions in a timely fashion. That means a few days, not four god-damned months."

"I don't know what you're talking about. There was no finding. What there was was an investigation, ongoing, to try to determine how much was being transferred to the Israelis." Polanski produced another pause. "And most likely to the Soviets."

"So you are telling me that you and the President did not run Joshua Stock as a spy against Israel, and that there was no finding about this extraordinary covert activity. Is that what you are telling me?"

Polanski did not answer.

"Stonewalling? Okay. Let's look at it from what you *have* told me." Falcone stood, made fists of his hands, and angling his body toward Polanski, leaned on his knuckles in the posture of a prosecutor at a courtroom table. "You are telling me that you had Stock under investigation as a spy, a *senator* under investigation as a spy. And while he is under investigation he is murdered. Yet it takes days before the FBI even acknowledges any interest in his murder."

"I see you read the Washington *Post,*" Polanski said, speaking calmly again. "I'm surprised that you believe what you read. The Bureau is very deep into that murder investigation. At this juncture, it is our belief that there is no connection, absolutely no connection, between Stock's spying for Israel and his death. It was merely a criminal murder with no foreign angle."

"And who else do you have under investigation, Polanski? What else are you keeping from me and my committee?"

"At this point, we do not have any alternative but to investigate every possible lead. And you, Senator, would be the first to criticize the Bureau if we did not do exactly that." Polanski stood and picked up his black attaché case, which Falcone assumed contained a tape recorder. For a moment the two men glared silently at each other.

"I don't believe a word," Falcone said, his face only inches away from Polanski's. "You tell your co-conspirator that."

Polanski turned away. Falcone grabbed his right shoulder. Polanski twisted around and raised his left fist. Falcone caught the fist in his hand and pushed Polanski's arm away. They confronted each other, Polanski slightly crouched, Falcone with his hands held chest high and slightly clenched. Then, as if by mutual signal, both men relaxed their stance. A door to Falcone's left opened slightly, and he realized that his suspicions were right. The room was under surveillance, and some overanxious security man had almost bolted in to rescue Polanski.

"Here's something else to tell Hollendale," Falcone said. "I'm going to get to the bottom of this. And then I'm going to go public and show the country that you are out to destroy the committee. You and Hollendale don't want anyone looking over your shoulder. You were running an illegal operation out of the White House—a *lethal* operation. I will prove it and I will expose it."

While Falcone spoke, Polanski turned away again, walked to the door, and left the room. A moment later an aide appeared and ushered Falcone out of the Situation Room.

Falcone maneuvered out of the bumper-to-bumper parking along the West Wing driveway and headed for Pennsylvania Avenue. He drove two blocks before he saw a street phone. He pulled up to the curb and made two quick calls, one to his office to say his return was delayed and another to Jack Bickford at CIA headquarters in Langley.

Fifteen minutes later he was walking across the stately, high-ceilinged foyer of the headquarters building. Halfway across the marble expanse he stopped and stood for a moment before the array of stars on the wall. Below them on a softly lighted shelf was a memorial book. On its pages were dates, names, and blank lines. For each star there was a name or a blank. Falcone recognized some of the names, and he knew the secret people and the secret deeds signified by the blank lines.

He headed to the left of the bank of security turnstiles where his escort stood waiting. She led him to the visitors' room, and after a few measured words of greeting and comments about the fine weather, she inserted and turned a key to summon the elevator to Bickford's office suite. Falcone noted that the elevator did resemble the one he had ridden in when he had been the guest of Michael Rorbach's. It seemed so long ago.

A security man met them in the anteroom. Rising from his desk, he peered inside Falcone's battered brown briefcase, wordlessly showed him into Bickford's office, and began talking to the pretty young escort.

Bickford came from behind his desk and joined Falcone in one of two chairs drawn up next to a large window that looked out over the top of a miniature forest. On the table between them were a thermal pitcher of coffee and a platter of sandwiches.

"I rarely get company when I eat in," Bickford said. "Glad you could join me. From your call I assumed you wanted to get over here and have a quick talk. But at least enjoy the view between bites."

"This is my second repast on the executive-branch budget so far today," Falcone said. He told of his request for a meeting with the President and the unexpected arrival of the belligerent Polanski.

"And what was Harry being belligerent about?" Bickford asked.

"I told him that I had reliable information that the White House had been running Joshua Stock as a spy. I'm convinced that is what got him killed."

"Jesus," Bickford exclaimed.

Before he could ask any questions, Falcone reached in his briefcase and took out the printout of Stock's memorandum. As he handed it to Bickford, he explained how he had obtained it and how he had seized the computer.

While Bickford read, both men began eating and sipping coffee. When Bickford looked up from the printout, Falcone said, "I have one question, Jack: What do you know about this?"

"Nothing. I swear, I know nothing. The White House running Stock? Incredible. I'd say impossible, but I'm holding the proof in my hand. What clinches it for me is Stock's mention of the defector film. That was the DIA's, all right. Even the Intelligence Committee hasn't been briefed on Kamamenov yet."

Reading the shock on Bickford's face, Falcone decided that he was not lying. But the look of shock instantly gave way to a grimace of anguish. And Falcone waited for an admission.

"Believe me, Sean, I did not know of Stock's involvement. But I did know that something stupid and probably out of control was going on at the White House. I just decided that it was amateur night over there."

"Do you mean you *knew* an illegal operation was going on?"

"Come on, Sean. Don't pull chairman-of-the-committee stuff on me. This isn't about laws. It's about people screwing up, people dying."

"You'd better tell me, Jack. Just me, Sean. Not the chairman."

"Okay," Bickford said with a sigh. "You remember the day you came out here about three weeks ago and made that very unusual request to check out that asset of ours in Israel?"

"Right."

"I formally asked the President if I could brief you. He gave permission and for some reason told me to give an identical briefing to my good back-stabbing friend Butch Naylor."

"Naylor? Why?"

"I had no idea. I chalked it up to White House power playing: 'You can't know something Butch doesn't know.' Whatever it was, it didn't bother me until we learned two days later that the asset had been killed by a car bomb. The Israelis, of course, blamed the PLO. It could have been coincidental, if you believe in coincidences. I don't. A Jesuit told me once that every coincidence can be traced back to an inevitability."

"What did you do when you heard about the car bombing?"

"We ran an extremely discreet inquiry and came up with noth-

ing, which is not unusual in the Middle East. If you look at the
report, you will see that our conclusion is something about 'assassin
unknown.' End of case." Now Bickford hesitated. "Are you back to
being the chairman?"

"I suppose I am, Jack. I'm afraid this is one that will keep
going on."

"My God, Sean. Not again. I don't think the country can take
any more hearings. Not the kind of hearings you probably have in
mind."

"This isn't the Agency, Jack. Once again it's the White House.
Do you know anything about a finding?"

"On what?"

"A finding authorizing the use of Stock as an intelligence con-
duit to the Israelis to ferret out a double agent."

"No, I know of no finding." Bickford shook his head. "It's just
stupid! Running another one off the shelf."

Falcone reached for the printout, which Bickford handed to
him. "I can't let you have this, Jack. I consider it committee property."

"Understood. I appreciate your giving me the chance to see it."

Falcone put the printout back in his briefcase and stood up.
"As I said, this one will not go away. I promise you that. Can I count
on you to cooperate if the committee looks into this?"

Bickford remained seated. He looked out the window wistfully.
"My job," he said, "is to make sure this Agency can continue to
function effectively. You'll have my cooperation. We lost a hell of an
important asset over someone's stupidity. But in this business you
learn to take what you get. When I saw that printout, I realized that
the White House bought the defector's story, which we didn't. The
President misled me, Sean, said he had another source. I know now
that the defector is bona fide. He was telling the truth. The *Canaan*
he told us about is real. Somehow, *Canaan* killed our asset."

"So *Canaan* is definitely a Soviet agent inside the Mossad? You
accept that professionally?"

"I'll have to play this out delicately to our Soviet watchers in
the Middle East. But yes, for now I certainly buy it."

"Well, isn't killing the asset kind of strong, even for the Soviets?"

"Yes. That bothers me some. I think that you can count on

there being more, much more, to this." Bickford stood and pointed to the briefcase. "I know you have a personal stake in this. I know you and Stock were close friends. But we may be talking about big, big stakes here, Sean. Don't let your passions rule this one."

"I'm not going to move hastily on this, Jack. I promise you that. And I'm playing it close to the vest. I'm planning to go to Israel. It's legitimate business. I'm carrying out a commitment Joshua made. I want you to clear the way for me there. I want a briefing from Ambassador Barrington and our country team. I want to meet with our chief of station. I want to meet with the head of the Mossad, and possibly the Prime Minister. I need your help. I expect nothing out of the White House. If anything happens to me, I want you to know that I've been working with Philip Dake on this. You know that he's not going to take a dive for anyone."

"I'll handle the Israeli details personally, Sean. Before you leave, make all contacts with the Agency through me. I will advise you on who to see when you get there. I have mixed emotions about Dake being in on this, though. I guess he's your insurance policy."

Nodding at Bickford, Falcone said, "Yeah. And he's probably going to demand a big premium."

"That's what bothers me about Dake."

35

F<small>ALCONE</small> WENT INTO
the office early, for a breakfast meeting that had been scheduled
with some Massachusetts municipal officials. He wanted to pacify
Tim O'Brien and lift staff morale even as his own was sinking.

The officials had come for the same reason everyone else came
to Washington—to shake the money tree. They wanted a balanced
federal budget but a "fairer" share of the federal pie. Lip-service
conservatives, liberal practitioners . . .

Falcone signed mail and discussed briefing memos with his
staff until ten o'clock, when a group of presidential classroom schol-
ars stopped by. He spent twenty minutes discussing issues, then
provided them with a photo session. Next he was off to a joint
session of the Governmental Affairs and Banking committees. He
found banking to be one of the most arcane and complex subject
matters to master—and one of the most tedious, unless you happened to like green eyeshades, which he didn't. He asked two or
three questions drafted by his staff, then left for the Republican
policy luncheon.

Before he arrived, the chairman of the Policy Committee had

announced that the cost of the weekly luncheons would go up to six dollars per meal. As he entered S-211 in the Capitol, he heard groans, moans, and low whistles from his colleagues.

Colby Sugarman pulled himself up with the help of his cane. "Goddammit, I'm not going to pay more for lunch unless the quality of the food in this place goes up with it. I'll brown-bag it first!"

Cheers and huzzahs went up. Sugarman, a millionaire, didn't have to worry about the price. He was standing up for a principle, one they all shared but didn't dare express for fear of looking cheap.

During lunch, Jack Prescott, a lanky, hard-boned lawyer-minister, rose and launched into a powerful speech about the United States' loss of control of its destiny. "We fritter away our lives hustling between committee hearings and filing bills to keep our names in the paper. We have some fundamental choices to make. Do we believe in a growth economy, and if so, how do we reconcile it with environmental concerns? Are we willing to fight for anything? If so, where? Fundamental!" Prescott slapped his hands together to drive home the urgency that he felt.

Everyone in the room knew he was right. But everyone was a prisoner of a schedule made up mostly of the trivial.

At two o'clock Falcone went to the Senate floor. A vote to break a filibuster had been ordered. Bob Drexler, the majority leader, had introduced a bill—as he had done each of the past four years— commemorating the slaughter of the Armenian people at the hands of the Turks from 1915 to 1918. The Turkish government had threatened to retaliate if Drexler's nonbinding resolution passed.

"Bob," Falcone said as he approached Drexler, who was sitting on the edge of the table in front of the Senate's marble dais, counting the votes of his supporters. "What in hell is so important about this? Christ, every year it's the same thing. The Turks are going apeshit."

"Don't tell me you favor genocide?" Drexler cracked. He knew he wasn't going to win the vote, but he wanted to see who his friends were. Rumor had it that an Armenian doctor had saved his life after he was wounded in World War II. He owed him.

"Okay, okay," Falcone said, threatening to hold his tie in the air to show the press gallery that he was facing a hanging. He then shouted in a loud voice, "Aye."

The rest of the afternoon was consumed by the debate of the

Health and Human Services budget. Ted Wheelright, who was leading the effort to block $56 million in budget cuts made by Eric
Hollendale in the health field, engaged in a fiery, thumping speech
that encouraged members to storm the White House and rip off the
containment caps Hollendale was trying to impose on Medicare and
on veterinary and nursing schools. He huffed and puffed, but even
with Falcone's support, he could not blow down Hollendale's walls.
He lost, 55–42.

After the vote Falcone returned to his office to meet with a
group of dairy farmers who were demanding higher price supports
for their milk. When he came out of the conference room into his
private office, he found a letter that Tim O'Brien had taped to the
back of his chair. From a disgruntled Massachusetts voter, it read:

Dear Senator Falcone,
        May a thousand camels relieve themselves in your drink-
ing water.

                                        Sincerely yours,
                                        Francis Xavier Mooney
                                        A dedicated Republican

Real touch of the frigging poet, Falcone thought as he snapped
the letter off the chair, tossing it onto a large stack of unanswered
mail. He had every intention of replying in kind to the jerk who sent
it, but it could wait until tomorrow. Or next week. He didn't much
give a damn.

36

Paris, August 9

AVI NESHER'S SECRE-
tary, the only person on earth who could mock him, had shaken her
head and said, "Sure, sure. You have to fly to Paris. Sure, sure.
You've got to go there in August. How come you never go to places
like Liverpool or Alaska in the winter?" As usual, their conversation had consisted of her mocking words and his glaring silence.

She could not have been more wrong this time, he thought now,
remembering the conversation. *This city is the last place in the world
I want to be.* He had never liked Paris, never liked the frivolous
people, the frivolous history. To him, the Arc de Triomphe was
where the Nazis marched. To him, the cafés were where the Nazis
drank and whored with Parisians who put more value on style and
pleasure than on courage and honor. To him, the Sorbonne was a
hatchery for soft-brained intellectuals who sneered at Israel and had
diplomatic love affairs with Israel's Arab enemies. The only admiration he had for anything French was his grudging respect for the
Mirage jet and the Exocet missile—and, he had to admit, France's
no-nonsense approach to intelligence operations: no parliamentary
inquiries, no newspaper headlines.

His apparent reason for this hasty trip to Paris was an unannounced inspection of the Paris residency for a firsthand account of the attack on Yitzhak Rafiah. Angrily turning aside the pleas of Mossad officials, he had left Tel Aviv without bodyguards. He had promised that he would pick up a security man as soon as he stepped off the El Al plane in Paris. But he had not notified Paris in advance. If anyone wanted an explanation, he would claim a need for surprise. He had indeed held a meeting in the early morning with a truly surprised Mossad station chief. Now, below the basilica of the Sacré-Coeur, in the Montmartre cemetery, he stood by the grave of Hector Berlioz and waited for Ptor Kornienko.

Nesher knew that Kornienko would be apprehensive and probably angry. This was the second time Nesher had called—demanded —a face-to-face meeting, and as he knew, in the choreography of running an agent, it was the controlling officer who was in charge, not the agent.

Such meetings are dangerous, for either or both parties may be followed. Even the procedure for putting out a signal was dangerous: a message through a third party or a coded phone call, which may set up a double-cross of the controller. Then the prearranged response, the instructions for time and place, which may expose the agent, deliberately or in some unforeseen way. Nothing that the controller and the agent ever do is more fraught with danger and mistrust than an unscheduled face-to-face meeting.

As a controller, Nesher had seen it happen so many times: A rendezvous like this, called suddenly and inexplicably by an agent, almost always meant that the agent wanted to run and hide. The emergency signal was a sign of fear, a prelude to panic. And Nesher had always responded by putting the agent out of business as soon as possible. *The best way,* he thought now, *is not by killing them. The best way is to say goodbye with a guarantee of security, a kind of pension, a string, so that someday perhaps I can yank them back.*

He knew he was professional, and he had to assume that Kornienko was, too. But he was still frightened, and he was trying to control that fright by making it sharpen his instincts. He reached under his jacket, put his sweaty hand in the back pocket of his slacks, and touched the .22-caliber Beretta.

Then Nesher saw Kornienko walking up the path, in the mists from the morning rain, an ordinary man strolling nonchalantly. He walked past Nesher without acknowledgment. Nesher waited a few moments and then walked along the same path, wandering off it occasionally to see the grave of Zola, the grave of Offenbach, but always looking down the path, making sure that no one was trailing Kornienko. Satisfied, he began following the route he had memorized, checking at each place to see if he was being followed.

Not quite two hours after seeing Kornienko in the cemetery, Nesher slipped into a booth in a café near the Opéra de Paris Ballet School.

Kornienko, raising his coffee mug, greeted him with "Shalom" and then continued in his heavily accented Hebrew. "I thought that you might like the scenery," he said, gesturing with his mug to a nearby table, where four slim, softly chattering girls sat.

"There is nothing I like about this city," Nesher said. "I am here because I am under obligation to be here."

"And I am here because of your . . ." He groped and stumbled through Hebrew, then used what Nesher recognized as the Russian word for emergency. ". . . signal." He summoned a waiter and said, in French, "For my friend."

"Tea," Nesher said in English.

"Tea," Kornienko repeated, scowling. He did not speak again until the waiter turned and made his way through the cluster of tables in the center of the café. Kornienko leaned forward, his bulky clothing casting a shadow across the table. "And what is it that you want to tell me?" Before Nesher could answer, he continued. "Are you afraid? Here. I hold your hand." He grabbed Nesher's right hand, squeezed it hard, and held it down on the table.

In a smooth, swift series of motions, Nesher reached his left hand around his back, drew the Beretta, and, shielding it between his legs, jammed the barrel against Kornienko's right knee. "Let go of my hand," he said in Russian, "or I'll shoot your balls off."

Kornienko released his grip and folded his hands next to his empty cup. He sat motionless for a long moment and then said softly in Russian, "Very good Russian. Even *balls*. I am impressed. Now please put away your gun."

"I was making a point," Nesher said, still speaking Russian. He put the gun into a side pocket and, imitating Kornienko, folded his hands. "I am not one of your back-alley agents. I am an intelligence officer. I do not meet you because of fear. I have a need, a vital need, for information."

Kornienko, his eyes hidden behind his tinted glasses, allowed himself to look startled. "Information? About what?"

"The attempt to kill Rafiah. The killing of the American, Senator Stock."

"As you say, Avi, you are an intelligence officer. So you will recognize the doctrine of compartmentalization. These events have nothing to do with what goes on between you and me, between my country and your country."

"These events, as you call them, have a great deal of importance to our countries and to us. They have endangered what we are doing."

"How?" Kornienko asked. The waiter reappeared, served them, and went away. Kornienko laughed and said, "I think he thinks we are having a lover's spat. It must happen often here."

"You ask how it endangers us," Nesher said. "It is causing people to ask questions. And I am expected to give answers."

"So give answers. Senator Stock? A martyr to the Israeli cause. Rafiah? Terrorists."

"Soviets," Nesher said. "Soviets did both."

"That is a very unprofessional conclusion. You talked to your Mossad man today. Evron, is it not? Nachman Evron? He surely investigated the Rafiah event. It happened almost on his doorstep. Does Evron say Soviets?"

Nesher did not wish to acknowledge Kornienko's identification of the Paris station chief, but he was right. Evron had not named the Soviets as suspects. In fact, he had said that he had got nowhere. Paris was not a helpful city for the Mossad.

"The attack is still being investigated," Nesher replied.

"Allow me to help you and Nachman Evron," Kornienko said, smiling. He raised his cup as if in toast, said, "To pleasing our superiors," and sipped. He put it down, cast down his eyes as if in thought, then looked up and said, "We have information from an extremely reliable and highly placed source. Rafiah was a stupid vengeance strike. Typically Arab. The opportunity came and an assassination team was put together from locals."

"Vengeance for what?"

"It could have been for many things, over many years. Rafiah, as you know, lost a son to the Arabs. And you also know what happened next. I believe you have *detailed* knowledge of what happened next."

"That's history," Nesher snapped. "I find it hard to believe that the vengeance still goes on."

"Our information," Kornienko patiently resumed, "is that it was a Qaddafi gang." Seeing Nesher about to speak, he held up a hand. "Please. I know you are going to say that we have had certain operational relations with Qaddafi. But some of Qaddafi's deeds are beyond anyone's control, certainly beyond Soviet control. Believe me, Avi, we did not do this. You have my personal assurance."

"Rafiah suspected something," Nesher said. "He was angry, distrustful."

"Yes," Kornienko said, his voice sharp. "Yes. I can believe that he was. Because of that unfortunate incident with the car bomb, no? And that, too—was that the work of the terrible Soviets?" Nesher did not answer. "Or perhaps it was the Americans? As I told you once before, my dear Avi, the KGB report on that incident puts the blame on the PLO. Just as the Mossad report does."

"And Stock?" Nesher asked.

"Perhaps you could tell me about that incident."

"What do you mean?"

"What I mean is that Moscow believes this was a Mossad wet job. Possibly with CIA help."

"Impossible," Nesher said angrily. "We work very rarely with the CIA these days. And never on . . . never on what you call wet jobs. Our intelligence services do not have wet jobs."

Kornienko smiled and nodded his head. He drained his cup and held it up to signal the waiter. "Our profession, Avi, is best performed not by those who tell the truth but by those who know how to use the truth. Do I believe you? Do you believe me? Does it matter? What matters are our masters and their work. Tell your masters, Avi, that Qaddafi's men attacked Rafiah. As for Stock"—again he smiled—"well, he is dead. And is it any business of ours?"

Later that afternoon Kornienko made his way to an alley where he was picked up by a florist's panel truck. The truck drove to the back door of an apartment house where many middle-rank employ-

ees of the Soviet embassy lived. After backing up to the delivery
dock, the driver got out and walked up the side steps of the dock.
He opened the wide rear doors of the truck, entered it, and picked
up three palm trees in large green tubs. The truck's wide doors and
an overhanging roof gave Kornienko cover from any French surveillance man who had enough curiosity to watch the apartment house's
door. As soon as he was inside, the driver closed the doors, got in
the truck, and drove away, leaving the palm trees on the dock.

Shortly after six o'clock one of the embassy's vans left the
compound and drove to the apartment house, where it dropped off
several Soviets at the front door. Three people, one of whom was
Kornienko, entered the van for the routine trip back to the embassy's underground garage.

Among the reports contained in that day's cable traffic was one
doubly coded and set in burst format. Embassy code clerks could not
read it, though they did recognize the format and knew that it was
reserved for eyes-only delivery to Viktor Borovlev, director of the
KGB. The message said:

> *Canaan* demanded meeting. He is nervous, angry, perhaps
> soon ineffective. Suspicious of origins for recent incidents here
> and in Washington. Believe I convinced him incidents work of
> independent Libyan group and PLO. But must now question
> *Canaan*'s future reliability. BURAQ may be endangered. Sug-
> gest disinformation effort aimed at keeping *Canaan* occupied
> defending Mossad counterintelligence operations to his superi-
> ors. Flying to New York.
>
>   Kornienko

37

Moscow, August 9

THE ZIL LIMOUSINE HAD just exited the Kremlin's Spassky Gate and entered Red Square when Viktor Borovlev ordered his driver to stop. "Come, Dyukov," he said, motioning for his deputy to get out of the car. "I think it would be good for us to get some exercise."

It was not exercise that Borovlev wanted but escape, escape from the giant ears the Americans had fixed in the heavens over Moscow. Spiked balls, invisible to the eye, hovered in the black silence of the universe, listening, recording, whispering. His apartment, dacha, and office had obviously been targeted for snooping. No doubt his limousine had been, too. But out in the nine-hundred-yard square, filled now with hundreds of people, it would be impossible for these "rabbits" to hear him. *Well, perhaps not impossible,* he grunted to himself, *but more difficult at least.*

The two men walked slowly and in silence. The sun hung low in the early evening sky, a huge red ball about to slip below the horizon. A thin layer of clouds, soft as dove feathers, caught the sun's deep glow and turned amber, ready to ignite, it seemed, and burn into wisps of nothingness.

They passed Lenin's tomb, where the changing of the honor guard was in progress. Young soldiers shouldering bayoneted rifles, their chins held high and eyes dead ahead, goosestepped their way to and from sentry duty. *A meaningless ceremony*, Borovlev thought bitterly. It was a tourist attraction that amused those who had neither memory of nor respect for the man entombed inside, the father of the Bolshevik Revolution.

Off in the distance, at the far end of the square, loomed the brilliantly striped, onion-shaped domes of St. Basil's Cathedral. Borovlev emitted a soft sigh. That is what foreigners could never understand—the depth and paradox of the Russian soul. It was at once mystical and murderous; capable of poetry so lyrical, so profound, that it set one's heart vibrating, and capable of violence so brutal it could freeze the hearts of millions in a tundra of fear.

Finally Borovlev spoke, reciting words that might have been his own.

"Know this: He who fell like ashes
   to the ground,
He who was ever oppressed,
Will rise higher than the great
   mountains,
On the wings of a bright hope.

"Did you know that Stalin was a poet, Dyukov?"

"No, Comrade Director. What we learned of Josef Vissarionovich Dzhugashvili did not relate to his creative talents." Dyukov had not intended any sarcasm, but as soon as his words were out, he realized that they might be misinterpreted.

"Stalin held a muse in one hand, a sword in the other. Not like those who pretend to lead our people today. He had passion, Dyukov, a magnetism that inspired, called forth the best from our hearts. Sacrifice. Order." Borovlev swung his arms suddenly in a wide arc. "Look around. What is it we see?"

Dyukov remained silent, not knowing what to say.

"Tourists in Bermuda shorts," Borovlev snapped in disgust. "With their Japanese cameras, looking at our monuments as if they were fossils."

Surely, Dyukov thought, the first deputy secretary of the KGB did not leave the meeting at the Palace of the Congresses just to speak of bad poetry and faded glories. Enveloped in his brooding silence once again, the young deputy grew increasingly uncomfortable.

At last Borovlev said, "The Libyan woman—I assume she is no longer in Washington."

"No, Comrade Borovlev. She returned to Paris immediately after her assignment. At the moment, she's actually in Strasbourg."

"But some of her relatives are still in Washington?"

"Of course."

"It's important that the American should not go to Israel at this time. He need not be killed. Not yet, at least. Consider that you are doing him a favor. You'll be saving his life by preventing him from going to Israel."

"Yes, sir."

"Cause him difficulties with the law. Washington is drowning in drugs. Perhaps Senator Falcone picked up an addiction in Vietnam. Something to kill his pain . . ."

"I'm sure that can be arranged."

"We are too close to BURAQ and do not need to risk any complications with Falcone stumbling around. In a few more days, no American official will have much desire to travel to the colony of Jews."

Borovlev turned and motioned to his driver, who had followed close behind, that he was ready to return to his office in Dzerzhinsky Square. Pausing to cast a final glance at St. Basil's Cathedral, he said, "Tell me, Dyukov, do you believe the story?"

Dyukov's eyes widened in puzzlement.

"The story that Ivan the Terrible blinded the architects Barma and Postnik after they constructed the cathedral so they might never again create anything so magnificent?"

"I think it is legend."

"Perhaps," Borovlev said. "But legend is more powerful than fact, Dyukov. Legends live in the imagination. They tantalize us with their power, their reach, their wondrous possibilities. More than facts, they touch the Russian soul. It's a pity that General Secretary Voronsky has never understood that this has been the source of our greatness. Russia has always been a land of legends."

38

T HE ROUTE TO DECEP-
tion was familiar.

An urgent meeting, called by Director Borovlev himself, with the highest-ranking officials of the KGB's Directorate K.

Then operational meetings in Directorate K's Service A, known in the West as the Department of Disinformation.

Then a long, urgent cable to the KGB resident in Bonn.

Then a call from a second secretary at the Soviet embassy in Bonn to his frequent tennis partner, a consular officer at the U.S. embassy.

Then lunch for two (the U.S.'s turn to pick up the check) at Latraverno, a restaurant favored by diplomats in a Bonn suburb.

Then an urgent report, filed right after lunch, from the consular officer to the embassy's State Department intelligence section. (The CIA resident showed little interest in anything coming from a State source.)

Then an urgent cable to the Soviet and Eastern Europe section of the State Department's Bureau of Intelligence and Research in Washington.

Then a conversation in main State between a senior analyst in the Bureau of Intelligence and Research and a junior analyst on the staff of the assistant secretary for Near Eastern and South Asian affairs. "They tell me," the senior analyst began, "that you're the gal I should talk to about those religious nuts in Israel."

And so the route of deception ended. But a new route of information had opened . . . for Philip Dake.

She had called from a phone booth, asked for Philip Dake, and said, "It's about Senator Stock's murder."

Now it was eight o'clock the next morning and they were meeting in the coffee shop of the Madison Hotel on Fifteenth Street, almost directly across the street from the Washington *Post*. She recognized Dake. He did not ask her name, but he did ask enough questions to establish that she had the State Department job that she said she had. Although he did not ask her anything personal, she volunteered that she was forty-one years old, divorced, and had been an employee of the State Department for nineteen years.

"I was Phi Beta Kappa at Stanford. Third in my class."

He wondered if this would be another waste of time. He had seen so many like her in recent years: bright, attractive, tired of not getting promoted, complaining about this department or that bureau. Usually they were whistle-blowers, and sometimes they had a tip or a document that would lead him to a good story. He tried to look interested, but he refrained from taking notes.

"As you may know," she continued, "there's a class action suit building up at the State Department over discrimination against women."

"Sure. I've heard about it."

"But there's been nothing in the *Post* about it. Not even a couple of paragraphs on the federal page, where you bury dull civil service stuff."

"Maybe there isn't a story. Maybe our State Department reporter—"

"There *is* a story, an important story. I would like to see a major story on what's going on at State." When Dake did not reply, she looked annoyed, but went on. "I am proposing what I suppose you'd call a deal. I'll tell—"

"I'm sorry," Dake interrupted, "I don't make deals. But if you have *two* stories, as I imagine you have, then tell me about both of them and I'll give each an honest evaluation."

She used the time it took to order—coffee and toast, unbuttered—to think about his reaction. The waitress did not ask Dake what he wanted. It was always the same: coffee and a blueberry muffin.

"Well?" he asked.

"I don't really like deals either," she said, reaching out her hand. Dake shook it and held it for a moment. She squinted when she smiled, and a faint web of lines appeared around her eyes. She did not use eye makeup. She looked trim, and somehow balanced within herself. He could imagine her running around the Tidal Pool on her lunch hour or in a glistening condo kitchen, stir-frying chopped vegetables and tofu.

She spoke first about the proposed class action suit. She gave him documents, a lawyer's name, her name, and the names of three other State Department women who would be co-plaintiffs. They agreed that he would not discuss the story with the *Post* State Department reporters. He said that he would pass her information along to a general assignment reporter on the Metro staff, a woman. He promised to keep watch over the story and help the reporter develop follow-ups.

She then switched to the story she had called Dake about.

"A man from INR—Intelligence and Research—who rarely consults me—he calls me 'dearie,' 'honey,' 'gal,' that sort of thing— phones me yesterday. He says he wants to talk about a major development in what he called the Stock case. Well, we meet in his office, of course, his *corner* office. And he closes the door and leers a little and makes a big joke about closing the door. And finally he gets down to what he wants to talk about. He tells me that INR has received a report that Stock was killed by a hit team from Israel."

"How reliable is that information?" Dake asked. His thoughts leaped ahead to the legwork he would have to do to pin this one down.

"I'll get to that," she replied. "Let me tell you first what he said. He told me that the killing was engineered by the Kach. You know about the organization?"

"A little. Started by Rabbi Meir Kahane. He was born in the

United States, arrested here a couple of times for harassing Soviet and Arab diplomats. Wound up in Israel. Wild right-winger. Became a member of the Knesset for a few years and then got himself expelled. An Egyptian-born New York City employee permanently expelled him with a bullet behind his ear after he gave a speech at a rally in Manhattan."

"You did a lot better than my friend from INR, who had never heard of the Kach. There's more about Kahane, of course. I'm told he did some intelligence work for the FBI, made a rather bizarre connection within the Mafia, moved to Israel, and under the Law of the Return, immediately got citizenship. He started the Kach sometime around 1975, and among other things, allegedly fire-bombed a mosque. He never calmed down after he got into the Knesset. Kept yelling 'Death to the Arabs' every chance he got. That's why he got the boot. Funny thing is that he had more support after he was expelled from the Knesset than he had while he was in it.

"After El Sayyad Nosair nailed him in New York, Kahane became a martyr to a whole lot of people in Israel. And now his successor, Solomon Ben Israel, is even more radical."

"Maybe this new guy is good copy," Dake said impatiently, "but before I could write a word about him, I'd have to—"

"Wait a minute. I'm not selling you this fairy tale. The point is that the whole thing the INR man told me looks terribly phony, so phony that I have to believe somebody planted it. *That's* the story: Somebody's trying to make it look as if Israelis killed Stock."

"What makes you doubt the story?"

"First of all, I have little faith in any INR report that comes in without any support from any other source in the intelligence community."

"From what I've seen," Dake said, "I'd have to agree. The INR's like the Defense Intelligence Agency—parochial, good at getting information that supports policy."

"Right. The Arabists at State would love to hang Stock's murder on Israelis, even nonestablishment Israelis like Kach. But I think there is something else to this." She paused to finish her toast. "The report seems to have originated in Europe, which makes me suspicious. If it were genuine, I would expect it to come out of the Middle East. And it had a little embroidery."

"What kind of embroidery?"

"My friend, with another one of his leers, said the INR was also told that Stock was having an affair with a Libyan seductress—that was his word, 'seductress.' Don't you love it? Well, this seductress was supposedly passing secret information that Stock gave her in pillow talk to Israel's enemies."

"She is supposed to be *Libyan?*"

"Yes. You sound as if you've heard otherwise."

"What I heard was Middle Eastern, not Libyan," Dake cautiously said. He wondered how much trading of information he would have to do.

"Libyan is almost too good, isn't it?" she asked, not expecting an answer. "Just like the Kach. Another bit that is almost too good. Right?"

"You're the analyst. What do you figure this all comes down to?"

"Disinformation. Somebody wants us—State, the CIA, the White House, the whole government—to think that Israeli right-wingers killed Stock because Libyan bad guys, or at least a Libyan bad girl, had been tricking him at Israel's expense."

"And the somebody putting out this stuff is the KGB?"

"Right. What I am telling you is a *non*story. I wanted you to hear my analysis before you get it from someone who thinks it's true."

"I have trouble believing in disinformation as something that happens in the real world," Dake said, pointedly pocketing his pen and notebook.

"Sure. Like most of the people in the media, you think disinformation is just something dreamed up by right-wing Soviet-bashers to keep you all from writing anything positive about the Soviet Union. But the fact is that disinformation does exist and it does work."

"Not with me, it doesn't."

"Don't be too sure. But anyway, it is not aimed primarily at the media. Take this one. If it circulates high enough in U.S. government circles, it blurs our perception of an important matter. State, thinking it is doing Israel a big favor, will undoubtedly share the report with Tel Aviv. Israel will move against the Kach, and maybe do something rash to Libya. The Mossad will be in an uproar, start looking for moles and scapegoats and other species of confused spies. All because we fell for a phony story that wasn't put together too well in the first place."

"You said all this to the INR guy?"

"This and more, much more. My opinion is based on highly classified information, which I cannot, of course, share with you."

"And he didn't accept your analysis?"

"He declared my analysis top secret, as if he were some kind of bishop banning a book or something. He told me not to make a written report about it for my files, and then he said, and I quote, 'Nice talking to you, sweetie. But you've got the KGB heebie-jeebies. I wish your thinking was as good as your legs.' End of quote. I *did* tell my boss, of course. But he just shrugged and chalked it up to an INR ploy to get mentioned in the presidential daily brief."

They talked for a few minutes more about women in the State Department, and then Dake, picking up the check, said, "Well, thanks for the nonstory."

"And the story. Don't forget that one."

"I won't. I'll be calling you."

She left the coffee shop and turned toward the lobby doors, where she could get a cab. Dake began walking in the opposite direction, toward the door nearer the *Post* building.

"Wait," she called after him. He turned and headed back toward her, forcing himself not to look at her legs. "One more thing," she said, keeping her voice low. "I'll bet you another coffee that before the day is over, there'll be a wire service report on this, quoting from a West German newspaper. That's a classic end to the disinformation route."

"The bet's on," he said. This time he waited for her to turn and walk away. He felt a moment's remorse for staring in admiration.

As soon as he got to his office at the *Post* Dake tried to call Falcone, but all he was able to reach was an answering machine at Falcone's apartment and an uncooperative secretary at his office. He dutifully briefed the Metro reporter on the State Department class action suit, wandered about the newsroom, took the Metro reporter to lunch, and returned to find a message to call a Mr. Cotton.

Dake called a number at CIA headquarters. Following the

usual arrangement, "Cotton" answered and, as usual, told Dake he had the wrong number. "Cotton" had been doing this for about three years. Dake had never met "Cotton," whose name he always mentally put between quotation marks.

Because the tips had been good ones and because they seemed eventually to serve some national or CIA interest, Dake had a theory that the caller was a tipster who had Bickford's unofficial blessing. Precisely at seven o'clock, Dake knew, "Cotton" would call from a pay phone to one that Dake would answer near the newsstand in the Madison Hotel.

At fifteen minutes to seven, Dake still had not been able to locate Falcone. By then he also knew that he owed the woman from State a cup of coffee. Early in the afternoon, a story datelined Frankfurt quoted a German newspaper as saying just about what the woman had told Dake at eight o'clock that morning. Dake convinced the news editor to spike the item. (It appeared in the final edition of the *Post* because, as the night editor later explained to Dake, all three television networks had used it.)

Dake let the phone in the Madison ring twice.

The caller was brief: "This is for you and your buddy Falcone. I assume you have a pencil. Write down Rachmella Rafiah, a.k.a. Aviva Kamakovich, a.k.a. Esterly Daniloff, a.k.a. Rachel Yaeger. Got all that?"

"Yes," Dake replied. "She's Mossad?"

"You're a genius." He hung up, as he always did, without saying goodbye.

Dake immediately called Falcone's apartment. Again he got the answering machine. He called Falcone's office.

"Ms. Moresi's line," a voice said.

"I need to speak to Senator Falcone," Dake said, hoping he sounded as desperate as he felt.

"Everyone here seems to be gone for the day," the voice said.

"Who is this please?"

"Victoria Aaron. I'm a summer intern."

"Well, Victoria, you can do me and the senator a big favor."

"And what is that, sir?"

"I've been trying to get him. We're supposed to have . . . dinner. But my secretary didn't remind me of the restaurant. Now she's gone for the day. So, Victoria, would you please go to his desk and look in his appointment book?"

"Just a moment, please, sir."

Dake heard the sound of a phone being gently placed on a desktop, a door opening, the faint tap of shoes on wood as Victoria crossed from the rug to the wood near Falcone's desk, and what he strained to believe were pages rustling. There was a click, and for a split second he thought Victoria had hung up.

"I'm on the phone on his desk, sir," Victoria said. "All it says for tonight is 'Rachel.' "

"God!" Dake exclaimed.

"Is something wrong, sir? Do you know where Rachel is?"

"Yes, I do. Thank you, Victoria. Goodbye."

Dake went back to the *Post*. By working the phone for nearly an hour, he was able to find first the company that supplied the maintenance for Falcone's apartment building and then the night watchman. He managed to get a message taped to Falcone's apartment door: "Call me at once. Music Man." Then all he could do was go home and wait.

In the late afternoon, when Falcone had called Rachel to confirm the time he should pick her up, she had told him that she had been handed an unexpected assignment and she would have to go directly from the embassy to the restaurant in her car. She took his directions and promised to meet him there at seven o'clock.

Now, nursing a bourbon at Positano's, Falcone waited. *For what?* he asked himself once more. Ever since she had said she would drive her own car he had been suspicious. *What·was she planning?*

Positano's was beginning to fill. It was a Friday night; Washington was an early town, even on weekends. She arrived at ten minutes after seven, and the eyes of everyone in the restaurant followed her as she strode to Falcone's table against a wall at the rear of the room. She wore loose dark slacks and a gauzy pale gold blouse that draped about her, somehow both veiling and revealing her body.

He stood and reached for her outstretched hand, but she brushed aside his hand and touched his shoulder, leaning toward him to kiss him lightly on each cheek. She brought with her the scent of some exotic flower, faint yet piercing.

They hardly had a chance to speak to each other before Luigi Traettino and his wife Angela embraced Falcone as if he were their son. "Welcome, welcome, Senator. We got a special table for you. And tonight, tonight Angela she make fresh cheese, especial for you." Luigi and Angela plied Falcone and Rachel with cocktails and a plate of antipasto.

"What was the cultural operation that kept you on overtime?" Falcone asked when the Traettinos finally disappeared. He emphasized *cultural.*

"We call them events, Senator. Our Army has operations. Oh, it's so very exciting. I was planning the guest list for a reception at the Kennedy Center, for an Israeli dance troupe. The ambassador will be making one of his rare public appearances. Do you wish to be invited?"

"As your guest?"

"A possibility."

"I'll have to check my schedule. I may be—"

"You cannot be too busy, Senator."

"Sean."

"Sean. Your Senate will not be in session."

"But I remain busy."

"Every evening?"

"I must travel. In fact, next week I'll be in Israel. I am honoring a commitment made by Joshua Stock. He was to dedicate a building at Hebrew University."

Rachel raised her eyebrows, and Falcone smiled, admiring her acting. He had to assume that she knew.

"You certainly are full of surprises. I would think that Israel would be your least favorite place on earth. Well, perhaps next to Russia."

"Why do you say that?" Falcone didn't like the sudden edge in her voice.

"I base it on your record, on your so-called neutrality toward Israel."

Falcone could feel his neck grow warm in anger. "It's not so-called. It *is* neutrality. I don't want another country running my country's foreign policy."

"Neutrality toward Israel is favoritism for its enemies. It wasn't neutral to give more AWACs and F-15s to the Saudis."

"And it was neutral for Israeli aircraft to attack the *Liberty?*"

"The *Liberty*. Scratch an anti-Israeli American and you get the *Liberty*. And what was your warship doing in Israeli waters? It was helping your friends the Egyptians in the middle of a battle."

"We were in international waters. And no matter where we were, you had no right to kill innocent Americans."

Rachel laughed sardonically. "Innocent? Like the Iranian civilians your warship shot out of the sky?"

Their words got so loud that Luigi hurried over to the table with a bottle of wine and interrupted the argument to propose a toast to his new granddaughter. This move broke the tension. Falcone and Rachel returned to small talk, and by the time the coffee arrived were even smiling again.

The evening had not gone the way Falcone had hoped. He had wanted to probe, to use his prosecutor's skills—rusted skills, he now ruefully told himself—to find out where Rachel fit into the puzzle surrounding Joshua. Instead, his temper and hers had flared and burned away any chance for him to delve into her background, her knowledge of Joshua.

There was also the barrier of her cool radiance. Looking at her, trying to fathom her mind, he could not escape the undertow of her beauty. Why did this exotic, alien woman so remind him of Karen? *Enchantment,* he thought. *It's a matter of sinister enchantment.*

They said goodbye, with pecks on the cheek, under the canopied entrance, and then stepped out into the night and walked off separately toward their cars.

To head back into town, Rachel had to make a U-turn. As she did, she saw a car emerge from a side street, turn sharply on Old Georgetown Road, and follow Falcone's car. Her professional training prompted her, almost without thinking, to make another U-turn and, at a distance, follow it. Next to the driver was a passenger. Another man was in the back seat. She identified the car as a Ford Fairlane. She could see what looked like an Avis sticker on the back window.

Twenty minutes later, Falcone turned onto Crystal Drive in Crystal City and drove toward his apartment house, which rose, in layers of windowed darkness and light, above the river. The second car slowed to a stop, with its engine running, at the curb, a hundred yards from the apartment house. Rachel pulled into a parking space on the other side of Crystal Drive, switched off her lights, and waited.

Falcone turned into a driveway that led to an underground garage. Rolling down his window, he reached out to insert his security card into a slot in a box on a stanchion. A steel mesh gate— *Modern America's version of the portcullis,* Rachel thought—lifted. Falcone's brake lights blinked off, and his car disappeared down the steep driveway. As the driver of the Ford inserted a card into the slot, Rachel sprang from her car, leaving the door open, and sprinted across the drive, clutching her black evening bag.

She got to the gate just as two men leaped out of the Ford and pounced on Falcone, who had parked and was turning to close his car door. One pushed him against his car. He kicked out at the man, momentarily driving him back. The other whirled, raised a blackjack, and struck Falcone on the top of his head. Falcone slumped down, his back still against the open door of his car, his legs sprawled on the concrete floor.

As the man raised his arm again, Rachel, bracing her Beretta against the mesh, fired three shots. The .22 was quiet—the firing produced only a muted pop, a soft echo in the cavernous garage. One bullet pierced the man's forehead. The others exploded into his chest. He was dead before he hit the floor.

The other man rose, ran behind Falcone's car, dashed to the Ford, and jumped into the passenger seat as the car roared up the driveway. The rising gate scraped its top as it careened past Rachel, who, hunched behind a wall, fired again. The bullet lodged in the passenger's door.

Rachel saw that Falcone was now conscious, on his feet and rubbing his head. Deciding that her car's diplomatic plates would attract too much attention, she ran back to it and drove directly to the embassy. There she wrote an incident report for the Mossad resident. Attached to the report was a request for all information regarding Falcone's trip to Israel and a recommendation that she accompany him on the plane "in the interests of his personal security." She attached a self-sticking removable note on which she wrote, "We can't afford to be blamed for allowing any harm to come to a U.S. senator."

———

Falcone pulled himself up from the floor, saw the unconscious man, and tried to remember what had happened. Groggy, his head pounding, he leaned against the car and looked again at the man. He was swarthy; he had longish black hair. He was in his mid-twenties. Slim. Black jersey, jeans, dirty sneakers. Half his skull blown away. *Gunfire? Did I hear gunfire?* He could only dimly recall the motions and the sounds. *Two men. Were there two men?*

He stumbled to the elevator, inserted a security card that permitted it to drop to the garage level, and took it to his floor. There was something on the door. A paper. He ignored it. Fumbling with his key, he staggered into the dark entranceway. He switched on the light, touched his throbbing head, winced, and jerked his hand away. He looked at it. Blood. He tried again to remember.

The other man. There were two men. He made his way into the kitchen, his bloodied hand smearing the hall's beige wall. Opening the refrigerator, he pulled out the vegetable bin, where he kept—wrapped in a dish towel—a nine-millimeter Colt handgun that a Massachusetts company had given him. He wanted it now.

The phone rang. He ignored it. He wanted a drink. *Not with a head wound.* He leaned over the sink, vomited, and let water trickle into his mouth. *Rachel. She was there. She set this up.* He felt himself growing faint.

He wobbled to a chair, reached up to the wall phone, and hit 0. After what seemed like an hour, an operator came on. "I want the Capitol Police," he struggled to say. "The U.S. Capitol Police. Not the number. I can't manage to phone. I'm wounded. Not 911, operator. I am a senator. Get the Capitol Police on the goddamned phone." In the briefings for the committee, the security types had stressed this: If there was any threat, any suspicious incident, call the Hill first and request protection from the Capitol Police. Initially, at least, don't trust anyone else.

He heard buzzes and clicks and then a voice. "Sergeant Driscoll," the voice said.

"Sergeant?" Falcone murmured. "You sound like Rachel."

"Sergeant Lillian Driscoll," the voice said. "Who are you?"

"Sorry, Sergeant. Always treat sergeants respectfully. You

never know . . . This is Senator Sean Falcone. I've been attacked. Head wound . . . gunshots. My gun . . . Man bleeding."

"Stay on, Senator. First tell me where you are."

"Apartment. My apartment." He gave the address, and said that building security would let the Capitol Police in.

"We're on our way." He could hear her speaking to someone else. "We'll get in. Don't worry. There will be four officers, and a doctor and an ambulance following. Do not open the door to anyone but us. Do not use the phone. Can you tell me what happened?"

"I don't know. I was attacked. Beaten on the head. Man—no. Two men. Man down. Gunfire. Here, in the garage."

"Okay. We'll notify the Alexandria police. They'll attend to him. We're taking care of you. Clear?"

"Clear."

"Sit tight, Senator. We're on the way."

The rest of the night Falcone later remembered only in patches, as in a fog: four Capitol Hill officers in flak jackets, carrying automatic weapons, bursting into the apartment; a frightened-looking security man, a keychain in his trembling hand; a doctor; a stretcher; questions; soft voices; Sergeant Driscoll.

She was standing by his bed when he awoke: a short, stocky woman with black hair and black eyes. He tried to remember the color of Rachel's eyes. It was somehow important. He moved his head to scan the room. Pain shot through his brain.

A door opened and a doctor came in. Falcone thought he recognized him from the night before.

"Now," the doctor said, leaning down so close Falcone could smell the coffee on his breath. "Now we are going to answer some questions." And in a singsong voice he led an increasingly irritated Falcone through a recital of his name, the day of the week, his birth date, his favorite color. "And now we will tell just where the pain is."

"I have a pain in the top of my head and a distinct pain in my ass, doctor. I know who I am. I know what day it is. Now I want to know where the hell I am."

The doctor reared back. The sergeant smiled and said, "In a private hospital in Alexandria, Senator. Under protection until we sort this out." As she spoke, the doctor slipped out of the room and a nurse entered, carrying a breakfast tray. She propped him up, watched him eat, and gave him a capsule to put him back to sleep.

He awoke in what he assumed to be midafternoon, somewhat muddled, dry-mouthed, but in no pain. Sergeant Driscoll was still there. He wondered if she had been relieved while he was asleep.

"Good afternoon, Senator," she said. "How are you feeling?"

"Hungry," he said. "I could use a hamburger and a beer."

"No beer," she said. "You're still under medication. But I think I can arrange the hamburger." She hesitated, and Falcone could sense that she had more to say.

"Anything wrong?"

"There's an Alexandria detective outside. He wants to ask you some questions. Are you up to it?"

"Sure. I'm getting bored with nothing to do. Show him in."

The detective entered, took a seat next to the bed, and looked up at Driscoll. "I'm staying," she said softly.

"With my forbearance," the detective said. "You have no jurisdiction here."

"Check the U.S. Code, detective, and see what it says about an attack on a federal officer or elected official. Forbearance my ass."

"Good enough, sergeant. I'll be sure to go to a law library on my way back to headquarters." He turned toward Falcone. "My name is Detective Walter Hendricks. I'd like to ask you a few questions."

"Fine."

Hendricks took a small looseleaf notebook from his suit coat pocket. "First," he said, "I'd like to hear your story."

Hendricks's last word alerted Falcone. *Story?* His memory of the attack was clearer than it had been the night before. He told it as accurately as he could: A car had followed his into the garage. As he got out, two men attacked him. He kicked at one. The other hit him with something. As he went down, he heard shots—"Three, I think. Pops. Small caliber, I think, and—"

"Just a moment, Senator. Three shots?"

"Yes. That's what I remember. I was out for—I don't know, a couple of minutes, I think. I got up—I was groggy—and I saw one man lying there. He had been shot. I decided I had to get out of there. I don't remember how I got to my apartment. I just remember arguing with a telephone operator and then I was talking to Sergeant Driscoll. And that's about it."

"About it," Hendricks repeated. He turned back a few pages in his notebook. "Your conversation with Driscoll was taped and time-clocked. The Capitol Police arrived at your door fourteen minutes later. Did you return to the garage while waiting for them, Senator?"

"I certainly did not."

Hendricks again consulted his notebook. "In your conversation with Driscoll, you said 'My gun.' Do you remember saying that?"

Falcone did remember, but he said nothing. The gun was unregistered. He had no need to raise that complication.

"Senator, last night we found a nine-millimeter Colt pistol in your refrigerator. Is that your gun?"

"It was . . . it was a souvenir."

"We find no record of a registration, Senator."

Driscoll reached over and closed Hendricks's notebook. "I think the senator has had enough questioning for a while."

Hendricks ignored her. He reached into his pocket and took out a transparent plastic envelope containing a piece of paper on which was written: "Call me at once. Music Man." "Do you know what this means?"

"No," Falcone replied. "I don't. Wait. I saw it; I think it was on the door when I unlocked it."

"And did you call this Music Man?"

"No. My only call was to the police."

"Yes. The *Capitol* Police. Why didn't you call the Alexandria police, Senator?"

"I can answer that," Driscoll said. "Because we instructed him and all members of the House and Senate to call us first in the event of an incident like this."

"And why is that, Driscoll?" Hendricks asked.

"Because we think we can provide better protection."

"Oh, I'm sure of that," Hendricks said, standing. "I'm sure of that." He turned and walked out of the room.

"Do you know what the hell that was all about?" Falcone asked Driscoll when the door closed.

"From what I can gather, Senator, your man on the floor was killed. Shot in the head and chest. At first the Alexandria cops were thinking that the rounds came from a nine millimeter, maybe even from the one you keep wrapped like a piece of meat in your refrigerator. We later persuaded them that they were .22-caliber, high-explosive shells. And another thing. Six packets of cocaine were found on the body of the dead man."

"My head is beginning to hurt again. What the hell is going on? What's in the *Post?*"

"Nothing about this, Senator. I talked to a man named Fulwood on your staff. He's on his way out here. He says that this is all a national security matter, and he's taken steps to keep it quiet. The Alexandria chief of police is cooperating. There's nothing on the blotter for the media to see. The chief will sit on our boy Hendricks until this gets straightened out."

Fulwood arrived a few minutes later. Falcone brought him up-to-date but did not mention Rachel. "Obviously somebody is trying to smear the facts a bit," Falcone said. "I don't know why those guys attacked me or why one is dead."

"Classic," Fulwood said. "Beat you up to intimidate and impede you—to keep you from your travel plans, for example. And somehow one guy was killed. Maybe by the other, who took off. It looks as if something got messed up. But there's a lot of organization there," he continued. "I've got to think it was something more than punks. It could have been an operation on the professional level—KGB, PLO."

"Or Mossad?"

"Funny you should say that," Fulwood said. From his briefcase he took the *Post.* Circled on page A-31 was the item from Frankfurt. "I think you should get out of town for a few days. This thing may blow sky high."

Falcone knew just the place. A place where no one would find him.

"I've got your ticket, passport, and visa. Alice packed a suitcase for you. I booked you on an El Al flight out of New York."

"El Al?"

"Alice insisted that you're supposed to fly American only. I overruled her. El Al is the safest way to get there. No bombs. No terrorists. No hostage-taking. Of course," Fulwood said, looking at the newspaper, "I'm assuming that you still want to go."

Falcone nodded vaguely, no longer sure why he was going there. He knew only that he had to go.

39

Washington, August 11

WHEN DAKE TURNED ON
the computer in his *Post* office, a flashing signal in the upper right
corner of the screen told him he had a message in the electronic
mail system. He hit a couple of keys and the message appeared:

> Police source says Sean Falcone in shoot-out at Crystal City
> apartment. Va. police seem to be bagging report. You have
> anything? Taylor, Metro.

Dake typed an acknowledgment to the message and rushed to
the newsroom, which was beginning to come to life. It was shortly
before 11 A.M.

"Where can I find Taylor?" he asked the Metro news assistant,
a thin, bearded young man who always, whatever the season, wore a
sleeveless maroon sweater. He squinted up at Dake from a pile of
Virginia and Maryland newspapers, which he was clipping. At the
moment he was the entire visible staff of the corner of the newsroom
called the Metro desk. He sat at a table with a telephone and the

newspaper pile, too low in rank to rate one of the computer terminals blankly glowing in Metro's dozen workstations.

"Home," the news assistant said.

"I assumed that. He works nights," Dake said. "He left an
overnight for me."

"Right. He left an overnight here, too. On Falcone?"

"That's it," Dake said. "Anybody working it?"

The Metro desk was responsible for news in the District and
the Washington metropolitan region. Dake, like most of the *Post*'s
eminent reporters, had begun his career there. He remembered the
years fondly, treated young Metro reporters with respect, and was
often cited by the bosses when Metro reporters got impatient about
serving on the paper's least glamorous editorial section.

"Nobody around," the news assistant said, his glance taking in
the empty workstations.

"You're around," Dake said. "What's your name?"

"Sid. Sid Frankel."

"Do you have a copy of the overnight, Sid?"

"Sure." He took the Metro log from a desk drawer and opened
it. It looked like a messy ledger book, stuffed with handwritten notes
and printouts. He rifled through the papers, removed one, and
handed it to Dake.

> Re Falcone. Cop tipster says Alexandria PD made late-
> night call on 8/10 at apartment where Falcone lives. Man shot
> in garage. Apparent homicide. Drugs—cocaine?—on body.
> Rumor that Falcone connected with shooting. Nothing on blot-
> ter. No info from dispatcher or homicide dicks. Apparent
> clampdown on orders from chief's office. Efforting police
> sources. Spaulding.

Taylor was holding out on the drug angle, Dake noted, smiling.
Wants to keep it in Metro. Can't blame him. Dake tried to remember
what he had heard about Joyce Spaulding, a northern Virginia reporter who usually worked on political and community news. She
was solid, competitive, and new. If she got this from a cop, it was
not because she had worked the police beat a long time. Some
pissed-off cop, probably a homicide detective, called her, probably
anonymously. There was no reason to make it up. Dake decided that

the report was true. He gave the memo back and said, "Well, Sid, how would you like to give me a hand?"

"I—I don't know, Mr. Dake. Mr. Tarica will be in soon, and . . ."

"I'll handle Tarica, Sid. And call me Phil. All I want you to do is get over to an address I'll give you in Crystal City. It's Falcone's apartment house. Try to find out where he is. I spent most of yesterday and last night trying to find him. There's a woman on the desk there named Agnes—yellow hair, hates nosy people. Tell her . . . well, tell her what you need to tell her. Try to get where Falcone is, and see if you can find out what the hell happened over there last night. And—"

"Like what?"

"Like what happened in Joyce Spaulding's memo."

"But I thought that if anything really serious happened, like a crime, the police put it in the blotter and it's a public record and—"

"It doesn't always work that way, Sid. Somebody, maybe the Secret Service, probably told the Virginia cops a national security matter was involved, and the cops temporarily bagged it. Don't worry about that. Just sniff around at the apartment."

"When do you want me to go, Mr. Dake?"

"Please, Sid. Phil."

"Phil."

"Right away. Take a cab."

Sid stood, took his wallet out of a back pocket of his brown corduroy pants, and looked forlorn. That look, Dake hoped, would help bring Agnes around. "How much is a cab to Crystal City?"

Dake smiled, gave Sid the address and two twenty-dollar bills, and went back to his office. He called Taylor and listened politely to a recital of what was in Joyce Spaulding's memo. Dake did not reveal that he already knew the facts in the report, and Taylor did not tell him that the tip had come from Spaulding.

After that, Dake made another short phone call, and a few minutes later he left the *Post*. He found a cab in front of the Madison Hotel, and with grunts, taps on the shoulder, and finger pointing directed the driver, an Afghan three weeks in Washington, to a parking lot beside the Potomac River. He waited until the cab left the lot, then walked along the river edge to a gangway that led to the lower deck of a two-deck restaurant-bar.

The hostess, a friend, chatted with him for a few minutes and then led him to one of two chairs flanking a narrow table. He ordered a beer and looked out through a glass door at the riverfront marina. On the nearest dock he recognized the houseboat on which a congressman had once kept his mistress. Farther down the dock was *Stardust II,* a yacht that belonged to a local drug dealer. A delivery boy was pushing a large wagon, presumably full of provisions for it. Shifting in his seat and leaning forward to get a better look at the boy's jacket, Dake took out a notebook and jotted down the name of the caterer. That night a note would go into one of his files on the District's flourishing narcotics trade.

Dake was halfway through his beer when he saw Becker enter. He looked, as usual, uncomfortable. His face was a splotchy red-and-white scowl. His buttoned suit coat strained against his belly, and his flowery yellow-and-black tie was askew. He made his way slowly across the floor with the waddling gait of a man whose feet were always sore. He did not look like an FBI agent, but he performed extremely well as one. Dake knew him as one of the best counterintelligence agents in the Bureau. But he was a go-it-alone operator, an outspoken man in an organization that revered conformity. Five years ago, when the FBI tried to get rid of him, ostensibly because of a physical disability, Dake had stopped the move with a single *Post* story.

Becker still worked for the FBI, but he no longer carried a weapon or FBI credentials. Publicly, he worked for the Chesapeake & Potomac Telephone Company and even coached a C&P–sponsored Little League team. Actually, in a building not far away he was a phone tapper, or what the FBI euphemistically calls a technical agent.

Dake ordered a beer for Becker as soon as he saw him. The beer arrived just after Becker lowered himself into the chair opposite Dake. He took off his suit coat and draped it over the back of the chair. His short-sleeved blue shirt was dark with sweat. "Jesus, Phil," he said. The rest of his remark was interrupted by a long pull on the beer. "Jesus! I told you, you want me, you don't call me from the *Post.* Better still, you don't call me period. Jesus!" He took his glasses from his shirt pocket and contemplated the menu. "Not much more than hamburgers."

"They're good here," Dake said. "And big."

They both ordered hamburgers, with french fries and another beer for Becker.

"I'm sorry I called you from the paper, Greg, but it was an emergency."

"It's always an emergency with you. If anyone knew . . ."

"Come on, Greg. If you can't make a telephone call not exist, nobody can."

"Still," Becker said. "Still." He looked around at the other tables, measuring the distance from his mouth to others' ears. Bending over the table and speaking almost inaudibly, he said, "I can't give you any information. Nothing."

"You don't even know what I want."

"Doesn't matter. I can't give you anything."

"Well, at least let me tell you my problem. It's about Falcone, Senator Falcone." Becker had turned his head toward the window. Slightly raising his voice, Dake continued, "I'm trying to find out what happened to him."

Becker turned and bent over the table again. "For God's sake, keep your voice down," he whispered. "And no names. Jesus."

"The gentleman in question is an object of your organization's special technical services, as you know."

Becker drew back and again looked out the window.

"I think something may have happened to him," Dake said, waiting for a reaction. There was none. "Look, Greg. I *know* about the tap. I've talked to your boss. He told me you're tapping him."

Caught by surprise, Becker asked, "Anderson? You're telling me you talked to Anderson? Bullshit."

"Not Anderson. Not your goddamned shift boss. I talked to Polanski. *He* told me about the Falcone tap."

Becker thrust his head forward at the mention of Polanski's name. "For God's sake," he said. "No names. And not *that* name."

Dake described his meeting with Polanski at length, knowing the verisimilitude would be convincing and would wipe away Becker's skepticism. "So," he concluded, "you believe me?"

"Okay. I believe you about that. But—" Becker was interrupted by the arrival of the hamburgers. He waited until the waitress walked off. "But so what? If you want to know what's on the record, all you've got to do is talk to your pal Harry P."

"I can't do that, Greg. Harry P. is pissed off at me because I haven't written a story telling the world that a certain senator is in big trouble with your organization." He paused. "Greg, I'm holding back on that for the good of your organization. Harry P. is setting up *his* boss for big trouble. Harry P. is going to take a fall, Greg."

Dake knew that Becker hated Polanski and loved the FBI. "Your pal is in trouble," Becker said. "Harry P. knows it. So okay, why shouldn't you know it?"

Dake waited a moment, trying to decide whether a question from him would break the spell. He thought it would. Instead of speaking, he nodded.

"He made a call—to the Capitol Police. Said there had been a shooting and he got conked on the head. Sounded bleary. Then a little while later, cops used the phone. It sounds like your pal was taken off somewhere, maybe to some hospital. Those Capitol cops, they know about phones. They were leery. The Alexandria cops, they came later—and used the phone. Some detective got the chief out of bed. He mentioned a dead man in the garage—no identity— and said something about your pal having an unregistered gun. Also something about dope on the body. Even from my distance I say the dope's a plant. I guess the chief did, too. He told the dick to bag it with a confidential report—verbal—for the time being."

"The detective must be talking about this," Dake said. "The *Post* got a garbled tip on it."

"Maybe he talked to whoever left a sticker note on Falcone's door."

"Who?"

"Someone who calls himself Music Man."

Dake smiled. "I put it there. I was trying to find him. He never called me." There was another pause, another quick appraisal. "Any other names mentioned?"

"Like what?"

"Like Rachel. A woman named Rachel."

"No. But they've talked. She's Israeli embassy."

"Oh?" Dake said, looking up from his hamburger, hoping he appeared surprised.

"Yeah. It looks like they're both going somewhere."

"Where?" Now Dake did look surprised.

"From what we make of it, your pal is booked on a flight to Tel Aviv that leaves next week. And so is she."

There is always a moment, Dake knew, when the talking, the real talking, is done, a moment when the source decides that there will be no more. That moment had come for Becker. Dake acknowledged it by switching the conversation to the Baltimore Orioles.

After lunch, back at the *Post,* he booked a seat on the same flight that Falcone and Rachel were on. Well aware that people on the payroll of any government usually travel tourist class, he got a first-class ticket, the better to stalk his quarry.

Around the time that Dake got the message on his computer, Harry Polanski was in the Oval Office briefing President Hollendale on what had happened to Sean Falcone.

Hollendale let Polanski finish telling what the FBI knew, then began asking questions.

"Who was the man in the garage?"

"Mustafa Rashish. Turns out he's a cousin of the guy the D.C. cops found strangled beside Rock Creek. They were part of a nest of Libyan students living in an old apartment house over in Arlington."

"Any suspects?"

"No one yet, Mr. President. The preliminary medical exam indicates that he was hit with high-explosive .22 slugs, which looks very much like the work of a professional assassin. Someone just drilled him while he was working over Falcone."

"Are you saying that Falcone was involved in killing this guy?" Hollendale glared down from his high-backed chair, the desk between him and Polanski as dark and menacing as a moat. "Why the hell would he want to do that? And how would it fit into what he's been up to?"

"Again, this is speculation. From our . . . technical information, we know he was supposed to be going to dinner with this Rachel woman. Someone may have decided he was nosing around too much and wanted to discourage him from going to Israel."

"Stop him, but not kill him, right?"

"Right. The man had a blackjack. You don't try to kill people with a blackjack these days."

"And this Rachel?"

"We figure that she may have fingered him. The guy attacks him, and there's gunfire and—"

"And you figure she was involved, Harry."

"We're working on it, Mr. President."

"Yes, with the usual Bureau alacrity. Did Falcone see this woman last night?"

"Yes. The restaurant owner says they left about ten-thirty. He says he thinks they were in two cars." Polanski took a sip of coffee, then held up the cup as if he were contemplating the presidential seal. "We, of course, were not surveilling them."

"Damn right. I told you I don't want FBI shadows on U.S. senators. Now, what about the drugs?"

"High-grade coke—cocaine—and—"

"I know what coke is, Harry. What I want to know is what you think about it. A plant?"

"Well, Mr. President, I certainly can't say for sure, but . . ."

"Come on, Harry. It looks phony to me. Somebody is trying to send us a message. I agree that maybe the Israelis don't want him going there. But a blackjack? Drugs? Murder?"

"There's his gun, Mr. President. He keeps a fully loaded semi-automatic handgun in his goddamned refrigerator. It seems to me—"

"And how do we know that? Illegal entry?"

"Please, Mr. President. As I've said before, leave details to me."

"Sometimes, Harry, I worry about that," Hollendale said, looking at his watch. "I can't spend all day on this. Without asking you *how* you know, can I ask you *what* you know about the gun?"

"We traced it directly to the factory. It's unregistered. An unregistered handgun. How about that?" The President impatiently waved a hand, and Polanski continued, speaking more rapidly. "It was a gift from the manufacturer, who lost out in competition to produce a new sidearm for the military to replace the .45."

"God, I remember that fight very well. It's a wonder they didn't use that gun on him. Okay, Harry. Now, what do you plan to do?"

"As I see it, Mr. President, we have a man who was mugged by a Libyan who is now very dead, a Libyan who had drugs in his possession. We have a man who is about to leave the country, and so—"

"That *man* is a United States senator. If you are about to suggest that your boys are going to go out and *arrest* him, well . . ."

"That's my recommendation."

"What?" Hollendale was looking and sounding angrier by the second. "Goddammit, Harry!" He slammed both hands down on the gleaming top of his desk. "Stop this! I know your publicity ploys. You tip the media to an arrest. The TV cameramen even know where to stand for the best close-range shots."

"Let him leave the country, Mr. President?"

"Yes," Hollendale replied, speaking slowly, asserting his authority. "We will let him leave the country. We will have Bickford alert the CIA station chief in Israel. We will keep our eye on him there. He may even lead us to *Canaan*"—Hollendale's voice began to rise—"and that, as you may remember, is the reason you started this whole thing. That will be all, Harry."

Polanski placed his coffee cup on the table next to his chair and stood. Hollendale was looking down, reading from one of the folders stacked on his desk.

"There's one more thing, Mr. President."

Hollendale looked up and sighed. "And what might that be?"

"Dake. I told you about the message on the door. It had to be Dake. He's in this pretty tight."

"Oh, so you want to arrest Philip Dake, too?"

"No. Not that, Mr. President. I think we'd better keep an eye on him. He's got a cute little partnership going with Falcone. He just might be going to Israel, too."

Hollendale, with a tight smile, shook his head. "Harry, if you had your way, you'd be keeping an eye on everybody in this town. No, I don't want another bad news story in the *Post* about the FBI, or another call from Claire Greisham about phone taps. Just keep an eye on yourself, Harry." He turned back to the folder, and Polanski left the office.

40

For ANATOLY VORON-
sky, August should have been the kindest month. For five days he
had remained at the Soviet President's official vacation home on the
Black Sea. With the sun and wind on his face, he had sailed, fished,
read. Or done absolutely nothing. There were briefings from top
advisers, to be sure, and plenty of phone calls to make and receive.
But time there was measured by the tides, and the waves breaking
relentlessly on the shore induced a tranquillity that no narcotic
could match.

Voronsky had left the capital reluctantly. There was too much
unrest. A surge of violence was running all the way from Moscow to
Moldavia—a violence that held little respect for vacations. The last
thing he wanted was to be hundreds of miles away from the Kremlin. And yet if he broke the summer ritual and stayed in Moscow, it
would signal the world that fear had stalked and overtaken him, that
he was finally losing control. And the smell of that fear would excite
his political enemies. No, he had to play out the role, exude confidence, pretend that he was fully in charge of his nation's affairs as
he played with his eight grandchildren and frolicked in the sea.

"You will not have many moments like this, Mr. President. You should not squander them with worry."

Voronsky smiled at Oleg Kutznetzov, who looked more like a clown than a scholar, barely visible now under a blue terry-cloth robe, dark sunglasses, sneakers, and a baseball cap. At his age, Kutznetzov wanted no love affair with the sun.

"Nazdrovya," Voronsky said as he lifted a tall glass filled with ice and Stolichnaya. "You know me too well, my friend. I worry too much, I know. But there is much to worry about."

Kutznetzov looked off into the distance at the billowing sails of the boats gliding through the water. The flesh from his chin hung to his chest, like a pelican's, thought Voronsky.

"I spent an interesting evening with Mao Tse-tung many years ago. He spoke of the Americans at that time. He said they act like a flock of starlings at the coming of a storm. They shriek and fly anxiously about." Kutznetzov paused and sipped from his drink. "But nothing they do, not all their clamor and noise, can prevent the coming of the storm."

"Meaning?"

"Oh, Mao had many meanings. But I suppose that it's important to know the difference between the avoidable and the inevitable and act accordingly."

"So what are you saying, Comrade Oleg? That I am a starling, or that a storm is coming?"

"That the turbulence that we are witnessing was inevitable. The Soviet Union was sliding like a dinosaur into the ooze. There was no choice but to change. Political change is joined at the hip with economic change. You cannot have one without the other. It is a dynamic process, and it must be managed with skill. One must know when to apply pressure, when to release it."

"Perhaps I should be applying more pressure." Voronsky sighed, not really wanting Kutznetzov to agree.

"No. The Cheka is gone. Stalin cannot be resurrected from the grave. There can be no mass purges."

"The Chinese seem to think so. Maybe they understood Mao better."

"Bah. China is walking forwards backwards. They will always have one foot in the last century." Kutznetzov finished his vodka in a long gulp, then turned to Voronsky. "Next week you will be in

Washington, signing another agreement with the Americans. The world will applaud. Soviet citizens will take great pride in your leadership. So tell me, Anatoly, what is it that's really on your mind?"

Voronsky shook his head, embarrassed that he was so transparent. "Stalin may be dead. But Viktor Borovlev lives on. He's still pressing on BURAQ. He claims he has the votes. He persuaded the council members that we have more to lose than gain in the chemical weapons agreement. American spies, posing as scientists, will be roaming all over the country, jeopardizing some of our most secret programs and sowing even more dissension among our people."

"But he agreed to sign off on the agreement," Kutznetzov said.

"Yes. But for a price from the others."

Kutznetzov hefted himself out of his lounge chair and waddled over to the portable bar, where he poured himself a second drink. He carried the bottle of Stolichnaya back, but Voronsky waved him off. Finally he said, "Let's look at it analytically. What if BURAQ proceeds? Worst case?"

"The Saudis have long-range missiles and an excellent air force. The Syrians have chemical weapons. The Libyans have long-range aircraft, and the Iraqis still have tons of chemicals and, as you know, biological weapons, along with some of our Scud missiles. There'll be a war," Voronsky said, shaking his head with despair.

"Possibly. No doubt that would suit Borovlev. He views it as a win-win proposition for us no matter what happens. Israel may no longer exist. And even if Israel should win, it will pay a heavy price: massive casualties and a burned cinder of a country, as popular as a leper colony. Because of our historical friendship with the Arab nations, we would dominate the Persian Gulf states if they remain on the map. And if there are no Arab oil fields left, we'll become the major supplier of the world's energy—at our prices."

"And what if the United States comes to the rescue of its ally?"

"The Americans will not risk war with us over a nation that has outraged the world."

"But what if they do, Oleg? Assume the improbable."

"First of all, as soon as BURAQ went operational, you would order our forces to go on high alert, giving us an immediate strategic advantage. The United States might try to bluff us, like Kennedy did

during the Cuban missile crisis. But that would never work. Not
now."

"So you would have me roll the nuclear dice?"

Kutznetzov waved the fingers of his right hand as if he were
flicking off a gnat. "No, President Voronsky, you are raising hypoth-
eses that are not realistic. Think about it. You will be in Washington
at the time, signing a chemical weapons agreement. You will call
upon the Arab nations to show restraint in the face of a catastrophe
—a call that they will ignore. The United States will have no choice
but to join you. It could prove to be an enormous political coup for
you as well as an economic one for the Soviet Union."

Voronsky searched his old friend's eyes for a long time, looking for what, he wasn't sure. A hint of doubt? Skepticism? Fear?
Was resignation masquerading as enthusiasm? Voronsky still
thought BURAQ was crazy, but he knew it was beyond rational
argument. In the long run Soviet prosperity would depend on the
ability to produce not oil but manufactured, value-added, high-quality goods. But that would take time, and time was running out on
Voronsky, on his country. It was falling apart. There were too many
graveyards between then and now. Maybe . . . maybe Borovlev
was right.

Finally Voronsky said, "Oleg, you argue like a good lawyer
with a bad case. All sound and fury and no merit."

Kutznetzov dipped his head and peered over the rims of his
glasses, acknowledging the flattery with a chuckle.

The tension in Voronsky's neck eased as he considered
Kutznetzov's reasoning. But doubts continued to flock about him.
Playing devil's advocate, he asked, "What if the Arabs trace
BURAQ to us?"

"That's unlikely. Only a few people know. Borovlev will leave
no fingerprints. There would have to be a traitor among us, and even
then there would be no proof. We have complete deniability. But
assume the worst. What could they do? Go to war with us? Who
would be the first to strike us?"

"You think, then, Oleg, I should agree with Borovlev?"

"I think," Kutznetzov said, looking up at several sea gulls
screeching in the distance, "that it is well to embrace the inevitable
and let it carry you."

41

ALICE MORESI PICKED
up Falcone at the hospital, handed him a sheaf of urgent letters to
sign, and drove him to his car, which she had parked a few blocks
from his apartment house in Crystal City. He handed her back the
letters, told her to refer all committee inquiries to Ed Fulwood, and,
as he was getting out of her car, added, "Between now and my Israel
trip I'm unavailable. I may go to Israel without touching base here.
Don't ask me where I'm going now." He slammed the door and
headed for his car.

Alice leaned across to open the door and shout, "I can guess."
As she closed the door she muttered, "No voters, but lots of trees."

He turned to wave and smile, then got into his car. His head
throbbing, he tried to keep his mind on his driving. He went first to
Dulles International Airport, parked in the area reserved for members of Congress and justices of the Supreme Court, and walked into
the lower level of the terminal. He took the escalator to the upper
level and walked to the battery of glass doors that led to the departure deck. A taxi was dropping off a young couple and a boy about
three years old. The father unloaded three suitcases and a pet car-

rier with a barking dog inside. As soon as he slammed down the trunk, the driver leaped from the cab and said something that sounded like "Twenty-two dollars." After a brief shouting match, the father reached in his pocket, pulled out a wallet, shoved some bills toward the driver, and stalked off, suitcases and carrier flapping.

Falcone slipped into the passenger seat, and before the driver could say that this was not an authorized pickup point, he handed him a twenty-dollar bill. "Crystal City," Falcone said. "And there's ten more when you get there."

He got out of the cab near the Marriott Hotel, then, as the taxi pulled away, circled around an office building and entered the Crystal City subway stop. He bought a ticket at the fare machine, passed through the turnstile, went down an escalator, and ran toward a train marked National Airport.

At National, he had time for a stand-up beer and grilled cheese sandwich before walking down to the shuttle area. There, using his American Express card, he purchased a ticket for the New York shuttle. Then he walked to a gate that had a direct flight to Boston. When a flight attendant collected his ticket and noticed it was for New York, Falcone acted embarrassed, returned to the counter, and paid the difference in cash.

As soon as he could reach a telephone at Logan Airport, he called his Boston office, which he assumed was not yet tapped. The phone was answered by Wayne Pelham III, a bit too Harvard and a bit too reserved for campaign work but a brilliant caseworker who masterfully aided constituents in their bouts with the Washington bureaucracy.

"Wayne. You know who this is. I need wheels. Pick me up at the usual place. I'll pay for the speeding ticket."

"Of course. I'm on my way."

Pelham arrived at the airport pickup point fifteen minutes later. Throwing his suitcase into the back seat of Pelham's blue BMW, Falcone said, "Let's go to the parking lot."

"You look dreadful, if I might say so."

"You might, Wayne. I've had a rough couple of days. Committee matters."

"I have no need to ask what committee," Pelham said with a sigh, cutting off a taxi and executing a U-turn to the nearest parking lot. He did not approve of the Intelligence Committee because it served no obvious constituent needs. "I assume you are not going to pay one of your rare visits to our little office."

"That's right. I'll take a rain check. I need to rent a car. So will you—"

"So," Pelham interrupted, "will I go to the Avis counter and rent a car with *my* driver's license and *my* credit card? Correct? And then I assume I am to give you the keys and send you on your merry way, wherever that may be. Very, very cloak and dagger."

"If I might say so, Wayne, you're no dummy."

"You might say so, Senator," Wayne replied. A tight smile appeared on his thin lips and quickly vanished. "And if some enemy of the republic inquires about you, I shall say . . . ?"

"You shall say that all inquiries about the senator are to be handled by Alice, all inquiries about the committee by Ed."

"Very well, *mon capitaine.*"

Pelham parked in the short-term lot and, as he got out of the car, handed Falcone a thick manila envelope. "Some selected constituent reading," he said. "You may as well make use of the time while you're waiting. Jot down some comments."

Pelham returned a few minutes later, tossed a set of keys to Falcone, and drove him to the Avis lot. Falcone picked up his suitcase and headed for a green Dodge Daytona. "My God!" Pelham exclaimed. "Green! How vile! I had no idea."

A little more than an hour's drive north of Boston, Falcone pulled off U.S. 95 at a WELCOME TO MAINE sign. In the men's room of the tourist information building he changed to jeans, battered black sneakers, and a red cotton shirt. He slipped on a blue windcheater, neatly folded his suit, shirt, and tie, and placed them in the suitcase, which, with his shiny black shoes, he put in the trunk of his car. The island ritual had begun. At that moment he remembered what he had said to Joshua before his first visit to the island: "The first thing you've got to do is shed Washington."

The next step in the ritual was a stop at a supermarket, another hour and a half north, in Brunswick, Maine. Falcone rolled a shopping cart rapidly up and down the aisles. Steak, a bag of rolls, canned beans, canned soup, a chunk of cheese, coffee, oranges, bananas, butter, yeast, flour—no, flour would be there, and sugar would be there, and those cans without labels—a six-pack of expensive beer, batteries for the flashlight . . . At the checkout counter he got a tide table and saw that he had just over two hours of tide left.

From Brunswick he took a blacktop road to one of the fingers of land that form the ragged edge of the mainland. The road continued across a short causeway to Orrs Island and down Orrs to a cribstone bridge, humped in the middle to allow boats to pass underneath. The bridge, which linked Orrs Island and Bailey Island, was built of granite blocks arranged with spaces between them for the tides to flow through.

At the crossing of the bridge came the next ritual: the sighting of the island. He parked the car at a big red barn on whose side ANTIQUES was neatly painted in white, man-high letters, with a smaller BOATS GAS just below it. Standing here, looking out into Casco Bay, he could see, two miles from shore, the low, dark mound that was Spruce Island.

The island had belonged to a retired general who had inherited it from his father. The general, a widower now too old to enjoy it, had simply mailed the deed to Falcone after reading about Falcone's heroism in Vietnam in a Boston *Globe* feature. "A place where you can be alone but never lonely," an accompanying note had said. Falcone had mailed back the deed with a polite letter explaining that he could not accept gifts. But the general had insisted on taking him to the island, convinced that its spell would change his mind. A month later they met at the general's club in Boston, and Falcone bought the island for $3,000, which the general promptly signed over to the Army Relief Fund.

Falcone entered the barn through a small windowed door that had been carved out of the sagging barn door. Mr. Custer, the proprietor, was seated in a straight-backed chair by a cold stove with an enormous gray-and-white-striped cat on his lap. There was never an exchange of pleasantries with Mr. Custer, who, as far as Falcone knew, had no first name.

"Sittin' at the end of the dock," said Mr. Custer by way of greeting. He was the keeper of the island's boat, a Cape Ann dory built by the general and powered by an antique outboard motor.

"But no one told you I was coming."

"Correct. My nephews put my boats in weeks ago. Figured I'd have 'em do yours at the same time." Mr. Custer stood, dropping the cat to the scrap of carpet by the chair. He stepped to the counter (behind which hung a 1967 calendar), reached for a ledger, and briefly consulted its tidy pages. "It's all here." He began filling out a bill, and looked up. "Parking how long?"

"Counting today, three, maybe four days. Put me down for four days."

"Put you down for *three*," Mr. Custer said, carefully writing in the ledger and then on the bill. He reached under the counter again, took out a set of keys labeled Spruce Island, and handed them to Falcone. "Another day, pay me then. I know where you are." He looked down at the bill. "Gas?"

"The pump's fixed?"

"Wouldn't of asked if it weren't."

"Yes. Six gallons. And a pint—"

"—of oil," Mr. Custer said, turning to the shelf behind him and picking up a can, which he thumped down on the counter. He made another entry in the ledger, added another figure to the bill, and handed it to Falcone, who, knowing the ways of Maine, paid in cash.

In two trips down the ramp to the floating dock, he loaded the boat. Then he emptied the oil into the outboard's tank and filled it from a rusty, once-red gas pump. The motor started on the fifth try, and Falcone was on his way, weaving through red and green and white lobster buoys, passing under the bridge, spotting the swallow's nests that were always there, seeing the sea and sky through the crimstone latticework, then heading the prow of his nameless dory out of Bailey Island's bay and toward Spruce Island.

The island seemed to grow from the sea as he approached, the dark mound changing to a silhouette of pointed spruce and glistening granite. Closer, the shoreline came into focus, a jumble of huge, wave-lashed rocks that offered no opening. Falcone slowed and pulled within twenty yards of shore. The surging seas tugged him toward the rocks. He twisted the throttle on the motor tiller, and the motor groaned at a higher pitch as the boat fought the drag of the sea and crept along the shore, pitching in the waves. A towering black rock loomed up in front. Pulling the tiller hard right, Falcone swung around the rock, catching the wash of a wave full in his face.

The sea swirled around the black rock, which stood off a few yards from a rock wall thrusting outward from the island. The wall, scored with cracks, looked as if it were made of a giant's building blocks. Another, taller rock wall rose just beyond. Between them was the narrow channel to a natural harbor. Falcone pulled the tiller hard left and, borne on a cresting wave, hurtled toward the opening, which was scarcely wider than his boat.

The dory plunged into an egg-shaped cove whose still water mirrored the cloud-flecked sky. The sound of the motor startled dozens of herring gulls strung along a stone-upon-stone jetty. Squawking and flapping, they flew up in a blur of gray and white.

Falcone pulled the boat alongside the jetty and cut the motor. After unloading his supplies, he tied the dory's painter to the outhaul rope, which looped from the jetty to an iron ring attached to a rock on the other side of the cove. He pulled on the outhaul until the boat was in the center of the cove, carefully positioning it so that it could swing in a full circle without banging the jetty or the cove's rock-wall border.

Falcone stood for a moment on the jetty, savoring not only the air and the sky and the silence but also the awareness of memory and ritual. Nearly every move he had made today was a move he had made before, a move made rarely and nowhere else, yet one well remembered and well executed because it was needed to attain this so nearly unattainable place.

A path wound from the jetty to a sloping meadow of knee-high grass and wild roses in pink-and-white bud. It crossed a pair of logs spanning a brook, then rose slightly, and a stone house came into view. Falcone hurried now, anxious to reach the house and settle in before it was time to raise a beer ceremoniously to the sunset flowing over the sea and the rocks.

Next morning the gulls and sunlight woke him. For a moment he did not know where he was. He sat up and looked around. A bed covered by a faded quilt. An oil lamp on the driftwood box next to the bed. The sun pouring through a casement window. Beyond, a skyline of dark, jagged green. The low, constant murmur of the sea. Spruce Island.

His day was chopping wood and cooking and fetching water

from the well, walking the rocks and scaling smooth stones into the cove, crouching at a tidal pool and watching a starfish slowly open a mussel shell and . . . Only at that moment did he think of where he had been and what he had to do.

He walked back to the house, which, except for the nearby silvery gray shed and outhouse, was the only structure on the island. The house was squat and square, with a slate roof that was low and sharply peaked. The thick stone walls looked as if they had grown out of the rocky soil and would stand, shouldering the wind, forever. The general had told him that eighteenth-century coins had been found in the shallow dirt cellar. One of the many things Falcone had vowed to do someday was to dig for treasure in the cellar.

He opened the thick wooden door and entered the kitchen. After he got a fire going in the black stove, he went to a counter under the room's only window. The propane-powered hot plate and tabletop refrigerator seemed out of place in that ancient room, but Falcone welcomed the luxury of quick coffee-making and chilled beer. He took a beer now and sat on a driftwood bench at the table, a slab of wood bolted to four driftwood legs. He remembered words from a poem by Edna St. Vincent Millay, who once lived on a nearby island: "Care becomes senseless there . . . and thrift is waste."

But care came, and questions ran through his mind. *I have to leave tomorrow, get back. Talk to Dake. Talk to Clarke. Find out about her. Maybe Bickford can help.* He glanced up, saw the sky filling with reds and oranges and purples, and left the house to walk down to the cove. The boat, motor tipped up, lay as if sleeping on the dark earth and tendrils of seaweed that the sea had hidden. It would be about twelve hours to full high tide, Falcone calculated. He could leave as early as five o'clock tomorrow morning, but perhaps he would wait, spend some more time here, thinking, wondering . . .

He climbed up on the rock wall overlooking the jetty. Great chunks of granite were changing color—gray, beige, tawny, golden —as the shifting light played on the minerals captured in the stone. The sun, with what seemed like quickening movement, descended toward the distant seam of sea and sky. Then there was a last arc of throbbing red, a spreading band of gold, and the coming of night.

Three hours after sunset, and only a few minutes after beginning an Agatha Christie by the oil lamp's light, Falcone was asleep.

On the island he lived by the sun and tides, and he rarely awakened before dawn.

But at some moment during the deep darkness of this night he was suddenly awake. The gulls were squawking. He sat up, listening to their cries, accepting the alarm they were spreading along the shore. His heart began pounding, and the wound on his head began throbbing. *Someone is out there.*

He tried to dismiss the idea. A night landing was almost impossible. *Almost.* No one knew he was here. *Except Alice and Wayne and . . .* A goddamned owl could set off those stupid gulls. *In nesting season. Not now.*

He was out of bed without realizing he had moved. He pulled on jeans and sneakers and grabbed the flashlight, but did not turn it on. He walked into the kitchen and felt his way along a high open shelf to a tin breadbox. He reached in and pulled out a .45 and a full clip, both wrapped in an oily rag. Sometimes, on the ocean side of the island, he threw bottles off a cliff and shot at them while they bobbed in the waves. He slammed the clip into place and chambered a round.

The gulls were still squawking. He slipped out the door and, pocketing his flashlight, instinctively crouched in the darkness. Even starlight could silhouette a target. He listened to the gulls, trying to read their alarm. The loudest shrieks were coming from the cove.

Keeping low, he made his way down the path. When he reached the rise, he raised himself high enough to look down to the cove. A light was moving around. Someone was there, getting out of a boat, looking for the path. Maybe more than one. His old combat skills had returned unsummoned, for without realizing it, he was sensing more than seeing.

He rolled off the path and lay in the grass on his stomach for a moment, listening. Footsteps. Clinking. One man. But maybe another down at the boat. He pulled himself up, crouching at the edge of the path, waiting.

Through the tall grass he could see a flashlight's beam angling along the path. He coiled, and when the flashlight's beam was opposite him, he sprang.

For an instant he had his left arm around someone's neck and his gun jammed into someone's belly. Then he was whirling through the air and was flat on his back. A flashlight was shining down on his face. He twisted his head and raised the gun, aiming it just above the light.

The light went out, a foot kicked his wrist, and as his hand involuntarily opened, the foot kicked away the gun.

"Sean! It's me! Rachel!" The flashlight came on again. She was holding it under her chin, eerily illuminating her face.

Falcone spun over onto his stomach and groped in the dark grass for the gun. He painfully closed his hand around it and again aimed at the light. "Don't move a goddamned muscle," he said. He stood and with his other hand pulled his flashlight from his pocket. He shone it on the gun for a moment, then turned it to Rachel's face.

She moved, almost imperceptibly, then froze. He had an instantaneous impression that she would have made a move for the gun if she had felt her life depended on seizing it.

He motioned with the flashlight toward the cove. "Who else is down there?"

"No one. I am alone, Sean."

The gulls had calmed down. He decided to believe her.

He wagged the flashlight again, this time toward the house. "Get moving. We've got some talking to do."

Falcone shoved her through the door and into the cool darkness of the house. She stepped out of the beam of his flashlight, and for an instant he again sensed that she was on the verge of making an aggressive move. "Take one step forward," he told her. "Place your hands on the table in front of you." He directed the flashlight toward a small washstand table by the door. "Don't move."

Keeping the flashlight on her, he backed into the kitchen and with one hand managed to light the oil lamp on the table. "Walk slowly toward me and sit in that chair," he said, pointing the flashlight toward a straight-backed chair pulled up to the table.

Rachel sat and stared up at him. "Please, Sean. Put down the gun. I'm exhausted." She leaned forward, folded her arms on the table, and started to pillow her head on her arms.

"Sit up straight and put your hands, palms up, on the table." She hesitated. He bent over her and waved the gun. "Move!" He sat on the bench across from her and kept the gun aimed at her. "First thing," he said, "is how you found me."

She looked down at her palms, up to his face, then down at her palms. "It wasn't that hard. Your office—Alice, isn't it?—said you were not available. So I took it to mean that you were in hiding for some reason. But I had to find you." She looked up again. "Don't you want to know why?"

"I want to know how you found me."

"Politicians always have hideaways. I checked our files and—"

"*Mossad's* files?"

"I checked our files and went through your financial disclosure forms. Public records, as you know. You own only three pieces of property. A house in Framingham, which you rent out. The condominium in Crystal City. And"—her gaze swept the arc of light— "this." She paused, seeming to relax.

He looked at her closely for the first time. She was wearing a shiny yellow jacket with a white stripe running down the left sleeve. The jacket's hood was down, and her hair, softly golden in the lamplight, fell in tangles to her shoulders. Her eyes were sea green, almost emerald, tonight.

"Go on," he said.

"I figured you were either here or at some hideaway in your state. I called your Boston office and spoke to a charming man. I'm afraid I said there had been a slight accident and I needed to reach you. The man—Pelham? A young man, I assume?—sounded agitated. He said 'Avis? Is this Avis?' And—"

"Damn!" Falcone exclaimed.

"And," Rachel continued, "I said yes, I was Avis, and he said, rather arrogantly, I believe, 'That automobile, miss, is being driven by a United States senator, Senator Sean Falcone, and any problems you have should be addressed to this office in my name.' I said I wished to confirm the license number and he gave it to me. He also gave me what he said was his private home phone number and suggested that I call him if I ever get to Boston. I then—"

"Goddamned Wayne. He's a good office manager, but . . ."

"Too naïve?"

"Too full of himself," Falcone said, shaking his head and lowering the gun to the table. He kept his hand on top of it. "Keep talking."

"I flew to Boston. At the airport it seemed only appropriate to rent a car from Avis. And I drove to Bailey Island. I am good with maps."

"I bet you are. And?"

"And I saw the Avis car parked next to that barn. I rented a boat from that charming Ian Custer. I then—"

"*Ian?* His first name is *Ian?*"

"Yes. A charming man. I assured him that since it was getting late, I would not try to get to the island until morning. I checked into a motel. But I felt restless, and so I came back to Ian Custer's and said I wanted to try out the boat. He said in case I started out too early in the morning he would tell me how to get here. He told me about the big black rock and the—what is it, the inhaul?"

"Outhaul."

"Yes. Outhaul. I had a map and—"

"A chart. On land it's a map. On water it's a chart."

"Thank you." She had taken her hands from the table, and lacing her fingers together behind her head, she arched her back and shrugged her shoulders. "So you have tea, Sean? Coffee?"

He picked up the gun and put it down again. "Both."

"May I?" She nodded her head toward the hot plate.

He picked up the gun, reached in his pocket with his other hand, took out his flashlight, and handed it to her. "Use this. There're matches next to the burner and the coffee and tea are on the shelf above your head. There's also a lamp."

Rachel had already found the lamp and was lighting it with the same match she had used to light the hot plate. She found the big white enamel pitcher, poured water into a saucepan, and put it on the burner. "It's quite lovely here," she said. "Do you come here often?"

"As often as I can, which isn't often enough." He stuck the gun in his belt and stood and stretched. "So you got in the boat and then what? If you started before dark, you should have been here long ago."

"I got lost in a sudden bit of fog near Bailey. I seem to have gone past the island. I had no compass, and the darkness came quickly. I was heading, I believe, toward Portugal." She turned and laughed.

Falcone smiled. "Same thing happened to me the first time I came here alone. What did you do?"

"I used the stars—they are quite beautiful tonight—to head back in what I figured was the way I came. I would at least be going toward Maine. It would be better than going toward Portugal. And then I heard surf and decided to come closer. I saw the lights on Bailey, saw the rocks of an island—or heard them, and the gulls. I . . . got my bearings? And I looked for the big rock Ian had told me of. In starlight, your eyes begin to see."

"Yes," Falcone said. "They do."

She returned to the table and sat down. "And now may I tell you why I came?"

While brewing the tea and finding bread and making cheese sandwiches for both of them, Rachel told Falcone that she was Yitzhak Rafiah's daughter and that she worked for the Mossad.

"You're a spy assigned to Washington?" he asked, munching on the sandwich. His voice had lost its edge, and his well-honed instinct for survival had vanished, along with the gun, which was back in the breadbox.

"I am an intelligence analyst assigned to Washington. I believe that there is a connection between Joshua Stock's death and the attack on my father."

"What connection?"

"Some answers may be in Israel. I am going there to talk to my father. I have been informed that he is no longer in a deep coma. He may be able to speak. At least to me."

"What has this to do with me?"

"It is very possible—very probable—that you are in danger because you are trying to learn what happened to Joshua Stock. When you were . . . missing, I felt I had to find you and tell you at once. You are, I believe, involved in something that is very, very dangerous."

"I suppose I should thank you," Falcone said, rubbing his right wrist.

"Then please do so."

"Thank you."

"You are entirely welcome." She smiled at him over the edge of her cup. "There is one more thing."

"What is it?" he asked sharply.

"I dropped my bag on the path. There is a bottle of brandy, Israeli brandy. Shall I get it? Or am I still your prisoner?"

"We'll both get it," Falcone said. "Prisoner and warden."

They walked down the path and found her blue-and-white El Al bag. Falcone gently shook it. "Nothing rattles," he said. "I think we have a nightcap."

"Can we stand here a moment?" she asked. "It is very beautiful here." She opened her arms, encompassing the island—the stars, the chilly night, the light of the lamp glowing in the window, the occasional soft mew of a gull, the never-ending whisper of the sea.

"You have made it more beautiful, Rachel," Falcone said.

"I am glad I am here, Sean."

He stepped closer, took her arms, and placed them on his shoulders. He felt her shudder as she touched his shoulders, and he pulled back.

"No," she said, pulling him closer. "No. For a moment, a memory." She looked up at his puzzled face. "Only a bad memory."

He embraced her, his lips brushing her neck. They stood for a long moment, then turned and walked back up the path to the house.

Seated side by side on the kitchen bench, they sipped brandy from jelly glasses and talked, Falcone about the island and a little about his life, Rachel about her father and even less about her life.

"It's getting cold," Falcone said eventually. "I'll get a blanket."

"We could go to where the blanket is," she said.

"There is only one bed. But in what I call the parlor there is an armchair, and I thought . . ."

"I imagine that you also have been thinking something else," she said, smiling and clinking his glass. "Last call."

He poured them each a drink, put down the bottle, and gently kissed her. She drew him close, his face between her hands, and they kissed again, deeply, tongue seeking tongue. Falcone pulled back and started to speak. She touched his lips and said, "No words."

He stood and took her hand. He blew out the lamp on the table and then the one on the counter. In the darkness they walked to the bedroom, undressed, and lay down on the brass bed.

She was close to Falcone now. That's what she had been trained to do: get close. That's what Ambassador Dimcha had said he wanted her to do. But for what? Rachel was no longer sure of her motivations or the reasons she had come all this way. Guilt, she knew, was part of it.

Falcone was on to something, something that someone didn't want him to pursue. Two nights ago, in the garage, that someone had arranged to send him a message. Break a few of his bones. Set him up with some phony drug deal. She could have disabled his attackers easily, but in that split second before she fired, she recognized one of the men, the one with the blackjack. He was the same man she had been tracking. He was to be her next target. In that moment of decision, she fired not to wound or disable but to kill. It was all so perfectly convenient. *Pfff, pfff*—the man was gone.

A cakewalk. Except for Falcone. It was not until after she had returned to her embassy and started to prepare a report that the first twinge of guilt had slipped up on her.

Retribution. She knew they would come for him now with more than a message. They would track him down, maybe all the way to Jerusalem. She could not let that happen. Not in Israel.

Falcone, his face partially illuminated by the diffuse starlight, touched her face and ran the back of his hand gently from her ear along her jawline until his fingers rested on her lips. Excitement ignited deep inside her, a small flame that grew in intensity, forcing her to fight for control of her thoughts.

Guilt, yes. But it was more than guilt that brought her here. More than the need to protect him had pulled her to this island. She had recognized something in Falcone: a wound that emptied into unfathomable darkness, a place where demons and gargoyles lived, where a chorus of obscene voices cackled at the absurdity of it all . . .

Falcone pulled her toward him and kissed her. He moved his hands and cupped her breasts. The flame deep inside her began to leap up and burn the back of her throat. Her mouth went dry. She swallowed. Then she let go, let fall the last strings of resistance. She allowed her mind to float out into that vast darkness where nothing beyond the moment mattered and she felt only a pulsing white heat moving inside and carrying her into the infinite night.

At dawn, awakened by the stirring gulls, they made love again, and Rachel drifted back to sleep. Falcone slipped out of bed and, standing naked in the kitchen, brewed coffee and began making pancakes. The aroma of the coffee tugged Rachel awake, and she appeared in the kitchen cloaked in the quilt. She stepped next to him and, flinging open the quilt, drew him toward her. Enwrapped on the bench, they sipped coffee until Falcone, complaining of cold feet, got up, poured the first pancakes onto the griddle, and streaked into the bedroom to dress.

As soon as there was water enough under the boats, they set out on a calm sea for Bailey Island. Boston was next. Then New York. Then Israel.

PART III

"I saw a man chasing the horizon,
Round and round they sped.
I was disturbed at this;
I accosted the man.
'It is futile,' I said,
'You can never' —
'You lie,' he cried,
and ran on."

—*Stephen Crane*

42

En route to Israel, August 14–15

TWO HOURS OUT OF Kennedy, an El Al cabin attendant touched Falcone on the shoulder. "A gentleman in first class asked me to give you this," he said, handing Falcone a folded piece of paper. He opened it and read, "Sean: Nothing is what it appears to be. Come see me quietly. Phil."

"What is it?" Rachel asked.

"A constituent," he said, rising. He leaned against the backrest of the seat, feeling slightly faint. They had called it a slight concussion. He called it a very bad headache that was going away slowly.

"Is something wrong?" she asked, looking up at him, her face concerned. He wondered again about what she knew, what she had done, what she intended to do.

"I was startled by the tap on the shoulder, I guess. I was just dozing off. Well, I'm off to first class, where the importuning voters always seem to be. I'll try to get rid of him as soon as I can. Can I bring you back a drink?"

She shook her head and picked up *Newsweek* from the pocket of the seat in front of her.

He began making his way down the aisle toward the blue curtains that separated the classes in airliner democracy. So far on the flight Rachel and he had talked little. Falcone had been lost in thought. It was not guilt that crowded in on him but nagging doubts about what had happened in Maine. Something was not right about Rachel. The way she had found him, flipped him in the dark; her strength, her speed. Why did he go to bed with a woman he knew so little about, one he had come to suspect? It had to have been her that night in his garage . . .

Now, suddenly, he had to start thinking about what he should say to Philip Dake. He remembered the paper on the door: "Call me at once. Music Man." Now this note. He had been keeping Dake in the dark. *And now,* he thought with a smile, *I'll have to pay.* Keeping Philip Dake in the dark was not a good strategy for anyone in Washington, especially not for people who were in trouble and in the dark themselves.

Falcone pushed aside the curtain. Dake was in a window seat near the front. When Falcone came alongside the seat, the reporter glanced up and motioned to the empty seat next to him. "Sit down, Sean," he said. "We have to clear some accounts."

"I'm sorry about not getting back to you," Falcone said.

"Not getting back to me?" Dake repeated, laughing. "That's the understatement of the week. Let's try vanishing act. What the hell is going on? I thought we were working together."

"We were. We are. Look," Falcone said, gesturing with his right hand and smiling faintly, "we're even on the same airplane."

"I'm on this airplane primarily to warn you about your girl-friend. Give me back the note. She might pick it from your pocket as part of her training."

Falcone handed over the note, which Dake put in his pocket. "What are you talking about?" he asked, trying to sound indignant.

"I assume you know her as Rachel Yeager. Her real name is Rachmella Rafiah."

"So?"

"You know, Sean, I've talked to enough politicians to convince myself that they can't all be as dumb as they sometimes try to sound. 'So?' Yitzhak Rafiah. Ring a bell?"

"Don't be a smart-ass with me, Phil. She told me all about her father. He got shot in Paris recently."

"He was shot the same night that Stock was murdered. I suppose she told you that they were quite close. Maybe even working for the same company."

"That's not fair!" Falcone exclaimed. The attendant, who had been hovering near, rushed up. Falcone waved him away.

"This probably won't come as any surprise to you, unless you're as innocent as you're pretending to be. She's a Mossad agent."

Falcone tried to feign surprise, quickly changed his mind, sighed, and said, "Look, Phil. I've been around the block a few times. I knew . . . well, I was damn sure she was Mossad. They've got her keeping an eye on me. So what?"

"So watch your ass. Joshua Stock wound up with a beautiful woman too. And he's dead."

"Thanks for your concern. I've been watching my ass for a long time and it's still there."

"Let me try again. Rachel is one of the Killer Angels. Ever hear of them?"

"I've a vague recollection."

"It's no motorcycle gang, my friend. Your new girlfriend can take you out while sticking her tongue down your throat."

"Nice, Phil. Real nice." Falcone exhaled slowly to show his impatience. "Okay. What's this all about?"

"Right after the Black September terrorist group massacred the Israeli Olympic team in Munich in 1972, Israel formed its own liquidation force. Elite teams were trained to carry out the execution of Arab terrorist leaders wherever they could be found. Membership in these assassination squads was pretty selective. Only the brightest young men and women could apply; only the best of the brightest could qualify. Not only did they have to be skilled in languages and possess nearly photographic memories, but they had to have the physical abilities of Israel's best athletes. Perhaps most crucial of all, they had to possess an essential cruelty—to be able to kill, not from a distance but up close, with a garrote, a knife, or a gun inches from their victims' faces. They had to be able to hear them plead for mercy, scream for life, weep for their families, and then put a bullet in their brain or slice a razor across their jugular."

Falcone almost winced at Dake's last words as the image of Joshua's ravaged throat flashed instantly in his mind. "From what little I know about it," Falcone said, coming down hard on *know*, "that's all something of the past. And most of it propaganda."

"Wrong, Sean. People out at Langley tell me they are very much alive. They've got the full logistical support of military intelligence at their service as well. There's a real system to it, nothing random. First they identify their target. Then they track him—or her—for weeks, sometimes months. They study travel routes, habits, peccadilloes, you name it—everything is put under a microscope. Intelligence boys forge identities for them, provide them with transportation, maps, hotels, safe houses, communication, weapons, disguises, escape routes."

"And you're telling me that Rachel is one of the Angels?"

"My information is that your friend may have helped on a job in Brussels a few years ago, the one that took out that Canadian who was helping the Iraqis build the long-range Tammuz missile they were going to aim at Israel. Her latest, as far as I have been able to find out, was Yassir Mohammed Abu Kattish. The FBI is also looking into the death of Ahmed Jooma, the Libyan they found strangled in Rock Creek Park. Turns out he was a cousin of the guy they found nailed in your garage."

"Jesus." Falcone sighed, slumping deep into his seat, his mind spinning in confusion. "What in hell is going on?"

"You tell me." Dake handed Falcone a glossy three-by-five photograph. There were four people in the picture. "What do you see that looks unusual?" Dake asked sarcastically. "Let me help you. That one there," he said, pointing to a tall, scholarly-looking man, "is Yitzhak Rafiah. I can't make out the man standing next to him in the shadows, but you should have no trouble with the other two."

Falcone stared in disbelief. There was Joshua with his arm around . . . Rachel.

"I'll bet you didn't know they were so chummy."

Falcone just shook his head, too stunned to speak. In the long silence that followed, a thousand thoughts went roaming around his mind, but not one of them made any sense.

"I said I wanted to clear accounts, so let me start. Here's what I've got. The FBI believes someone was leaking classified stuff to Israel. I'm told Stock was on the suspect list. Stock had a meeting with Hollendale in April. It was never recorded in the White House logs. Polanski was there, too. But there was no record of his presence."

"And what do you think is the significance of that?" Falcone asked, trying to sound surprised. He was not sure he fooled Dake.

"Either they wanted something or they were using him for something. And maybe that something killed him. Whatever it is, Polanski is suddenly very chummy with me. I'm practically being courted by the FBI." He hesitated and turned to look directly at Falcone. "I told you before, they are tapping your phone. You didn't believe me. Now I'm telling you they've got you on the suspect list, too."

"What?" Falcone grabbed the armrests. He lurched toward Dake. "What? What the hell are you talking about?" The attendant took a step closer. Again Falcone waved him away.

"Polanski himself told me. I didn't believe it, but I confirmed it for myself." He patted Falcone's arm. "Look, I know it's bullshit. But it means something. Just like the attack in the garage. The Virginia cops hushed it up, but news is getting around. You've got poor Agnes all worried. You should send her a postcard."

"What did Polanski tell you about the attack?"

"That's just it, Sean. Initially, I got nothing from Polanski on that. What I first found out I got from one of his boys, and indirectly from Agnes, who, by the way, may think you have a long-lost nephew named Sid." He paused for effect. Falcone settled back in his seat. "Then, three hours before I leave for the airport—as if they *know* I'm just about to leave for the airport—I get a visit from the same Division Five guys who took me to Polanski the last time. I tell them I'm in a hurry, and as I said, it's as if they know. They say they'll take me to the airport. I say no thanks. But I go to Polanski's office and there we are, just him and me in his office, and he's telling me all about the shooting—the drugs on the guy's body, the place where you like to keep guns . . . It's obvious that Polanski is trying to feed me from menu A to keep me from seeing the really good stuff on menu B." He looked hard at Falcone. "And I am sure that you know what's on menu B."

"Extended metaphors confuse me," Falcone said. "Besides, how do I know you're not interviewing me for a story about how Polanski suspects me of being a spy?"

"Polanski's given me so much stuff that I'm suspicious. Very suspicious. I don't want to be used by that sonofabitch. Don't worry, there's no story. I only wish there was. I'm writing memo after memo to my boss to make him understand that I'm not spending all this time and money for nothing."

"Maybe there never will be a story, Phil."

"Meaning?"

When Falcone failed to answer, Dake grabbed his arm. Falcone twisted away and began to rise from his seat. "I've got to get back," he said. "She'll be wondering."

Dake grabbed his arm again. "Wait a minute, Sean. I thought our original deal was that we would share information. It looks like I'm doing the sharing and all you're doing is getting deeper into whatever this is. Let me sum up. Your friend may have been an Israeli spy who got murdered. And now you're on your way to Israel in the company of a professional killer, who, I might add, seems to fit the description of a woman Detective Clarke tells me was seen leaving Stock's house the night of the murder. Now then, don't you think it's about time you told me what the hell is going on?"

"Joshua Stock was no spy," Falcone heatedly replied. "And neither am I. Polanski's trying to cover up another one of those goddamned off-the-shelf White House operations that went off the tracks. I'll tell you this much. Joshua wasn't working for the Israelis. He was working for Polanski."

"What?" Dake exploded, not believing what he had just heard.

Falcone got out of his seat and leaned toward the reporter. "Like you always say, nothing is what it appears to be." He slapped Dake's shoulder and then headed back to the tourist class.

When Falcone returned to the rear of the aircraft, he found Rachel asleep—or pretending to sleep. He slipped down into his seat, trying to keep as much distance from Ms. Mossad as possible. Inches somehow seemed to matter to him just then.

He found himself unable to sleep during the long flight. He ordered two Jack Daniel's from the attendant. He dozed, blinked awake, dozed again. He hoped reading might serve as a tranquilizer, but it was no use; his eyes remained fixed on pages that might as well as have been blank. He sat up and stretched his neck left and right, trying to stretch out the stiffness in his shoulders. Then he went to the bathroom, returned to his seat, stared into the darkness around him.

Exactly what had Joshua gotten into? Gotten him into?

Questions continued to move past him in the gloom that enveloped him. He could hear the jet engines' soft whisper outside the cabin. He was hurtling through the night, sheathed inside a thin aluminum membrane, heading for what? Looking over at the woman beside him, he thought, *Maybe for hell.*

Falcone stepped off the plane at Ben Gurion Airport outside Tel Aviv. Following Rachel's lead, he moved rapidly past the line of passengers who were queuing up for customs inspection. He searched vainly for Dake's face and assumed that the first-class passengers had already cleared. He had two bags, both carry-ons. Rachel had checked her luggage, but retrieved it with surprising speed at the baggage section. Speaking Hebrew and flashing an ID, she escorted him quickly past a customs officer and the waiting crowd of relatives and friends.

Outside they were greeted by a blast of hot air—hot, but surprisingly, not as humid as Washington's. Horns were blowing as taxis and buses pulled up, disgorging or receiving passengers. The air was thick with diesel fumes, and the noise from the traffic and people waiting for passengers was almost deafening.

Falcone looked out into a sea of Semitic faces. He presumed that most of them were Israeli, but they might just as well have been Arab. The men were dark, narrow-hipped. Many had on designer jeans. All wore open-necked cotton shirts. Anyone in the area wearing a tie had to be a tourist.

Falcone pushed through the crowd. He was tense, uneasy. It reminded him of his days in Vietnam. He could never tell who the enemy was.

Rachel paced back and forth near the curb. Standing on her toes, she shielded her eyes with one hand while looking for someone. Minutes passed. They seemed like hours to Falcone. He wanted to get away from there.

What in hell was he doing here, anyhow? Was Rachel setting him up now? Maybe to be hit by some commando team posing as

PLO terrorists, a trick to enrage Americans and drive them back to Israel, away from the Arab cause?

Falcone was shaken from his thoughts by Rachel, who was tugging on his arm. "Hurry, this way. That's our car, over there." She waved at a black Peugeot.

"Shalom, Kobi," she bubbled at the driver when they got to the car. "I'm glad to see you." She embraced him briefly.

The square-jawed young man, his black eyes shining, flashed a wide grin, revealing even white teeth against his dark skin. "Shalom, Rachel. Sli'ha li she'icharti k'zat."

"No, Kobi." Rachel laughed. "You are not late. The plane arrived early."

Kobi opened the trunk, took their bags, and set them inside. Falcone and Rachel jumped into the rear seat as horns of taxis scolded them for tying up traffic. As Falcone looked past Rachel, she noticed a look of surprise on his face. "What is it, Sean?"

"Over there," he said, motioning with his head. "The man over there, getting into the limosine. What's he doing here?"

"Michael Rorbach?" Rachel said, turning to look out the rear window. "He's a big benefactor of Israel. Do you know him?"

"Not really."

"He's a long-time friend of my father's. The new wing at Hebrew University is being named after him. He's probably here for the dedication ceremony."

Maybe, Falcone thought. But somehow he just didn't believe it.

During the thirteen-mile drive northwest to Tel Aviv, Falcone remained silent, his body turned away from Rachel. She noticed that his mood had changed ever since he returned from visiting with that constituent of his on the plane. Something the man said must have upset Falcone. Or maybe, she reasoned, he was merely tired. She engaged in small talk about the weather, the traffic, familiar landmarks, missile craters, plans for seeing her father.

Soon they arrived at the Hilton Hotel, where Falcone had a room reserved. As he got out of the car, Rachel suggested that they have dinner that evening.

"I'm not sure I can. I've already made plans to visit our ambassador. But right now what I need is some rest. Call me tomorrow. I'll try to plan something for tomorrow night."

Kobi retrieved Falcone's bags from the trunk and handed them to him. "Tiyeh bari, Senator."

Falcone looked puzzled. Kobi was smiling, but it was a face whose lips contained a certain hardness. He was certain that Kobi was more than a driver.

Rachel leaned her head out the open rear window. "He said, 'Stay well,' Sean," she explained, then chastised Kobi for speaking Hebrew.

"Thanks. I thought he was looking for a tip," Falcone responded, without much mirth.

Kobi slammed the trunk down, returned to the driver's seat, and pulled away. Falcone, refusing assistance from a bellhop, disappeared into the hotel lobby. Ten minutes later he was in his room on the fifteenth floor of the hotel, which faced the Mediterranean. He unpacked quickly, took a long hot shower, donned a monogrammed terry-cloth robe, and stepped out onto a small tiled balcony. Below him, a clean-looking beach stretched north in a smooth line. It was dotted with sun worshipers, who walked along the shoreline or played in the surf. Not far from shore were dozens of sailboats moving rapidly across the dark blue water. In the distance he could see merchant ships chugging slowly toward the port cities of Jaffa and Haifa.

A strong breeze touched his face with a warm, sensuous caress. Below, the sunbathers were folding their chairs, gathering blankets, towels, and children, preparing for the solemn trundle through the sand back to their cars.

Stepping into the air-conditioned room, Falcone went to the small service bar and unlocked it with the key provided by the hotel. He extracted two one-ounce bottles of bourbon and poured them over ice in a short glass. Then he called the American embassy and spoke with the ambassador, Reed Barrington III. Ordinarily, Falcone made no attempt to feign cordiality toward people he disliked. But he needed information now and he hoped Barrington might be able to provide it.

Drinking deeply from his bourbon, Falcone begged off his appointment at the embassy, saying that he was jet-lagged and needed rest. Barrington, playing a your-wishes-are-my-orders role without a hint of annoyance, said that the team briefing that had been arranged for Falcone could be easily rescheduled for the next day.

Falcone exchanged a few insincere pleasantries with him and said that he might need some help from one of the embassy staffers with a few appropriate remarks at the dedication ceremonies. Finally he asked Barrington to recommend a good restaurant in Tel Aviv.

"That's like coming to New York and asking about a good play," Barrington said with a laugh. "French? Italian? Israeli? What's your preference?"

"Jewish Italian?" Falcone asked in mocking disbelief. "Now that sounds interesting."

"Well, there are at least ten that I could recommend, but I've found Da Sergio to be consistently good. The cheese dishes are homemade, the sauces are light, the vegetables are fresh, and there's a good selection of wines and homemade ice cream and zabaglione. It's an Arab house, right in the heart of old Jaffa."

"Sounds terrific."

"Speaking of homemade, how about if Kibby and I put something on for you over here? She makes the best pasta in Tel Aviv— maybe in all of Israel."

"No. No. It's very kind of you, Mr. Ambassador, but I've got some plans already."

"How about if I send a car over and a staffer to escort you?"

To watch me, you mean, Falcone found himself thinking. "Many thanks, but I'll be fine. If I run into any problems, I'll take you up on it. Actually, I could use a car to bring me to the embassy tomorrow, though. See you then, Mr. Ambassador. Looking forward to it. Best to your wife."

Falcone set the receiver back into its cradle. Then he picked it up again. He called the hotel's concierge and asked for the street address and telephone number of Da Sergio. Then he called the restaurant and made dinner reservations for two at eight the next evening. It was a reservation that he knew he was not going to keep.

Falcone finished his bourbon, then lay back on his king-sized bed and drifted off into a long dreamless sleep.

43

"GOOD MORNING, SENA-tor," the ambassador said, enthusiastically grasping Falcone's right elbow as he pumped his very best handshake. It was a well-practiced gesture to convey sincerity. But Reed Barrington III was not known as a sincere man. Ambitious and calculating, yes. But hardly sincere.

Barrington was tall, lanky, and raw-boned. He swept his graying hair straight back and held it in place with some designer glue. His blue eyes were deep-set. There was a coldness to them, Falcone decided, and more than a touch of cruelty could be found there, too. But the cruelty was subtle. It was hidden behind Barrington's urbanity and refined speech.

His speech—that was what annoyed Falcone the most. Barrington spoke with an accent that seemed to become more affected with each of his diplomatic assignments. It was calculated to set him apart from the vast middle class—or classless middle—of Americans, to remind his audience of long bloodlines, of a toughness cut on rugby fields, of wisdom acquired from gold-leafed, leather-bound books, of visions much broader than those of ordinary men because they had been acquired from superior heights.

When Falcone had met Barrington, in El Salvador, he experienced an almost immediate contempt for him. There was excitement in Barrington's voice as he spoke of the prospect of America's sending troops to bolster the Salvadoran army against the FMLN. To Barrington, San Salvador was Saigon in Spanish, this time without the mistakes. But that's what men like Barrington always thought.

It was well known that most Israelis considered Barrington's professed intellectual neutrality nothing but the mask of a bigot. He was not necessarily pro-Arab, but he was not pro-Israel either. Perhaps it was just that he reminded them too much of their experience when the British controlled Palestine under the mandate.

Falcone forced something that approximated a smile as he returned Barrington's handshake. As the ambassador escorted him over to a sofa, he glanced quickly around the private study. There were the obligatory photographs of President Hollendale and Secretary of State Shanahan. A family portrait of Barrington's wife, two children, and mandatory golden retriever rested on a dark mahogany credenza behind an old, ornately carved oak desk that was not government issue. The walls were covered with a tan grass cloth, except for one that contained a floor-to-ceiling bookcase. Falcone scanned some of the titles: Kissinger's *The White House Years,* Brzezinski's *The Grand Failure,* Nixon's *Nineteen Ninety-Nine* . . .

A ficus tree and two potted plants added a soft ambience to the room. A window faced onto a small garden surrounded by a high concrete wall. Falcone imagined that the room was frequently filled with the music of Mozart or Chopin. In fact, Barrington preferred Mantovani.

Falcone recognized a large box constructed of vanilla-colored wood, with Barrington's initials carved boldly on its top, resting on the desk. It had been made in the Philippines. Falcone had one nearly identical to it. It contained, he suspected, fresh, hand-wrapped, and absolutely foul-tasting cigars, a Christmas gift from some retired Army colonel still living in plantation splendor somewhere outside Manila.

Barrington engaged in the usual small talk. "Smooth flight? Jet-lagged, are you? Senate in recess? . . . Important times, you know . . . Washington must be excited with Soviet President

Voronsky coming next week for the signing of the chemical weapons agreement, hmmn . . . Nice of you to participate in the dedication ceremony at the university. A United States senator's presence means a great deal to the Israelis. Frankly, I didn't know you had an interest . . . in such matters."

Such matters? Was this a probe? "I'm just helping out a friend," Falcone said without elaboration.

Barrington offered coffee from a polished silver serving set.

"Yes. Please." Falcone quickly refused to extract a cigar from the open box that Barrington extended to him.

Barrington explained that his deputy and top foreign policy expert had had an unexpected call to meet with some key Israeli officials in Jerusalem, but he would be back in the afternoon, if Falcone wanted to meet with him. "What can *I* do for you during your stay, Senator?" he then asked, after lighting a long, thick cigar with a wooden match that he had struck with his thumbnail.

It was a curious gesture, Falcone thought—the act of a common man, transformed by Barrington into one of swaggering condescension. "Tell me what's going on here," he replied. "Politically. Militarily. The diplomatic relationship with the Soviet Union. A general overview."

"I'm not sure I can add much to what you already know, but . . ."

This meant, Falcone reasoned, that Barrington did not feel free to give him more than a superficial analysis. He remembered reading that back in the early fifties, the Israelis had planted a microphone in the ambassador's office. There had been telephone taps attached to the military attaché's residence, another time. But that was long ago, when the relationship was less solid. Still, most ambassadors, in hostile or friendly countries, usually acted on the assumption that someone was listening to their words.

Of course, maybe Barrington was just signaling that he intended to be minimally helpful.

"The Israelis are staggering through what is no doubt the greatest crisis of their existence. They are confused and demoralized. Bewildered, actually," Barrington said, lifting his right eyebrow. It was a gesture so practiced that it very nearly seemed genuine. Falcone noticed that Barrington had allowed a certain weariness to attach itself to his words, as if he were carrying the tragic burdens of *his* state upon *his* shoulders.

"The United States would like Labor to win control of the government. But Labor's leadership is split into two warring camps, and there aren't any new political stars on the horizon. The Likud is hanging on by its fingernails. And while Gerstel may not be President Hollendale's favorite overnight guest at Blair House, the people coming behind him are more rigid and even harder to deal with. If we undermine Gerstel, Labor won't be able to pick up the pieces. The Likudites will fry Gerstel and we'll end up with a new wave of hard-liners who will never give an inch of land to the Palestinians."

Oddly, Barrington seemed pleased with his description of Israel's political travails. He paused, sipped his coffee, and drew deeply on his cigar, careful not to inhale the smoke, which he released through pursed lips.

"Labor and Likud are united in how to deal with the external threat to Israeli forces," he continued. "Thanks mainly to our Western allies—Germany, primarily—chemical weapons have become a major component of the arsenals of Syria, Iraq, Iran, and Libya. And we believe Iraq still has substantial quantities of biological weapons—"

"Supplied by us," Falcone interjected sarcastically. He had been furious when he discovered that the American Type Culture Collective, in Rockville, Maryland, had supplied Iraq during the 1960s with tularemia, a bacterium that in weapon form was ten times more lethal than anthrax.

Taking the official State Department line, Barrington replied, "That's not entirely clear. It's possible that Iraq acquired the bacteria sample from any number of countries, including Hungary, Czechoslovakia, and Bulgaria."

"Maybe," Falcone said, "but I doubt it." He knew that the United States had obtained the bacteria from the Soviet Union before the Geneva Biological Weapons Convention was signed in 1972. Conceivably, the Soviet Union had shared them with some of its client states. But Falcone thought it unlikely.

"In any event," Barrington continued, dismissing the significance of the origins of biological weaponry now in Arab hands, "Israel's security problems have been compounded by enhanced delivery systems now in the hands of its enemies. China has continued to sell ballistic missiles to Saudi Arabia. The Soviets still provide short-range Scuds to the Syrians, who upgrade them so they can put them on top the library at Tel Aviv University."

Falcone decided against interrupting again. No mention was made of the United States' participation in the arms sales orgy. As Joshua had frequently pointed out during Senate debates, we Americans always rationalized that if we did not sell arms, our allies would. And they, of course, were not quite so sympathetic to Israel and would be less inclined to use any leverage to restrain Arab animosities and aggression. If we stayed out of the arms action, it did not mean that the arms merchants stayed out of the Middle East. Nothing had been learned from our experience with Saddam Hussein.

"In spite of tremendous numerical odds, Israel is still able to cope with this external threat." Again Barrington paused long enough to sip coffee and puff on his cigar. "But its military is no match—I should say, is mismatched against Palestinian children. The *intifada*, the uprising, has the Israelis completely befuddled. Their young front-line soldiers have been trained in aerial, ground, and tank combat. Turning them into riot police only degrades their military skills. But when the Israelis bring in middle-aged reservists for extended duty, the reservists—who are a bit out of shape, I might add—rebel against the time they have to spend away from their families and professions and resent being forced to brutalize children and teenagers. That's what is draining Israel, Senator. There are no more heroes to fire the imagination of the people. No more Weizmanns, Yadins, Dayans. The Palestinians have all the passion, the martyrs."

Barrington stood up, stretched, and walked to the window. He struck something of a thoughtful pose and then leaned against the edge of his desk.

"Israeli leaders careen back and forth. One day they offer olive branches, the next an iron fist. When they raze Palestinian houses and shoot rock-throwers, world opinion turns against them. When they seem willing to negotiate indirectly with the PLO, the Palestinians see it as a sign of weakness and redouble the violence. Complicating the matter is the power of the religious fundamentalists, who seem to be gaining numbers and influence at a rather surprising rate."

Everything Barrington said conformed to what Falcone had heard during Intelligence Committee briefings. What bothered him was the ambassador's manner: his bloodless tone, the structure of his words, the damn arch of that brow, as if he were a professor lecturing a student in some safe ivy-covered campus hall.

"I gather you don't see any solution . . ."

"Ah, Senator," Barrington said, relishing the chance to lecture his guest. *"Solution* is not a good word to use with reference to the Israelis. Their conflict with—"

"Forget the word then," Falcone snapped, unable to contain his resentment. "What answer do you—the State Department, the President—propose to help end the war? And don't play word games with me. I do mean war. *Conflict* is a word that diplomats use when someone else is doing the fighting and the dying."

"The answer, Senator," Barrington said stiffly, "is that there is no answer. The 'peace process' that we keep referring to with such misty-eyed hope is a mirage, an illusory oasis in the desert."

Falcone knew he had struck a tender spot. The ambassador had managed to avoid the Vietnam "conflict," initially through a series of deferments from the draft while in college and graduate school. When the deferments expired, he was injured in a hunting accident that ruptured his right eardrum, disqualifying him from military service.

"The Palestinians want the West Bank, East Jerusalem, and Gaza. Neither Likud nor Labor will ever agree to such concessions. Any settlement, or solution, if you will, can only come about if Jordan can bring about some sort of joint rule with the Israelis on the West Bank. This *could* provide some measure of territorial rights to the Palestinians and security to the Israelis.

"The problem is that Likud is willing to permit local elections in the West Bank only if there are no indications of what ultimate concessions might be made and only if the *intifada* is stopped. While you might not like to hear it, Senator, I think the prospects for breaking the cycle of violence are not promising."

The phone on Barrington's desk rang. He reached over, picked up the receiver, and winced slightly, as if he resented being interrupted by outside forces. "Oh, yes. Tell him I'm running a bit late. I can talk with him in just a few more minutes. Thanks, Donna. Sorry," he said, turning back to Falcone.

He's not sorry, Falcone thought. He knew the call had been well planned. Barrington's secretary had deliberately interrupted, would gauge her boss's response, and would know whether he wanted her to break off the meeting with another call three or four minutes later. Falcone had used the tactic in his own office many times before.

"Now, you mentioned something about Israel's diplomatic relations with the Soviet Union. The Israelis probably have multiple motives. Theirs is never a simple agenda. No doubt they were unhappy that many Soviet Jews passed through Vienna hell-bent for Los Angeles or New York rather than Jerusalem, and pressured the United States to help stop them. The Israelis wanted to reduce the number of Jews in the Diaspora, not simply witness a change in Zip Codes.

"It may be they're cozying up to the Soviets to put more pressure on Congress to provide them with greater financial and military assistance. Or perhaps they're trying to shove a finger in the eye of the Arabs as well. After all, the Soviets have not exactly taken a blood oath with the Muslims. The Arabs serve a useful strategic purpose, but the Soviets would turn on them in a moment if they saw it was in their interest to do so."

"I know you're busy, Mr. Ambassador. Just a couple of questions. A Colonel Mizrahi was killed with a car bomb recently. Any word on who was responsible?" Falcone hoped that the mention of Mizrahi's name might prompt some recognition in Barrington's eyes.

Barrington revealed nothing. "That was the work of Arab terrorists, I'm told. Several groups have claimed responsibility. It's difficult to tell in these things, but Ahmed Jibril's group, the PFLP-GC, is a strong suspect."

"Well, thank you, Mr. Ambassador. You've been very helpful," Falcone said as he pushed himself up from the couch.

"Any time, Senator. As I said, I think it's important that you're here. If there's anything we can do to help, just call. The switchboard is open twenty-four hours."

The two men shook hands. As Falcone started to leave the room, he turned. "Just a final question, if I might. We have a program called SUNDANCER, with the Israelis. It involves their missile defense system. Are we on track with it? Have there been any hitches?"

Barrington hesitated—only momentarily, but enough to satisfy Falcone that he knew exactly what the program was about.

"Sorry, I can't help you on that. I'm not keyed in to military programs, Senator. Perhaps," he added, trying to sound resourceful, "the Agency's chief of station might be able to assist you. I can set up a meeting this afternoon, or tomorrow, if you'd like."

"No, it's not really important. I can get an update back in Washington. But thanks for the offer."

As soon as Falcone left the embassy, Barrington picked up his telephone and pressed the intercom button. "Donna, I want you to place a call to Washington. This one should be on the secure phone. Butch Naylor, the national security adviser. Tell the White House switchboard that it's important that I speak with him."

44

Tel Aviv, August 16

FALCONE DECIDED TO walk from the embassy back to his hotel. He had not realized that it was so close. He crossed Herbert Samuel Street so he could stroll along the beach.

It was a bright, sun-drenched day. A light breeze was coming off the Mediterranean, easing the effects of the humidity that had settled in the air during the meeting at the embassy. The beach was teeming with people. There were paddle tennis and Frisbee players. Bikini-clad women, the kind seen on advertisement posters in travel agencies, frolicked with beach balls in surf that was dazzlingly white. Lifeguards peered approvingly at them through dark wraparound sunglasses. In open-air showers and half-gazebos, bathers sat chatting away. He passed a sidewalk restaurant with more people, more talk. Talk seemed to be a national pastime.

Across the street, Falcone could see the effect of the salt air on the buildings. Many were made of stucco or cement, and most seemed to be chipped or peeling, their decorative iron gates rusting. Shiny cars, mostly new Peugeots and Subarus, roared past. Everywhere, people were on bicycles, licking ice cream, sipping cold drinks. As Falcone approached his hotel, a lavender-colored bus pulled into the driveway. Across its top a sign read JEWISH COMMU-NITY RELATIONS COUNCIL—MEDIA MISSION.

Falcone did not know quite what to make of the scene. This was not the Israel he had imagined, a sacred and sad nation under arms, under siege. He might just as well have been on Cape Cod or at Rehoboth Beach.

Thanks to the humidity and the vigor of his walk, he was perspiring heavily by the time he reached the Hilton's air-conditioned lobby. But his thoughts were not about the weather or the casual languor of Tel Aviv. He was thinking about Barrington. The man had been perfectly pleasant and perfectly unhelpful. Maybe Barrington resented the fact that Jack Bickford had arranged for Falcone to meet Prime Minister Gerstel. That was Secretary Shanahan's job, or President Hollendale's. DCIs have no business mucking about in the business of diplomacy. It was a clear breach of protocol. No doubt Barrington had sent a cable back to Shanahan in protest.

Actually, the thought of that pompous hawk stomping about in his gilded cage with ruffled feathers rather amused Falcone. And the sudden outburst—"The answer is that there is no answer"—now that was going to make some interesting reading for the Israelis.

Falcone was still smiling as he stepped into his room. Immediately he sensed that something was wrong. Someone was in his room. How stupid could he be? Walking around in a foreign country, accompanied—no, followed—by a Mossad agent, looking for what? Moles? Secrets? Assassins? And he had gone stumbling around laughing at some aristocrat's petty vanities.

"Hello, Senator." The voice startled him. His body tensed, waiting for an attack. Would there be one in front and others behind him, like that night in his garage? Then the voice's familiar resonance, its mocking tone, caused his arms to go slack.

"Jesus Christ! How the hell did you get in here?" Falcone's embarrassment quickly turned to anger.

"Thanks for the compliment, Sean. I'm afraid you overestimate my talents. No walking on water. No loaves of bread. No miracles. Sorry." Dake shrugged his shoulders and held out his hands, palms up, as a smile broke across his lips.

"You didn't answer the question."

"I tried calling you, but your line was busy all morning. Now, knowing you to be a man of few words, I began to worry. I thought something might be wrong. When I came to your room, the cleaning lady apparently thought I was you. She apologized and left, so I decided to wait here. Nothing more complicated, or sinister, than that."

"So you're here. What was so important that you decided to impersonate me?"

"No impersonation—I simply didn't offer to correct her mistake."

"What's the point? Why are you here?"

"The point is that I wanted to forewarn you. I'm doing a story that your friends here aren't going to like."

"About what?"

"It's about the Gaza massacre. I filed the story before I left Washington, but I had to check one source over here before I let it go to print."

"So that's why you were on the plane!"

"That's *part* of the reason I was on the plane. You know, I can work on more than one story at a time and chew gum, too."

"What about Gaza?" Falcone said, with increasing irritation.

"It's better that you read about it. Otherwise the Israelis might think you're the one who leaked it to me."

"Jesus, you're impossible!"

"But right, Sean, and you know it."

"Okay. Okay. I'm forewarned." Falcone moved to the sliding glass doors and looked out at the water.

"Are you going to see her again?"

"Who?"

"Cut the shit, Sean. You know who I mean."

"Tonight. I'm taking her to dinner."

"Want company?"

"If she's as good as you say, then I don't think your little spiral notebook is going to offer much protection. I think I can handle Lizzie Borden alone."

"Okay. It's your funeral." Dake rose, brushed some lint from his pants, and headed for the door. "I always figured I'd have to finish the investigation on my own. Politicians have a way of screwing things up. Just a piece of advice, Sean. There's a difference between stubborn and stupid. I think it would be wise right now for you to stay closer to our side than to hers."

For several seconds Falcone stared at Dake. So far the relationship had been pretty much a one-way street—all taken by Falcone, little given to Dake. He was in a foreign country, and the prospects were at least even, maybe better than even, that he wouldn't leave it alive. Someone wanted him dead. Maybe the Mossad. Maybe the KGB. Hell, maybe even the FBI! This thought caused Falcone's throat to go dry.

The only other person who knew about what Hollendale and Polanski had done was Jack Bickford, director of the CIA. And where did his loyalties lie? If Falcone ended up on a slab in an Israeli morgue, would Bickford lay his career on the line by releasing the diary? Would he confront Hollendale and force him to go public with the full story? Bring down an American President, maybe the Israeli Prime Minister, in a scandal bigger than Watergate and Irangate combined? Or would he be loyal to an unwritten code of the intelligence world, one that said that laws sometimes have to be circumvented or broken in the name of national security?

Joshua had already been burned. Why should Bickford run the risk of toppling the White House, canceling SUNDANCER, maybe even severing relations with Israel? Why not just drop Joshua's story right into the Agency's shredder?

Falcone held up his hand, motioning Dake not to leave. "Phil, wait. There's something I want to give you."

He walked over, picked up his briefcase, and spun the combinations on the double locks—006 on the left, 008 on the right. The latches popped open. He extracted a large sealed envelope that bore a Senate stamp and a facsimile of his signature in the right-hand corner. Handing the envelope to Dake, he said, "This is a copy of Joshua's diary. The information in it is the most sensitive—"

"Goddammit!" Dake exploded. "You've had this all along. I've been feeding you everything I had, and you've been holding back. All that bullshit about trust, working together. Goddammit."

"Hold on, Phil. For Christ's sake, let me explain."

"Yeah, sure," Dake countered, not willing to contain his anger. "Explain, explain."

"The information in there, if it's true, could rock Hollendale— maybe even Gerstel—right out of office. It could be the biggest

scandal ever to hit either government. Advanced technology going to
the Soviets. Moles in the Mossad. A senator used as an agent. Assas-
sinations. Cover-ups. This could cause such a furor that we would
dump Israel as an ally. Christ, we have no way of knowing what it
could lead to."

"So you decided you couldn't trust me. That I don't have a
patriotic bone in my body. National security be damned, I've got a
story, so crank up the presses! Is that what you thought? Did I run
the story on the videotape? Or mention the fact that the FBI was
investigating you as a prime suspect? Or that Joshua was screwing
around with some Libyan? Jesus! Do you have any idea what Brad
Bentley will do to me when he finds out that I've been holding back
on this story? He's going to be absolutely bullshit! He'll say that
I've compromised journalistic principles once too often, that . . ."

Falcone hadn't thought about Dake's predicament or future.
Never convinced of the reporter's trustworthiness, always suspicious
of his motivations, he had used him.

"You don't trust anyone, do you, Falcone? You're the Lone
Ranger, with your secrets all bottled up inside. The sole judge and
jury of what's important."

"There's one other person who knows," Falcone said lamely.
"I showed Jack Bickford a copy of the diary before I left Washington."

"What?" Dake was fuming now. "You trusted Bickford with
this? The man who keeps or shreds all the secrets? But you didn't
trust me! Damn. Damn." His reddened face looked ready to explode. He paced back and forth across the room like a caged cat.
Falcone could not tell whether he was going to hurl the envelope
back or run with it to the nearest telephone.

"I need a favor, Phil."

"Lotta nerve. Lotta nerve," Dake said, continuing to stalk
around the room.

"You've got to promise me that you won't file this story, not
until after I meet with Prime Minister Gerstel. There's a chance that
we might be able to find the mole before this whole thing blows. If
we can do that, there'll at least be some redemption for Joshua."

Dake did not let Falcone finish. "No, Senator. No more promises. I couldn't care less about your buddy Stock and whether he is

redeemed or not. I care about the truth. Period. Not Hollendale. Not Gerstel. And especially not you."

Clutching the envelope tightly under his arm, Dake spun away from the window and stormed out of Falcone's room.

Falcone sat motionless on the couch. He knew Dake had a right to be outraged. But he had never violated his oath of office, the one he had sworn with his hand upon the Bible that day eleven years ago in the Senate chamber. Never once had he broken a confidence, revealed a secret. Well, maybe that time with Joshua. But that was different. He thought he was serving the nation's interest, not undermining it.

Falcone had no idea what Dake would do now. He could only hope that the reporter would give him another twenty-four hours, long enough to meet Gerstel.

Dake had given Falcone a warning, a warning that bothered him. Dake had said to stick close to our side. *Wonderful,* Falcone thought. *Stick to Hollendale? Polanski? Bickford? Reed Barrington III? Just wonderful.*

What had made him come here? Was he playing Sherlock Holmes? Assuming that Rachel, Rachmella, or whatever her name was didn't provide him with a unique experience tonight, he was scheduled to meet with Gerstel tomorrow morning. To what end? Was he going to confront the Prime Minister about Israeli espionage in Washington? Tell him that President Hollendale was running a U.S. senator against Israel? That this little covert operation had led to the execution of Stock, the attack on Rafiah, the car bombing of Colonel Mizrahi?

In his mind's eye he could see Gerstel asking in a deceptively understated way, "Why, Senator Falcone? Why?"

And would Falcone then tell him the truth? That the United States believed that technology from SUNDANCER was being shipped to Moscow via Israeli Federal Express? That we had to find the mole without alerting the Israelis for fear of tearing the Mossad apart, as we had done to the CIA in the seventies, looking for a mole that may have been a phantom?

We had to alert you, Mr. Prime Minister, or cancel the program. Those were the two choices, he could hear himself saying. *Well, the President or Polanski, bless his fat head, decided upon a third option: to use Joshua to trace the line of communication through channels and then confront you with the evidence. Stupid? Idiotic? Indeed. Done in good faith, but incredibly stupid nonetheless.*

Falcone could hear the hollowness in his mental voice as he rehearsed what he would say. He sounded unconvincing even to himself. He winced at the weakness of his words.

Would Gerstel rage? Or just hang his head in silent despair that two allies had come to such skulduggery, that an American President and an Israeli Prime Minister could no longer trust each other with the truth and had to resort to the conduct reserved for their enemies? Double agents. Shadows. Lies. Betrayal.

And Falcone thought of his own conduct. He could be charged with a violation of the Logan Act, a law that prohibited private citizens from conducting diplomacy with another nation. He was not just a private citizen, but he had no authority to affect relations between the United States and Israel. But was telling the truth an act of diplomacy? Diplomats who told the truth were thought to be fools or liars!

Logan Act or not, Falcone knew that at the very least he would be violating the Senate's rules concerning the disclosure of classified information. The penalty could be expulsion from the Senate, maybe even prosecution by the Justice Department or a special prosecutor. Censure, at the minimum.

"To hell with politics," Falcone muttered to himself. Let them expel or prosecute. He'd take the case to the public and tell them what a sewer had been constructed inside Murder Capital, USA! He could feel a surge of adrenaline pumping through his veins. Fighting was the thing he always did best. It was a skill that had fallen largely into disuse since he had entered the Senate. The constant need to massage egos, slap backs, cater to the institutional narcissism that paraded around as civility, strike compromises, water down principles and call it a legislative triumph—all this had deadened his need to fight.

He had become just like all the others, just like the ones who had maintained their silence and pandered to public opinion during the Vietnam War, who had compromised daily while he and others who believed they were fighting for someone's freedom were getting their asses shot off, who had refused to let fighting men fight except on the enemies' terms, who wouldn't declare a victory or defeat and just walk away. Moral ambiguity. Indecision. Deception. Defeat.

No more, Falcone decided. This was one fight that no one was going to walk away from.

Shortly after Dake stormed out of the room, Rachel called. Falcone said that he had just returned from the embassy and asked if he could call back in a few moments. After some hesitation, Rachel gave him a number, saying that she always screened her calls through a recording machine so he should not hang up when the machine activated. Falcone quickly consulted a travelers' guide to Tel Aviv. Dizengoff Street sounded like a perfect place to go. It was close by and loaded with restaurants and sidewalk cafés. Throngs of people would be milling about. Falcone wanted lots of people— witnesses—around him.

He took the elevator to the lobby, turned right, and walked to the bank of telephones near the concierge's desk, where he dialed the number Rachel had given him. After two rings, a machine clicked on. A voice, not Rachel's but some strange, unidentifiable voice that sounded as if it had been produced electronically, apologized for the homeowner's absence and requested the caller to leave a date, message, and telephone number.

As Falcone began to speak, Rachel picked up the phone. Falcone was brief, almost curt. He said he had made a reservation for dinner at Kassit. "Do you know the place?"

"Of course, Sean. On Dizengoff. It's one of Tel Aviv's most famous restaurants. Poets and artists love it there. We can eat inside if you like, but outside is better if you like to people-watch. Of course, it will be warm outside."

"No problem. Let's plan on outside. The reservation is for eight. I'll meet you there."

After hanging up, Falcone called Kassit, praying he could get a reservation. Luck was with him. Then he returned to his room and planned how he would confront Rachel.

At seven o'clock that evening, Falcone stepped off the elevator and walked through the hotel lobby's glass doors. The heat outside was oppressive. He was glad he was wearing a short-sleeved knit polo shirt. The dispatcher signaled for a cab. Falcone noticed that it

was parked separately from the others. The driver flashed a smile—
a little too eager a smile, Falcone thought.

He ignored the driver and instead walked across Hayarkon
Street. There he hailed another cab. He knew it was foolish to think
that he was not being watched and followed. But by whom? CIA?
Mossad? KGB? PLO? It was equally stupid to think that he was
skilled enough to escape them. But he didn't have to make it easy.

He had almost an hour before he was to meet Rachel, so he
instructed the driver to take him to Da Sergio. Turning to look over
his left shoulder, he saw a dark sedan make a quick U-turn on
Hayarkon and follow him. The driver's face was obscured, but Falcone thought he looked very much like Kobi.

As the cab approached the restaurant, Falcone glanced at his
watch and shook his head. He told the driver he had miscalculated
the time. Could the cabbie take him to a nearby bar?

"No problem, sir," the driver said in accented English that was
quite lyrical. He gunned the engine, making a noisy turn. "On Rothschild Boulevard there are many bars. Young crowd. Old crowd.
Many people." His eyes were fixed in the rearview mirror on Falcone. "But I should tell you the best places do not really come alive
until after midnight. Deja Vu. Taboo. Hamisba. In these places you
will find music, dancing, everything."

Nicely put, Falcone said to himself. *No doubt he thinks I'm
looking for action and willing to pay.*

A few minutes later the driver pulled up to the Mann Audito-
rium, indicating that it was a good place to sightsee. Falcone
thanked him and gave him a good tip, then stopped in a café called
Apropos and ordered a drink. He asked directions to Kassit. "It's
not far," a waiter sniffed somewhat rudely. "A ten-minute walk.
Stay on Dizengoff."

Falcone drank his bourbon slowly. This could prove to be a
long night, and he wanted to remain alert. Apropos was starting to
get crowded, and he felt some pressure to make room for other
patrons. But he was enjoying the music coming from the piano near
the bar.

He waited a half-hour, paid his bill, and started to walk northwest on Dizengoff. It was slow going, but he was in no hurry. The
streets were now packed with young men and women. They looked
mostly like students. All were in a uniform of sorts. The men wore

tight-fitting jeans, baggy shirts, and white tennis shoes; the women, cotton slacks or cut-offs and lightweight Reeboks, the kind advertised for aerobic dancing. They shared a genuine gaiety. Laughter emanated from dark faces. Eyes glistened. Startlingly white teeth flashed. Now that darkness had enveloped the city, sensuality slipped out of its work clothes and eased into the heat of Tel Aviv nightlife.

Israel's religious fundamentalists were furious with what they saw as the absolute decadence of their youth. The young people were behaving like Americans, narcissists obsessed with sex, alcohol, drugs. Jews were not supposed to dance with the devil! And if God did not smite them, perhaps God's servants would do so. Falcone had read that several movie theaters and newspaper stands that operated on the sabbath had been firebombed and a number of students beaten by dark-suited men. One man wearing a long beard and earlocks had rolled a hand grenade into a sex shop. Another had bombed a grocery store that sold razor blades, which posed an "incitement to sin" to ultra-Orthodox men, who followed a religious tenet not to shave. All acts of terrorism were traced to Keshet, whose name was the Hebrew acronym for "the uncompromising group."

But the Israeli youth refused to be intimidated. They formed their own protective groups—gangs—and struck back, defiling the walls of synagogues. One group placed a pipe bomb in the small van driven by the wife of an ultra-Orthodox rabbi who engendered acts of terrorism against university students. Her legs had had to be amputated as a result of the blast.

Jew against Palestinian. Jew against Jew. Zionists who wanted a Jewish state. Ultra-Orthodox Jews who insisted that such a state would violate the Old Testament. It was too baffling for Falcone. As he snaked his way through the crowd of lithe bodies, he wondered how long the American people would continue to support a nation that was drifting rapidly into either political or religious authoritarianism.

When he finally managed to squeeze his way to the entrance of Kassit, he saw Rachel sitting at one of the wrought iron tables outside. She was facing the street but not looking in his direction. How long had she been sitting there? And why did she seem so preoccupied, so locked in thought? He stared at her. He had never seen her so unguarded—or so beautiful.

As he approached the table, Falcone felt awkward. He would feel foolish shaking her hand, but he was not about to embrace her and begin the evening with a light kiss on her cheek. He was there for answers. Still, he felt something in his chest—a short stab. It was not pain, not in the physical sense. Rather, a sudden emptiness, a hole that opened up in the darkness, then closed, offering a brief glimpse of the abyss into which Falcone fell at the oddest of times. There were moments of unspeakable happiness when he felt a surge of sadness overwhelm him, as if noon suddenly turned to midnight and owls hooted at the sun. Times when everything was turned inside out.

Now, at the very moment when he was angry enough to hurt this woman, this Killer Angel, he had the absolute desire to wrap his arms around her, feel her warmth, inhale her fragrance. He wanted to untie the bow that held her hair, which gleamed like the sun under the streetlights . . .

It passed. The night and the owl were back. He was in charge of his emotions. He smiled as he greeted her—a formal, forced smile; a full moon smile, he thought, shining but cold and hard.

Rachel seemed genuinely glad to see him. There was an excitement in her eyes. This was her country, her city, her language, her home. But the enthusiasm she extended fell flat. She could see it in his eyes, behind the smile, in the turn of his shoulders. There was an abrupt coolness in his voice, subtle but unmistakable. She could feel her own face turn into a mask of formality.

There were only two chairs at the table. Falcone didn't want to sit with his back to the street. He wanted to see the activity, to people-watch, to be in a position to identify friend or foe. What he meant was to identify enemies. He had no friends in Tel Aviv. But Rachel, seeing his hesitation and discomfort, made no offer to change places.

A waiter appeared as soon as he was seated. "Kir," Rachel ordered. "Extra cassis. I have a sweet tooth!" Laughter returned to her voice, with the musicality that Falcone had noticed before. She seemed determined to enjoy the evening.

Falcone ordered Jack Daniel's on the rocks. "Yes, with a lemon twist."

The drinks arrived quickly, and Rachel was the first to raise her glass. "Welcome to Tel Aviv, Sean. *L'chaim*—good health!"

Good hunting, Falcone thought as he touched her glass. "Thank you, Rachel," he offered, trying to sound sincere.

He looked directly into her eyes. Light from a nearby gaslamp danced in them. She was breathtaking. He decided to postpone the confrontation.

During the meal Rachel rambled on gaily. She spoke of the weather, the humidity. She praised the food (which Falcone found too heavy and filling), described the movies that were playing— dubbed in Hebrew, naturally—and laughed at the thought of Tom Cruise and Eddie Murphy speaking Hebrew. An hour passed. Falcone had another bourbon. Rachel switched to red wine. Over the vehicular and pedestrian traffic, they could hear the sounds coming from Agam's Circus Symphony. Against every instinct, Falcone found himself relaxing.

"How did your meeting at the embassy go?" Rachel asked.

She is always the first to inquire, the last to answer. Never to answer, Falcone thought. "Oh, it was pretty tame. Barrington gave me his overview of the Middle East. He tends to speak from great heights."

"And?"

"And while he didn't say it, it seemed pretty obvious that he thinks Israel can't win its battle against the Palestinians."

"Americans are such hypocrites," Rachel said. Her voice was suddenly flat. There was an anger in it now, an anger that cut quickly, like a new razor. "Saddam Hussein thumbed his nose at the United States and George Bush launched a full-scale attack on Iraq. And your Ambassador Barrington thinks Israel should engage in suicide to pacify the PLO's Yassir Khalef. Sometimes, Sean, it is just too much." She paused and sipped from her wine glass. "American television—that's our biggest problem. It glorifies the 'children of stone,' the little Davids. They even steal our Biblical heroes."

"It's not just Americans or television. Israelis themselves are divided. Many of them think the Palestinians should have a homeland." Falcone did not sound convincing even to himself.

"The Palestinians have a home, in Jordan. Hussein is king of the Palestinians! Americans don't understand. We are caught in your echo chamber. You see our division, which is something quite normal for a democracy, and use it to justify backing away from us. We see you backing away and begin to doubt ourselves." Rachel's eyes started to mist up, as if she were on the edge of tears. Crimson rushed up from her neck into her face, deepening her color, giving her skin a burnished glow.

Falcone stared at her, momentarily mesmerized, forgetting who she was, what she had done. Then he decided it was time.

"Tell me, Rachel. Tell me about Killer Angels."

Her expression changed instantly. Now it was a mask again.

"Tell me what Rachmella does for her living. Or is it for pleasure?" Falcone thought that several hard jabs might shake her. He misjudged her. Rachel's eyes did not break from Falcone's. She was a cool—no, cold—professional. This woman was no sabra, prickly on the outside but sweet on the inside. Just the opposite. She was so extraordinarily beautiful to look at, but hard as steel.

"What exactly were you doing in Washington? And who put you up to following me?"

"First of all, I go where my government sends me."

"Mossad. Say, where the Mossad sends you."

"Where Israel sends me," Rachel replied, ignoring Falcone's interruption. "Second, no one put me up to anything. You're the one who approached me in Washington, remember? You invited me to dinner. Or did you manage to forget that minor detail?"

Falcone started to ask about her father and Joshua when he noticed that her eyes had shifted away from him. Not in embarrassment or guilt; something was going on over his shoulder. Her eyes were alive, scanning rapidly from left to right, right to left, like a radar beam, identifying intruders. He started to turn toward the street.

At that moment Rachel bent down, reaching for her ankle. Had something bitten her there? In a quick smooth motion, she swung back up, holding a .22-caliber semiautomatic pistol fitted with a silencer. Now he understood why she always wore full-cut slacks.

"Jesus!" Falcone shouted, thinking she was about to kill him. He remembered what Dake had said on the plane. *They have to be able to kill, up close to their victims' faces . . .*

Before Falcone could move, she fired two successive shots inches to the right of his head. *Pfft. Pfft.* They were little more than coughs, barely audible.

A second elapsed. There were another two shots. Then the patrons, stunned by the sight of her gun, started to scream.

Falcone turned to the street. Two young men were down, both shot in the head. He could tell from the pieces of skull and fleshy mass on the pavement that Rachel had used hollow points. A small automatic machine pistol lay near one of the men, and a bottle had smashed on the pavement. Falcone could smell gasoline. A Molotov cocktail! Now his senses were alive, screaming.

His instincts told him that if two had been sent to kill him—or Rachel—from the front, others would be behind. He swung around, just in time. A bearded man sitting directly behind their table, wearing a heavy gold chain and a Star of David (was he Jew or Arab?), was reaching with both hands behind his back.

Falcone picked up his table knife and whipped it hard at the man. The thick handle stuck him hard on the collarbone and he screamed in pain. Moving swiftly now, Falcone grabbed his thick hair with his left hand and yanked his head back. Then, with a doubled-up fist, he punched him in the throat, smashing his windpipe. Screams were reduced to raspy whimpers as the man gasped for air and fell rapidly into unconsciousness.

Falcone reached behind the man's back and pulled from his belt holster an Israeli-made .44 Magnum handgun. It was larger than the old Colt he had carried in Vietnam, and heavier. He liked the feel of the steel-blue metal in his hand.

"Sean, look out!" Rachel yelled. He caught a blur of motion coming from the entrance door of the restaurant as she fired three shots in rapid succession. All missed as the man ducked behind a stone column.

Falcone had only a split second to decide what to do. The pistol he held was not cocked. But he had to assume that the man with the smashed throat had chambered a round and then released the hammer so the gun wouldn't accidentally discharge in the restaurant. He hoped he was right. He had to be. All he had to do was pull hard on that trigger . . .

Baroom! It sounded as if a cannon had erupted. As fire flashed from the muzzle, the roar nearly split Falcone's eardrum. There was a slight kick, but Falcone had gripped the gun with both hands and aimed at the center of the man's stomach, anticipating a kick. The shot struck the man in the chest, knocking him into Kassit's plate-glass window.

Now there were more screams. Rachel was tugging on Falcone's arm, pulling him away from the panic-stricken patrons. He followed her mindlessly, not sure why he was running, or where.

A dark car had pulled up at the curb. The driver reached across the seat and flung open the rear door on his side. It was Kobi. Another man was in the passenger's seat. "Get in!" he cried. "Hurry!"

Rachel jumped in first, followed by Falcone. Kobi slammed the car into first gear, and the tires screamed and began to smoke as the rubber burned into the pavement. Over the roar Falcone could hear someone yelling. "Sean! For Christ's sake, Sean! Stop! Stop!"

Falcone turned and looked over his shoulder. It was Dake. How the hell had Dake known where he was going to meet Rachel? Was the reporter part of the hit team? Had he helped to set Falcone up? Now that Falcone had given him the only copy of Joshua's diary, maybe they had decided to take him out. Maybe that scene back at the hotel was all an act. But who were they?

Questions continued to tumble through Falcone's mind as Kobi weaved in and out of heavy traffic. He had stepped into a sinkhole. He was already a suspect in the murder of a man in his garage. Now he had killed one man, possibly two men, in a foreign country. Sweet Jesus! Had he been set up? Was this a Mossad trap to discredit him, jail him? How in hell was he ever going to explain this? Call Rachel, a professional assassin, to his defense?

Dake. Dake had seen what happened. He was an eyewitness. He could explain that Falcone had acted in self-defense! The thought depressed him. Maybe Dake was working for the Agency, had been undercover all along. *Maybe that explains how he's been able to develop those sources of his. How he's been able to bring down so many people. Maybe Langley has been running him all these years! Now he's got Joshua's diary, and he'll file a report that I killed a couple of Palestinians and ran away from the scene of the crime in the company of a professional killer!*

The passenger in the front maintained an ominous silence while Rachel and Kobi talked back and forth excitedly. They spoke in Hebrew. Falcone understood not a word. Instead he tried to keep track of the streets, as if they had some meaning or would be of

help. At that moment he felt it important to maintain some sense of
direction, even as events spun totally out of control.

Kobi turned left at the first intersection, then took another left.
He accelerated as they moved onto a wide boulevard. Falcone saw a
sign that read "Ben Yehuda." He knew this street ran parallel to the
sea. Kobi raced along, heading south, away from the Sheraton Hotel, which Falcone could see fading in the distance. They took another right at Bograshov, past Hayarkon. Now they were on Herbert
Samuel, the same street Falcone's cab driver had taken to Da Sergio.

As the car neared Old Jaffa, Kobi slowed down. Rachel explained that they were passing Tel Aviv's police headquarters—as if
that meant anything. Falcone could make out a tall clocktower
nearby. It was nine-thirty.

Kobi made a wide loop and headed north, back toward the
center of the city. Falcone recognized several landmarks he had seen
earlier. They turned onto Rothschild Boulevard. Where in hell were
these people taking him?

Seeing the confusion and anger in his eyes, Rachel reached
over and grasped his arm. "Be patient. We're almost home."

Home? Whose home? It was probably someplace with insu-
lated walls where they could work him over, squeeze the chairman
of the Intelligence Committee for all they could get. Then what—a
bullet in the head? A razor across the jugular? Set him out in the
Mediterranean as a source of protein for the scavengers to pick at?

Falcone had tucked his newly acquired .44 into the top of his
trousers. Now he gave some thought to jamming it into the back of
Kobi's skull. But what would he demand? That they take him—
where? To the police? To Reed Barrington III? To the airport? The
temptation passed quickly. Besides, there were three of them. He
might be able to take out Kobi and Rachel, but the gorilla in the
front probably had an Uzi glued to his hand and would like the
chance to waste him. He decided he had no choice but to go along
with them—for now.

At the corner of Shinkin and Ahad Ha'am, Kobi stopped the
car. Again he and Rachel spoke in Hebrew. Then she said, "Come
on. Let's get out of here. The apartment is just a few blocks. We
should walk." Slipping her arm through Falcone's, she led him to
the curb.

Of course. Just an innocent stroll. Two lovers out for the evening. Kobi and his fellow goon could park and follow them to make sure there were no late pursuers to see them enter the—not "her"— apartment.

They walked slowly past the Tamar, another café that was brimming with what looked to be young professionals, Israeli yuppies. Farther along there were scores of small shops crammed together—pharmacies, newspaper and art supply shops, bookstores. It reminded Falcone of Manhattan's Upper East Side.

Finally Rachel said, "Here. Up these stairs."

They were in front of a tall, elegant building that looked to be at least fifty years old. Rachel produced two keys from a small purse that she had managed to hold on to during the melee back at the Kassit. She opened the two locks easily, and they entered a high-ceilinged apartment with plaster walls, filigreed moldings, and thick green drapes held back by sashes from tall windows. Several abstract paintings in slim gold frames hung on the walls. The room had a professional's touch, but there was something missing: life. It was sterile. This was not Rachel's apartment, Falcone knew. It was everyone's and no one's. It was a safe house. Safe for whom? For Rachel, to be sure. But not for Falcone.

Rachel led him down a narrow hall, past a modest kitchen, toward the rear of the apartment. The hall opened to a large study/ bedroom area. A king-size bed covered with a light blue spread occupied the center of the room. Off to the right was a couch covered with corduroy, and next to it a matching chair deep enough to swallow up most occupants. A tall reading lamp stood next to the chair, along with a teakwood rack filled with magazines. On the other side of the room was a small writing desk with a black leather inlay. A modern Swedish-designed telephone sat on top of the desk, and next to it stood a magnificent rosewood wall unit. One of its doors was open, displaying a bar with a good selection of liquor. Behind the bed, to its left, was a bathroom, which Falcone judged to be quite large.

"Make yourself comfortable, Sean," Rachel said as she tossed her handbag onto the bed. "Oh," she muttered, noticing for the first time that she had torn her silk blouse. Striding directly toward the bathroom, she said, "I'm going to clean up a bit."

Falcone started toward the bar. He needed something to calm him. However, he was distracted by something in the corner of the room, just two or three feet from the wall unit: Rachel's suitcase. Obviously she had been there earlier, but for some reason had never unpacked. Falcone was not in the habit of rummaging through other people's belongings, but something had caught his eye. Something dark and shiny. It was hanging out over the unzippered lid of the suitcase, partially exposed.

Falcone walked over to the suitcase and lifted its top. *Damn!* A wig. He pawed through the suitcase quickly and found two sets of plastic containers. He opened them: contact lenses. One set brown, the other blue. *Damn!* he thought again.

Acrylic fibers—that's what Detective Clarke had told Dake they had found in Joshua's bed. Now the pieces were starting to fall into place. Now Falcone was sure that Rachel had killed Joshua. She was an Israeli masquerading as a dark-eyed Moroccan or Libyan. All that travel, jetting in and out of Washington. A perfect cover . . .

A shower curtain snapped along an aluminum rod. Water hissed loudly. Falcone walked across the room, holding the wig as if it were a dead animal. Now was the time to strike, he thought, while she was unprepared, unarmed.

He slipped quietly into the bathroom. It was clouded with steam. Quickly he surveyed the countertop, making sure that no knives or scissors were handy. Moving stealthily, he slipped his hand behind the shower curtain and twisted hard on the right-hand knob, releasing ice-cold water. Rachel, her face covered with soap, shrieked, sputtered, then reached blindly for the shower knobs.

In one swift motion, Falcone ripped away the plastic curtain and wrapped it around her like a straitjacket, so that her arms and legs were immobilized. He had taken her completely by surprise. She struggled helplessly as he pushed her roughly to the floor.

"Now," he shouted at her, after wedging his knee deep into the small of her back while he pulled her head back by her hair. "Now you're going to start talking, or I swear, I'll break your neck."

Rachel told Falcone everything. Not out of fear; she knew that Kobi and Nathan, the other passenger in their car, were outside, guarding the apartment. Falcone was in a prison without bars. He had nowhere to run and no one he could trust. She owed him the truth.

Her parents had both been teenagers when their families had
fled with them to Israel in 1939. Rachel was born in Israel in 1960.
She attended schools in Tokyo, London, and wherever else her father was assigned as a diplomat. After two years of mandatory service in the military, she completed her studies at Tel Aviv University. The Mossad had recruited her upon graduation.

"Why were they interested in you?"

"It was the other way around." Rachel went on to explain how
her brother, Moshe, had been killed in Munich in 1972, how she
had vowed that she would avenge his death. She had approached the
Mossad. And when they learned about her linguistic and athletic
skills—and her hate—they knew instantly she could be a candidate
for their elite antiterrorist unit: the Killer Angels.

"Why were you assigned to Washington?"

"There are some Libyan terrorists living there. My government
discovered that they were planning an attack on our Washington
embassy. I was assigned to terminate a man named Ahmed Jooma,
one of their assassins."

Terminate. She sounded so clinical, as if she were just a latex-
gloved doctor completing a surgical operation in which the patient
had died.

"I came back to Israel when my father was shot. I stayed for
days, but there was nothing I could do for him but pray. The prayers
may have saved his life. Now the doctors and physical therapists are
struggling with him, to help him regain his speech. That is the best
that can be hoped. He will never walk again." There were tears in
her eyes as she related what had happened to her father.

Yes, she had known Joshua. She had met with him on several
occasions, and she had delivered materials from Joshua to her father. She knew they were classified documents, but she knew nothing more about them.

Falcone believed her. If she had killed Joshua, then why would
she have saved him that night in the garage? It had to have been
her. After seeing her in action at the Kassit, he had no doubt about
it.

He released her, pulled her to her feet, and gently wiped soap
from her face with a towel. Suddenly conscious of her nudity, he
helped her slip into a large terry-cloth robe. It was an innocent

gesture and yet one that stirred him erotically. His spine began to tingle.

And then the unexpected happened. Suddenly Rachel was in his arms. He kissed her eyes, let the salt run onto his tongue. He parted her lips, felt the moistness there, nibbled gently, pushing, probing, as he ran his hands inside her robe. He was tender with her, loving. Rachel responded, pressing her body against him, gently at first, and then harder as a hunger inside was released.

Falcone stripped his clothes off. They stumbled to the bed. Falcone was on fire. His hands flashed across her breasts, her neck. He tugged on her loose hair.

They were both exhausted, but when their bodies fused, each suddenly became energized, driving, accepting, moaning in an incredible frenzy, building to orgasm, a crescendo of release that reaffirmed a center of warmth that burned inside them, reaffirmed not animal instinct but a desperate need to touch, reach, communicate . . .

When it was over, they laughed. Together, at each other, as if they had been silly teenagers groping for each other's loins in the back seat of a family car. Yes. And how good it felt! To be alive again. To be touched to the core, quickened by another human being.

Before his night on Spruce Island with Rachel, he had felt barren, emotionless. He had slept with other women to be sure. He liked Tina, but she was not enough for him. Or maybe she was too much. Six years in prison had not intensified his desire. So many of his nights had been filled with thoughts of Karen; he had dreamed of being with her again, making up for the love he had lost, the guilt he felt in leaving her. When she died, he died inside. Tina provided release, but it was a momentary connection, an excitement that lasted no longer than an erotic spasm. Nothing stirred inside. His soul remained a scarred battlefield, with leafless trees and the smell of smoke.

He had rationalized that politics had deadened him. He was all packaged up in blue pin-striped suits, consumed with the commonweal, with never a lustful or loving thought to touch his heart. He had to be an idol, which voters could not visualize locked in the embrace of a woman. But that was a lie, he knew. Anger and guilt had wrapped around inside him, tapeworms feeding off any feelings that remained there.

Rachel turned off the lights. In the darkness, she began to run her fingers over his body. She touched the lines of a face that was wide and strong, handsome, but in a rough way. She could feel several thin scars just over his eyebrows and a nose that had been broken more than once. She rubbed her fingers over his as if to memorize the swirls of his prints. She was an artist stroking a canvas with her brush.

Falcone stirred, came alive again. He was the sun, pure energy, volatile, explosive. The center of light, pulling her into his flames.

45

FALCONE HAD JUST started to dream. Or at least he thought so. Pictures were forming. People were talking. He could hear the voices so clearly. Then came a harsh ring, an annoying interruption, shattering their coherency, pulling him up through the dark layers of sleep.

Coffee. The sharp aroma awakened him. Rachel was hovering nearby, holding a tray table. He could hear the radio in the kitchen. The voices carried an unmistakable excitement, even though he could not understand a word being spoken.

"Not your typical New England bed-and-breakfast," Rachel apologized, forcing a smile. Next to the coffee were two undernourished slices of bread and a deeply bruised apple. Rachel looked radiant, but her eyes revealed something Falcone had not seen before.

"Trouble?"

She nodded.

"Did we make the morning news?"

"Not exactly." Rachel handed him a newspaper. Pointing to a column buried on page nine, she translated for him.

Three terrorists were killed and a fourth severely wounded in a gun battle that took place on Dizengoff Street.

The terrorists have all been identified as members of the so-called Party for the Liberation of Oppressed Palestinians, a radical group believed to be under the control of Fatah.

According to witnesses, an unidentified man and woman, believed to be undercover police officers, shot and killed two of the men as they were about to attack the patrons seated at tables outside the Kassit restaurant.

Witnesses were able to give only a partial description of the couple, who were seen speeding away from the scene in a dark sedan.

Falcone drank deeply from his coffee cup and then refilled it. "It could have been worse. It's hard to believe that no one remembered anything about us."

"The police probably have a good description but withheld it from the press so they could locate us before any more terrorists do." Rachel spoke matter-of-factly, confident that the police would not expend much effort to find them. "There is something else that is not in the paper but is in the news. Kobi called a few minutes ago."

What Falcone had seen in her eyes, he could now hear in her voice.

"Nathan went off duty around three o'clock this morning. Kobi called to tell me that he was found an hour ago. He was . . . tortured to death."

"Jesus."

"There's more." Rachel hesitated. "Your friend Phil Dake has been arrested."

"What?" Falcone exploded, nearly knocking over the tray, which was resting on his lap.

"Somehow Dake found out about the massacre in Gaza, that a poison gas had actually been used. The Voice of America has been pumping it all over the airwaves."

"They've thrown Dake in jail for violating censorship laws?"

"No. He's being held as a material witness to the terrorist attack last night at Kassit."

Falcone had been startled when he had seen Dake at the restaurant. He had even begun to think the impossible: that Dake was the one assigned to follow him to Israel. He kept asking himself, *By whom, for what?* And the answer kept coming back: *to get the only existing copy of Joshua's diary.* But he resisted the notion that Dake was a plant.

There could be only one reason that Dake was in jail, though. Someone wanted Joshua's diary. And that someone wanted Dake out of the way so he could find it.

"Hurry, Sean," Rachel said, handing him his clothes. "You can shave and shower later. It's important that we leave here quickly."

Falcone looked puzzled.

"Nathan may have told his killers about us. And whoever is trying to kill you—or me—may know that we are here. We should leave for Jerusalem."

It took a little less than an hour to drive to Jerusalem. Because of a hastily called Cabinet meeting, Falcone's appointment with Prime Minister Gerstel had been postponed until the afternoon. Dake's report on the Voice of America alleged that the Israelis had used a deadly poison to kill the Palestinians in the Gaza massacre and that the Israeli government had deliberately lied to the public. Several members of the Labor Party were calling for an independent investigation, and some were demanding Gerstel's resignation.

Rachel called Teddy Kollek, the venerable mayor of Jerusalem, and a suite was quickly reserved for Falcone at the King David Hotel. Falcone remembered Joshua telling him that this was the hotel that Menachem Begin and the Stern Gang had bombed back in 1946 when Palestine was under British control. Rachel had picked it because it was near the Prime Minister's office. Besides, as long as they had several hours to kill, she wanted Falcone to visit the Old City, which was only a few minutes' walk from the hotel.

As they passed through the Jaffa Gate, Falcone noticed an Arabic inscription over the entrance. Rachel translated. "There is no god but Allah, and Abraham is his friend." Then she slipped her arm through his and they plunged into the Old City.

Almost immediately Falcone felt as if he had stepped into a time warp.

"The city is divided into four quarters," Rachel explained with the enthusiasm of a tour guide, "Christian, Muslim, Jewish, and Armenian." Turning left, they walked through the Christian quarter, past the Church of the Holy Sepulcher where Jesus had been buried, then right on the Via Dolorosa, the Way of the Cross, the path Christ had stumbled along to reach the place of his crucifixion. Falcone glanced over his shoulder and saw that Kobi and his new companion, Ariel, were not far behind.

They turned left on El Wad, then right again as they passed into the Muslim quarter. Rachel pointed out each station that marked Christ's cruel walk. At the sixth, she pulled him to a stop. "Here," she said, slipping her arm out of Falcone's and touching his temple gently, "is where Veronica wiped the blood, sweat, and dust from Christ's face. Do you know the legend?" Before he could answer, she continued, "His features were said to have left an imprint on her cloth."

"Thus the name Veronica, which means 'true image.' "

Rachel laughed, leaning her head on his shoulder. "I'm sorry. I do babble on."

"It's about the only thing I remember from Bible studies." He could not understand how she could be so relaxed and unafraid. Someone might be lining them up in his gun sight at that very moment, and yet she was completely calm and unguarded. But Falcone knew that her eyes took in everything.

They continued along the narrow cobblestone streets, two ordinary tourists, both wearing sunglasses and Rachel in a kerchief, gathering in the sights and sounds of history.

"We're lucky to be here early. By this afternoon the streets will be packed with today's pilgrims, tracing Christ's footsteps."

Falcone said nothing. He remained mostly silent during the walk, trying to comprehend the significance of this historic, magical city. It was such a jumble of contradictions to him, a haphazard mixture of the old and new. Holy sites were engulfed by merchants like some plush garden under assault by galloping thickets of ugly weeds. There were alleyways, arches, courtyards, stairwells, stone walls; gold and silver jewelry, cameras, sheepskins, Maltese crosses, and Stars of David. The smells of herbs, spices, and frying meats filled the air. Not more than fifty steps beyond the Ecce Homo Basilica was an Armenian pottery shop. Catholic nuns and Russian monks mingled in the streets with gnarled-fingered hucksters trying to pass off junk as ancient or holy relics.

They stopped at the Abou Sein Bakery for baklava and thick Turkish coffee. Again Rachel slipped her arm through Falcone's and tugged him to the right. He wanted to believe it was a gesture of affection. Or was she just pretending that she and he were merely another couple taking a romantic tour of the Old City?

"Come," Rachel said. "You must see the western wall. For us, it's the most important place in all of Jerusalem. The Wailing Wall."

Within minutes they approached a large open square patrolled by Israeli border guards dressed in green fatigues and sporting green berets. Each carried either an Uzi machine gun or a large-calibered pistol, but the preferred weapon seemed to be a baseball bat wrapped in thick tape. In the distance was a towering wall constructed of massive, rough-surfaced stones. Rachel explained that it was all that was left of the temple that had been erected on Mount Moriah. Actually, there had been two temples. The first had been destroyed by the Babylonians, the second by the Romans. The wall wasn't part of the temple itself, but only a retaining wall. According to historians, the Emperor Julian had started to build a third temple in the third century, but it was destroyed by a mysterious fire. "According to Jewish faith, when the temple is rebuilt, then the Messiah will come."

"What's holding up construction?" Falcone asked, not trying to hide his sarcasm. "Can't get a building permit out of the mayor?"

Rachel poked him in the ribs and laughed. "It gets a bit complicated. You can't quite see them from here, but beyond the wall, over there, are the Dome of the Rock and the al-Aksa Mosque. Inside the Dome is the rock on which Abraham prepared his son Isaac for sacrifice, where Solomon built his temple. Some even believe it is the very place where the Holy of Holies, the Ark of the Covenant, was kept. And Christians believe it is where Christ taught, where he threw the money-changers from Solomon's temple."

Rachel paused, inhaling in a way that expressed a long sorrow. "It's also the place where the Muslims believe Mohammed ascended to heaven on a winged horse named Buraq after traveling from Damascus. It's the third holiest site in Islam. The Temple Mount, known to the Arabs as Haram al-Sharif, is under control of the

Muslims, the Waqf. We are not allowed to pray there. You were joking just now about construction, but it's not a joking matter. Rabbi Meir Kahane's followers, who are now led by Solomon Ben Israel, have threatened to blow up the Dome so they can build a new temple. I used to think it was a ploy to get them more publicity. But I'm convinced now they're serious. And they have lots of people supporting them—not only Jews, but evangelical Christians. Millions of them."

"I don't understand."

"The Christians believe that the Biblical prophesy of our final days is approaching. They want to accelerate the event. They believe that once the temple is built, they will witness the second coming of Christ. For Jews, the rebuilding of the temple will bring forth the Messiah."

"That's a nice partnership."

"In more than a theological sense. There have been a number of plots to blow up the Muslim shrine. Bombs, rockets, mines, explosives—all have been confiscated. They are paid for, we believe, by American Christian fundamentalists. Of course, our government will never let the zealots succeed."

"Why not?"

"It would mean a *jihad*, an absolute holy war, against Israel. That's why we allow the Waqf to patrol the Temple Mount. But they are unarmed and have only the illusion of control. We are the ones who guard the ramparts against our own."

Falcone shook his head in bafflement. He stared hard at the dark-suited men stiffly bobbing back and forth near the wall. Some were tucking rolled paper into the wall's crevices.

"Those are *kvitels,* prayers," Rachel said.

"Who retrieves them? Or do the holes just keep multiplying?"

"Sean, you're too cynical."

Rachel tugged on his arm, pulling him in the opposite direction, as a group of a dozen or more men appeared on top of the wall. They ran about wildly, screaming as they lifted large rocks over their heads and hurled them at the people standing at the base of the wall. Pandemonium broke out.

Two men, one elderly, were knocked bleeding to the ground by the stones. Several people rushed to assist them. Others ran for safety. Then shots rang out. Israeli soldiers wearing helmets and flak jackets rushed at the men on top of the wall. Firing at point-blank range, they killed four and began to bludgeon the others, who tried to escape. Sirens began to ring in the square as Israeli police poured in to cordon off the area.

Kobi and Ariel moved up quickly behind Rachel and Falcone. As he pushed them toward the Jaffa Gate, Kobi spoke in rapid Hebrew. *"Hava nehlayeh!"*

Falcone needed no translation this time.

46

"Y OU'RE DISAPPOINTED?"
Although Rachel tried to make it sound like a question by inflecting
her voice slightly, it came off as a conclusion, one that carried its
own sadness. "Come on, the truth."

The truth? Falcone thought to himself as he gazed past her.
They were sitting on the veranda of the King David Hotel, eating
lunch, shaded by a large umbrella centered in a metal-edged Plexiglas table. Above them the steep hills were covered with sleek stone-
and-glass condominiums, as modern and expensive as any to be
found in the Western world. Below was the Old City, sealed off from
the centuries by its towering walls. From here Falcone could see a
large gold dome and a smaller silver cupola: the Dome of the Rock
and the al-Aksa Mosque. They shimmered like precious metals in
the merciless sun. Israeli police now patrolled the top of the western
wall, preventing Arabs from entering their place of worship.

The truth? All that history trapped in the narrow alleys of hate
and hucksterism. Wooden slivers from the cross Christ bore on his
back? Nails that anchored his feet and hands to the cross? Hairs
from the tail of the beast that carried Mohammed from Damascus?

"I'm just confused," he finally said. "I don't understand it." He sipped from a glass of iced tea, weighing his words. "You call it the City of Peace. But how many wars have been fought here? How many invasions have there been? Babylonians, Persians, Romans, Crusaders, Turks, Jordanians . . . I've read descriptions of the battles. Some of them make the Khmer Rouge look like Boy Scouts. I just don't understand. What is it that drives men insane with hate over here?" It was a question that he had asked Joshua. "I mean, Wailing Walls, temples, Mecca once removed. Everyone clawing each other for . . . for what? Heaven? Salvation? Killing each other for the right to worship Yahweh, Mohammed, Christ?"

"Maybe if you had lived under the pharaohs or the Nazis, you'd understand what it means to Jews to have a place where we don't have to fear a knock on the door at midnight or hear the shattering of crystal."

"So now you worry about children with slingshots or pipe bombs. Or Palestinians grabbing the wheels of your buses and plunging them into ravines."

Falcone tried to say this in a noncombative way, but his words struck Rachel like stones. She moved back in her chair and stiffened. Falcone reached across the table and grasped her hand. "Rachel, it's not just me. There are a lot of people in the United States who are equally confused about what is happening here."

"Most Israelis no longer care that Americans are confused."

"You care about our money."

"Of course. We want your support—money, if you will—but we no longer count on it. We hear your pledges of friendship and loyalty, but the words are hollow. We know that one day you will betray us. Abandon us."

"No. That's not true and it's not fair."

"Unfair perhaps, but true, Sean. Every time there is the slightest crisis, we hear that America is losing confidence in us. When we captured Sheik Abdul Karim Obeid, who conspired with Hezbollah terrorists, congressional leaders blamed us for Colonel William Higgins's murder. Rather than condemn Hezbollah, you condemned those who have the courage to do something other than appease the terrorists."

"We didn't condemn you. Some just thought you should con-

sult with us before doing something that jeopardized innocent people.''

"Everyone took it as criticism. Besides, you know that it would
be impossible, foolish, for us to consult with you. That would mean
that you control us. It would be an open invitation for terrorists to
kidnap more Americans and demand concessions from us! Sean,
surely you understand that, after all that you've been through?''
Rachel's tone was beseeching.

Falcone slipped off his sunglasses and looked at her for a long
time, his eyes meeting hers, holding them. The sun caught her hair,
dancing on it the way the sun does on water touched by the wind,
casting ingots of gold up from its infinite depths. He wanted nothing
at that moment to erase the night they had shared together. He
knew that something long ago had burrowed deep inside her, crowd-
ing out everything else. It wasn't love. And it was surely stronger
than anything she could feel for him. He knew it was vengeance.

Finally he sighed. It was the sound of resignation, of agreement. Then he slipped his sunglasses on, not wanting her to see the
pain of loss that he knew was coming, had already come.

"We understand that Americans like the idea of Israel—the
stories of Entebbe, Exodus, Leon Uris's suntanned warriors fighting
for their lives—but you don't like the reality. The Begins, the
Shamirs, the Gerstels—war-toughened men with blood on their
hands—offend you. You think they wear flak jackets around their
hearts. And then your networks show the Palestinians tear-gassed,
beaten, or shot with rubber bullets, and you're conscience-stricken,
horrified at our brutality.'' Rachel kept her voice flat and unemotional even as she felt a familiar anger welling up inside. "Americans weep over the names carved into the Vietnam Memorial. Think
about it, Sean. If we were to build a Holocaust wall, it would have to
be twice as high as the Washington Monument to hold all the names.
Can't you understand why we say 'never again'?''

Falcone stared at Rachel but said nothing.

"It's easy for you and President Hollendale to speak of land for
peace,'' she said. "You have thousands of miles. Our existence is
measured in feet, in inches.''

Falcone wanted no more confrontations, but he had to make
her understand why sentiment was shifting against Israel. "Democ-
racies are not always governed by truth, Rachel, but by perceptions

and public opinion. And public opinion is shaped by what people see."

"Or think they see."

"Fair enough. But right now, Americans see the Palestinians as the underdogs who also should have a homeland."

"But Sean, don't *you* see? It all sounds so fair, so democratic, but giving them a homeland will turn ours into a wasteland! Yassir Khalef tells America what it wants to hear. He talks about peace, coexistence. But to the Arabs he whispers that a Palestinian state is just the first stage of Israel's destruction. What do you think will happen when the Arabs in Jaffa or Galilee demand to join this new state? Israel will become another Lebanon, Jerusalem another Beirut! Why can't—"

Rachel was cut off in mid-sentence by a melee that erupted around them.

A man had approached the table where she and Falcone were sitting. When Kobi grabbed him roughly by both arms, a scuffle ensued. Four men, wearing sunglasses and dressed in dark gray suits, rushed to wrestle Kobi to the floor. Ariel pulled out a large semiautomatic pistol and began to brandish it at the intruders, but Falcone leaped up and swatted the gun away, sending it rattling across the tile floor.

"For Christ's sake, what are *you* doing here? Trying to get yourself killed, or me?"

Jack Bickford straightened his jacket, which had been pulled nearly off his shoulders while he wrestled with Kobi.

"We've been looking all over for you, Sean," he rasped, slightly winded. "You certainly have a way of finding—or starting— trouble."

"Meaning?"

"Meaning last night. The police have a pretty good description of you."

"Jack, someone's trying to kill me. That was a professional hit squad that came at us." Falcone glanced over at Rachel. She was impassive, coolly serene. Bickford was on her territory, and she needed to offer no explanations.

"Self-defense or not, it's not going to look great to the Virginia police who think you aced that guy in your garage."

"You know I had nothing to do with that."

"I *believe,* Sean, I *believe.* But there are a few folks back home who don't. Maybe," Bickford said, staring now at Rachel, "it's just the company you keep. Look, I need to talk to you."

Even before he finished speaking, Rachel had slipped gracefully out of her chair. She ignored the director's snide reference. Resting one hand on Falcone's shoulder, a gesture that signified their intimacy, she said, "Senator, I'll be in the lobby. You should leave in about ten minutes. The Prime Minister, I am told, appreciates punctuality."

Falcone motioned for Bickford to take Rachel's chair. Then he ordered iced tea for both of them.

"Jesus, Sean. That woman is pure trouble. Do you know who—what—she is?"

Falcone nodded. "Yeah. Mossad. Killer Angel. I also know she saved my life last night. And probably in my garage, too."

"Did it ever occur to you that it might be more than just coincidence that people start dying whenever she's around?"

Occur to him? The thought had haunted him ever since Dake had said she fit the description of the woman seen leaving Joshua's house. He had come to suspect that she was Joshua's assassin. But last night—last night he had been sure that he was wrong. Even as Falcone looked at Bickford, images floated languidly through his mind. Rachel's lithe, supple body melting into his. Lips full as ripe fruit, taking forever to close. Eyes that pulled him into another galaxy, into the heat of a soul that said yes to him . . .

"I trust her. Enough said," Falcone snapped. "By the way," he said, switching subjects, "Phil Dake's in jail."

"I know. We got word early this morning. The Israelis are holding him as a material witness."

"Bullshit, Jack. They're holding him so they can search his room or force him to tell them what he knows about Joshua."

"I know. I went to see him. He's hopping mad. And he wanted no part of me helping him to get out of jail! Said it would look as if he were on the Agency payroll, which would be the kiss of death to him as a journalist."

"That sounds like Dake," Falcone said, allowing himself to smile at the thought of the reporter pacing around behind iron bars.

"I'll get him out. One of Barrington's boys can arrange his release in a couple of hours."

Falcone glanced at his watch. "Jack, I'll have to run in a few minutes. You said you had something important."

Bickford leaned over the table and dropped his voice to a conspiratorial whisper. "Two things. I don't know if it has anything to do with Joshua's murder or not. But it might. Before he was killed, *Peg Blazer*—Colonel Mizrahi—told us there was something strange going on with the Soviets' policy toward Israel." He paused and swiveled his head back and forth to make sure that other patrons, and especially the hotel's waiters, could not hear what he was about to say.

"One of our analysts had a hunch," he continued. "She had been keeping an eye on the flow of Jewish émigrés out of the Soviet Union. As you know, before the direct flights to Tel Aviv began, the route had been Moscow to Vienna, Budapest, or Prague, where the overwhelming majority chose to go on to the United States rather than Israel. But she noticed that there had been a slight change in percentages. Not much, but steady."

Bickford then told how the hunch began evolving into a premise when the analyst put it on the Soviet East European electronic mail system, a network of computers at Agency headquarters that could instantly communicate with each other. "The computers are much more responsive than interoffice memos in those perforated brown envelopes," Bickford said. With a few keystrokes, an analyst watching émigré matters put a query to a couple of dozen other analysts, including one charged with keeping track of Soviet *spetsnaz* forces—supersoldiers trained in language skills and unconventional warfare.

The *spetsnaz* analyst, Bickford said, had noted that several members of a Soviet track team had not been on the schedule at a Soviet-French track meet, and three tennis players from Soviet Georgia had failed to show up at a West Berlin tournament. The analyst knew that *spetsnaz* soldiers, who operate under Soviet military intelligence, often traveled as athletes. But in recent weeks, *spetsnaz* patterns had been changing, and he wondered why.

He was asked by the first analyst, called Friedel, whether he had any ideas or reasons to explain a slight but steady shift of Soviet émigrés to Israel instead of to the United States. The *spetsnaz* specialist, a brilliant linguist named Sokolov, in turn asked whether he could get a quick and dirty demographic breakdown of the émigrés who went to Israel. He bet two beers that most of those breaking out of the pattern were males between the ages of twenty and thirty-five.

Friedel responded that the demographics were on the button. Then she offered another two beers for the premise.

"Well," Bickford concluded, "the premise—that *spetsnaz* were being slipped into Israel—tied into broader intelligence that we already had. The Soviets had been letting hoods, ex-convicts, even major criminals, go to the United States. There's a Russian Mafia, into protection, loan-sharking, even counterfeiting, blossoming in New York. The FBI had some material on it, but it hadn't gone anywhere with us. Too domestic. But Sokolov had been looking at *trained* bad guys. He started poking into the use of émigrés by the Soviets. And what we have as a result is a fairly neat proposition."

"Which is?" Falcone asked, trying not to sound too interested. His mind was convoluted enough to wonder whether Bickford had dropped Sokolov's name so that Falcone would recruit him for the Intelligence Committee staff, which would give the CIA a penetration agent there. He filed away the thought.

"Which is," Bickford replied, "that a major Soviet covert operation is planned for Israel. Soon."

"How soon?"

"No idea. But *spetsnaz* troops are hit-and-run boys—killers, saboteurs. They wouldn't be very good for a long sleeper mission. Besides, the KGB handles that kind of operation. These are GRU, probably on temporary loan to the KGB."

"I don't understand, Jack. Why are you telling me this now? Why not run it past the director of the Mossad?"

"It comes back to the whole problem with SUNDANCER. We don't know who or how high up the Soviets' man is in the Mossad."

Bickford's choice of words hit Falcone like a ten-wheel truck. "Holy Christ, Jack. Do you know who you sound like? Polanski. That's just what that bastard said to Joshua. That's what started the whole stupid plan to use Joshua to trace the mole! 'We can't go through the Mossad, might tip the wrong man, remember Kim Philby . . .' Do all of you guys read from the same goddamned script?"

Bickford's face flushed with embarrassment.

"If you don't even trust the Mossad's top dog, then why doesn't the President just call the Israeli Prime Minister? Or do you think he's a Soviet agent, too?"

"He can't, Sean, don't you understand?" Bickford pleaded. "Gerstel might think it's an Agency ploy. Or figure that Hollendale's trying to extract some more concessions from him. Besides, he'll want to know why we've been tracking people going into Israel. That puts the President in a tough spot. He's got to have some cover."

"Okay. Okay. So you want me to tell Gerstel he's got a big problem. Is that it? Gives the President deniability. Right?"

Bickford sat back in his chair and shook his head. "You know I can't ask you to tell the Prime Minister anything about this. It's all code-word information, and only the President can authorize declassifying or discussing it."

"Which he, of course, won't do." Falcone's voice took on the edge of a scythe. It was ass-covering time for the director. "All right, Jack, stop screwing around with me. You can't tell me to tell Gerstel what you want me to tell him. Okay, I understand the game you're playing."

Bickford remained silent, embarrassed that he felt the need to protect his own career while asking Falcone to risk his. And he felt foolish that he was so transparent.

"But I'll tell you something, Jack. I'm not going halfway. I'm going to tell him everything—Joshua, *Canaan*, Mizrahi, Rafiah. Every goddamned bit of it."

"That would be unwise, Sean. It would open a whole can of worms. Gerstel would be in a hell of a position to hurt President Hollendale. He could demand some kind of quid pro quo."

Falcone started to laugh, a laugh without mirth, a laugh that turned quickly to a sneer. "What you want is for me to do your dirty work so you can disavow that it was an official disclosure. Circle the wagons around the White House. Protect the President."

"Sean, you came to me once when you wanted something, and you got it."

"Pay-back time?"

"I wouldn't ask you if it wasn't important."

Falcone signaled the waiter for the check. "Okay. I guess it does come round, as they say."

Bickford said nothing, just stared off in the direction of the Old City.

"But I'm surprised that you don't recognize what you're doing, Jack."

Bickford turned toward Falcone, puzzlement stamped on his face.

"You're using me. Just like Hollendale and Polanski used Joshua."

47

AT PRECISELY TWO
o'clock, Falcone was escorted into Prime Minister Shimon Gerstel's
private office. It was a long narrow room, spartan in appearance. A
dark wood conference table ran perpendicular to Gerstel's desk.
Behind the desk was a credenza adorned with several framed photographs of what appeared to be the Prime Minister's family. To the
right of the credenza stood the Israeli flag.

Falcone had met Gerstel once before at a reception held for
him by the Senate Foreign Relations Committee. More than twenty
senators had stopped by Room S-207 in the Capitol. Some had
tough questions they wanted to press. Others wanted only an obligatory photograph they could send back to their home-state newspapers as evidence of their status in the field of international affairs.

Falcone wanted neither. The questions he had could not be
asked in that room and not with so many present. And most of these
so-called give-and-take sessions were nothing of the kind. The questions would be wrapped in so much diplomatic gauze that they hit
the visiting dignitary with the force of a snowflake. And the visitor,
knowing that his "off the record" responses would be in reporters'

notebooks before he entered his armored limousine outside the Capitol, offered up little more than vapid, well-rehearsed platitudes.

Gerstel had surprised them. A man of medium height, with short wavy hair that he combed neatly back from a deeply lined forehead, the Israeli leader displayed an impressive presence. Almost immediately, Falcone could tell that Gerstel was not given to ceremony. It was in his eyes—dark, intelligent eyes that seemed to absorb everything and reflect nothing. It was in his voice—deep, guttural, lyrical. And it was in his attitude—he meant business.

The chairman of the Foreign Relations Committee, Ralph Kondracke, first welcomed Gerstel, then asked whether he had any observations on the pending sale of Hawk antiaircraft weapons to Jordan.

Gerstel made a stab at diplomacy. "I am a guest in your country, Mr. Chairman, and therefore think it inappropriate to inject my opinions into your political decisions." *Much as I expected,* Falcone remembered thinking at the time. But then Gerstel's manner shifted. His voice took on an edge. "Perhaps I should follow a Jewish custom of answering a question with a question," he said, flashing a smile that was quite foreboding. It was the smile of a shark, Falcone had thought. "As you know, my country is surrounded on three sides by heavily armed neighbors who have declared a holy war against us. Three wars have been fought. A fourth is under way from within. In addition, Saudi Arabia has acquired ballistic missiles that can strike us. Iraq still has vast amounts of chemical and biological weapons. Libya has acquired from the Soviet Union SU-24 bombers with an in-flight refueling capacity."

Gerstel paused, his eyes searching those of the senators, who had stopped nibbling the hors d'oeuvres in front of them.

"Let us assume that Canada and Mexico were to turn against the United States and declare its existence illegal. Let us assume that Israel, America's loyal and steadfast ally, proposed to sell Canada or Mexico, or both, sophisticated weapons that could complicate its defenses, perhaps even assure America's destruction. Israel might say it was doing so because it wanted to pursue an even-handed policy with nations in the western hemisphere. And besides, if Israel did not do so, China, the Soviet Union, Japan, and others would. What would be the position of your President? What would you do, Mr. Chairman?"

Gerstel's question hung like a dagger on a string of silence right over Kondracke's head. He had assumed the Prime Minister would artfully dodge his question. Now his face was scarlet. He forced a smile that looked silly.

Several senators, not knowing what to say, reached for water pitchers or poured hot coffee into porcelain cups that bore a blue Senate seal.

Gerstel had gone too far. *But diplomacy be damned,* his eyes said, flashing in the light from the ornate chandelier that hung over the baize-topped conference table. Israel was not going to swap a German gas chamber for an Arab one—not with American complicity!

When Hollendale heard what Gerstel had done, he went into one of his patented rages. He sent word to Gerstel that he considered the Prime Minister's conduct a breach of faith. To little avail— the proposed sale of weapons to Jordan was defeated by a wide margin.

Now, two years later, Gerstel still seemed robust, even though the lines of fatigue around his eyes were deeper. He and Falcone exchanged pleasantries for a moment while coffee was poured for them. Falcone began, thanking Gerstel for the meeting, particularly under such trying circumstances.

"It is my pleasure, Senator," Gerstel said, setting his coffee down. Then, smiling, he remarked, "I'm told you had an interesting evening."

Is he baiting me? Falcone asked himself. *Is he talking about Dizengoff Street or Rachel's—the Mossad's—apartment? Has Rachel told them about our lovemaking? Did she have to, or is it all on film?* Suddenly his mind was filled with Joshua as he appeared moments before his throat was slashed.

"Mr. Prime Minister," he said, "let me be as direct now as you have been with us in the past. Trust has broken down between us. We have started to behave more like enemies than allies." Falcone went on to reveal that the United States suspected that Israeli intelligence had been penetrated by the Soviets, and that information about SUNDANCER had been passed to Moscow. A stupid plan to detect *Canaan* had backfired, resulting in Joshua Stock's murder and the attack on Yitzhak Rafiah.

As he listened to Falcone, Gerstel's face reflected no emotion.

His eyes swept back and forth as if they were printing the words on his mind. Finally he said, "You've been very candid, Senator. But you have not told me everything. Obviously, if Senator Stock was giving us information, someone requested it. I had no knowledge of this—I am truly offended by the very thought, but I accept full responsibility. There is no excuse for this activity. Apologies are insufficient for what has happened, but I am truly sorry." He paused, and Falcone was certain that he was pondering how he was going to explain this to his Cabinet. It was certain to be leaked to his political opposition.

"There's more, Mr. Prime Minister. Our intelligence people believe that some of the Soviet émigrés may not be what they seem." *God*, he thought to himself, *I sound just like Dake!* "They may be *spetsnaz* troops."

Gerstel looked as if he had been kicked in the chest. If the information was accurate, he knew that Israel was in grave danger, immediate danger. His mind was racing, trying to draw connections between Falcone's words and what had been happening in his country. Anger gathered in his face, even as he tried to appear calm. "You've been most helpful, Senator."

Falcone knew that at that moment Gerstel wanted to be very much alone.

"Sir, I know you don't need any more burdens to carry right now, but I have two requests that only you can help me with."

"Of course. If I can," Gerstel said.

"I need to see Ambassador Rafiah," Falcone said. "He's the only one who can lead us to *Canaan*. I've been told that he's under heavy guard and I need your permission to see him."

"I'm afraid that you'll be disappointed, Senator. Ambassador Rafiah has made some progress in recent days, but he is completely paralyzed and as yet has not been able to talk. He is alert, but our physicians say that he suffers periods of deep depression because of his condition."

"I think it is important that I see him," Falcone insisted.

Gerstel moistened his lips, then pursed them. Finally he nodded.

Falcone moved his chair away from Gerstel's desk, rose, and thanked him for the meeting. Then, just as he began to leave the room, he turned to the Prime Minister. "There is just one other thing."

"Yes?"

"The police have a friend of mine in jail in Tel Aviv—Philip Dake. He's being held as a witness to a shooting last night on Dizengoff Street. I would appreciate it if you could arrange for him to be released."

"Your friend has made things very difficult for me, Senator. There will be consequences for me with Americans if he's held and consequences with Israelis if he's released."

Falcone nodded, acknowledging the political vise Gerstel was in.

"I can promise you only that I'll resolve the matter soon."

Perfectly candid, and perfectly ambiguous, Falcone thought as he left the Prime Minister's residence and joined Rachel outside.

48

"COLONEL NESHER, I'VE just received information—not yet verified, mind you—but suggesting that among the thousands of recent émigrés from the Soviet Union are not only professional agitators but Soviet soldiers. Specifically, *spetsnaz* soldiers. What would you make of it?"

The words came from a large man with a soft oval face. Dark horn-rimmed glasses framed blue eyes that lurked under heavy eyelids. His manner and voice were those of an English aristocrat, but David Ben-Dar was no aristocrat and no Englishman. He was Israel's top intelligence officer, the director of the Mossad. His words, so calmly uttered—fashioned nearly as a mere Socratic inquiry—came flying at Nesher like knives.

"Impossible, Director," Nesher answered reflexively. Then, stammering, as if he knew the rejection came too quickly, "Well, not impossible, but highly unlikely. We expect the Soviets to plant intelligence agents among the émigrés. That is something they've done virtually everywhere. But *spetsnaz* are used only if there is a major military or paramilitary attack plan." The very thought of it suddenly loomed like a dark cloud in Nesher's mind. "Our diplomatic

relations with the Soviet Union are excellent. In fact, they are im-
proving every day."

"Of course. But it's well to remember that Stalin thought he
was on rather good terms with the Germans," Ben-Dar said, tamping
tobacco into a meerschaum pipe, then lighting it.

Nesher started to panic. Ben-Dar had not called him in to
engage in a discussion of history or philosophy. Why had the director asked him to visit? Domestic counterintelligence was not his
province.

"True," he said, trying to keep the growing terror out of his
voice. "There is not much that any of us can say with certainty. But
I am aware of absolutely no information that would lend any cre-
dence to such a story."

Ben-Dar exhaled, pushing a small puff of smoke through his
lips. "Of course, I realize this is not your bailiwick. Shin Bet and
Immigration have that responsibility. I just wanted to get your
thoughts on it. I agree that it does seem rather far-fetched."

"It's the kind of rumor the enemies of Israel might start, Director." Nesher tried to sound convincing. "Plant a story that a bottle
of aspirin contains cyanide tablets or that Israeli oranges have been
injected with a deadly insecticide. Instantly"—he snapped his fingers to dramatize the point—"all aspirins are pulled from the
shelves, all Israeli oranges are barred from being sold. It could very
well be an Arab plot to prevent us from bringing more of our people
out of the Soviet Union. Remember how they tried to stop Aeroflot
flights into Tel Aviv."

Nesher's heart was thumping so hard that he feared Ben-Dar
would hear it. He could feel beads of sweat popping out along his
hairline. *Of course. It all made sense now. The poison gas . . . Colonel Mizrahi . . . Rafiah . . . Stock. They were no accidents, no random acts of terrorism. They were all part of a terrible plan to betray
him. Betray Israel. But why? Why?*

"Yes. Yes, of course, Colonel. A very good point. Still, I think
it's serious enough to check out with Reuben Sharett. Shin Bet
should be aware of the rumor. I appreciate your coming."

As Nesher turned to leave, Ben-Dar spoke as if he had had an
afterthought. "Oh, Colonel. I've been told that you've been spending time traveling to Paris lately. Anything I should be aware of?"

Now the knives were being twisted. Ben-Dar had to suspect

him! In the private moments of his morning walks along the beach, Nesher had constructed in his mind a cathedral of lies, with balustrades and arches so intricate and rich in design that they would have the appearance of absolute authenticity. But now, looking into the owlish face of one of Israel's most brilliant men, his fabrications turned to rubble. One lie, one false step, and he could trigger a booby trap. But half the truth would not be a lie. Half the truth might be enough to protect the rest of his secret.

"Nothing serious, Director. I've tried to keep in regular contact with our counterterrorist unit in Paris. As you know, there's been an upswing in anti-Semitism there, more violence toward Jews. I want more information about what happened to our friend Yitzhak Rafiah."

"Of course, Colonel. Yes. That's important, thank you," Ben-Dar said, sounding not the least bit skeptical.

After Nesher left, Ben-Dar returned to his desk. His mind was racing through the implications of what Senator Falcone had said an hour earlier to the Prime Minister. Soviet and U.S. moles in the Mossad. SUNDANCER compromised. A senator murdered. The attempt to assassinate Rafiah. Had paranoia and conspiracy run like headless horsemen in an endless circle of insanity? Was he staring into a hall of mirrors, the reflection multiplied a million times so that he was paralyzed by contradiction and doubt? Was the threat of *spetsnaz* soldiers a cruel hoax concocted by Arabs, as Nesher had just suggested?

Nesher. A war hero. A patriot.

Ben-Dar opened a file that had been prepared for him only that morning. He slowly reviewed a series of black-and-white eight-by-ten photographs that had been supplied by the Service de Documentation Extérieure et Contre Espionnage, the French counterintelligence service. Thank heavens for the special liaison relationship the Mossad maintained with its sister organizations.

There was Nesher huddled in a café, talking to another man. The same man was seen walking past Nesher near Zola's grave. The French had identified him as Ptor Kornienko. They had traced a call from the bar of the Raphael Hotel on Avenue Kléber to the Soviet embassy in Paris. With the cooperation of one of the hotel's bartenders, they had identified Kornienko as the caller. They did not know much about him. They assumed that Kornienko was a cover name, and some doubted that he was a Soviet academician.

Ben-Dar found it curious that Nesher had made no record of his encounters with this Kornienko. Even more curious was why Nesher had taken such elaborate trade-craft measures to avoid surveillance. As far as the Mossad's files were concerned, the meetings had never occurred.

Tapping the dying embers from his pipe, Ben-Dar decided that he needed to know why. Now, at this very moment.

49

Naked and bound by his wrists to a heavy metal chair, the man did not look very much like a fierce *spetsnaz* warrior. Nesher had wasted little time after leaving David Ben-Dar's office. Two heavily armed security men had driven him to Avram Koshinsky's apartment. Bursting in on Koshinsky while he slept, they quickly subdued him with a massive dose of sodium pentathol. Then they transported him to a secret interrogation room in the basement of a metal fabrication company owned by one of Nesher's friends. There no one would hear the sound of voices. Or screams.

Nesher knew that he had to move quickly. Time was running out. His country was going to be attacked. *But where? And why?* he kept asking again and again. *What have we done?*

He knew about *spetsnaz* soldiers. They were young, war-hardened. Most had served in Afghanistan or Africa. Their physical condition was superb. They were airborne-trained, skilled in martial arts, scuba diving, archery, demolition. Capable of surviving extreme cold or heat. Able to live off the land like animals. Patriotic. Willing to die before compromising their secrets, their country.

That was the key. Was Koshinsky really willing to die? Nesher, who had considerable interrogation skills, didn't think so.

"Sergeant Major Koshinsky," he began, in a voice filled with cold fury. The room was completely dark except for a spotlight that was so bright that it forced Koshinsky, who was stirring to consciousness, to keep his eyes closed. "I have no rubber hoses. No pliers to pull out your fingernails. No electric wires to scorch your testicles." In the darkness, Nesher's voice took on a strangely ethereal quality, as if it were completely detached from his body.

Koshinsky said nothing.

"I know you are trained to endure great pain—"

Koshinsky's jaw muscles twitched. His body stiffened, as if ready to receive impending blows.

"—but I have little time to test your ability to withstand the punishment you deserve. So I've decided that you can either tell me the names of your fellow saboteurs and the exact nature of your plans, or you will die. Very simply. But very slowly."

Sensing the menace in Nesher's voice, Koshinsky remained rigid, contemptuous.

Nesher was not by nature or practice a cruel man. He had fought heroically in three wars. He had killed many men, but he had always fought by the rules, fiercely but fairly. He acknowledged the courage and loyalty of those called to battle. He mutilated no corpses, mistreated no prisoners of war.

Now he was desperate. There was no time left for psychological games. He stepped abruptly into the cone of light. With surprising deftness—and to the horror of the security men—he sliced through the veins of Koshinsky's right wrist with a sharp knife.

"It will take several hours before you go into shock and then experience convulsions. With each heartbeat, you will push out another drop of life." Nesher was surprised that he sounded so ruthless. "If you decide to cooperate, I'll be in the next room, waiting." With that he turned, motioned for the others to follow, and snapped out the spotlight, leaving Koshinsky in total darkness.

It was not long before Koshinsky experienced the sensation of black walls closing in, confining him to a coffin. The drip of his blood onto the tile floor was amplified by the darkness. Each drop exploded like a bullet in the terrifying silence. Twenty minutes passed. Thirty. Maybe if he struggled, he thought, he could pump the blood out faster. But his arms and legs were taped to the chair in a way that permitted no movement. *Death,* he silently prayed, *be merciful. Come quickly. Take me. Take me . . .*

He began to get lightheaded. His whole body seemed to spin in the darkness. Desperate thoughts came. Who would tell his mother? His girlfriend, Raisa? Would he lose control of his bowels? No. Please. He didn't want to die in his wastes. Bile started to creep up the back of his throat. He gagged. There was only one way to stop it. He bit down, hard, screaming.

Nesher, who had no intention of letting Koshinsky die, was surprised at how quickly he broke.

But as he entered the interrogation room, he heard a different sound. Koshinsky was no longer screaming. He was choking! Blood was streaming not from his wrists, but from his mouth. He had bitten off part of his tongue, and it was lodged in his throat!

Now Nesher was screaming frantically. "Stop him! Stop him! He's choking to death."

They could not move quickly enough. Koshinsky had clamped his jaws like a vise. They slapped his face and pounded his chest, but nothing they did could pry his jaws open. His tongue was wedged in his throat like a piece of meat, shutting off all air to his lungs.

His chest heaved momentarily. Then Koshinsky slumped forward, dead.

Nesher stared at his body, transfixed by the horror of what had happened. He had just lost the only person who might have helped him.

50

Jerusalem, August 17

LATER IN THE AFTER-
noon, on the way to the hospital, Rachel spoke optimistically about
her father's improved condition. Now that he was out of his coma,
they would learn who was responsible for all the mayhem that had
brought Falcone and Rachel together. Falcone was cautiously enthusiastic, staking out a supportive position he could retreat to if
Rafiah's condition proved too unstable to rely on.

That was what he had learned in prison camp—cautious enthusiasm. It was what separated him from the other men, whose skepticism and disappointment were the usual commodities exchanged
during the years of waiting. Falcone had learned patience while
many learned despair. It was only in the years since the war that he
had begun to lose faith in the distinction.

Falcone followed a few steps behind Rachel and Dr. Benjamin
Rosenthal as they stepped off the elevator on the third floor of
Hadassah Hospital. Rafiah's room was located at the end of a long
corridor on the west side of the hospital. It remained under heavy
guard. Rachel was anxious to spend a few moments alone with her
father, to prepare him. Falcone was equally anxious for her to do so.

He hated hospitals. They were all crisp and white and sterile. But disinfectant and that clipboard efficiency could not remove the smell of sickness, the chalk-white skin, the matchstick-thin bones; the flowers and get-well cards could not conceal how death had once sat, a vulture on a tree limb, over his father's door.

After his father's death, Falcone had formed a cynical view of hospitals. Hospitals were the way stations you passed through before you were admitted to death. You were cleaned and monitored. You were examined under subdued lights to the tune of whispered voices and hopes forged out of desperation. And all the while you found yourself saying, "Look what modern science has done for me." You found yourself cautiously enthused, and utterly helpless.

Five minutes passed. Finally Dr. Rosenthal appeared in the doorway and motioned to Falcone.

As he entered the room, Falcone knew immediately that Rafiah was one of those patients doomed to live in the prison of his body. He wasn't going to recover and he wasn't going to die—at least, not soon.

Rachel was sitting on the edge of her father's bed, as if her legs had suddenly become too weak to hold her. Her eyes glistened, a dam threatening to break loose.

"Look, Father," she whispered. "You're alive." She hesitated before touching Rafiah, looking at Dr. Rosenthal instinctively to be sure that she wouldn't hurt her father with a kiss or a tender laying-on of hands. Dr. Rosenthal was benign about such shows of affection, preferring to let the relatives of the infirm come to their own peace with the condition of their loved ones. How anyone could ever come to peace with Rafiah's condition was beyond Falcone, however.

Rafiah was strapped into a wheelchair that had been backed against a large window. The afternoon sun streaming through the glass caught a wispy fringe of white hair in such a way that it appeared to be a halo.

This was not the vital man whose photograph had once rested on Joshua's office bookcase. This man's life force had been ravaged. He looked emaciated. Blue veins ran through skin so translucent that it seemed the sunlight passed through it. His eyes, like melting ice, had loosened, so that the edges of his irises merged with the surrounding whiteness. The bib tied around his neck was stained with saliva.

Rachel spoke slowly, explaining that Falcone was a friend of Joshua Stock's. It was important to learn the identity of the person who had asked him to obtain information from Joshua. "Father," she said, her voice so thin, so full of pain that it cracked, "the Prime Minister would like you to help Senator Falcone. Help us. Father, we haven't much time. Please try."

Rafiah's head was completely immobilized by the straps that held it to the high back of his chair, but he seemed to understand. His facial muscles moved, and his tongue extruded between his lips as he struggled to speak. The sounds were garbled, unintelligible. He stopped, then tried again. Stopped. Rachel moved to press a glass of water to his lips.

Dr. Rosenthal intervened. "I'm sorry," he said wistfully, "he is unable to swallow. He can only take food intravenously."

Once more Rafiah struggled to speak, but the words remained trapped in his mind. It was no use.

"I'm sorry. Now please." Dr. Rosenthal signaled that Rachel and Falcone should leave. As he ushered them toward the door, Falcone felt like tearing into him, but he decided that he would do better to comfort Rachel.

At the door they were met by a nurse, a small woman with birdlike features. Her eyes moved about the room, searching out what would need to be rearranged and cleaned after the intrusion of bothersome visitors. Something in the way her eyes darted back and forth struck a chord with Falcone. As Rachel left the room, he checked her with his hand. "Wait," he said. "Let me try something. Just this once." He asked the nurse for the clipboard she was holding, turned over a sheet from the pad, and began to print the alphabet in large block letters.

Rachel stared at him, baffled.

"Senator," Dr. Rosenthal warned, impatient with any attempt to undermine his authority.

"You've had your say, doctor," Falcone said. "Now give me mine." Finished, he walked over to Rafiah. "Ambassador," he said gently, "if you understand me, I want you to blink your eyes. Blink them twice."

Rafiah blinked twice in quick succession. Falcone suddenly felt the exhilaration he had felt in the Calcutta Room when he had first communicated with his fellow soldiers. They'd devised a system of tapping on walls to reach each other from solitary confinement during the days and nights. On the few occasions they were together in a lineup, they'd devised a way of speaking as Falcone was trying to do now, with blinking.

"Sean?" Rachel asked. "He can hear you, can't he?" Her enthusiasm was almost as welcome as Rafiah's response.

"I think so," Falcone said. "Now," he continued speaking to Rafiah, his pulse quickening with expectation, "I'm going to point to the letters on this sheet. Whenever I touch a letter that's in the name of the man or woman who asked you to get information from Senator Stock, I want you to blink twice. This may take some time, but we need to spell out his full name."

Again Rafiah blinked. His eyes were alive, brimming with tears.

"Rachel, you've got to help me with this. I'll need the groupings of common vowels and consonants."

Rafiah blinked twice after Falcone pointed to the first letter. "A?" Falcone asked. Rafiah blinked twice again. On the second letter there was no response. Falcone passed halfway through the alphabet, then Rafiah blinked once. Falcone stopped to make sure he hadn't passed over the next letter in the name they were seeking.

"Is *m* the second letter?" Rachel asked her father. Rafiah made a fruitless effort to speak, and Rachel turned to Falcone expectantly.

"You're taxing what few powers he has," Dr. Rosenthal said. "You may kill the ambassador if you don't stop."

Falcone looked to Rachel for the next step. She knew her father was strong. "He wants to help us, Sean."

"Were you just blinking to clear your eyes?" Falcone asked Rafiah. That was the correct question. Rafiah blinked twice with relief.

They made it all the way to the letter *v* before Rafiah blinked again. Before Falcone started on the third letter, he blinked more fluid away from his eyes. Rachel had the nurse bring some tissues, and she dabbed at the corner of her father's eyes and smiled reassuringly. Then she kissed him on the forehead, saying, "I love you, Father."

Rafiah's eyes shone brightly, and Rachel had to dab away tears before they could communicate further with Falcone's letters. *I* was the third letter. After this Rafiah tried again to speak until Rachel quieted him.

"Avi?" she said. "I think the man's first name is Avi." Rafiah blinked twice in succession.

Slowly, for the next fifteen minutes, Falcone moved his finger back and forth across the letters.

Finally, over the protests of Dr. Rosenthal, who felt the procedure was too slow, too exhausting, for Rafiah, they had it.

"I don't believe it!" Rachel exclaimed. "Avi Nesher? The chief of counterintelligence? You're sure, Father?"

Rafiah blinked again, then struggled to speak. Suddenly he began choking as his throat muscles went into spasm. Moving quickly, Dr. Rosenthal pressed an intercom switch and called for emergency assistance. Within seconds, a nurse burst into the room and handed him a syringe. Injecting its contents expertly, he said, "It's just a muscle relaxant. He'll be fine. But I insist that you leave now. This has been very exhausting for him."

Rachel hugged her father, then took Falcone's hand in her own and walked quickly out of the room, not looking back.

Moments after they left through the hospital's front door and got into the car Kobi was driving, a nurse, the one with the birdlike face, stood at a public pay phone on the third floor. "Uncle," she said, "I have some news. Your friend is doing much better. He remembered you to his daughter and her American friend. Now that he is doing so well, you should think about taking better care of yourself."

51

AVI NESHER SAT IN HIS apartment overlooking Merom Zion Street, letting his vision adjust to the end of day. A half-empty bottle of Scotch rested near the right-hand side of his desk. Wanting to be alone, he'd dismissed his bodyguards earlier in the day. His world was coming to a close. Soon he would die.

He'd betrayed his country, his people. If it were up to Israel, Nesher would most likely be tried and shot for conspiring with the Soviets. He almost had to laugh at the lofty intentions that supported his actions. What mattered in the intelligence world was results, not intentions. Loss and gain. Cause and effect.

Nesher had actually started writing a note that explained everything, how he'd only wanted to protect Israel, to revitalize his people with Soviet Jewish émigrés. Would anyone believe he could have been so naive? When the *spetsnaz* troops were activated, bringing Israel to its knees on whatever mission they were on, would anyone think him less a traitor because of his intentions? He had passed along technology to the Soviets, but what of it? Ronald Reagan had promised to do the same. What had Nesher done that was so awful?

This was all just vanity, this posturing, Nesher realized. It was time to get down to the real question of the evening—what to do. Should he go to the Prime Minister and reveal what little he knew about the *spetsnaz* troops? Try to plead for mercy in a messy situation by admitting everything up front? Or was it better to make a clean break of it, to perform a painless little suicide that kept his treachery absolute and intact? Would it be in Israel's best interests to have Nesher represent total treachery and villainy, the better to stand guard against such evil in the future? Did he want his whole life rewritten to show how he had arrived at this one awful point of betrayal? His thoughts were plagued with vanity. What had truly brought him to reevaluate his life this way?

More than anything else, Nesher hated to lose. His whole life he had served his people with self-righteous vigor. It was the only way he knew. Inattention, a slackening of concern—that would be the death of Israel. Nesher wished he'd known relaxation. His mind had never been at ease, not once that he could think of. He wondered what his life might have been like if he'd been a warrior anywhere else in the world, if he'd known relaxation. If, after a battle was won, he had truly believed that the world was a safer place, just for a moment.

Nesher had won more than one battle. But there was no such thing as victory in a permanent state of war. That was why he fought —to keep what he had won yesterday. If Israel had that, the Arabs would always have less. You needed vigor to keep up in a zero-sum game.

Vigilance. Only with your eyes open did you see the enemy. With his one eye, Nesher saw more than enough. He likened it to the blinking game—when you stopped staring, the game was lost. He had been good at staring, staring across the borders of Israel. Late at night, with caffeine in his veins, he would stare out his window, looking for ghosts. The Arabs were ghosts to him, a part of the nation's collective unconscious. He fully believed in ghosts. They never haunted him, though. Nesher never fully surrendered to sleep.

It was easier to live this way. Always doubting, never believing the war was won. It was the high road to security. To live securely within one's obsession was a real feat. If you managed things right, you could stifle paranoia almost completely. Of course, every true

Israeli was paranoid. You had to be. You used it to your advantage, though. You kept your eyes open, and the ghosts stayed at the borders. You looked at them. The test of your vigor was your eyesight.

That was what Nesher had always believed, before he lost his way. He had been running around the perimeter for so long that real paranoia had begun to set in. He could find no one else as vigilant as he, no one to take up the baton in the never-ending relay he'd been running. His worst fear had set in. His own countrymen had fallen asleep. There were too many ghosts to fight alone. That was what had begun to frighten him.

Ghosts and monsters had been dominating his thoughts. Lately Nesher had likened Israel to Frankenstein's monster. The United States, Dr. Frankenstein in this mad scenario, was faltering in its support for his country. The United States was Israel's doubting father. With everyone calling for the beast's destruction, wouldn't Dr. Frankenstein loathe his child after a while? Had that already happened? Nesher wondered.

Or had his paranoia gotten the best of him? Had he blinked too soon? Was it foresight or hallucination, his betrayal of Israel? He wanted more Jewish émigrés to come to his country. He wanted his people to come home. He wanted more eyes along the border to protect Israel.

Of course Nesher assumed there would be a few plants among the émigrés, a few Soviet loyalists collecting information. *Spetsnaz* were something else, though. These were the very ghosts Nesher feared, come to life. He had released the black plague on his own people. What was the most fitting way for a man brought to this end to die?

The shadows caused by the sun's steady drop crossed the floor of his apartment like black stormclouds on the horizon. It was the only movement Nesher had been aware of this evening. There was more movement in his apartment though, he realized. An intruder, a presence, something. There, by the window, he saw it again. It was someone, a man. Kornienko . . .

Nesher smiled. He knew the end had come. It would be all right after all. He was practically delirious, facing death this way. Who was this man, after all? A ghost?

Nesher got up from his deep-cushioned sofa and stretched his tired legs, never taking his eyes off the man who stood in front of the window.

"Why, Kornienko? Why did you betray me?" Nesher's voice cracked with stifled grief.

"It would take too long to explain, Avi," Kornienko said coolly, patronizingly.

"You owe me an explanation."

"Because we are friends? You're a fool. I owe you nothing. There are no friendships, only interests. You wanted Jews. We wanted technology. It was a straight trade."

"And you got what you wanted."

"We want something more. We want survival. Not on our knees, begging with a tin cup for aid. We want prosperity. And BURAQ will give us that."

"BURAQ?"

"Yes. Tonight, Avi—*Canaan;* perhaps you're entitled to know your code name—tonight we will enter the promised land." Kornienko laughed cruelly, mockingly.

Nesher took two steps and lunged at the ghost who had come to kill him. His instincts had taken over, but he was old now, half drunk, no longer an agile warrior. Kornienko stepped aside deftly and shoved him through the picture window of his fourth-story apartment, plunging him toward certain death. Here was Nesher, chasing ghosts, committing suicide.

Kornienko watched his victim's awkward flight disinterestedly. Such a spectacle was of no concern to him. To die so messily, crashing through a window, smashing head first through the windshield of some hurried commuter on the street—he did not approve. An insecure man, Nesher must have been, to need all that attention. It was better to go unnoticed, to keep death to oneself. Of course, the world of espionage was seldom that accommodating.

52

Jerusalem, August 17

In THE HOSPITAL LOBBY, just beyond the spectacular stained glass wall created by Chagall, Rachel found a public telephone. She placed a call to Mossad headquarters and asked to be connected to the Department of Public Information, History and Culture Division—the code for counterintelligence. Once connected, she asked to speak with the director of the office.

A flat anonymous voice refused to express more than a standard regret of the director's unavailability. Once Rachel identified herself, however, the voice changed immediately to one of friendly deference. "The director left early today. I'm afraid he was not feeling well. But he should be back tomorrow."

Rachel hung up, cutting the line abruptly. She knew where Nesher lived: an apartment in Bayit Vagon, an upper-class suburb populated by deeply religious immigrants from Iraq and Kurdistan. It was not more than five minutes' drive.

She and Falcone slid into the car that Kobi had pulled to the curb. "Hurry," Rachel snapped, unable to hide her fury.

Moments later they jumped out and ran toward Nesher's apartment on Merom Zion Street. A crowd had gathered outside the building, which caused a lump to work itself up into Rachel's throat. She glanced at Falcone, as if to ask what could possibly have happened in this quiet neighborhood. As she did so, her attention was momentarily diverted. She slowed her pace while Falcone raced on. The man walking away on the other side of the street—there was something familiar about him. Not his face. That was in profile and angled away from her. But his walk, his carriage. She could feel her spine literally humming. *You know this man. You know him.*

She followed him with her eyes until he turned the corner and disappeared down Haida Street. Her instincts told her to follow him, but a woman's piercing scream pulled her back.

Falcone had pushed through the knot of people and rushed to the figure that lay crumpled like some old rag doll amid the shards of glass. The man was bleeding profusely from the mouth. There was a dark empty hole where one of his eyes should have been. He was still alive, but Falcone knew it would not be for much longer.

He was trying to speak. The words came out in a whisper, a croak. Falcone leaned over to hear better. He didn't understand. The man was speaking gibberish. He said the word twice. "Borook . . . tonight . . . Borook . . ." Then he went still.

By the time Rachel reached Falcone, the man was dead. "Sean, did he say anything?" she asked. "Did you hear?"

Shaking his head, Falcone said, "Nothing that made much sense. He repeated a word. It sounded like Borook, or something like that. And he said tonight. That was it."

"Barukh? Is that the word?"

"I think so."

Barukh, Rachel thought. *A blessing? The bastard was praying? I hope he rots in the hottest circle of hell.*

The wail of a siren announced the arrival of the police. Rachel and Falcone moved away from the crowd. There was no time to get involved with their questions, and no time to get into Nesher's apartment.

"I have to go to Tel Aviv," Rachel said, "to meet with my superiors. Wait for me at the King David. It may take some time."

53

THE DRIVE TO TEL AVIV
was exasperating—and wild. Rush-hour traffic choked the main
highway. There must have been an accident. Cars crept bumper to
bumper like slow-moving cows heading to their barn.

Kobi drove like a madman, stomping on the accelerator, weaving back and forth among the three lanes. Motorists cursed him,
blew their horns, shook their fists. But Kobi, his eyes hidden behind
mirrored sunglasses, ignored them and pressed on.

More than an hour later, Rachel was in David Ben-Dar's office.
She told him what happened in the hospital, how her father had
identified Nesher. "He's dead," she hissed. "Someone at the hospital must have warned him. The coward must have jumped."

"Or been pushed," Ben-Dar offered, puffing on the pipe that
was never far from his lips. "Although we did find a draft of what
appears to be a confession or suicide note."

Rachel looked at the director, confused.

Ben-Dar explained what Falcone had relayed to Prime Minister
Gerstel. *"Spetsnaz.* It's possible that one of them got to Nesher.
Maybe in retaliation for what happened earlier this afternoon.

Nesher tortured a man named Koshinsky, who ended up choking to death on his tongue. Could be his friends found out about it. We're still trying to piece it all together."

Ben-Dar opened up the file on his desk and showed Rachel the photographs of Nesher and the man the French had identified as Ptor Kornienko.

Rachel felt her heart jump. "That's the man I saw walking away from Nesher's apartment." She riffled through the photographs quickly, shuffling them back and forth. Then she looked through more slowly. She studied every angle, traced every feature, every line in the man's face. Finally she looked up at Ben-Dar. "Can I borrow these for a few minutes, Director?"

Ben-Dar dipped his ample chin and peered over his glasses, which had slipped down slightly on the bridge of his nose. "Of course. Can you tell me why?"

"I'm not sure how or why, but I know this man from somewhere. I'd like to run the photos through Bari Yudin down at the identification center. Maybe the Wizard can work his magic and help me remember."

Rachel was in luck. Bari Yudin was working late. The first thing she noticed as she entered his windowless room was that it was at least ten degrees cooler than Director Ben-Dar's office. Bari was sitting on a low-backed chair with coaster wheels that allowed him to skate along a long bank of computer consoles. He was twenty-eight years old, but he had trouble passing for twenty-one. One thing about him went unchallenged—his brilliance in mathematics and computers. His classmates had dubbed him "Wizard" even before his bar mitzvah.

He greeted her warmly. "The director said you might need some help."

Computers were foreign to Rachel. They spoke an alien language, one she couldn't comprehend, never mind master. "Bari, I need two things. First," she said, pulling from her handbag the small photograph Falcone had given her last night, "I need to know if you can enlarge this photo so that I can see this man's face more clearly." She pointed to the figure standing next to her father. He had been just beyond the range of the camera's flash when the photograph was taken, so that his features were not clear. She remembered the night and she knew the man. But she had to be sure.

"No problem, Rachel," Bari said with a wide grin. "First, we take this little videocamera and focus it on the photograph. Then I crank up Mr. Macintosh here. This is the frame-grabber," he said, beginning to lift off into another world. "The grabber takes the camera output and creates a bit-mapped image. Digitizes it."

Rachel nodded knowingly, but the words meant nothing to her. "Can you make it brighter and sharper?" she asked, looking at the face that had appeared on the twenty-seven-inch monitor.

"Sure," Bari said, tapping away at his computer keypad with the absolute confidence of a concert pianist, never once looking down.

In the corner of the monitor screen, something called "Enhance Menu" appeared:

Enhance windows
Sharpen
Smooth
Edge Detection 1
Edge Detection 2
Vertical line
Horizontal line

"You see," Bari said, "the Histogram Equalization enhances images by evenly distributing the gray scale values of the pixels."

A Tower of Babel, Rachel thought. But her eyes widened as the face on the monitor emerged with absolute clarity.

"Bari," Rachel said, handing him one of the photographs Director Ben-Dar had given her, "would you split the screen and put this man's picture next to the one we've already got?"

Fingers flew again. *Click. Click. Click. Click.* The photographs were digitized, converted into bytes.

Side by side, the similarities in the photographs were dramatic. The faces were nearly identical—angular, thin-lipped, strong-jawed —except for the toupee and beard.

Bari studied the two faces. "Let's do this," he said, beaming like a brilliant boy showing off for visiting relatives. He called up an Image Calculator display which allowed him to subtract one image from the other, add the two together, and mix and match the pixels of the images. He removed the toupee and beard from the face on the left and shifted it over to the one on the right. Then he reversed the process.

It was almost perfect. The only remaining differences were the eyes. The man on the left wore tinted glasses, which obscured the shape of his eyes.

"Let's put this one's glasses over—"

"No. Do it the other way," Rachel insisted.

Clickety, click. Click. With a final flourish, Bari merged the two faces into one.

Rachel felt a cry nearly escape from her lips. She could feel her throat going dry, a burning sensation in her chest. Although she had suspected the truth, she now found herself thinking, *Not one of her father's closest friends! It had to be a mistake.*

Her mind was alive, snapping like an electric wire. Perhaps he was a deep-cover Mossad agent masquerading as a Soviet academician. Perhaps he had been tasked to find the mole and kill him for his treachery. But if that were so, Ben-Dar would have known him. And if Ben-Dar knew him, why would he have shown her the photograph and feigned ignorance about his identity? Was Ben-Dar testing her? No. This man was not Mossad. And Ben-Dar was not playing games.

But what if she was wrong? She could end up destroying the life of an innocent man, a friend. She had to be sure before she could confide in anyone, including Director David Ben-Dar.

"Bari," she said, taking the photographs back, "you are terrific. A true genius."

Bari blushed shyly, not knowing how to respond.

"It's important that I hold this information very tightly for the moment. *No one,*" she emphasized, making it clear that there should be no exceptions, "must know about this."

Bari nodded. "Say no more, Rachel." He tapped the Quit key. A Save As Dialog box appeared in the corner of the monitor. He hit the Cancel button, and the two images instantly disappeared from the screen, leaving no trace of their existence.

By the time he turned back to Rachel, she too had disappeared, as if she had never been there.

———

Ben-Dar was surprised to see Rachel return to his office so quickly. She had been gone no more than thirty minutes.

"Find anything of interest?"

"Yes . . . and no."

Ben-Dar shot her a quizzical look.

"I think I know this Ptor Kornienko. But I have to be sure. There's one more thing I need to check before . . ."

"Well," Ben-Dar said, returning the photographs of Kornienko to the file, "it will have to wait. While you were gone, the Prime Minister called me. He's setting up a special meeting tonight. A highly unusual one. He wants to meet in the Kiryat, and he wants you, your friend Senator Falcone, and the director of the CIA to join us."

"What for?"

"I think he intends to discuss the intelligence that the CIA has passed on through Senator Falcone about *spetsnaz* forces having infiltrated Israel."

Rachel was stunned. Sean had never mentioned anything about *spetsnaz*. "When did Sean . . . Senator Falcone reveal this?"

"Today. When he met with the Prime Minister."

Good God, she thought. If there were *spetsnaz* in Israel, that could only mean . . .

"Things are going to get a bit tense tonight, I'm afraid," Ben-Dar continued. "Apparently, Solomon Ben Israel has called for a rally at ten o'clock down at the Wailing Wall. He's protesting our failure to protect Israeli citizens from Arab terrorism. Two worshippers died from the stoning at the wall today. Ben Israel intends to make a very big issue of it. Come on," he said, hefting himself out of his chair. "You can ride with me."

Rachel needed no explanation for the reason for the rally. She and Falcone had been there when the riot broke out. She shook her head and sighed. "When is this ever going to stop?"

Ben-Dar merely grunted. It was obvious that he had no answer.

As they walked down the corridor from his office, Ben-Dar suggested that Rachel might go along with his bodyguards to his bullet- and bomb-proof car. He had forgotten a small matter. It would take only a moment.

Returning to his office, he searched through the list of telephone numbers that he kept taped to the inside of the top drawer of his desk. Scanning the list with his index finger, he picked out five digits and quickly dialed them. "Bari. Would you mind telling me what Rachel asked you to do?"

There was a momentary silence on the other end of the line. Rachel had said, "Tell no one." Of course, no one could not mean the director. He was someone. "She had me compare two photographs, one that came from our files and one from her purse."

"And what did they show?"

"They appeared to be the same man, Director."

"Did you make any printouts?"

"No, sir. In fact, she asked me to erase the images from the computer."

Ben-Dar remained silent for a moment, trying to figure out exactly what Rachel was up to. "Can you retrieve the images, Bari?"

There was a pause. "Yes, sir. It may take a little time, but I can get them back. Yes, sir."

"As soon as you do, call my office. My secretary will know where to reach me. And Bari—"

"Yes, sir?"

"Do hurry."

54

GERSTEL HAD ARRANGED
for the meeting to be held in the Kiryat, Israel's military headquarters in the center of Tel Aviv. Everyone had been instructed to meet in the room used by the war planners for their deliberations, a room that was eight stories underground.

Bickford briefed Falcone on the men as they began to gather in the room. "This is the Va'adat," he whispered, "the central body of the Israeli intelligence and security community."

"Like our National Security Council?"

"Something like that. There's David Ben-Dar, head of the Mossad. You met him earlier, although you're not supposed to know he's the director." Nodding, Bickford picked out a stodgy man with a bullet-shaped head. "That's Mordecai Gedalia, director of military intelligence. He's sitting next to the man on Gerstel's left—Reuben Sharett, the Shin Bet director. His name is classified, just like Ben-Dar's. He's a take-no-prisoners man."

Falcone's eyes did not stay on Sharett long, but he wondered whether the unshaven, sullen-faced man was anything like Harry Polanski.

Two more men entered and quickly took their seats at the oval dais that encircled the table where Bickford, Falcone, and Rachel sat.

"That's Etan Narkiss, the Foreign Minister, and Ariel Herzog —he's the equivalent of Butch Naylor, the top adviser to Gerstel on political and military intelligence and antiterrorist matters. And there's Eli Ben-Haim, the director general of the Ministry for Foreign Affairs. I think a couple of people are missing."

"I know Narkiss. I met him at a State Department dinner. Who carries the weight with Gerstel?"

"In theory, they're all supposed to be equal in status. Ben-Dar has the title of chairman, and that gives him the top spot. But the fact is that Gedalia overshadows Ben-Dar in power and importance. Gedalia's agency prepares the national intelligence estimates and evaluates all information dealing with the Arab nations. That gives him de facto power."

The last man to enter the room was David Zamir, the Minister of Defense, a former battle-tank commander, a brilliant strategist, and a particularly vicious soldier. His reputation on both counts was well deserved.

Gerstel opened the meeting, speaking first in Hebrew, explaining the presence of the three people who sat before the Va'adat. As Rachel translated to Falcone in a low whisper, he glanced around the room, somehow surprised by its lightness and modernity. The doors and paneling were made of wood lighter than teak, perhaps a Scandinavian birch. The walls were covered with huge maps of the Arab territories surrounding Israel. In the very center of a long wall was a floor-to-ceiling television screen.

Falcone's eyes were brought back to Gerstel when the Prime Minister switched to English.

"Gentlemen, I regret to advise you that we have a traitor in our midst, a traitor who has passed highly sensitive information to the Soviets. I have reason to believe that he was either directly or indirectly responsible for the death of an American senator—our friend Joshua Stock—and the attack on our own Ambassador Rafiah. The traitor is Avi Nesher."

Everyone but Ben-Dar reacted with shock and disbelief.

"Impossible," thundered Narkiss, slamming his fist down on the table.

"This must be a cruel hoax," protested Sharett. "Who gave you this information?" He eyed Bickford angrily.

Ben-Dar intervened. "It is no hoax. We have verified the information. Avi Nesher is dead. Either he was murdered or he was a suicide victim. We are not sure yet. At this moment we are looking for the man who controlled him."

Narkiss, a tall, angular man with pale blue eyes, persisted. "I'm not sure I understand. Assuming that what you say is true—and I'm not prepared to make that assumption—why does this necessitate the presence of our American friends and Miss Rafiah here tonight? I find this highly unusual. It is uncalled for."

Gerstel cut Narkiss off. "Because our *American friends* and *our* Miss Rafiah," he said, making it clear that he would tolerate no sarcasm, "have information that suggests we are in grave danger. Director Bickford believes that the Soviets have infiltrated an unknown number of *spetsnaz* forces among the recent émigrés. If so, it means they are planning some kind of military action in Israel. Against Israel. These are no ordinary PLO terrorists, Minister Narkiss, not rock-throwing children, but their very best special forces." Gerstel's deep voice rose until he was nearly shouting.

"Mr. Prime Minister," Bickford said in a deliberately gentle tone, trying to defuse the tension, "this is an extraordinary meeting, and I—Senator Falcone and I are truly grateful to you for permitting us to be here."

Gerstel's security advisers fell silent, but clearly they were still disturbed by Bickford's and Falcone's presence in the room.

"As Prime Minister Gerstel has said, we believe the Soviet Union is planning some kind of military or paramilitary action somewhere in Israel. Possibly tonight. It involves *spetsnaz* and very likely explosives."

"Somewhere? Very likely? Explosives? Is that the best information you have, Director?" Sharett asked.

"I have nothing more specific, Director Sharett," Bickford responded calmly.

"Well, Mr. Prime Minister," Sharett retorted, "if *you* believe that the American intelligence community's very general information is reliable, then we have no alternative but to place our forces on high alert!" He glanced over at Mordecai Gedalia, in search of approval.

The Prime Minister turned toward Sharett, fixed him with a cold stare, and said, "And who do you recommend we prepare to strike against? The Soviet Union?"

"There must be Arab complicity, at the very least," Sharett responded, somewhat less sure of himself now.

"That's possible. But the only complicity we know about is *Israeli* complicity!" Gerstel hammered his words hard at the head of Shin Bet. "Besides, if we go on full alert, the Soviets will know immediately and will tell our Arab enemies to mobilize. Each of us will then race to be the first to strike preemptively."

Gerstel allowed the consequences of another full-scale war with all of the Arab League nations to sink in before he turned to Bickford and Falcone. "My friends," he said in a lower, less combative tone that conveyed regret, "we also have to consider whether the story of an imminent attack on us is false. It could be a plant, disinformation. Perhaps it is sincerely believed to be true by American intelligence sources, but nothing more than a cynical plan to bring about a preemptive strike by Israel against its sworn enemies. Suppose Israel were to start a war on the very eve of a new treaty between the United States and the Soviet Union."

"So what are you suggesting, Mr. Prime Minister?" Gedalia asked with a display of irritation. "That we do nothing because we have no one to attack, or that we do nothing because there is no reason to attack? Have you called us here tonight to give you a mandate to do nothing? The Israeli people will never forgive you, or us, if in the face of a warning we decide to stand paralyzed with fear. With due respect, I think we should mobilize and prepare for the unknown. Prepare for the worst!"

Rachel listened to the exchanges between these tough-minded men in silence. Her mind kept playing over the day's events. The walk through the Old City . . . her father . . . Nesher. Nesher's words had to be the key. He said, "Barukh. Tonight." Blessed tonight. It made no sense.

Whether from inspiration or desperation, she couldn't be sure, Rachel leaned over to Falcone and whispered, "Sean, is it possible that Nesher said Buraq?"

Falcone gave her a puzzled look. "It could have been, yes. There was a lot of commotion going on. Buraq, barukh—it all sounds the same to me. What difference does it make?"

What difference! Rachel wanted to shout. *All the difference! A life-and-death difference!*

Buraq was the name of the winged horse that carried Mohammed to heaven. From where? From the Dome of the Rock.

Suddenly an idea that had been forming somewhere deep inside came rushing to the surface. The rock; men hurling rocks from the wall down on the worshippers below; Israeli troops shooting, arresting Arabs; a rally planned for ten o'clock tonight; Solomon Ben Israel to speak. All the scattered pieces were drawn like iron filings to a magnet.

The massacre in Gaza last April was just one part of the plan. Insert trained professionals, posing as Jewish émigrés, into Israel to swell the numbers of the religious fanatics, the radical right. Push them—or use sabotage if necessary—into violent action. Crank up the growing tension between Israel and the United States. Then covertly commit a truly monumental act of outrage and lay it at the feet of those who have proposed to do precisely the same thing. Blow up the Dome of the Rock!

"Mr. Prime Minister," Rachel said, "if you'll indulge me for a moment."

Gerstel was surprised by her interruption, but nodded for her to speak.

"I think it is unnecessary for you to mobilize our military forces," she said, her voice firm and unwavering. She then spent the next few moments explaining what Buraq was and what she believed it meant.

Protests erupted around the table. For the first time Ariel Herzog spoke, dismissing Rachel's theory as preposterous. Even Ben-Dar thought she was overreaching.

"No, Director," she responded. "What is the lesson our instructors drove into each of us? 'Think like the enemy. Take on his hatreds, his prejudices, his training. Think what you would do in his place.' "

"But he would know that destroying the Dome would start a full-scale war," Narkiss said, shaking his head to indicate he thought the very notion foolish.

"Precisely," Rachel shot back. "And what could be better than to have Israel blamed for starting a war in this fashion? Militarily, we will always be on our own. We know that. We should win, but who knows now, with all of the chemical and biological weapons in the hands of the Arabs? This time, though, it is certain that the United States would not be able to stand with us politically.

"Don't you see? The Soviet President is in Washington signing a chemical weapons agreement, promoting peace. We gas Palestinians! We blow up the Dome of the Rock! Do you think Washington could do anything but join in the absolute condemnation of Israel? Even if we win, we lose. No government would support us!"

Both Falcone and Bickford were persuaded by Rachel's logic and passion. They wanted to say, "Yes. Yes." But they sat in silence. This was a decision for Israel alone.

After a long pause, Gerstel said, "David. I want you to increase our alert status. But no mobilization of troops."

Zamir started to protest.

"No. I gave you an order. I'm the one who'll be held accountable, not you."

"Accountable to whom? How many Israelis will be left if you're wrong?" Zamir turned to the others, looking for support.

Gerstel moved quickly. Looking at Bickford, Falcone, and Rachel, he said, "If you'll excuse us, please, there are matters that we should discuss in private."

As soon as they left the room, Gerstel turned to Zamir in a rage. He knew that if there was any hesitation on his part, he could be faced with a mass walkout. Zamir had issued a direct challenge to his authority. His voice was cold as steel. "David, you are out! Fired, as of this moment! And anyone who shares his opinion," Gerstel shouted, scanning the faces of the other men, "may follow him out the door."

No one spoke. Or moved.

"And a word of caution," Gerstel said to Zamir, who sat in silent fury. "If you say a word to anyone, I'll have you arrested and tried for treason!"

Zamir, his face flushed with anger, heaved himself from his chair and stormed out of the room.

"Now, gentlemen," Gerstel said in a softer voice, "there is little time for us to act. Ariel, in Zamir's absence, I want you to get a rapid response team from Golani Brigade's Egoz Commandos to the Old City. All of the police and border guards who are guarding the entrances to the Dome of the Rock are to be relieved immediately.

Anyone who resists should be shot. All of those relieved should be held, temporarily at least, for questioning."

Even as he acted with swift assurance, Gerstel could not fully repress the doubt he felt. If he had made the right decision, the Israeli people would never know. There was too much at stake. Disclosure of the plot would place those émigrés already in Israel under a permanent shadow of suspicion. No, there could be no celebration. Buraq would have to remain a state secret.

But what if he was wrong? What if he had committed a monumental act of folly by placing confidence in the judgment of one woman?

More than his political career was on the line. Israel, assuming it still existed, would be in another war. Perhaps for the last time. And he had given up the one advantage that had helped Israel in the past—surprise, preemption. This time he had even given up preparation. He would go down in history as the one who had delivered them to the second holocaust . . .

55

AFTER THE FORMAL meeting of the Va'adat ended, Gerstel invited Rachel and Falcone to join him in a smaller office furnished with a desk, a leather couch, and chairs. The walls were dark mahogany, the lighting recessed and indirect. It was a room, Falcone guessed, where momentous decisions had been made. Solitary decisions. It was a room for waiting. For worrying.

The clock on the credenza behind the desk read 8:15. The silent sweep of the second hand was transformed in Falcone's mind to the pendulum of a grandfather clock, with each click touching the detonator of a bomb ready to explode. One more click . . .

Twenty minutes passed. Thirty. Finally the phone on Gerstel's desk rang, as loud as a fire bell.

"Yes?" the Prime Minister answered tentatively, trying to force the apprehension out of his voice. For the next few seconds he remained silent. But his eyes said everything: disappointment, defeat, despair.

"That was Director Sharett. All the men assigned to guard access to the Temple Mount have been replaced. None resisted. If there had been *spetsnaz* among them, they would have fought. As far as we can determine, all of the men are loyal to Israel. Either the CIA was wrong—"

"Or I was wrong," Rachel volunteered. "I'm sorry. It seemed so logical. All the pieces fit."

"You needn't apologize. I really had no option. Going on full alert would have started a war. I'm convinced of it." Gerstel lapsed into silence. Israel was in an impossible position. It was waiting to be attacked, but by whom? And how many?

Rachel was tempted to tell him about the man called Ptor Kornienko, but then he would think that she was truly crazy. She had already foisted one wild theory on him. She couldn't try another.

She excused herself, asking Falcone to join her outside so that Gerstel could be alone. Then she went into an empty adjoining room while Falcone waited outside. She called Mossad headquarters, got connected to the computer center, and spoke with one of the operators of the large computer that Mossad agents called Springs, because of its never-ending source of information. She gave the officer a man's name and asked him to check all the hotels in Tel Aviv and Jerusalem to see if he was listed as a guest in any of the hotels.

She was placed on hold for less than a minute. He was in Jerusalem, at the American Colony Hotel. Rachel looked at her watch. It was 8:50 P.M.

She knocked gently on Gerstel's door and entered. The Prime Minister's face was pinched with anxiety.

"Mr. Prime Minister, I have a request I'd like to make in my father's name."

"Rachel, you needn't do that."

"It's important that I get to Jerusalem as soon as possible. It will take at least forty or fifty minutes by car. I need to be there immediately."

"You would like a helicopter?"

"Please."

Gerstel found himself almost saying no. After all, what had this woman brought him? Ridicule, disgrace, national suicide? But he relented. She had lost a brother, nearly lost a father. She had paid her dues, risking her own life many times over. "I'm sure the Defense Minister can arrange it for you," he said.

Five minutes later, Falcone and Rachel emerged from the Kiryat. A military chopper was just setting down on the helipad adjacent to the headquarters. They ran toward it, ducking their heads to keep well below the sweep of the rotor blades. Once aboard, they quickly strapped themselves into their lap and shoulder harnesses.

The turbo engines roared as the pilots gave them more throttle. The whip of the rotor blades accelerated. At first the Huey lifted slowly, nose dipped forward, tail high. Finally they were off, skimming along at 150 knots, not more than a few hundred feet above the ground.

When Falcone first stepped into the helicopter, he felt a vague nervousness sweep through him. Then the anxiety became more specific. Twenty-five years had passed since the time he was dropped into a hot landing zone—the time he lost all of the men in his unit. Butterflies were going crazy in his stomach. Memories were rushing at him in the darkness like bats. His chest tightened. He tried to take deep, satisfying breaths, but his lungs seemed to be in a vise. Strapped tightly into the seat next to Rachel, he felt a slight tremor in his arms and legs. He hoped she didn't notice it.

If Rachel felt anything, she didn't say so. She sat strapped in her seat, a dark silent figure preoccupied with her own thoughts. *What if BURAQ has nothing to do with the Dome of the Rock? What if the* spetsnaz *forces—if they in fact exist—are here to destroy Israeli command and communication lines prior to a massive, well-organized assault by our Arab enemies? What if . . . ?*

The Huey's powerful engines drowned out any attempt to talk. Falcone slipped on the communications headset. The voices squawking over the intercom were flat, monosyllabic, robotic, but their cool professionalism calmed him. He was fully alert now, his mind no longer distracted. He looked out the window into the darkness and could see lights shining below like diamonds. He heard the subtle change in the sound of the rotor blades. The Huey feathered down so smoothly that Falcone barely felt the bump when the wheels touched the parking lot next to the Knesset. They had made it in fourteen minutes.

Rachel had called ahead. Kobi and Ariel were waiting for them.

The phone startled Prime Minister Gerstel. It was David Ben-Dar.

"Mr. Prime Minister, I'm sorry to disturb you, but I must know whether Rachel is still with you."

"No, David. She left for Jerusalem by helicopter. Why?"

"Sir, I'm afraid I have some very bad news. Rachel has been distraught over what has happened to her father—apparently, more deeply distraught than any of us knew. She was at headquarters today, matching up some photographs. It turns out she thinks a Russian called Ptor Kornienko may be our friend Michael Rorbach."

"Preposterous. Michael is—"

"I know. I know. But this whole business about the Dome of the Rock—I think she may have snapped. We're still checking this out, but she might have been the one who killed Nesher this afternoon. We have to stop her, Mr. Prime Minister. She may be planning to kill Rorbach, too."

Gerstel slumped back into his chair. He was expecting bad news, but not anything like this. "I'm afraid it may be too late, David. She must be in Jerusalem by now."

Kobi floored the accelerator. The tires burned as if they were on fire, their screams momentarily terrifying nearby pedestrians. He turned right, then left, racing through stop signs and red lights all the way down to Hazanhanum, then left again onto the old Nablus Road.

Moments later, Rachel and Falcone were out of the car, running into the hotel that a century and a half before had been the palace of an Arab pasha and now was the watering hole of visiting actors, playwrights, and traitors.

"I'm sorry, miss," the concierge behind the sweeping wood desk said, "Mr. Rorbach left not more than five minutes ago."

"Did you notice whether he took a cab?"

"No."

"Please, it's important that we see him. It's an emergency. A . . . family problem. Do you recall how he was dressed?"

The concierge paused for a moment, then said, "Yes. He had on a light tan suit, and he was carrying a brown shoulder bag. Slightly larger than a camera bag, as I recall."

Without bothering to thank the man, Rachel pulled Falcone outside the hotel.

"For Christ's sake, Rachel, are you going to tell me what in hell is going on?" Falcone shouted, refusing to move another step.

"Sean, you've got to trust me on this," Rachel said, desperation in her voice. Then she explained what she was certain was going to happen. She instructed Falcone to go down Salah Ed Din Street. She would meet him at Herod's Gate. "That's on Suleiman, the main street outside the north wall of the Old City."

Rachel looked at her watch, which now read 9:40. "Sean, if you see him, make him stop." Then, handing him Kobi's .44 Magnum pistol, she said, "Or kill him."

56

As HE PASSED ST. George's Cathedral, Falcone broke into a sprint. Pedestrian and vehicular traffic was practically nonexistent. He reached Suleiman in a matter of minutes and spotted Rachel rushing up on his left.

As they turned to cross the street, a string of buses brushed past, missing them by inches. The buses stopped and disgorged their passengers, blocking the street in the process. Weary tourists piled out, some of them beet red from their trip to the Dead Sea and Masada. There were some smiling faces. Others looked angry from too much sun and heat.

Rachel and Falcone got snarled in the crowd. They tried to twist away, but succeeded only in entwining themselves with more people. They bumped one woman, knocking her to the ground. A fat man shoved Falcone roughly. "Sonofabitch," he cursed. "What the hell are you doing pushing old people around?" Others began to shout angrily as Rachel and Falcone finally broke through the knot of tourists.

Rachel directed Falcone to continue up Suleiman and turn in at the Damascus Gate. She would go through Herod's Gate and then meet him where the Via Dolorosa intersected Al Wad. "It's not far from the place where we had baklava and coffee this morning," she reminded him. "And when you enter the Old City, walk quickly, but don't run. The police and border guards are expecting trouble, and we can't afford to be stopped."

As Falcone raced up Suleiman, the angry voices behind began to fade. The only thing he could hear was his own breathing. Then he slowed down and adjusted the .44 Magnum, which was tucked inside his shirt, so that its hammer no longer cut into his stomach.

As soon as he passed into the Old City, he experienced an eerie sensation. There were no people—no pilgrims, no teeming masses in search of history. The shops were all closed, shuttered up with antiriot shields. And it was dark. Street lighting was sporadic. He found himself stepping out of ink-black darkness into pools of soft light and then into darkness again. It looked like a lunar landscape.

Actually, he preferred the dark, once his eyes adjusted to it. He could move easily without becoming a target for Rorbach or any of his *spetsnaz* friends.

He picked up his pace, striding just short of running. All his senses were alert, strung out like high-tension wires. A cat's squawl startled him. He reached for his gun, then relaxed. He breathed out. Kept moving. Saw nothing.

The night air had not cleared away the odors of the day's activities. He could still detect heavy traces of fried meats and spices, and the faint smell of donkey shit, which had been ground over the centuries into the cobblestones . . .

Rachel arrived at their meeting place first. She had found nothing. Rorbach had vanished. "Maybe he isn't even in here." She began to lash out at herself. "What if I was wrong about him? About BURAQ? What if—"

Falcone cut her short. "Come on. We've still got time to find him. Besides, no one has a better idea of what in hell is going on or what to do about it." He didn't have to add that if Rachel was wrong, it wasn't going to matter much longer. His watch read 9:52 P.M.

They decided to take their chances with the police and border guards and broke into a run. They were halfway to the western wall now.

Then Falcone spotted him. A man in a light suit, with a shoulder bag on his left arm. A tourist on an evening stroll through the streets of a magical city. "There he is," Falcone whispered hoarsely. "There he is."

Falcone shot forward, whipping the gun from his belt. He was running fast now, up on his toes, his footfalls barely making a sound. He knew Rachel was not far behind, but he dared not look back for fear of losing Rorbach, who moved like an eel in the shadows.

He gained quickly on his prey, who was headed directly for the western wall. Thoughts kept rushing through Falcone's mind as he found himself gasping for air. Rachel was right. The explosives had already been planted somewhere in the network of tunnels that run under the Temple Mount. That bag had to contain a radio. Rorbach was going to send the signal.

Suddenly Falcone went down. Pain shot through his left ankle as if it had been touched by a hot wire. Tucking his shoulder just before he hit the ground, he rolled, hoping to avoid further injury. His gun clattered along the pavement. "Shit," he cursed, holding his ankle and scrambling on one leg to retrieve it.

Now Rachel was beside him, helping to push him along. Then she let go and began to sprint, driven by the fear that she was going to lose Rorbach. She was in full stride, her hair gleaming in the moonlight. A Killer Angel on the hunt, her prey another killer.

How many had Rorbach killed? Falcone wondered as he felt the pain in his ankle ease. How many would he kill tonight just by pushing a little button? Just a nation.

He could feel the adrenaline pumping through his veins. Rachel was only a few feet ahead of him now. Rorbach was almost to the Street of the Chain, almost to the wall. They had to stop him. "Kornienko!" Falcone suddenly shouted. "Kornienko!"

Rorbach turned instinctively, a flash of panic in his face. He spun around in a circle, then started to run, slipping the bag from his shoulder and carrying it under his arm like a football. He was almost there. One flick of his finger and it would be over.

Now Falcone and Rachel made no attempt to hide their weapons at their sides. Falcone stopped, dropped to one knee, and gripped the .44 in both hands, ready to bring Rorbach down. The tan suit was easy enough to pick out in the darkness. But as Rorbach crossed the Street of the Chain, he was suddenly swallowed up in a sea of yellow shirts. Falcone cursed and started to run again. Within seconds, he was beside Rachel.

"The Kach!" she yelled. "They're the settlers, mostly from the West Bank. They must be here for the rally."

There were scores of them, moving in clusters of thirty or forty. All were wearing yellow T-shirts over their street clothes. Like the Guardian Angels, Falcone thought, only with yarmulkes instead of berets.

Rorbach allowed himself to be carried along as if they were a school of fish moving through dark waves. They were all chanting in Hebrew.

In the far distance, Falcone could see a tall bearded man on a raised platform. He was shouting into a loudspeaker. "No more guilt! Tonight we pledge: No more Crusades! No more Inquisitions! No more Masadas! No more Auschwitzes!"

His anger ricocheted off the ancient stones. The crowd at his feet repeated each pledge, working itself to a frenzy.

"We choose to win! To live! And we don't give a damn what the world thinks!"

The fresh border guards were stationed near the western wall, blocking off the ramp that led up to the Temple Mount. They had been through this before. But tonight, they sensed, was different. Tonight the anger was more volatile. Tonight the Yellow Shirts might storm the Temple Mount, the place Orthodox Jews were forbidden to walk lest they trample upon the Holy of Holies. Tonight, Solomon Ben Israel and his followers seemed determined to reclaim Mount Moriah, to rebuild Solomon's Temple so that the Messiah could come.

It was all so clever, so simple, Falcone thought, as his eyes scanned the cluster of Yellow Shirts. The timing was perfect. Arabs were demonstrating over the use of poison gas, were stoning Israelis. Israelis were killing Arabs. A demonstration had been organized to start a riot, to blow up the Dome of the Rock. With a little help from friends, a wish would be fulfilled . . .

But why would Rorbach do this? Why would he bring the world down on Israel, even if the Jewish extremists didn't give a damn? Falcone didn't have the answer. He only knew that in seconds the course of world events was going to change, unless he could find Rorbach.

He raised the .44 in the air and fired. Once. Again. Again. It sounded like the roar of a cannon.

Pandemonium broke out. Yellow Shirts were everywhere, screaming, scrambling, pushing, trampling.

Then Falcone saw Rorbach sprawled on his knees, the bag knocked from his arms and kicked fifteen feet beyond his out-stretched arms. Rorbach started to crawl like a dog toward the bag, desperate to reach it. He was less than ten feet away from it. Falcone dropped to one knee, determined to pump whatever rounds were left into the man.

Then, from the corner of his eye, he detected movement. Some-thing was coming at him. He turned. A baseball bat. It missed his head by inches, but glanced off his shoulder. Pain shot through his arm, numbing his hand. He dropped the gun.

Two Yellow Shirts were coming at him. Both were burly and mean-looking, with hate in their eyes. If they were *spetsnaz*, he was in trouble. They'd kill him.

The biggest one attacked him first, with a wide swinging punch. Falcone knew immediately it was not the movement of a professional. These guys might be tough bastards, but they didn't know how to fight. He ducked easily under the punch and drove his left fist hard into the man's ribs, then in rapid succession hit him twice in the jaw, sending him crashing to the ground.

Now the other Yellow Shirt was on his back, choking him. Falcone, his right arm still numb with pain, jammed his foot sav-agely down on the attacker's instep, causing him to release his choke hold. Then Falcone snapped his head back, smashing the Yellow Shirt's face. He dropped him to his knees in pain.

The gun. Falcone still had time to get Rorbach. Where was the goddamned gun?

He looked up. Rorbach had reached the bag. He was fumbling with it . . .

She moved swiftly, like a cat going in for the kill. Rorbach never saw her before her foot crashed into his face. He screamed with pain, clutching his face, which had turned into a crimson mask.

He reached inside his coat. He had a gun.

Recognizing the bulk of a bullet-proof vest, Rachel buried her foot in his groin, doubling him over. Then she brought her knee up sharply into his face, sending him sprawling backward.

Rorbach struggled to his feet, staggering, blood spurting from his nose.

Falcone raced toward Rachel. It was over. Rorbach was helpless. Rachel had turned her back on him, but she was not walking away. Falcone could see her coiling herself, winding every muscle in her body into a spiral of energy. He sensed what she was going to do.

"Rachel!" he screamed, racing toward her. "No! You don't have—"

But before he could reach her, Rachel leaped high into the air and swung the entire right side of her body around in a wide, sweeping arc. The heel of her foot, cocked at a sixty-degree angle, struck Rorbach in the jaw with such force that it snapped his neck with a loud, unmistakable crack. It sounded like a pistol shot.

Rorbach's body went rigid, then crumpled onto the cobblestones like a puppet whose strings had been cut.

Falcone finally grabbed Rachel. She was still coiled tight with fury. "For my father," she cried, standing over Rorbach. "For my father."

Falcone was holding her in his arms when the border patrol seized them and roughly placed them under arrest.

57

They stood on the small balcony of Falcone's hotel room, looking out over the Old City. A nearly full moon had broken through the clouds, sweeping them away, leaving only a few gray wisps that moved off like thin vagrants into the night. The Dome of the Rock appeared silver in the pale, suffused light. Jerusalem had settled into a temporary calm. In another hour dawn would break, stirring the city into life, into motion and commerce, into episodic spasms of violence.

Rachel had been right. The *spetsnaz* soldiers had made preparations to destroy the Dome using semtex, a highly explosive *plastique* manufactured principally in Czechoslovakia. Altogether they had smuggled in more than two hundred pounds of semtex, more than enough to blast the Dome of the Rock and the al-Aksa Mosque all the way to Cairo.

Rorbach, a man above all reproach, had been planning to detonate the explosives. Why, no one was quite sure as yet, but David Ben-Dar, who was deeply embarrassed over his doubts about Rachel, had come up with a theory. He thought Rorbach was in fact a Russian, but not a Jew. He had been born in Bialystok and went with his parents to Israel before immigrating to the United States. His father was probably a Soviet intelligence officer.

Ben-Dar said it was not unlike the case of a legendary Czech who had been given the name Rudolph Herrmann. An immigrant from West Germany, Herrmann was sent first to Canada. He was accompanied by his wife, a German who had also been trained by the KGB. After several years as an up-and-coming intelligence officer in Canada, where his two sons were born, Herrmann and his wife obtained a U.S. visa and moved to Hartsdale, a suburb of New York City. As a "resident illegal," operating without diplomatic cover, he could travel freely throughout the United States, finding drop sites, the hiding places that intelligence officers and agents used for the exchange of messages, money, and pilfered material.

Herrmann free-lanced, with great success, as a photographer and filmmaker. He instructed his older son, Peter, in spy tradecraft and enlisted him in the KGB, which put Peter on a path that would lead from Georgetown University to a law school and perhaps ultimately to a sensitive government post or high elective office, all under KGB direction. But eventually Peter and his parents were caught. The FBI turned them into double agents, then gave them entirely new identities when the Soviets caught on to them.

Ben-Dar speculated that Rorbach must have been one of the Soviet's merchants of treason. He would know for certain in a few days. Meanwhile, the Mossad chief put together a cover story to account for Rorbach's death: He had been accidentally killed during a religious rally at the foot of the western wall. An unidentified man had begun shooting into the crowd, and Rorbach, in Israel to be honored by Hebrew University, was trampled to death in the melee that broke out.

The story just might hold. After all, it was almost true.

After they were released from custody, Rachel and Falcone returned to the King David Hotel. They were both exhausted, but once in the room, they were in each other's arms, holding, caressing, kissing, and weeping with relief, with joy. They made love, not with the urgency, the desperation, the hunger that had grabbed and locked them in a frenzy the night before, but slowly, and so gently

that only their souls seemed to touch . . . as if they both understood it would be their last night together.

As they looked out at the panorama of Jerusalem, Falcone
pulled Rachel tight against him. He kissed her hair, still damp from
the shower they had taken together. He could smell the fragrance of
roses.

A breeze came up, and he pulled her even closer. "Will you
come back to Washington with us?" *Say "with* me," Falcone said to
himself. *"With* me." But already he could feel his pride starting to
wrap itself up with protective words.

"Sean," Rachel said, lifting her head from his shoulder and
turning her face away from him, out toward the darkness. "I can't."

He brought her face back to his. "Would it make a difference
. . . would it be different if I were Jewish?"

Rachel's eyes filled with tears. "Oh, no, Sean, you mustn't
think that." She reached up and kissed him, her tears hot on his
face. Then she turned away once again. "My father needs me more
right now. One day I'll come back, but not now."

One day. The words echoed in Falcone's mind. She should have
said in a year or five years. *Don't tell me one day,* he wanted to say.
Tell me never. One day means never.

The thought of not seeing her again caused a sharp pain in his
chest, as if a burning cigarette were being stubbed out there. Not
since Karen had he met a woman who intoxicated him so. Her walk,
her eyes, her strength, her laughter, set him on fire. He wanted to
consume all of her, take her inside him, let her cleanse the lacera-
tions that still festered there, heal him so that he could start over,
leave his past behind like a useless skin that he had shed.

They had spent only four days together. But it was enough to
tell him that he could love her. Did love her.

But he knew she would never come back. It was not only her
father that kept her from him. It was her dead brother. It was Israel.
Falcone could never compete with them.

He kissed her again, a long gentle kiss. "Maybe one day, Rachel. Maybe one day."

It would have been a prayer, if he had believed in prayers.

58

Bickford's EIGHT-PAS-
senger Gulfstream III offered Falcone and Dake comfort and first-
class service. Even so, the flight home seemed to take forever. It was
eight hours to Mildenhall Air Force Base outside London to refuel;
another seven to Washington. Dake's foul mood didn't help. He was
furious over having to spend a second night in jail, and he couldn't
understand why the American embassy had proved so slow and
ineffectual in achieving his release.

As soon as Dake stepped aboard the plane, Falcone—over
Bickford's objections—briefed him on everything that had happened. He told him how Rafiah identified *Canaan*, how Nesher had
died, about the Va'adat meeting, about the meaning of BURAQ. The
information only seemed to deepen Dake's anger.

When Bickford tried to persuade the reporter of the extraordinary sensitivity of these events, Dake rebuffed him hard. "Save the
lecture. And for Christ's sake, don't start waving the flag at me, or
mention the words 'national security.' I've been sitting on this story
for months. Well, it's time the American people were told what in
hell the people they elected to represent them have been doing!"

Bickford turned to Falcone for help. "Senator, perhaps you can reason with him. There's more at stake here than a goddamned story."

"Sorry, Jack. I can't."

"Won't." Bickford snapped, effectively ending this line of conversation.

In fact, the three of them had little to say to each other during the long flight back. They read, ate, and napped.

Then, when they were just under two hours away from Andrews Air Force Base in Maryland, Falcone nudged Bickford awake. "Jack, I think we should see the President tonight."

The director looked at Falcone, then over at Dake, who was, or appeared to be, asleep. He could tell that Falcone was going to the White House with or without him. "I agree," he said simply, then moved up to the front of the aircraft, where a communications officer could place a call directly to the White House switchboard.

Shortly after nine-thirty that night, Falcone and Bickford were waved through the security check at the southwest gate of the White House. As they got out of the LTD sedan, they could hear music and laughter in the distance. A presidential state dinner in honor of Anatoly Voronsky was in progress. Falcone imagined he could hear the mindless banalities being exchanged, the champagne glasses being clinked, as Washington's beautiful people basked in a self-congratulatory glow.

Bickford had called ahead to alert Butch Naylor that they were coming to see the President. "Yes, it's important. No, it won't wait! And Butch, no one else is to be in the meeting. Not you. Not anyone."

They were escorted by a somber-faced White House aide up the back staircase and through the West Wing's reception area into the Cabinet Room, which adjoined the Oval Office. When Hollendale entered the room, his face was tight and grim. He was dressed in a formal, custom-tailored dinner suit and was perspiring lightly, presumably from dancing in the ballroom of the East Wing. He mopped his brow with a white monogrammed handkerchief. The evening's splendor had been disrupted. There was little doubt of his displeasure.

Bickford began to speak, too deferentially to suit Falcone, who interrupted. "Mr. President, let me get to the point real quickly. You and President Voronsky have a major problem. We found *Canaan*. We also discovered a Soviet plot to radicalize Israel's right wing with phony émigrés. They inserted *spetsnaz* troops to blow up the Dome of the Rock in order to start a bloodbath over there between the Arabs and Jews. They figured the destruction of the holy site would force us to drop Israel right into the Dead Sea. We also know that you and your friend Polanski are responsible for Joshua Stock's death. Maybe not in any legal sense, but I don't have to go to court to prove anything. I just have to tell the story."

Falcone had expected Hollendale to deny everything, to protest ignorance, or to insist that he was unaware of anything Polanski might have done. Instead the President just stood there in numbed silence. At first his face grew red, as if he were about to explode in anger. Then the color just drained from him, leaving him pale and slightly unsteady on his feet. But there were no protests, no denials, and no threats. Bickford remembered what Butch Naylor called Hollendale: Iceman. Yes, tonight he lived up to his name.

Finally he spoke, his voice a hoarse whisper. "Will I have enough time to sign the agreement?"

"Longer, Mr. President, provided certain things are done." Falcone then explained exactly what he meant.

59

THE TABLEAU WAS ONE
that Falcone would never forget. Eric Hollendale and Anatoly
Voronsky, shoulders squared, were standing tall and rigid on a
raised platform on the south lawn of the White House. The skies
were remarkably clear. Helicopters fluttered overhead; the Marine
Corps Band, buttoned up in their red, white, and blue parade dress
uniforms, played the national anthems—the Soviets' first, then ours.
Each leader's speech contained soaring, inspirational rhetoric about
new and deeper bonds of friendship, the horror of chemical warfare,
and the bold step that this agreement made toward a durable peace.

Most in the audience were misty-eyed, glowing with the hope
that we were winning the war against man's darker side. There was
talk that a Nobel Peace Prize awaited the two leaders. Even Falcone
felt a tingling creep up his spine at the sight of the Soviet and
American flags stirring in a slight breeze.

Few people had any notion of how exhausted Hollendale and
Voronsky were. Both men had been awake most of the previous
night, weighing Falcone's demands. The signing ceremony, scheduled for ten o'clock that morning, had been delayed several hours

while Voronsky engaged in heated discussions with his Foreign Minister.

The international press corps had worked itself into a near hysterical frenzy over the delay. Was the agreement falling through? Were the Americans trying to extract more concessions at this late date? Was Israel on the verge of starting a chemical war in the Middle East?

American and Soviet spokesmen assured everyone that Presidents Hollendale and Voronsky were working out some last-minute details that would make the agreement even more comprehensive and verifiable, and that the ceremonies would commence at two o'clock.

In the end, each leader had to capitulate. There really was no choice. Disclosure of the truth would have driven both from office and damaged relations between the superpowers, perhaps irreparably.

The ceremony lasted a little more than an hour. Then the last blare from the polished horns faded, the applause stopped, and the two most powerful men in the world were escorted off the platform into history's waiting arms.

As the elated guests began slowly walking off the south lawn toward the East Executive Avenue gate, Falcone felt someone touch his arm.

"Things are never quite what they appear, are they now?"

Falcone turned and stuck his hand out to Philip Dake. They shook hands warmly.

"Thanks for not going to the *Post* this morning with Bickford," Dake said.

"Word travels fast."

"There was quite a scene, I understand."

The director had arranged an early morning meeting with the publisher, Claire Greisham, and the executive editor, Brad Bentley. Bickford had assumed that the *Post* had everything—Joshua's diary and a full account of SUNDANCER and BURAQ—and was preparing to print every word of it. He claimed that if the *Post* published Dake's story, he would have the Justice Department prosecute everyone in sight for criminal violations of the National Security Act.

Bentley, who loved nothing more than a good fight with the CIA, was surprisingly uncontentious. He didn't know what Bickford was talking about. Dake had filed a story disclosing that Senator Joshua Stock had been working on a classified mission for the White House when he was murdered by a foreign intelligence agent. According to Dake, the President was going to award Stock the Congressional Medal of Honor posthumously. Then Bentley told Bickford that Dake had said he was suffering from deadline burnout, cleaned out his desk, and quit.

"How did you know I wasn't going to run with the story?" Dake said now.

"I didn't," Falcone responded. "I told the President that I would do my best to stop you. If you didn't print it, I looked good. If you did, well, you'd just live up to your reputation for being a stubborn, unpatriotic bastard who thrives on revealing our secrets." Falcone flashed a smile, then jostled Dake with his shoulder. "Besides, Hollendale really didn't have much choice."

"What did you get out of Hollendale?"

"In two weeks, Polanski will be history. A sudden attack of poor health. More time with his wife and grandchildren. You know the line."

"Yeah," Dake grunted. "And Hollendale?"

"I don't really know. But my guess is that he won't seek a second term next year. I think the idea of leaving office riding on the crest of this agreement looks pretty appealing. Plus, if the story ever gets out, Minnesota's probably going to be a better place to be than Washington."

"How'd you handle Voronsky?"

"He didn't take it well. He denied any knowledge of the Gaza massacre or BURAQ, and accused me and Bickford of being right-wing extremists trying to sabotage the chemical weapons treaty. He put on quite a convincing show, actually. Then I mentioned that the Mossad had solid evidence that Michael Rorbach, alias Ptor Kornienko, was a Soviet agent, and he got quiet. He stormed out of the room. That's why the ceremony was delayed."

"C'mon, Sean. What's the deal with him?"

"No deals, remember? You don't like the word *deals*. He had to negotiate an understanding with Prime Minister Gerstel this morning."

"And?"

"And the *spetsnaz* boys, along with all the professional political agitators, are going back to the good old U.S.S.R. Voronsky has agreed to establish full diplomatic relations with Israel, officially recognizing the legitimacy of its existence. And . . ." Falcone paused, teasing Dake with feigned drama. "As a measure of good faith, Gerstel insisted that Voronsky pull all Soviet advisers out of the Bekaa Valley and terminate military assistance to Syria."

"Some de— understanding," Dake said, a broad grin breaking across his face.

By this time they had passed through the gate and were heading toward Falcone's Mustang, which was parked in a reserved space.

"There's one thing I don't understand, Phil. Why did you quit the *Post?*"

"I know it's hard for politicians, Sean," Dake said mockingly. "It's a little thing called principle. There's not much of it around the Hill . . . I knew I had lost it as a journalist. My job is to report, not to judge. When I decided that this story was too good to report, I knew my objectivity was gone."

"What are you going to do?"

"I haven't the slightest idea. And you know what? I like the feeling."

He declined Falcone's offer of a ride. Instead he shook his hand, the broad grin replacing his perpetual half-smile, and strode off, suit jacket slung over his shoulder, toward Pennsylvania Avenue.

Falcone watched him until he disappeared from view. He wondered whether now they could be real friends.

60

Falcone drove along the George Washington Parkway, heading north. He did so instinctively, not knowing where he was going or why. He needed to be away from Washington and the exaggerated spirit of celebration that was consuming the city right then.

He rolled down both windows, letting the warm air rush through the Mustang's interior and blow his hair about uncontrollably. An hour later, out past the suburban sprawl, the houses thinned out and he caught quick glimpses of lush pastures and cornfields that would soon be ready to harvest. He could feel the tension in his neck ease, his repressed anger dissipate. He stopped at a rest area, sat on a bench, and tried to clear his thoughts, which were still filled with the horror of how close it had all been. Finally he got back into the Mustang, and after assuring that traffic was clear, he made a sharp U-turn and started back toward Washington.

There was a place he had never visited since arriving in the capital. He knew it was time.

He crossed Memorial Bridge, bore right around the traffic circle, and parked near the turnoff for the Lincoln Memorial. Dozens of tourists were climbing the wide marble steps, acolytes approaching a majestic stone deity who looked down upon them with a serenity that assured them that America had once been a place of heroes. The sun was a large, perfectly cylindrical ball that shimmered in the early evening heat, turning the white marble into soft hues of red and orange. It looked so close, so beguiling, that if you ran and jumped, you could touch it and never burn.

He laughed to himself, the very thought of it calling up his father's voice. He could hear it as clearly as that day in the car nearly fifty years ago. *Whatever you do, Sean, don't ever touch that. You'll get hurt bad, ya understand? Bad.*

He turned away from the sun and walked toward the place he had avoided all these years. Near a paved walkway he passed a kiosk where a uniformed park service employee stood behind a counter, leafing through a large bound volume, helping an older couple who had come in search of their son. Behind the kiosk, about fifty feet or more, a man stood on crutches. He was dressed in faded green-and-black camouflage fatigues and a soft Ranger hat, which was tied up rakishly on one side. His right pants leg was folded up and pinned in the back. There was a mixture of hostility and pride in his face. He stood there like a watchdog at the gates of hell.

As Falcone walked past him, their eyes met and locked momentarily. If the man recognized him, he did not let on. Falcone just nodded and kept moving.

As he approached the Vietnam Memorial, he noticed that it was cut below the earth, forcing him to descend symbolically into a mass grave. It was V-shaped, the angles of the marble slabs as brutal and sharp as a knife wound. Black marble. *How appropriate,* Falcone thought. *Black like the VC's pajamas. Black like the nights when they came for you. Black like death's foul breath, which filled your brain . . .*

Then the names started coming at him, like a blizzard of blood; names, not the wholesale numbers—light, moderate, and heavy casualties—the Pentagon used to cover up the horror. Names that spoke of young men whose bodies had broken and bled into this stone!

Falcone scanned the slabs, looking for names he might remember. He wanted to see the names of Bobby Miliken, Jeff Whalen, Alan Loane, and others in his company. But he couldn't find them.

The names were etched into the marble at random, not by alphabet, but by date of death. War's booby trap.

He watched others standing at the wall, tracing longitude and latitude lines, as if they were searching a piece of geography, until they came to what they were looking for. One woman held her granddaughter in her arms and stood there weeping for her son. A young man touched the wall and closed his eyes. He was praying for his father.

At the foot of the memorial there were bouquets of flowers, stick flags, photographs, and dog tags. Falcone stood there mesmerized by his reflection on the polished marble. The silhouette was shaped like him, but in the fading light it had no features. It was just a dark, anonymous shadow that stared back at him like a shrouded question mark. He wondered whether this was the burden that each of us carry. Was it his father? His son? Guilt? Or just the person he might have become?

He could feel tears welling up in his eyes and starting to spill down his cheeks. He had no prayers to stuff into this wall; here there were no crevices to stuff them into. He wiped his eyes with the back of his hand. Tomorrow another name would be added—not to this wall, but to the one out at the Agency. Bickford had promised him that Joshua Stock would be added to the list of those agents who had died serving their country.

He turned, walked up the ramp, and headed in the direction of the long Reflecting Pool, which ran toward the gigantic obelisk of the Washington Monument. He walked past a bronze statue of three soldiers. Two were helmetless. The third wore a bush hat and carried an M-60 machine gun on his shoulders. Two ammunition belts were draped across his chest, bandito style. These were the survivors. But there was a haunting vacuity in their eyes. They had been on a journey into the darkest part of man's heart, and what they had found there was so unspeakably horrible that their souls had turned to stone.

Falcone stood in front of the soldiers in the dying light. Unable to move. Unable to touch their eyes.

61

FALCONE POURED HIM-
self a Jack Daniel's and stepped out onto his balcony. The November air had a bite to it, forcing him to turn his jacket collar up. Drinking deeply, he could feel the bourbon spread its warmth down the back of his throat all the way into his chest.

He looked at the panoramic view below. Washington was a beautiful, breathtaking city, never more than at this hour. The night had fallen like a dark layer of cotton, softening the harsh sounds of the day. The jet planes taking off at National Airport seemed to whisper rather than roar, as they lifted off, arching gracefully into the darkness. The lights across the Potomac sparkled, starfish blinking on a moon-washed beach.

Falcone's eyes swept across Memorial Bridge, past all the monuments that glowed like a king's treasure. He stared off into the distance at the majestic dome of the Capitol, basking in floodlights, more radiant even than the one in Jerusalem.

Jerusalem's Old City—was it so different from this new city, this place cut into quadrants, dominated by a dome, its streets running with hatred and violence?

His thoughts drifted back to the events at the White House three months earlier. The faces of Hollendale and Anatoly Voronsky stayed with him, carved forever in his mind. The image they offered to the world was that of men of peace working together to promote international harmony. But how close we had come to the brink of war. Both men were prisoners of advisers and adversaries who spun webs of deceit and plans of destruction. SUNDANCER. BURAQ. HONEST BROKER. DECIMAL DEWEY. The names didn't matter. We were locked in an endless global chess match. My king, your queen. Check, checkmate. Could it ever stop?

Maybe it had.

When Voronsky returned to Moscow, his very first act was to remove Viktor Borovlev as head of the KGB. This came as a surprise to most foreign policy experts and was interpreted as a sign of Voronsky's move to consolidate political power. But then the Soviet President named Gennadi Dyukov to replace Borovlev. Intelligence reports indicated that Dyukov was a conservative hard-liner who in the past had paraded around in moderate clothing. If that was true, what did Voronsky have to gain by appointing Dyukov? Was he simply pacifying Viktor Borovlev's supporters in the Supreme Soviet while giving the Soviet people the impression that he, like Mikhail Gorbachev, was truly dedicated to change? Was it a change of face and not one of substance? And if the conservative ideologues in the Kremlin had retained their power base in the KGB, why were those same intelligence reports phrased in a way that subtly suggested that Dyukov was an improvement over his predecessor?

Falcone shook his head in puzzlement. Then he permitted himself a wild thought. Could Dyukov, the new head of the KGB, be an American agent?

He laughed at himself. It was foolishness. The bourbon must be getting to him.

Or maybe it was just that he had been wandering around too long in the secret world of intelligence, the bewildering land of a thousand mirrors, where he could never distinguish what was real and what was reflection, cover stories, false identities, front operations, proprietary companies, safe houses, double agents, triple lies. "Know the Truth, and the Truth shall make ye free."

Indeed. He knew but a small portion of the truth, and that knowledge had only imprisoned him.

He looked up and saw a shooting star drop in a fiery arc across the inky sky. He wondered whether that was all his life meant—a few seconds of blazing light, making no sound, leaving no scars. Was that how he was going to fall? Would he drop like a stone into the universe and leave no trace of having lived?

He drank deeply again, letting the alcohol drive away the vast loneliness that had begun to engulf him. He inhaled slowly, invigorated by the cool air. He looked out again at Washington, transfixed by its beauty.

Involuntarily, he thought of Rachel. About a month ago, he had read an item in the *National Intelligence Daily*. London police had found a woman who had been murdered in Hyde Park while she was out jogging. She had been shot once in the back of the head. The police found a number of false identities in her hotel room. One passport contained the name Elise Morney. She was rumored to have been having an affair with Sir Anthony Applegate, one of the Prime Minister's top advisers. There were no witnesses to the murder, and no suspects.

Could Rachel have done it? Had she avenged Joshua? Falcone looked down, remembering the night she had pursued Rorbach, her hair gleaming in the moonlight, flowing in the night wind, a righteous angel racing after the man sent to kill her people, kill Israel.

He pushed the thought away. It could have been anyone—a stranger, a madman, a jealous boyfriend. Sir Anthony Applegate. Maybe even the Libyans . . .

Looking out into the night, Falcone remembered the last night Rachel had been in his arms, how her love had touched him. And he found himself whispering, "One day, one day," wanting desperately to believe it.

ABOUT THE AUTHOR

WILLIAM S. COHEN, first elected to Congress in 1972, has been a U.S. senator since 1979. He served as vice chairman of the Intelligence Committee from 1987 to 1990 and is a member of the Armed Services and Governmental Affairs committees. He is the coauthor, with former senator Gary Hart, of a previous espionage novel, *The Double Man,* and, with fellow Maine senator George Mitchell, of *Men of Zeal: A Candid Story of the Iran-Contra Hearings.* He is also the author of *Roll Call,* a journal of his first year in the Senate, *Getting the Most Out of Washington,* and two volumes of poetry. Senator Cohen lives in Washington, D.C., and Bangor, Maine.